THE MERSEY DAUGHTER

THE MERSEY DAUGHTER

by

Annie Groves

Magna Large Print Books
Long Preston, North Yorkshire,
BD23 4ND, England.

British Library Cataloguing in Publication Data.

A catalogue record of this book is
available from the British Library

ISBN 978-0-7505-4527-3

First published in Great Britain 2017 by Harper
an imprint of HarperCollins*Publishers* Ltd.

Published in Large Print 2018 by arrangement with
HarperCollins Publishers Ltd.

Magna Large Print is an imprint of Library Magna Books Ltd.

Printed and bound in Great Britain by
T.J. (International) Ltd., Cornwall, PL28 8RW

ACKNOWLEDGEMENTS

A big thank you to Kate Bradley, editor extra-ordinaire, and agent Teresa Chris, for making this book possible.

PART ONE

CHAPTER ONE

Spring 1941

Kitty Callaghan drew her coat more tightly around her and wondered if she'd done the right thing.

It was an old coat, but then nobody could get anything new nowadays. She'd never had much new to begin with, so at least everyone was in the same boat, now that war had been raging for over eighteen months. The material was worn and bobbled where her bag usually rubbed against it. It wasn't much protection against the cold or the biting winds that blew in off the Atlantic. Well, she told herself, that wouldn't matter now. She would soon be far away from Liverpool and everything she was familiar with, all she had ever known for every one of her twenty-two years.

She caught sight of herself in the dirt-smeared train window. A pair of dark eyes stared back at her, set beneath waves of dark hair, which she had tried to control with a few precious grips. Her face was white. That would be the light making her look like that. It was nothing to do with the fact that she was full of trepidation at what she had done.

Kitty had been lucky to get a corner seat. She knew that it was going to be a long journey – nobody could say quite how long, as the tracks

13

were always getting damaged and then the race would be on to repair them. Her fellow passengers were in every sort of uniform. Soon she would be in uniform too.

Her decision to join the WRNS – the Women's Royal Naval Service, known as the Wrens – had been a sudden one, and had come about partly thanks to a chance encounter at the New Year dance at the Town Hall. Kitty had been doing her bit for the war effort already, managing the local Navy, Army and Air Force Institutes (or NAAFI) canteen on the dock road near her home in Bootle to the north of the city. At first she had enjoyed it, finding it a challenge, and was satisfied that she was helping out, even if in a small way. But, having seen the devastation caused by the bombs dropped on the docks and all around, she knew she needed to do more. Her home city had suffered terribly from attacks by the German air force, the Luftwaffe. Family and friends had been hurt, and forced to make heartbreaking decisions, such as whether to evacuate their children away from the most dangerous areas. Yet everyone had been buoyed by the bravery of the pilots in the Battle of Britain back in the summer and, once it became clear that the war was not going to be over any time soon, people had begun to dig deep and find reserves of courage. So when Kitty had bumped into a recruitment officer at the dance, she had decided to pursue the enthusiastic young woman's suggestion that she consider joining up.

'Penny for 'em!' One of the young lads, in an army greatcoat that was far too big for him, leaned across from the seat opposite and grinned

14

at her. 'What are you doing, then? Going to see your boyfriend?'

Kitty was no stranger to dealing with such comments – you couldn't afford to be standoffish in the NAAFI canteen. She had learned to give as good as she got. Fortunately, having three brothers at home, she had already had plenty of practice. But she also knew not to indulge in idle conversation when she couldn't be certain who might be listening, so she shook her head gently. 'Careless talk costs lives,' she said lightly.

The young man's face fell. 'Go on, a pretty girl like you must have a boyfriend,' he persisted. He looked about seventeen with his baby face without a trace of stubble.

'Don't pester the lady – she's right,' said one of his companions, whose own uniform showed he was a corporal, not just a private. 'You don't know if there's spies out there in the corridor or not. Sorry, miss, he don't mean nothing by it. No offence, like.'

'None taken,' said Kitty. She was going to have to spend many hours with these people and there was no sense in making a scene. Equally, though, she didn't want them larking about and chatting her up. She had some serious thinking to do.

Her own big brother had signed up almost as soon as war broke out. Jack was a pilot with the Fleet Air Arm and had already had a narrow escape when his ship went down after being attacked by the enemy. He'd been wounded by a bullet in the shoulder, but insisted he was better, and had returned to active service as quickly as they'd let him.

15

Danny, the brother who was just over a year younger than her, was in a reserved occupation on the docks, although at the moment he was recovering from an accident. It had nearly killed him, and could have taken scores of others with him. Kitty shut her eyes briefly at the memory. Danny had been the hero of the moment, taking the place of a firefighter who'd collapsed when trying to save a burning cargo ship. What Danny hadn't told anyone was that he'd been turned down by every one of the Forces because he had an enlarged heart, the result of rheumatic fever as a child. So when he himself collapsed soon after the exertion, Kitty and the rest of the family had had to cope with the shock of the accident and the additional news that Danny had a serious condition that would restrict him for the rest of his life. She shook her head a little. It was no good worrying. Danny was old enough to look after himself; and besides, he could talk his way out of just about anything.

As for Tommy ... Kitty couldn't contain a sigh at the thought of her youngest brother, just eleven years old. As their mother had died giving birth to him, and their father while alive had been a feckless drunkard, she had raised him almost as her own. He'd also had a rough time of it over the past year and a half since the war had broken out, but he'd finally agreed to be evacuated. Kitty had no concerns on that score; he'd gone to a farm in Lancashire where their neighbour Rita's children had been made more than welcome. He would be fussed over and pampered by the farmers Joan and Seth, safe from the attentions of the Luftwaffe

16

that had made life in Empire Street so perilous. While she knew in her heart of hearts he had wanted to stay at home for the excitement of collecting shrapnel and being in the thick of things, it was for the best. Little Michael and Megan from across the road were there to play with, and he'd be better fed than the rest of the family put together.

So why was she so full of doubt? Kitty mentally gave herself a shake. She should be grateful. She'd survived the bombings where so many hadn't. She'd been lucky to meet the kindest man in the midst of all the chaos at Linacre Lane hospital, where Danny and Tommy had been treated. Dr Elliott Fitzgerald was so far above her in social station that she sometimes had to pinch herself that he'd even talked to her, let alone taken her to a posh dance at the Town Hall and seen her whenever his rare time off from the wards coincided with her being off shift from the canteen. He'd been immediately encouraging about her joining the Wrens. Plenty of men would want the woman with whom they were developing a relationship to stay close at hand, but not Elliott. He believed she could do it, and be a success. He'd held her hand, looked into her face with his beautiful blue eyes, and said that she would be wonderful and exactly what the country needed. Just having him next to her made her feel more confident, more assured.

So why wasn't that enough?

Because, said a little voice in her head, he isn't Frank Feeny.

Suddenly the train jolted to a halt. Shaken, Kitty peered out of the window, but of course all the

17

signs at the station they'd just drawn into had been removed, for security. She'd never been this far from home before and didn't recognise anything.

'It's Crewe,' said the baby-faced private, but the corporal dug him in the ribs.

'Shut up, Parker. You know you're not meant to say that.'

'Only trying to be helpful,' said Parker, rubbing his side. 'That hurt, that did.'

'I'll give you more than that to complain about if you don't watch your mouth,' warned the corporal.

Just when Kitty thought it could be getting nasty, the door to the compartment opened and a young woman stuck her head through the gap. 'I say, could you shove up? Thanks ever so.' Without waiting for a reply she swung herself in and hoisted a very elegant case on to the overhead rack. Kitty only had sight of it for a moment, but that was all it took for her to recognise its quality, so very unlike her own shabby one beside it.

'I'm so glad to have a seat,' the woman went on, giving the occupants of the carriage a dazzling smile. 'I simply dreaded standing all the way to London. Now let me make amends for disturbing you by offering you some gingerbread. Mummy asked Cook to bake extra for this very reason.'

The soldiers immediately broke off from their quarrel and looked brighter. Kitty masked a grin. Maybe this journey wouldn't be so bad after all. It was a sign, she told herself. Push all thoughts of Frank Feeny firmly away – he thought of her as a pesky little sister, that was all. She was better off in so many ways now that Elliott had come into

18

her life. And, while she was nervous about what the coming weeks of training would bring, there was something else too. Excitement. Ambition. This was the start of something completely new, and she owed it to her family, her friends, but most of all herself, to make the very best of it.

CHAPTER TWO

'So why aren't you out helping Mam down the WVS?' Rita Kennedy, née Feeny, demanded of her younger sister Nancy. They were in the kitchen of the family home, even though neither of them lived there any more since their marriages. Then again, both marriages had turned out very differently to how they'd expected, and they both preferred the comfort of their mother's warm and welcoming kitchen to just about anywhere else on earth.

Nancy planted her elbows firmly on the old chenille tablecloth and sipped from her cup of tea. 'Because I'm minding Georgie. He's still having a rotten time with his teething. The last thing they'll want is a howling baby shouting the place down.'

Rita raised her eyebrows, knowing full well that Nancy would do anything to get out of hard graft. While their mother was a mainstay of the Women's Voluntary Service, as well as organising salvage collections, cookery classes, make-do-and-mend classes and being the auxiliary fire

19

warden for Empire Street, Nancy rarely lifted a finger if she could help it. She was perfectly happy to let somebody else mind her young son – usually their sister-in-law Violet, who, having no children of her own yet, liked nothing better than entertaining young George, who was not quite a year old. That suited Nancy down to the ground. Now she pouted at her big sister – a look she'd practised for many a year.

'You needn't be like that about it.'

'I didn't say a thing,' Rita pointed out, pulling out a wooden chair and sinking gratefully on to it. She'd been on her feet all day.

'You didn't have to,' Nancy complained. 'Your sour look gave it away. Someone's got to look after Georgie, and now Violet's thrown herself into the WVS as well, it'll have to be me.'

'What about Sid's mam?' Rita asked innocently, waiting for the firestorm that would follow. She wasn't disappointed.

'That old witch! I wouldn't trust her with a baby.' Nancy was incensed. 'It's bad enough having to live under her roof – we don't want to spend any more time with her than we have to. I don't know how she does it, but she manages to be a proper busybody and a big streak of misery at the same time. I mean, Sid's been a POW since Dunkirk, but every day she goes on and on about it like it's only just happened. It's as if nobody else has lost anyone in this blessed war. It's all about her, what a martyr she is, how it's destroying her health. It's enough to get your goat.'

Rita couldn't argue with that; Mrs Kerrigan always had been one of their nosiest neighbours, and she'd taken to the role of grieving mother as if she'd been born for it. Rita smiled to herself. Whatever disapproval anybody had for Nancy's ways was like water off a duck's back; she didn't seem to give a hoot about other people's opinions. Still, her sister could be remarkably callous about her missing husband, and Rita knew she was sailing a bit close to the wind these days. 'You're going to have to keep on the right side of her, though, for when Sid gets back,' she said. 'He'll have been through enough without coming home to find his wife and mother at daggers drawn.'

'Oh, I don't want to dwell on it.' Nancy tossed her head, making her red hair swing about her shoulders. 'We none of us know when he'll be back. It's too depressing to think about.'

More like Nancy didn't want Sid back to cramp her style, Rita thought, but decided to keep her thoughts to herself. It couldn't be easy for Nancy, rattling round in that gloomy big house with a mother-in-law who made no secret of disliking her. As for Mr Kerrigan, nobody ever saw him. He worked nights on the *Liverpool Post* and kept totally different hours to the rest of his family, which Nancy figured was to stay out of the way of his disagreeable wife. Nancy spent as much of her time as she could in her mother's house, and had even come back to live there for a while, before Violet had arrived and it had simply become too crowded to contain them all. Reluctantly she'd taken little George back to his other granny.

Rita sighed. She was hardly so squeaky clean herself. She pushed thoughts of the circumstances of her marriage to her husband Charlie out of her

21

mind, feeling too exhausted to think about it now. She loved her work as a nurse, but ever since the local infirmary had been bomb-damaged, she had been working at the hospital on Linacre Lane, a much longer walk away. She didn't mind the walk itself – especially now that the buses were so unreliable – but the journey there and back combined with long shifts and the weight of responsibility of being a nursing sister wore her out. She reached for the teapot before Nancy could help herself to a refill. Guiltily she realised she was drinking her mother's tea ration, though Dolly Feeny wouldn't have begrudged her eldest girl a cup. The whole family were proud of Rita, who'd kept at her post while the docks were bearing the brunt of the Luftwaffe's devastating raids.

Warming her hands on the cup, Rita leant back. 'That's better.' It was amazing what a drop of tea could do to restore your spirits. 'Have you heard Mam's latest?'

Nancy glanced up. 'No, what?'

'She's gone and put her name down for a victory garden. She was talking about it at Christmas and I thought she'd given up the idea, but no. Now the days are getting longer it'll soon be time to start planting seeds and I don't know how she'll manage.'

'Well, I suppose we could all do with more fresh fruit and veg,' said Nancy eagerly. Her mouth watered at the thought of strawberries in the summer. Even if there was no cream or sugar to go on them, they could always use evaporated milk.

Trust Nancy to jump straight to how she'd benefit herself, thought Rita. 'Yes, that's all very

22

well,' she persisted in trying to make her point, 'but how will she find the time? Look at how much she's doing already. She doesn't get enough sleep as it is – not that there's any telling her. We're all going to have to muck in.'

'You've got to be joking!' Nancy cried hotly. 'What, go grubbing round in the dirt? Lots of these gardens are just on dug-over plots where bombs have dropped, aren't they? They'll be filthy, not even like proper allotments. I'm not having anything to do with it. It'll ruin my nails.' She turned her hands to admire the latest shade of polish she'd managed to procure. It wasn't easy to come by and she had no intention of spoiling her careful manicure by wielding a spade.

'All the more for us, then.' Rita drained her tea. Even though her sister was annoying, it was fun to wind her up and it was better than the alternative – going back to her own house and her own difficult mother-in-law. But there was no getting away from it. She rose to her aching feet, steeling herself for the short walk to the corner shop across the mouth of the alley. 'I'll see you tomorrow, Nancy.'

Nancy nodded absent-mindedly as her big sister made her way out of the door. Truth be told, she had more urgent matters to worry about than whether she'd be needed to take a turn on the new vegetable beds. She was sure she could get out of it – she could usually wheedle her way into her mother's good books and persuade her somehow. There were some things, though, on which her mother wouldn't budge.

One of those was how the wife of a POW should behave. Both her mother and her father had been very angry with Nancy when her other sister, young Sarah, had accidentally seen her canoodling with a man in a bus shelter back in December. Sarah had clearly been torn in her loyalties and very upset about the whole thing, but in the end had spoken up, more because if anyone else had seen them it would have been ten times worse.

As far as Dolly and Pop were concerned, that was the end of the matter. Nancy had been warned in no uncertain terms that she'd have to watch out for her reputation. It was bad enough to be a fast woman, but to be one when her husband had been taken prisoner in the course of serving his country was not to be contemplated. They had spelled out to her just what sort of reaction she could expect if she continued down that route.

Nancy shut her eyes and remembered. It hadn't been just any man. It was Stan Hathaway, local boy made good. Even though his grandmother lived just around the corner from Empire Street and his family weren't anything special, he'd managed to go to university and was now a flight lieutenant in the RAF. If anyone deserved a bit of fun on his precious home leave, it was him. Besides, he made her feel something that no other man had – not even Sid, back in the days when she'd first fallen for him, before she'd taken off the rose-tinted spectacles and realised what he was really like. But by then it had been too late and she'd been pregnant with Georgie. But Stan ... he was utterly different. He was sophisticated and smart, and made her think she was those things too when she was with him. She could just imagine his arms around her, his persuasive whisper in her ear, the way her skin seemed to fizz with electricity at his touch.

She started suddenly as a wail came from the room next door. Georgie was awake again and it didn't sound as if his nap had eased his teething troubles. Carefully she got up, making sure not to catch her precious nylons on the chair. She'd have to wait until Stan's next leave to get new ones – he always seemed to know a way of finding them, and was only too pleased to give them to her. He used to joke that it was his excuse for finding out if they fitted her properly...

Guiltily she wondered if that tea had tasted right. Maybe she'd got another one of her upset stomachs. She'd had a few of those lately. That was all it was. She wouldn't even think about the alternative.

Rita pushed open the back door to the living quarters, which were behind and above the corner shop. She paused to listen. In days gone by there would have been the constant buzz of gossip from the shop, as her mother-in-law Winnie Kennedy extracted the juiciest morsels of scandal from anyone and everyone, before selling on her carefully hoarded luxury items that only a select few customers knew about. Sometimes it was as if rationing had never happened. Being so near the docks, there were always folk who could get hold of just about anything for a small consideration, even though this was strictly illegal.

Now there was only silence. Rita groaned inwardly. Winnie had changed, and it wasn't because of the destruction of so many homes around them or the loss of life that had shattered so many families around Liverpool in general and the docks in particular. In fact most people had become more defiant, nobody wanting to give in to the terror of the bombs. The people of Merseyside had come together and refused to be cowed. But Winnie had retreated into an angry shell.

She had always carried on as if she was a cut above everyone else, and had raised her son Charlie to feel the same. She'd never troubled to hide her resentment of Rita, who had never been good enough for her beloved son. Rita had married Charlie knowing all this only too well, but she'd had little alternative as she'd been pregnant with Michael. She and Jack Callaghan had been young sweethearts, but too young and naïve to realise what they were doing. When Jack had been sent away on his apprenticeship, Rita had panicked – making the worst decision of her life. Many a time over the past eight years she'd berated herself for the choice she'd made, but she had made her bed and now had to lie on it. The living quarters had been crowded when they'd all lived there, with Winnie's bedroom right next to Charlie and hers, and even more so when baby Megan had arrived on the scene. Rita had treasured the dream of finding a place of their own, away from Charlie's interfering, domineering mother, hoping that this would be the solution to the widening cracks in her marriage. She'd been foolish to think that, she now realised. Now she was wise to Charlie's callous and vicious nature, but here she was, trapped with the poisonous Ma Kennedy, Charlie goodness knows where, and her children far away from Empire Street.

She sighed at the thought of her children; she ached at being apart from them. However, she knew Megan and Michael were safe, away from the air raids, living on a farm in Freshfield all the way out in Lancashire. Tommy Callaghan was with them, which would liven things up, and she tried to visit them when she could, always amazed at how they thrived away from the air raids. They looked so different from the pale children of the city who remained; those whose parents couldn't bear to part with them and who now roamed the bombsites of Merseyside, exposed to many dangers. Thank God the farming couple had welcomed them with open arms, and Rita knew the children would have the love and security they needed – not to mention all those fresh vegetables and meat, and the cream of the milk and the rich golden butter they could never have hoped for in Empire Street.

She pushed open the inner door to the shop. Winnie was slumped behind the till, her eyes dead. 'Oh, it's you.' She could barely summon the interest to speak.

'Of course it's me. I'm late because the shift didn't finish on time.' Rita thought it best not to say she'd stopped off for a cup of tea next door. 'Shall I put the kettle on? It's freezing in here.' No wonder there were no customers, she thought.

'Certainly not. Tea's rationed, as you should know.' There was a trace of the old Winnie, snobbish and sharp. The fact that she had a case of tea stowed away in the cellar was not to be mentioned. Rita bit back the retort.

'If you're sure? Then I'll go and get changed.' Rita let herself out of the shop again and made her way upstairs.

Winnie's situation was all of her own making. She'd kept a secret for twenty years or more and it had only come to light during a terrifying raid just before Christmas. Dolly, as fire warden, had had to make sure everyone left their houses and went to the bomb shelter at the end of the street, but Winnie had resisted, even though the roof of the shop was alight. She'd been desperate to rescue a box of papers from the loft. Dolly, at great risk to herself, had managed to persuade her difficult neighbour to get to safety and had looked after the box. In all the confusion of the raid it had finished up in the Feeny family home. Both Dolly and Rita were now aware of its contents.

Far from relying on the income from the shop, it transpired that Winnie had been the owner of three properties: the shop and its living quarters, a large house in Southport and a guesthouse in Crosby. All those years Rita had dreamed of moving out – and Winnie had said nothing, like a dragon sitting on a pile of gold. She'd been far more keen on keeping Charlie tied to her apron strings, where she wanted him.

Charlie had had other ideas, and while his mother had boasted to all and sundry about his job in insurance, he'd used it to pay calls on well-heeled women on their own in the afternoons. Winnie had either turned a blind eye or refused to believe it was possible – just as she'd managed not to notice the marks on Rita when Charlie's rage turned against his wife. Charlie had finally taken off to the house in Southport, supposedly so the children would be safer, which was managed by a very accommodating woman called Elsie. He'd even put it about that she was his wife. Rita had eventually tracked them down and taken the children away – just in time, as a stray bomb had ripped the front off the once-grand house, and the children had been left standing in the road.

Rita's parting shot had been to hand Charlie his call-up papers. He was a coward, all bluster and smarm; the only fighting he was capable of was to hit a woman behind closed doors. She had no idea where he was now and she didn't care. That was Elsie's problem.

There had been one more document in Winnie's box that if anything had been even more startling. It was a birth certificate for a child called Ruby, born to Winnie Kennedy, but two years after her husband had died. The father's name was left blank. This baby would now be coming up to twenty-one years of age. And when Rita had tracked down Charlie and Elsie, the neighbours had been keen to point out that the couple were often in the pub of an evening – but the children were looked after by a young woman called Ruby.

So things had come to an uneasy standoff. The people of Empire Street were mostly a good lot, but prone to suspicion and gossip. Charlie's disappearance, and the fact that he'd never been seen in uniform, was a gift to the likes of Vera Delaney, who would love to wipe the smug smile off Ma Kennedy's face and take her down a peg or two. Only a few Feenys knew the full truth. Winnie was slowly going to pieces waiting for her big secret to be blown.

Rita, meanwhile, harboured a secret of her own. When she'd gone to rescue her children, she hadn't done it alone. Jack had taken her: Jack Callaghan, Kitty's big brother, her childhood sweetheart and – as she'd finally confirmed to him – Michael's real father. She'd tried to be a good wife to Charlie, to forget everything that had passed between Jack and her; they'd been too young, and fate in its many forms had made it impossible for them to be together. Now he was back doing his duty, escorting naval convoys across the vital supply routes of the North Atlantic. How she missed him. How she wished they'd somehow found a way all those years ago to overcome all the obstacles – but that hadn't happened. Now she had to face the fact that her feelings for him had never died, but that she could not have him. The fact that Charlie had broken every bond of duty to her as a husband was neither here nor there. Divorce wasn't a word you'd ever hear in Empire Street; no matter what a husband had done to his wife, she'd be expected to stand by him. The best she could do was to write. Rita had promised that to Jack and she wouldn't break her word. The letters were hurting no one, and if they kept his spirits up through those dark nights on the Atlantic, then that's what she'd do, and to hell with the holier-than-thou attitude of the rest of the world – couldn't they have those precious words to share, if nothing else? But now Kitty had left, she would have to find another way of receiving his letters to her. Next to the children she adored, the letters were the one chink of light in this miserable life she was stuck with.

A noise at the top of the stairs startled her. A slight figure with huge pale-blue eyes and a frizz of pale-blonde hair emerged, smiling nervously, almost like a frightened child.

Rita took a long look at her, and noted again how much she looked like Winnie, her mother. Not so much her hair, but her nose and her eyes were very similar, though the young woman's had a gentleness to them which Winnie's certainly didn't. Something else for the gossips to get their teeth into... Rita forced herself to get a grip and spoke steadily and comfortingly. 'Hello, Ruby, come and have a cup of tea, love.'

As Ruby tip-toed down the stairs towards her, Rita looked around her at the shabby, care-worn kitchen – she saw the loose tea that Winnie had tipped into the sink, the chipped cups on the drainer and the cold grate that had been left for her to make up herself. She sighed deeply – if she didn't have Jack's letters as a lifeline, then she didn't know how she would keep on going.

CHAPTER THREE

'Are you sure you don't mind me taking the top bunk?'

Kitty shook her head. 'No, I don't like heights at the best of times. I'm much better off down here.' She thumped the hard pillow into something she thought might be a more comfortable shape. It was never going to be soft, but at least all the bedding was clean. She'd heard horror stories about some service accommodation, and apparently the Land Army girls often had to put up with worse.

'Bit of a coincidence that we ended up being billeted together, isn't it?' asked the elegant young woman from the train, whose name was Laura Fawcett. They'd introduced themselves on the journey, Kitty explaining she'd come from Liverpool, and learning in turn that Laura, although from Yorkshire, had spent lots of time in London and knew it well. 'I'm glad we got the chance to get acquainted before the others turn up. Looks as if they're expecting a lot of new recruits.'

Kitty had been taken aback on arrival in the capital and had been glad to have the much more confident Laura to guide her to their new home in North London. Although she was well used to the bustle of Liverpool city centre, this place was on a different scale. The sheer number of people was overwhelming, many of them in uniform of one sort or another, all weaving around each other at baffling speed. Kitty had gripped her new friend's arm, totally disoriented. Laura had taken it in her stride, mildly annoyed to find that holes in the road meant she couldn't take the route she'd originally planned, but swiftly deciding upon a new one. She'd plunged into the Underground and Kitty had followed immediately behind, terrified at the thought of getting separated. That had been her introduction to the Northern Line.

Now Kitty glanced uneasily around the large room they were in, full of bunk beds in readiness for the arrival of trainee Wrens. She was used to sharing a house with her brothers, and not having a minute to herself, but her bedroom, basic though it was, had always been her sanctuary. She'd done her best to soften it with her eiderdown and the few bits and pieces that remained of her mother's possessions. Here there would be room only for the most functional items. She wondered what sort of bedroom Laura had had and what her home was like – nothing like Empire Street, she was sure of that.

Laura appeared to have no such doubts and finished packing away the small amount of clothing they were recommended to bring in no time, somehow managing to cram in some very elegant-looking frocks as well. 'This place must have been a school, just look at it. Certainly wasn't made to sleep in.' She glanced around at the huge windows and high ceilings. 'Bet it'll be freezing. Oh well, maybe they'll work us so hard we won't care. Can't be as cold as up north, that's for sure. I'm used to the wind howling over the moors so I probably shan't even notice. How about you?'

Kitty smiled, remembering the force of the westerly gales that came in over the Atlantic with such regularity. 'Oh, that won't worry me,' she said lightly. 'We have to put up with that all the time in Liverpool. At least they'll give us uniforms to keep out the worst of it. I've been wearing dungarees for work in the NAAFI and this uniform is much nicer – warmer too.'

Laura held up the bluette overall she'd been issued with. 'It's a bit stiff, isn't it? It'll be itchy as anything.'

Kitty grinned, thinking that her pretty new friend probably wasn't used to anything but the finest material, and would not have had to wear anything practical, certainly not like the often-patched clothes she'd had to put on for scrubbing down the NAAFI canteen after it closed every day. She smoothed down the blue-and-white bedspread on her narrow bunk, running her hands over the anchor motif. She couldn't help wondering what her brother Jack would be doing, out there on his aircraft carrier, facing God knows what.

'Let's go and see where that canteen is that they told us about,' Laura suggested, hanging up the overall once more. 'I shan't wear that until I have to. If this is going to be my last day in my own clothes for a while, then I'm going to make the most of it. Two weeks of basic training and then heaven knows what we'll be in for or what we'll have to wear.' She shrugged into her pale-yellow cardigan, which Kitty was fairly sure was cashmere. It perfectly set off Laura's mop of beautifully cut blonde curls.

They made their way to the lower floor and uncertainly down an echoing corridor, trying to remember what the officer who'd welcomed them had said. There were so many doors – but then the unmistakable smell of cocoa hit them and they followed their noses to what might once have been the school refectory. A woman in her forties was standing by a large urn. She wore a bright turban on her head and Kitty reflected that up until a short while ago this would have been her, greeting the servicemen and sometimes women who'd

34

come through the doors of her own canteen.

'Hello, girls,' the woman said, immediately friendly. Steam rose from the urn. 'I can do you tea or cocoa. What'll it be?'

'Cocoa,' Laura and Kitty said immediately. Kitty couldn't remember the last time she'd had cocoa. Before the war, at home in Empire Street, there hadn't always been enough to go round; it was ironic that rationing meant that some people were better fed now than before the war. Kitty's mother had died when she'd been a young girl, and Dolly Feeny, their neighbour, had been the closest thing to a mother she'd had since. Kitty's father had liked a drink – too much sometimes – often spending down the pub what was intended for the housekeeping. Thank God for her brother Jack, and for Dolly, who'd made sure that the Callaghan kids didn't go without. The Callaghan and Feeny children had been as thick as thieves growing up. Eddy had been like a brother to her – and Frank, of course, though in the last few years, Kitty knew her feelings had changed into something deeper, something enduring. Kitty pushed thoughts of Frank Feeny from her mind again – he'd never see her as anything other than a little sister, and it was time to put away her childish dreams and look to the future. The smell of cocoa drifted tantalisingly up to her nose. This was a treat not to be missed.

Gratefully they warmed their hands on their cups as they made their way to a battered wooden table next to a window. Through it they could see a curving drive and, beyond that, down the hill, London was spread out beneath them. Kitty took a tentative sip to see how hot the drink was and smiled. 'Delicious. Haven't had that for a while.'

Laura smiled back ruefully. 'Strange, isn't it? How quickly one gets used to not having the everyday stuff.' She took a sip too. 'Heavenly. That's made it worth joining up already.'

Kitty eyed her new companion curiously. She seemed to be about the same age as her. 'Why did you? Join up, I mean?'

Laura paused. 'Well, I suppose it's a case of doing my bit. And I was tired of sitting at home, doing nothing.'

'Did you really do nothing?' asked Kitty. Even though she hadn't known this young woman long, it didn't seem very likely.

Laura snorted. 'Oh, nothing much. I knitted for the troops and went to some WVS meetings with my mother, but that's not really a lot of help, is it, when we're facing a fight to save our country? I knew I could do more. Well, I hope so anyway. I don't know what they'll decide I'm best at, but I look forward to finding out.' She took another sip. 'What about you?'

Kitty gazed out at the trees coming into bud, swaying in the breeze. 'I think it was seeing what my brothers were doing and realising I didn't have to look after them any more. Jack's with the Fleet Air Arm, Danny's on the docks, though he's off sick at the moment, and Tommy's been evacuated. I've run around looking after them for years and now they don't need me so much, I wanted to do something more – something that will make a difference.' She met the other woman's gaze. 'I don't know what I'll be best at either. I hope it isn't cooking. I've done that and I've loved it but I want to try something different. I've never left home before. Even though we're at war, I can't wait to see a bit of London. D'you think we'll have time?'

'We'll make time!' Laura declared. She raised her cup and chinked it against Kitty's. 'I know exactly what you mean about doing more... Here's to having fun, and damn the war. Those Germans aren't going to put a stop to me showing you the delights of our capital city. Freddy used to show me around every chance he got.' She stopped suddenly.

'Who's Freddy?' Kitty asked shyly, hating to be nosey but keen to get to know this force of nature. Being around Laura was exciting in itself; she made it seem like anything was possible. 'Was he your chap?'

'No, nothing like that.' Laura's voice caught but then she cleared her throat. 'No, he was my brother. Is my brother. He's missing in action, has been since November. He's a pilot.' She looked away quickly to the faint outlines of the buildings on the horizon. 'He was only a year older than me, we did everything together – or at least we did until he was sent away to school and I had to stay at home and not bother my silly little head about serious subjects like maths and things like that. Still, we went everywhere together when he was home. He even taught me to drive.'

Kitty felt a bit awkward. She'd only known this woman a few hours, but they were going to be sharing a room and intimacy couldn't be avoided. She desperately wanted to be a part of this new life and being shy wasn't going to get her anywhere. She reached out her hand and took Laura's shaking palm in her own. 'Look, I realise it's easy to say, but you mustn't give up hope. I know. It happened to my brother Jack; his ship went down and we didn't know where he was or what had happened to him. It was awful. It felt like a lifetime, but in the end we got news that he was alive and on the way home. He was shot but he says he's better now and he's back in active service. Don't ever give up hope; it's what keeps us going.'

'Thanks.' Laura seemed to give herself a mental shake and then smiled with determination. 'Nothing I can do about it. Sitting around moping won't help and Freddy wouldn't stand for it, so I must buck up. Mummy's furious with me for putting myself in danger but I told her not to be silly. They won't actually let us fight, so I might as well go and make myself useful in whatever way I can. And if one of those ways is showing you around London, then all the better. Anyway, what about you – do you have a chap? With your looks you're bound to have, hope you don't mind me saying.'

Kitty furiously tried to stop herself from blushing. She'd got used to being called all sorts of things when behind the counter at the NAAFI, and fielding outrageously flirtatious remarks from many of the servicemen, but to have her appearance commented on by this smart and very attractive young woman was another thing entirely. 'Sort of,' she admitted. 'Well, nothing formal or anything, but I was walking out with a lovely man called Elliott.' She could hardly believe she was going to say the next words. 'He's a doctor. He looked after my little brother Tommy when he was ill once.'

'Oh, well done you!' Laura beamed. 'A doctor – that's jolly nice. Oh God, I sound like Mummy. But you know what I mean. Doesn't he mind you going away? Did he beg you to stay at his side?'

'No, the very opposite. He said if it was what I wanted, I should leap at the chance,' said Kitty, aware now that pride had crept into her voice. She knew she was lucky to have such support from him. 'Also, he's from London, so he wants to come and see me when he next has some leave.' Her face fell as she remembered his workload. 'That doesn't happen very often though. And even when he thinks he'll have time off, he's often called back to the ward for an emergency. We really have been through a lot over the past few months. The bombing felt non-stop over Christmas.'

'Oh, I know.' Laura's face was instantly sympathetic. 'Even though they never give the name of the city on the radio, just say it's in the northwest or wherever; we only heard about it afterwards, though word sort of gets around, doesn't it?'

Kitty nodded sadly. 'Should we even be talking about it now?' She glanced around nervously. There was hardly anybody else in the room, as so many of the new recruits wouldn't arrive until tomorrow, but all the same she was aware that the least said the better.

'Well, it's over and done with,' said Laura pragmatically. 'I don't suppose it can do much more harm. But anyway, that's wonderful that your chap might be down to visit. Maybe he can show us some places I don't know about.' Her eyes brightened. 'He can take us out on the town. D'you think he'd like that?'

'I'm sure he would. He's very kind – and he's a very good dancer.' Kitty smiled but felt an odd prickling of something else – not pride, not anxiety but ... could it be jealousy? Wouldn't Elliott be far better off with a girl from his own background, someone exactly like Laura? No, she mustn't think like that. Elliott had been surrounded by gorgeous young nurses from every walk of life and yet he had chosen her. She had nothing to worry about. And, furthermore, if she was prepared to feel jealous, then that must mean she was over Frank Feeny, mustn't it? But, as she settled herself into the unfamiliar bed that night, it wasn't just the strangeness and excitement of her new surroundings that give her a fitful sleep, but the blue of Frank Feeny's eyes that seemed to invade her dreams.

CHAPTER FOUR

Rita stared at herself in the mirror in the bedroom she used to share with Charlie and thought how much weight she'd lost. It was no wonder: rushed off her feet all day, walking to and from work as often as not, serving in the shop when she wasn't on duty, and all on less food than she was accustomed to. By the dim light of the overhead bulb she could see her clothes were beginning to hang loosely on her, but she couldn't exactly go out and buy a whole new wardrobe in a smaller size. She had once been proud of her curvy figure, and Jack had loved it ... now there wouldn't be much left for him to catch hold of. That was if he ever came back. And anyway, she wasn't going to go down that route again; there was no future in it but heartbreak. So really it didn't matter what shape she was, as long as she could keep body and soul together. Shivering, she knew it meant that she felt the cold more keenly. Still, it was March now and the weather would soon turn warmer.

There was a gentle knock at the flimsy door. Rita started. It wouldn't be Winnie, that was for sure. She would just barge in – or at least the old Winnie would have. Now she no longer bothered, which was a relief. 'Come in,' Rita called.

Ruby stepped into the room, as cautiously as a mouse peeping out of its hole to see if the cat had gone. 'Rita? Um ... can I come in?'

Rita wondered what this was about – Ruby usually kept herself to herself, and in fact she felt she knew the younger woman no better than when they'd first met, three months back. Even though they shared the same house, they barely saw one another, as Ruby kept to her attic room and Rita rarely had time to sit around downstairs. She sat down on the bed and patted the space beside her. 'Come on in, Ruby. Make yourself comfortable.'

Shyly the young woman stepped forward and then sat where she'd been asked to, all without looking directly at Rita. Even though she was nearly twenty-one, she acted like a child, a timid

41

one at that. Rita didn't know if it was because there was something wrong with her, or because of how she'd been treated all her life. Being raised by that hard-faced Elsie Lowe would have been no picnic.

'What's wrong, Ruby?' Rita could tell something was bothering her, and her naturally warm heart went out to her. 'Take your time.'

Ruby jerked her head away and muttered something before she managed to say, 'I've not done nothing wrong.' She turned to face Rita and her huge blue eyes glittered with unshed tears. 'Honest, I haven't.' She began to shake violently.

'Ruby, of course you haven't. Who said you did? Why are you saying this?' Rita asked gently, wondering what could have frightened her. Everyone had been living with frayed nerves during the bombings, but those had tailed off recently. Was it the fear of the planes returning that had upset the young woman so much? 'Don't be scared, you can tell me.'

Ruby took a deep breath. 'The police came.' She looked away again. 'I haven't done nothing, really I haven't.'

'Police?' Rita's hand flew to her heart, immediately wondering if anything had happened to her children. Then she reasoned that they would have come to the hospital to tell her if it had been that. 'Did they say what it was about?'

Ruby gave a big gulp. 'I ... don't know. I heard them. They had loud voices. Mrs Kennedy shouted at them. They were very angry. I could tell but I didn't go down. Then Mrs Kennedy went away with them.'

Mrs Kennedy! Rita had to stop herself from exclaiming out loud. Winnie was this poor girl's mother and yet she wouldn't even allow her to call her by her first name, insisting on the full and more formal Mrs Kennedy. And surely she hadn't just shut the shop in the middle of the day? Even though she was a shadow of her former self, she still had an eye for profit.

'You don't need to worry, Ruby,' Rita said, thinking fast. 'It will have nothing to do with you. Otherwise they would have asked to speak to you, wouldn't they? You haven't done anything bad. They will have wanted to speak to Winnie. Maybe one of the customers has caused trouble, something like that.' But Rita didn't believe that for one minute. If it wasn't the children, then there was only one person who was likely to bring trouble to this place.

'So they don't want to take me away?' Ruby gasped. 'They aren't going to put me in prison?'

'Of course not. Why would they do that?' Rita tried to keep her voice reassuring, but she wondered just what Winnie had been saying to the poor girl while she was out of the house. Winnie loved to have control over people and here was a sitting target for her malice, daughter or no daughter. There was no telling how deep her spite ran.

Ruby's face had just begun to brighten when the all-too-familiar air-raid siren began to wail. 'Oh no, not again,' Rita exclaimed without thinking. Then she said, 'Don't panic, Ruby, just go and get your bag – you do have it ready just in case, don't you? – and then meet me downstairs. We'll go to the shelter at the end of the road. I'll

43

see what we can take to eat, to keep our spirits up.' Wearily she began to shrug into the coat she'd not long taken off. Eight thirty in the evening and she hadn't had a proper meal all day.

Down in the kitchen she put her hand to the kettle and found it was still hot, so she quickly set about making a flask of tea. She knew Winnie kept packets of biscuits where she thought nobody could find them, and hastily bent to put a couple into her bag. A shadow fell across her as she stood up.

'And what do you think you're doing?' Winnie spat.

'Getting ready to go to the shelter,' Rita said shortly. She didn't intend to waste time or energy on her mother-in-law. 'You'd better grab your things and come with us.'

'Go to that shelter again? I'll do no such thing,' Winnie protested. 'You get all sorts in there, all squashed in together – it's not hygienic. You don't know where they've been.' She caught sight of Ruby hovering in the doorway. 'My point exactly. I'm not going anywhere where I'll be seen with her, for a start.' Her eyes gleamed. 'I'll be safe enough in the cellar.'

'In that case I'll take that pie for Ruby and me,' said Rita, catching sight of a pastry crust under a dome of white netting. 'We all know you've got enough to feed an army stocked away down there.'

'That's my pie...' Winnie began to protest, but Rita was too quick for her.

'That's my supper. I only just got back from my shift and I opened up the shop first thing this morning, if you remember.' Rita wrapped the pie

44

in a clean tea towel and added it to her bag. She was about to head out of the door when she paused. 'Winnie, what were the police doing here? Weren't you going to tell me?'

Winnie's head snapped round. 'Oh, someone's been gossiping, have they?'

Rita thought that was a bit rich, coming from the vicious-tongued old woman. 'Just explain to me what happened.'

'It's you who's to blame,' Winnie hissed. 'Going round saying things about my Charles that aren't true. It's all a mistake. They won't be back here again to bother me. Not unless you start telling your pack of lies again.'

'What are you saying?' Rita was momentarily shocked into silence. Then the penny dropped. 'I see, they've come about him being a deserter, haven't they? His papers arrived in December and I bet he hasn't shown up to enlist, so they've come for him at last.'

'He's in a reserved occupation,' Winnie insisted, with whatever misplaced dignity she could muster. 'He would never stoop so low as to desert.'

'Winnie, this is Charlie's wife you're talking to, not one of the customers you're trying to impress,' Rita sighed in exasperation. She finished fastening her bag. 'Since when is being an insurance salesman a reserved occupation? And he didn't even do much of that.' She buttoned her coat. 'And he's already well practised at deserting – he left me quickly enough for his fancy woman, don't you remember? Why don't you tell that to your customers – the ones we have left, anyway. Listen, Ruby and I don't have time for this, we have to go.

45

Stay in the cellar if you have to ... and,' she added in an uncharacteristic moment of sharpness, 'do look after that precious box of documents, won't you? You wouldn't want them to fall into the wrong hands.' Leaving Winnie open-mouthed, she hastily took Ruby by the arm and ushered her through the side door and on to the pavement.

Empire Street was lit by a beautiful full moon, but Rita didn't have time to stop to admire the bright silver light. She knew it would make the bombers' task easier – although the anti-aircraft gunners would have a better chance of hitting a well-illuminated plane. People were pouring out from every door of the short street, hastening to the communal shelter. There was Violet from her parents' house, her gawky frame easily recognisable. She waved and came over.

'You on your own?' Rita asked her sister-in-law in surprise. The Feenys' place was usually bursting at the seams.

'I am,' said Violet in her strong Mancunian accent. 'Dolly's out fire-watching, Pop is on ARP duty, Sarah's at the Voluntary Aid Detachment post down the docks and Nancy went back to her mother-in-law's after supper, taking baby George with her. I've just locked up, so it's as safe as I can get it.' She smiled ruefully.

'No sign of Frank?' Rita asked.

'No, he's at his digs. He's doing a lot of night shifts this week,' Violet said. 'Hurry up, I don't like being out in this, it's like daylight.'

As the alarm continued to wail, the three women broke into a run towards the shelter. Once safely installed alongside their neighbours, they un-

46

packed their provisions and settled down, knowing it could be a long night. Rita was full of admiration for Violet; she never seemed to tire and her spirits never seemed to flag. She led them all in a singsong, though Rita thought the notes of 'Run Rabbit Run' and 'Pack Up Your Troubles' sounded rather gloomy as they fought with the rumble from the guns and incendiaries outside. And none of it could hide the whispers and mutterings occasionally directed at Ruby from some of the ruder elements among the street's residents. Rita pulled Ruby closer towards her and made soothing noises to calm the strange girl as they waited, for what seemed like an age, for the all-clear.

Warrant Officer Frank Feeny hurried down the concrete steps of Derby House, ready to show his ID for the second time since entering the building. Nowhere in the entire country was security taken more seriously than in this fortified bunker in the centre of Liverpool, which was now home to the command for the Western Approaches. It was no exaggeration to say that the fate of the war relied on what happened in these two storeys of underground offices, mess areas, and the vital map room, which served as the nerve centre for the Battle of the Atlantic.

He checked his watch as he handed over his pass. Just about on time – he hated to be late, as did everybody involved in this high-level operation. Even though today he would have had a valid excuse. Last night's raids had caused damage to the city centre, with the General Post Office being hit and the telephone exchange being affected; emergency exchanges had been at work ever since to ensure there was no breakdown in communications, but it was still a major cause for concern. Derby House had its own direct telephone line to the War Cabinet down in London, as top-secret news had to pass between the two centres at all hours of the day and night.

Frank rubbed his eyes, berating himself for feeling tired. After all this time in service he should be used to the demanding shifts by now. Despite the loss of his leg, he was still young and fit, even if he'd never be a champion boxer again. He needed to keep alert and all his wits about him. There was no room for anyone to make a mistake, here of all places.

'Good evening, Frank.' One of the teleprinter operators looked up as he passed by and gave him a cheeky smile. 'Manage to catch up on your beauty sleep today, did you?' She raised one eyebrow, and if Frank hadn't known better he'd have thought she was flirting with him.

'Can't you tell? I'm handsome enough already,' he managed to say automatically as he headed for the next room along. She was quite pretty, he recognised, with her hair in its victory roll, just like his sister Nancy liked to style hers. But he didn't have time to think about girls. They were a distraction and he couldn't afford that. One small slip and the consequences could be fatal in this line of work.

He was glad he'd settled into service accommodation rather than move back in with his family. He told himself it was because they were full enough, now his brother Eddy's wife Violet lived there while Eddy was back at sea with the Merchant Navy, and even his little sister Sarah was little no longer and serving her own shifts as a trainee nurse. They didn't need him waking them up at all hours. He'd have loved the comfort of his mother's cooking and the reassurance of his father's hard-earned wisdom, much of it gathered from the last war, but that was an indulgence he couldn't afford.

He didn't want to think about the other reason he stayed away. He would have had to look across the road at that other front door and know that Kitty was not going to step through it. When he'd first learnt that he was going to be stationed back in Liverpool, his heart had soared, despite his best attempts at reasoning, at the prospect of being near her. Somehow over the past couple of years she'd gone from being almost another sister to the one woman who made his pulse race, whose face he looked for in every crowd. But then he'd lost his leg and he knew no woman in her right mind would look at him twice. He had his pride; he wouldn't beg. And he absolutely would not hold her back. In his current state he would be a burden to any woman and he didn't want that – least of all for Kitty. It would be unbearable. He knew she was friendly with a doctor now, someone who had his full complement of limbs in working order, and whose job was to save lives; he was a lucky man and Frank hoped he knew it. But he cursed to the heavens above that just as he had returned to his Merseyside home, longing to see her again, Kitty had enlisted and been posted to the other end of the country.

CHAPTER FIVE

Nancy heard the flap of the letterbox rattle against the door and rushed to see what the postman had brought. She made a point of being the first to do this as she didn't trust her mother-in-law not to open her letters; for an old woman who complained she was ill all the time, Mrs Kerrigan was surprisingly quick off the mark. She had just managed to stuff the two envelopes bearing her name into her waistband and cover them with her cardigan when, sure enough, her mother-in-law emerged from the dining room.

'What is it?' she demanded. 'Is there anything from my poor boy?'

'Must have been the wind,' said Nancy brightly. 'There's nothing there. We can't expect Sid to write all the time, can we? He'll have other things on his mind. Oh, that's Georgie crying again, I'd better go.' She almost ran through the parlour door, ignoring the venomous look Mrs Kerrigan shot at her.

The parlour was gloomy, but at least it was Nancy's own space, which she rented from her in-laws in addition to the room she'd shared with Sid and insisted on keeping. She'd go mad without some privacy in the daytime. They had plenty of room, which was about the only good thing she could say for the cold, unwelcoming place. Now she drew a chair as close to the window as she could, to catch what meagre daylight managed to filter through the heavy net curtains.

Georgie looked up expectantly, crawling over and trying to pull himself up with the help of the chair leg. Nancy regarded him sadly. It was a shame that Sid would miss his son's first steps – it wouldn't be long now. Then George would be all over the place and she'd never have a moment's peace. George had never known his father, and she had almost forgotten what he looked like herself. She glanced over at the picture on the mantle of them both on their wedding day. She smiled at the picture, admiring her own shapely figure and the way the fashionable dress hugged her curves. It suited her to ignore the memory of the swell of Georgie in her tummy and how it had taken several goes to zip up the dress, and the bitter tears she'd cried that morning over the revelation that Sid had been carrying on with a fancy woman in the run-up to their big day – if she hadn't been in the family way then they'd never have made it up the aisle. Her smile drained away. Sid, well, he just looked like Sid, didn't he. 'Good boy,' she said wearily. 'Mummy's just going to read her letters, then she'll play with you.'

She opened the first envelope with its familiar handwriting. Mrs Kerrigan must never see this, must never know that Stan Hathaway was still writing to Nancy. The pilot's looping script was instantly recognisable and it would be evident to anyone who saw it that the letter came from someone in the services – not something from a POW camp forwarded by the Red Cross. She hoped the postman could be relied on for his

51

discretion, but she was far from sure he could. Her heart was hammering as she tore open the flap, careful not to rip the flimsy paper inside.

It was a short note, as Stan claimed he didn't have much time. Still, he wanted her to know he was thinking of her – Nancy could just imagine the gleam in his eye as he wrote that and exactly what he was thinking of – and couldn't wait to see her again. He wasn't able to say exactly where he was, but he was being kept busy, defending the skies. He wasn't sure when his next leave would be but maybe in another six weeks or so, if he was lucky. Nancy sighed with longing. She remembered how his touch made her feel, the sheer delight of being held by him making her reckless. Six weeks seemed like for ever. She didn't know how she'd be able to sneak past the dragon-like figure of her mother-in-law but she'd manage somehow. She'd have to. Nothing could keep her from the warm embrace of the gorgeous Stan Hathaway. Carefully she folded the precious piece of paper and reached to tuck it in her skirt pocket. She'd hide it away in her bedroom later. Mrs Kerrigan would think nothing of coming into the parlour if she was out and snooping about to see what evidence of her daughter-in-law's flightiness she could uncover.

'Mmm-mmm-mm.' Georgie reached for his mother's pocket, keen to see what the fuss was about.

'No, that's not for you,' Nancy said shortly. Then she saw her son's face fall and the trembling of his chin that heralded another bout of wailing. Hurriedly she relented, bending down and scooping him up to place him on her lap. 'Look what Mummy's got. This is a letter from Aunty Gloria. Shall we see what it says?'

She opened the envelope with the huge handwriting on it and George snatched it from her, happily tearing it in two and stuffing one bit into his mouth. Nancy debated whether to take it from him, knowing that even used envelopes should be saved as paper was so scarce. Then again, it was keeping him quiet, and as long as he didn't actually swallow it, it would probably do him no harm.

She unfolded the letter from her best friend, written on lavender-coloured notepaper and bearing a faint trace of Gloria's favourite perfume. Even though there was a war on, she'd never gone short of it, as there had always been an eager queue of men willing to do anything to present her with a bottle or two, no matter how it had been come by. Nancy felt a twinge of jealousy. She knew she was pretty but Gloria Arden was something else, with her natural silver-blonde hair and her golden voice. She looked like a film star and carried herself like one, for all that her parents ran the Sailor's Rest pub at the end of Empire Street. She had gone to London and been taken on by a leading impresario, who was arranging far more glamorous concerts for her than her old regular spot at Liverpool's Adelphi Hotel.

Nancy skimmed the page and gasped. The concerts had been a roaring success, Gloria reported, and she'd been asked to do more and more. London just loved her. The impresario, Romeo Brown, was talking about getting her to make a record. In order to whet the nation's appetite for that, he'd suggested a tour. She'd be heading up north, and a date had already been booked in Manchester. So she was going to persuade them to add a date in Liverpool. Then she would be able to stay for a while to see her family and, of course, her best friend.

Nancy was torn between the envy she always felt at Gloria's success and anticipation of her visit, when she would be able to bask in her friend's reflected glory. Life with Gloria was never dull, that was for certain. Trouble and adventure seemed to follow her around wherever she went. Nancy paused guiltily as she remembered that Gloria hadn't had it easy these past few months, as her posh pilot boyfriend had died saving her, shielding her from a blast during an air raid. Giles had only just proposed and it should have been the happiest night of Gloria's life, but tragedy had struck right at the moment of her triumph. So perhaps it was only to be expected that she would throw herself into her singing career.

'Well, Georgie, things are going to liven up a bit at last,' Nancy cooed to her son, as she retrieved the soggy paper from his mouth. 'Let's see what Granny Kerrigan says about *that*.'

And, she thought to herself, Gloria would know what to do about the other matter that was bothering Nancy. Not that there was really anything to worry about. But just in case it did turn out to be what she feared...

'Winnie not well again?' asked Vera Delaney, her lips pursed as she rubbed her finger along one of the shelves in the shop. 'That's a shame. Without her behind the counter this place is going to rack and ruin.' Dramatically, she held up her fingertip, which bore a trace of dust. 'Still, I suppose you've got more shelves to clean now there's not so much stock.'

'Well, there is a war on.' Rita struggled to keep her welcoming smile in place. 'What can I get you, Mrs Delaney?'

Vera hesitated. When Winnie was in charge she could get all manner of extras under the counter, but she was convinced nobody else knew about this, so she had no intention of asking Rita for any favours. She was all too aware Winnie distrusted her daughter-in-law. 'I'll just get my sugar ration,' she said, pursing her thin lips.

'Awful how it goes so fast, isn't it?' Rita said, trying to make conversation. She hated it when the atmosphere in the shop felt unfriendly.

Vera ignored her comment. 'Still no sign of your husband, then?'

Rita looked up from the counter. 'I'm sure Winnie told you, he went away to look after the children safely.'

Vera rolled her eyes. 'Dodge conscription, more like.' She reached for her sugar and handed over her coupon. 'Don't you try to lie to me, young lady. Word is out that your man is a deserter, plain and simple. I feel for Winnie, really I do, but when I think about what danger my Alfie is in down the docks it makes my blood boil.'

Rita didn't reply as she took the coupon, even though there was plenty she could have said about Alfie Delaney. True, he had a job on the docks and was therefore in theory in the most dangerous place on Merseyside, but he spent most of his time appropriating goods for the black market, some of which found their way into Winnie's cellar. He was far from the only dock worker helping himself to any extras that were available, but Alfie took it to a new height. When he wasn't doing this he was usually skiving. Admittedly he had performed one heroic deed, saving Tommy Callaghan from a burning warehouse, but that had been months ago. Vera couldn't resist mentioning this again.

'And him pulling that young rascal from the flames, when he had no call to be there! Putting his own life at risk like that! That's something we won't find your husband doing, I'll be bound.'

Rita smiled tightly, knowing that to say anything would be to give Vera even more ammunition. Somehow she had to ride out these snide remarks and hold her head high. She cursed Charlie for his cowardice. His reputation threatened to ruin her own, but she couldn't let that show.

Vera drew closer. 'Maybe you could let me know when Winnie will be back at work?'

Aha, thought Rita, that's what she's after – her usual parcel of ill-gotten luxuries. Before she could say anything, the shop door opened again and a gust of wind blew sharply down the narrow aisle.

'Morning, Rita!' Violet's lanky frame appeared silhouetted against a rare burst of sunlight. 'Hello, Mrs Delaney. Cold out, isn't it? Brass monkeys, as my brothers would say.' She threw her head back and gave her braying laugh – which took some getting used to – and her bright scarf slipped sideways on her poker-straight hair.

Vera shot her an infuriated glance. 'Well, if you'd tell Winnie that I asked after her...' She beat a hasty retreat. Violet beamed at her cheerfully.

'Bye, Mrs D, sorry you couldn't stop!' she called as the door slammed shut. She turned back to Rita. 'Horrible old bag, what did she want?'

Rita shook her head. 'Her sugar ration. Or that's what she said, anyway. Really she wanted to carp about Charlie and to find out when Winnie's back in charge so she can get bits and bobs on the QT.'

'Still no word from him then?' asked Violet sympathetically. She had never met the man, but had heard all about him from the rest of the family. Nobody had a good word to say about him.

'Not a dickie bird. He's as good as vanished,' Rita confirmed. She couldn't bring herself to mention the shame of hearing about the visit from the police. 'I can't pretend I'm sorry, and the children never even ask about him. We're better off without him. I just wish people wouldn't tar me with the same brush.'

'No, you mustn't think like that,' Violet said, immediately reassuring. 'Everyone knows how hard you work. How are Michael and Megan? Have you heard from them recently?'

Rita's expression changed at the thought of her beloved children. 'Yes, they write all the time – well, Michael writes, and Megan mostly sends drawings. They love it down on the farm. Joan and Seth, that's the couple who run the place, spoil them rotten. Now they've got Tommy as well, they're made up. He's big enough to help out with the animals. They'll never want to come home.'

She shook her head. 'I miss them of course. It's like going around without one of my limbs. But knowing they're safe and happy helps.'

'Can't you go and see them?' Violet wanted to know. 'You can't be at that hospital every day, week in, week out.'

Rita bit her lip. 'It's just that bit too far to do on my own. You can't rely on trains or buses and they're rather out in the sticks. Also, I get called in for extra shifts all the time – you know what it's like. Every time there's a direct hit on the docks or anywhere around here I could be needed and I hate to say no.'

'Of course,' Violet nodded. But she could sense her friend wanted to say more.

Rita glanced behind her, as if to check the inner door was firmly closed. 'Besides, I'm needed here,' she said quietly. 'Winnie's not been herself ever since I got the children back. She used to run this place like clockwork, but now she doesn't seem to bother about anything – not the orders, or the cashing up, or filling the shelves. I have to try to keep on top of that as well as everything else.' Her expression gave away just how tiring she was finding it.

'Oh, I'm sorry to hear that, I hadn't quite realised,' Violet said. 'You can't do everything, you know. Maybe I could help? I'm not very organised but I can talk to the customers all right.'

Rita smiled in gratitude. 'I know you could; you'd charm them and they'd love it. But you're so busy already, what with helping with little George and the WVS, and aren't you helping Mam with the new victory garden too? You've got your hands full.'

Violet shrugged. 'That's as may be, but you think about it. If I can be of any use I will – as long as you don't expect me to do any sums. I never was any good at maths, just you ask my Eddy.'

'Oh, I will, next time we see him.' Rita cheered up at the mention of her brother, who everyone thought of as the quiet one in the family, but who had a wicked sense of humour. 'Don't let me keep you. Did you want anything?'

'Some strong string,' said Violet, reaching for her purse. 'I'm going to mark out seed drills in the new plot. One of the old fellows from the Home Guard showed me how. We'll all have fresh carrots and be able to see in the dark.' She waved brightly and was on her way.

Rita grew solemn again as soon as she'd gone. Violet was a breath of fresh air, all right, but she'd feel bad asking her to help out any more than she already did. Besides, it was the sums that most needed attention. Rita had only just realised that the shop wasn't making anything like the income it had before Christmas, and she had no idea what to do about it. They needed the money – now Charlie had given up any pretence of providing for them. But there was no time to think about it now. She checked her watch, knowing that she'd have to set off for the hospital any minute.

'Winnie!' she called through the inner door. 'Are you ready to take over? I've got to get going.'

There was a shuffling and then Winnie slumped reluctantly along the corridor. 'When are you going to give up that ridiculous nursing job?' she demanded. 'Your place is here, looking after the shop and me. Now you've driven Charles away, it's the least you can do.'

Rita closed her eyes for a moment and prayed for strength. She would not rise to the vicious old woman's bait. 'I'll see you later,' she said instead, picking up her bag and jacket and making her way through the meagre stock to the outside door. She wrinkled her nose. It was still morning – but was that sherry she'd smelt on her mother-in-law's breath?

CHAPTER SIX

'Blast!' Laura sat back on her heels and groaned. 'You must think I'm a waste of space, Kitty, but this is much harder work than I'd ever have imagined.' She wrung the grey water out from her damp cloth over the galvanised bucket. The sleeves of her overall were dripping from where they'd come unrolled.

It seemed that all they'd done since arriving was to clean the building, scrubbing and polishing, even though it had evidently been scrubbed and polished to within an inch of its life already by the previous band of new recruits, and alternating this with gruelling rounds of PT. The girls had also been sent on errands around London, taking urgent papers between offices, dishing out tea at important meetings and generally making themselves useful. Kitty had found it a shock to the system. She'd been accustomed to lifting enormous heavy pans of stew around the NAAFI canteen, but running around on her feet all day, minding her p's and q's whilst learning the ropes had been exhausting, and it had been almost impossible to take it all in. To begin with it had been hard to adjust to sleeping in their dormitory – which they were told to call a cabin. Soon they would also embark on a series of classroom lectures to learn the rules and regulations of the service, along with the endless jargon everyone used.

Kitty couldn't help laughing at her friend. 'It's easier once you're used to it,' she said warmly. 'Believe me, I know. I've been scrubbing floors since I was eleven – that's when Mam died and I had to take over. Or even before that, as she couldn't bend down when she was expecting our Tommy.' A cloud passed across her face at the memory. 'Anyway, they won't have us doing this for long. It's just to make good use of our time until we're allocated our new positions.'

'I hope you're right,' said the young woman who'd been assigned to clean the corridor with them. 'This stuff is making my hands red raw. I wasn't sure what to expect in our first week but it wasn't this.'

Kitty regarded their new colleague with interest. She was slight, and had very pale skin and a smattering of freckles across her small upturned nose. While she was not conventionally pretty, she had striking looks and an air of determination and energy about her that somehow reminded Kitty of her old friend Rita back in Empire Street. 'I bet they think that as long as they have a group of women together they might as well set us to clean up the place,' she said, shaking the bristles of her scrubbing brush with vigour. 'But I'm sure they'll start training us to do something else once we're all here and the place is shipshape. What did you do before?'

The girl raised an eyebrow. 'I was a teacher.'

'A teacher!' Kitty gasped. 'You don't look old enough ... sorry, I don't mean to be rude, but...'

'I'm older than I look,' said the girl. 'Don't worry, everyone says the same to me. I'm twenty-three. I trained for two years, and then all the kids got evacuated, and I thought, "Marjorie, my girl, you'd better find something else to do with yourself and do it sharpish." So here I am.' She shrugged.

Kitty couldn't help staring. Nobody from Empire Street had ever been a teacher, much less any of the women. Hardly anyone stayed at school longer than they had to; they were all needed to go out and work, or help raise the families, or both. It was all she could do to stop her mouth gaping open. 'Well, at least you'll be all right with these lectures we're going to have to go to. I can hardly remember the last time I sat at a desk – I'll probably be useless. Don't you miss your job?' she managed to say after a moment.

Marjorie looked wistful. 'I'd be lying if I said I didn't. I had to fight tooth and nail to do my training. My family thought I was crazy, spending all that time studying for my Higher Cert and then going to college, when I'd only end up getting married and having to give up anyway.' She shook her head. 'Well, that's not going to happen. I prefer teaching to going out with men and I'm not ashamed to say so. When this war ends I'll be back in the classroom like a shot. But meanwhile I'll do whatever's needed here. It's just a pity that happens to be scrubbing floors, or ferrying urgent messages backwards and forwards, never mind the endless PT lessons. I know we'll have to be fit, but at the moment my muscles don't know what's hit them.'

'Too true.' Laura sloshed the water around in the bucket and went back to the task in hand. 'You must have been really determined to get to college, Marjorie. I must say I envy you. I'd have loved to be allowed to study like my brother, but my folks wouldn't hear of it. My father still thinks that women get ill if they have to think too hard. Doesn't want me coming down with a fit of the vapours.' She rubbed at the tiles. 'There, that's better. Do you think they've ever been so shiny?' She sat back on her heels once more. 'I probably shouldn't say it, but if there's anything good to come out of this war, then maybe it's going to be people like us having the chance to find out what we're good at and to get on and do it. I've always been terrible at sitting around in drawing rooms and making polite conversation. There must be more to life.'

Kitty giggled. 'I'd have loved to be made to sit down and talk to people. We never had time for that.' The very idea was completely opposite to what she'd known in her life so far. Perhaps that was no bad thing. She wanted to be fully prepared for whatever was going to happen to them next. If their future survival was going to depend on their physical fitness in any way, she wouldn't complain about the seemingly pointless rounds of PT.

Marjorie looked at them both and smiled. 'I was always too busy studying or marking to do much of that either. So what are you good at, Laura? Apart from your budding ability to clean a floor?'

Laura pushed up her sleeves again. 'I, my dear, am good at having fun.' She grinned mischievously. 'Stick with me and I'll show you how, you see if I don't.'

Danny Callaghan sat at the kitchen table and felt the silence echoing around him. He couldn't get used to it. He'd never experienced anything like it in this house – there had always been Kitty bustling around, Tommy bothering them both, and now and again Jack striding about and giving him advice, whether he wanted it or not. Then there had been all the friends and neighbours popping in and out, passing the time of day, sharing cups of tea. He could hardly believe it was the same place. There was the kettle still in its spot on the hob, there were the cups and saucers and plates, steadily getting more chipped, but there was no delicious smell of baking from when Kitty miraculously managed to procure the ingredients for one of her delicious cakes or pies, and no pile of scraps that Tommy had salvaged from a bomb site and brought home to keep in case they were useful.

He couldn't stand the thought that everyone was out doing their bit for the war effort when he was confined like this. He wasn't usually given to self-pity or despair, but if he allowed himself to think too far ahead he could feel all hope draining from him. He was young, he was enthusiastic, he didn't know the meaning of fear, and yet all because of a ridiculous twist of fate he wasn't allowed to fight for his country's freedom. It hurt him bitterly.

Sighing, he drew the newspaper towards him. This was his one regular piece of routine: ever since coming out of hospital he had made himself do the crossword every day. He'd never seen the point of it before, but during the long, empty hours convalescing on the ward, a fellow patient had introduced him to the challenge of filling in the gaps, solving the complicated clues. He'd bonded with the older man and somehow their shared interest had overcome the difference in their backgrounds. It turned out that the man was a high-ranking officer, who'd now returned to some shadowy behind-the-scenes, hush-hush role, whereas of course Danny had never been able to join any of the armed services, thanks to his damaged heart. But for those few moments the two men had been united in tracking down the perfect solution, and Danny had been bitten by the crossword bug. He'd made himself do one a day ever since. It was strange in some ways. He'd been no slouch at school, but had been too restless ever to settle down and make the most of his studies. He knew he had a good brain but had preferred to use it coming up with the latest scheme to make money or have some fun while working on the docks. Now all that was denied him, for the immediate future anyway, he took refuge in the pastime of thinking for its own sake.

He was absorbed in what he thought must be an anagram when there was a knock at the door. He almost jumped, he'd been staring so intensely at the arrangement of letters, willing them to form a recognisable word. He shook himself and shouted 'come in', as the door opened anyway and Sarah Feeny stepped inside.

The youngest of the Feenys, Sarah shared the no-nonsense, get-up-and-go attitude of her mother. She'd taken to her VAD nurse training like a duck to water, despite being so young. There wasn't much that shocked or surprised her – having all those older brothers and sisters meant she'd heard it all before. Now she looked about her and grinned. 'Blimey, Danny, it's as quiet as a church in here.'

'Tell me about it.' Danny made a face. 'Cup of tea? The pot's around somewhere.'

'Oh, I can see it, I'll do it,' Sarah offered at once.

Danny rose. 'I'm not dead yet, I can still make a pot of tea,' he told her, more sharply than he'd intended.

Sarah's face fell. 'I didn't mean it like that, you know I didn't. I was just trying to be helpful.'

Danny groaned inwardly. He knew he was over-sensitive to everyone trying to molly-coddle him, and that's why he hadn't told anyone about his condition in the first place – anyone apart from Sarah, who'd found out. She was the last person he wanted to snap at and he felt bad about it, but that's what came of spending too long on his own with only his puzzles for company.

'I know,' he said, his face softening. 'But it'll do me good to stretch my legs a bit. You make yourself comfortable, you must have been rushing round all day. Take the weight off your feet, I'll only be half a mo.'

Sarah sank gratefully into the chair that until recently had been Kitty's. 'It's so nice to have a bit of peace! No, don't look like that, I mean it. People have been shouting at me all day at work and my head's fit to burst with all the things I'm meant to remember. Then I come home and there isn't a spare inch of space. Nancy's in a mad flap because Gloria's coming back for a visit and she hasn't got anything to wear if they go out. Rita's there because Mrs Kennedy's driving her round the bend. Violet's going on and on about the victory garden – you'd think she'd been a farmer or something before she married Eddy. Mam's got piles of old rags everywhere, which she says are for her make-do-and-mend classes. Mam and Pop are bickering like they always do. It's like a madhouse.' Her hand flew to her mouth. 'Oh, don't listen to me, I don't mean it. I love them all, you know that. But sometimes it gets to me, I can't help it.'

Danny smiled. 'A bit of a contrast to here, which is like a monastery. You're doing me a favour keeping me from going crackers rattling around here on my own.'

Sarah beamed. 'Good, I'll put my feet up then. Don't suppose you've got any sugar? I know we aren't supposed to have any in our tea now as it's not patriotic, but some days it's the only thing that'll keep me going.'

Danny turned to the corner cupboard. 'Don't tell anyone, but I've got a secret stash of it in

67

here. What's the point of working on the docks if you can't sweeten your tea now and again?' He passed it across. 'Just don't make a habit of it, all right – it might have to last for the rest of the war, however long that'll be. My contacts aren't what they were, not since the fire.' He smiled ruefully.

'Don't worry, this is a treat,' said Sarah, stirring the precious sugar into her drink. 'I'm not encouraging you to go on the black market, Danny. Not like that Mrs Kennedy, we all know what used to go on in her shop.'

'Used to?'

Sarah looked up at him, registering how pale he looked, his face white in contrast to his dark wavy hair. 'You haven't been in there recently, then? It's driving Rita mad. Winnie's hardly ever behind the counter, Rita's left to open up and shut the shop, and it's hardly making any money any more. She never has a moment to think straight, let alone visit the children. I think missing Michael and Megan is making it worse.'

'But they're happy on the farm, aren't they?' asked Danny. 'Our Tommy's having the time of his life. Or so I gather from his letters. His handwriting isn't the greatest, but he goes on and on about the animals, they're turning him into a right farmer. At least he's making himself useful digging for victory. He loves it, so I bet the others do too.'

'It's not that so much as being apart from them,' said Sarah. 'Honestly, Danny, they're all fine. Rita showed me one of Michael's letters – they couldn't be in a better place. But she misses them like mad, even though she knows they're

68

safer there than just about anywhere.'

'Can't she go and see them?' asked Danny, then cursed himself for his own stupidity. What had Sarah just told him? The shop wasn't making money and Rita had hardly any spare time. Of course she couldn't just up sticks and catch a bus out to the country – always supposing there were buses running anyway.

Sarah shrugged. 'You know it's not that easy. Pop would take her in his cart but he's never home either – he's on ARP duty all the time. When he isn't, he's sleeping off the night shifts. You know how it is.'

Danny nodded. He remembered all too well the effects of working night shifts. Your brain didn't feel as if it was your own. Then the idea struck him.

'Why don't I take her?'

'Well, I'm sure it would be a lovely thing to do but...' she began.

'No buts,' said Danny, suddenly seeing that this was the ideal solution. 'Come on, Sar, it'll be doing me a favour. I get to leave the house, but I'll be sitting down the whole time so won't need to worry about me ticker – while Rita gets an escort to see the kids. I get to see Tommy, check he hasn't run too wild. Everyone wins.' He stood up.

'Danny, what are you doing?' Sarah set down her mug.

'Well, you just said they're all there. We'll go and tell them now. No time like the present.' And before she could stop him, Danny headed out of the door, a new spring in his step.

CHAPTER SEVEN

'Now are you sure you'll be all right?' Rita was torn between wanting to get going as soon as possible and anxiety that her sister-in-law wouldn't be able to manage. She hastily buttoned her coat against the chilly spring breeze blowing through the open shop door.

'Of course!' Violet assured her. 'Don't even give it a thought, I'll be absolutely fine. What can go wrong? You get off and see those children. There's Danny now with the cart. Go on, stop mithering, I'll see you later.' She all but pushed Rita out of the door.

Rita hopped up on the cart beside Danny, tucking a loose strand of red hair behind her ear. 'If there are any problems just make a note and I'll sort everything out later,' she called. She waved as Danny lifted the reins and the horse began the steady clip-clop that would take her to her beloved children.

Violet waved back cheerfully but gave a sigh of relief as she shut the shop door. She was sure that she could cope, but somehow not having Rita around made her feel more worried than she expected. She glanced around the place. Rita had dealt with the early morning rush, when the dock workers came in to get their newspapers, cigarettes and other essentials, and now everything was quiet. This was when Winnie would normally take over, but she'd gone back to her bed in a huff once she learnt that Violet had been drafted in to help, muttering what were most probably insults as she retreated up the stairs. Violet could have sworn the older woman had been unsteady on her feet, her eyes red, but she wasn't going to dwell on it. She'd rather face a day in the shop on her own than share the cramped space with Winnie, who in their short acquaintance had been nothing but unpleasant. Still, she wasn't going to let that upset her; according to Rita and Dolly, the miserable old bag was like that to everyone.

Violet decided the shelves could do with a clean. Poor Rita, she must never have the time to do it, so this would be something she'd appreciate. Violet wasn't scared of hard work and elbow grease and she soon had the surfaces gleaming. Beaming, she looked around in satisfaction. That was a big improvement. Working in a shop was a doddle, she decided, as she put her duster behind the counter and smoothed down the front of her printed overall. Rita had been fussing about nothing.

No sooner had she settled herself on the stool behind the counter than the bell rang and a plump figure in a plaid headscarf came in. Violet recognised Mrs Mawdsley, a friend of Dolly's from the WVS. She was a bit of a dragon when you first met her but nice underneath.

'Oh, it's you, dear!' Mrs Mawdsley peered short-sightedly over her round glasses. 'I didn't expect to see you here. Has there been an emergency? I do hope everyone's all right...'

'Nothing to worry about, Mrs Mawdsley,' Violet said hurriedly, cutting off her customer before she

71

could work herself into a tizz. 'Rita's gone to see her children for the day and so I'm standing in. How can I help you?'

The older woman undid her scarf and came closer. 'Well, that's very good of you, dear. That's what families are for, though, isn't it? I won't keep you for long. I'm looking for some clothes pegs.'

Violet smiled in relief. 'Well, you won't need ration coupons for those.' She'd been slightly confused by Rita's explanation of which goods were rationed and which weren't, and how the system worked, but this request should be simple enough. 'Household goods are on these shelves here – but I expect you know that better than I do.'

Mrs Mawdsley beamed at the suggestion she knew her way around the shop better than the staff. 'I do indeed, dear. Oh, someone's made this look nice. Was that you? Dolly's always saying what an asset you are around the house, and I expect Mrs Kennedy will be delighted.'

Violet smiled back but said nothing. She doubted Winnie would be delighted about anything.

'Here we are, then. I'll have two sets, a small and a large, just in case.' The woman fiddled with her purse. 'Now, I'm afraid I have no change, but I hope that won't be a problem.'

'Of course not.' Violet held out her hand and Mrs Mawdsley gave her half a crown. Violet's smile began to falter. Mental arithmetic was not her strong point. It was bad enough that there were two things to add up, but they were at different prices, and that made it more difficult. She looked around for a notebook. Maybe if she wrote it down it would be easier.

The doorbell rang again. A frail old lady stepped inside, drawing her shawl around her thin shoulders. 'Hello, Mrs Mawdsley,' she said in a tremulous voice. 'And ... it's not Rita, is it? No, I can see you have different hair, young lady. My memory's not what it was, you'll have to–'

'It's Violet, Mrs Ashby,' said Violet, recognising the oldest inhabitant of Empire Street. 'I married Eddy Feeny, you know. Haven't seen you since we were in the shelter together for the last air raid.'

'That's it!' The old lady's face lit up. 'So you're helping out here, are you? I'm glad to see you. Now maybe you can help me with my sugar ration. I like it when Rita does it, she's always very fair, but sometimes,' she dropped her voice, 'Mrs Kennedy gets it a bit wrong and there never seems to be enough in the packet.' She reached into her battered handbag.

'Don't you fret, Mrs Ashby, I'll see you right,' Violet assured her. 'Let me see, I know the stamp for the coupons is back here somewhere...'

Mrs Mawdsley leant across the counter and tapped the front of a small drawer. 'In here, dear. I think you'll find that's where it usually is.'

'Oh yes, that's the place, Rita did show me.' Violet was getting really flustered now. 'So, you give me your coupon...'

'But I just did, dear.' Mrs Ashby's voice shook a little but she was adamant. 'One moment ago. You've taken it already.'

Violet clapped her hand to her forehead. 'Silly me. What am I like? Yes, you gave me the coupon, now where...'

73

'It's by the till where you put it,' Mrs Mawdsley explained. 'Right next to my half-crown. You've still got to give me my change.'

'Yes, so I have.' Violet stared at the counter. 'It was two packs of pegs, one large and one small, so that's … that's…'

'You owe me one and six, dear,' said Mrs Mawdsley, taking pity on Violet's inexperience. 'You do know what that looks like, don't you?'

Violet wilted under the gentle sarcasm then drew herself up straight. 'Of course I do.' She pinged open the till. 'Here you are. And here you are, Mrs Ashby.' She carefully cancelled the precious coupon. 'Shall I put the sugar in your handbag?'

'Thank you, Mrs Feeny,' said the old lady, her eyes bright. 'Oh, doesn't it sound funny to say that. But now Dolly isn't the only Mrs Feeny on Empire Street. Your Eddy beat his brother Frank down the aisle, who'd have thought it? He's a dark horse, your young man. But you must be very proud of him.'

'Oh I am, Mrs Ashby.' Suddenly Violet found there was a lump in her throat. It was so long since she'd seen her husband, and being in the Merchant Navy he was putting himself in danger every minute of the day. But it wouldn't do to show her fear for his safety. She forced herself to smile. 'He's one in a million, my Eddy. I'll tell him you were asking after him when I next write.'

Mrs Mawdsley gave her a knowing look. 'Chin up, that's the spirit. Give him something to be proud of when he comes home. It's not easy having your man away, is it? I remember when Mr Mawdsley was away during the last war…' She

74

fell silent for an instant and her face became unexpectedly tender. 'Ah, well. It doesn't do to dwell. You'll soon get the hang of this place and it will be a big help to Rita.' She linked her arm with that of the old lady. 'Come along, Mrs Ashby, I'll see you home.'

As soon as the door swung shut behind them, Violet collapsed on the stool. She couldn't believe how tricky that had been, and it was only two customers with simple orders. How did Rita do it, serving all the dock workers practically at once? She supposed it was all a question of practice. Well, she had given her word that she would help out and she couldn't back out now. Her pride wouldn't let her – and she wouldn't give Winnie Kennedy the satisfaction.

Back home after his day out, Danny shivered as he tried to coax the fire alight. Who would have thought it could be so cold riding on Pop's cart? His hands were freezing. But it had been worth it, to see the pleasure on Rita's face and the delighted smiles from Michael and Megan. Of course Tommy had been there too and he'd loved having his big brother coming to visit, and had shown Danny round every inch of the farm. Danny had to admit he'd been impressed; Tommy had sounded as if he knew what he was talking about when he'd explained how he looked after the animals and what some of the machinery did. All three children were pictures of health, thriving on the good food that Joan and Seth, the farming couple, could provide. Rita had almost cried at the sight of Megan, who she'd confessed she was most

75

worried about. Megan had hated it when Charlie had taken her away from Empire Street and had become nervous and withdrawn. Now she was running around non-stop, her cheeks rosy and her eyes shining. It was her job to check for fresh eggs every morning, which Joan then scrambled for them all with loads of butter. Danny's mouth had watered at the description of their breakfasts. It had been a long time since he'd had loads of butter, even with his connections on the docks.

Finally he got the fire lit. Then he turned to the bag that Joan had insisted he take back with him: there was some of the famous precious butter, a box of eggs gathered by Megan, some of Joan's home-made bread and scones, and some vegetables straight from the field.

Tommy had laughed when Joan had handed it over. 'Danny don't know how to cook,' he'd said. 'Kitty did all of that for him.'

Danny had pretended to clip him round the ear. 'How do you think I've been managing all this time? I'm not completely useless, I'll have you know.' But now, looking at the bag of treats, he had to admit that Kitty would have known exactly what to do with them. He sighed; surely it wasn't beyond him to make a vegetable stew? He could ask Rita for advice.

His thoughts turned to what Rita had said on the way back. On the outward journey she had talked of nothing but the children, her worries for them and her fears of what damage Charlie's behaviour might have caused. Seeing the pair of them so happy and settled had calmed her anxiety on that front. So on the way back their conversation had become more personal.

Danny had known Rita all his life and she was almost like another sister to him – particularly as she was so close to his own sister, Kitty. He'd never had much time for her husband, thinking that Charlie was too full of himself, always ready to look down on everyone, and with very little cause as far as Danny could see. But he'd been too busy with his own life to take much notice of what had gone on nine years ago. He'd known Rita had been walking out with his big brother Jack back then, but that was about as far as his interest went.

On their journey back, as they had sat together on Pop's old cart, Rita had asked him for a favour.

'I have to tell you something, Danny,' she'd said, nervously retying the knot of her headscarf. The worn material had slipped back over her wavy red hair and her hands shook slightly as the wind grew chillier. 'I swore to your brother Jack that I'd write to him now he's away and I want to keep my promise. He's been writing back to me. The thing is, he always wrote care of Kitty...'

'Oh, right,' Danny had said, not sure in which direction this conversation was heading. If two old friends wanted to write to each other, who was he to stop them? But he couldn't see what it had to do with him.

'Well, now she's not here any more,' Rita went on, pausing a little and then resuming when Danny didn't get the hint. 'Look, I don't want him to send them direct, as Winnie would get hold of them and then have the wrong idea.'

True enough, Danny thought, nodding. Winnie

was mean enough to use that sort of thing against her – she would do anything to stir up spite and hurtful gossip.

'There's nothing bad in them, Danny,' Rita had assured him, her eyes brimming with tears. 'We aren't doing anything wrong. It's just two friends writing to each other. He gives me such good advice about the children, and now Charlie's not around... It means the world to me to have his letters. Sometimes, when Winnie's getting me down and I'm tired out from doing a late shift then working in the shop ... well, it peps me up to hear from him. I don't want to ask you to do something you don't feel is right but ... would you mind ... could he send them to you? Then I could pop by and pick them up.'

Danny could see that this made sense. If Rita found Jack's letters a comfort, then who was he to deny her that? He could see how Jack's advice would be valuable to her, as his big brother had always been the steady, reliable one, unlike himself in the good old days before the fire when he'd had lots of carefree fun with numerous girls. Jack had always been sensible. Rita needed someone like that outside her own family, where nobody could say a thing without the entire house knowing. Jack would be the voice of reason. So he'd agreed. Jack would be pleased that Danny was prepared to help; he'd maybe even think his irrepressible younger brother was finally growing up.

Danny had just made himself a sandwich with Joan's bread and butter and some Spam he'd found in the cupboard when there was a knock at the door. Some instinct made him shove the bag of farm produce away out of sight before going to see who it was. Usually he wouldn't have bothered, but somehow his suspicions were raised.

He opened the front door and there was Alfie Delaney.

Danny groaned inwardly. His former colleague from the docks was the last person he wanted to see. But he couldn't exactly turn him away.

'Evening, Danny,' said Alfie, all smiles. That had to mean he wanted something. 'Aren't you going to ask me in?'

Danny grunted and led the way back into the house, to where the fire was now burning brightly. He pulled up a chair and sat beside it. Alfie didn't wait to be asked but did the same. 'Oh, this is nice. Lovely warm fire, Danny. Proper little housewife, aren't you?'

Danny glared at him. 'Come round this late just to say that, did you, Alf?'

Alfie looked up. 'No need to take that tone with me, Danny. I was paying you a compliment.'

Danny shook his head, knowing it was no such thing. Alfie reserved his compliments for when they were useful, when they would get him something he wouldn't be able to have otherwise. Danny wanted the man out of the house as soon as possible, not to have him making himself comfortable in front of the fire. 'So, what's this about, then? What's brought you sniffing around here?'

'I'm concerned for your welfare, Danny,' said Alfie, a sly smile on his face. 'Haven't seen you down the docks for ages, and we all know you've been ill with your dicky ticker. Heard you were all alone in here so I thought I'd better see that you

79

were all right.'

'Very kind of you, I'm sure.' Danny eyed his visitor warily.

'And of course I wondered if you'd had any more thoughts on that little proposition we spoke about,' Alfie went on, his voice as light as if he was just talking about the weather.

Danny wasn't fooled for a minute. 'If you mean am I going to take the medical test for you, the answer is no and it's going to stay that way. It's fraud and we could both end up in hot water. You know it as well as I do.' Alfie had been keen to dodge the call-up, and knew that if Danny took the regulation medical exam in his place, he'd be granted exemption. There was no way Danny's heart could pass for normal.

'Danny, Danny, you aren't making any sense,' sighed Alfie. 'You having a bad heart could be a golden opportunity. I'd make it worth your while. Come on, make the most of this gift – it's been handed to you on a plate.'

Easy to say when it wasn't your heart that was damaged, thought Danny sourly, but he was far too proud to complain about his condition to the likes of Alfie Delaney. 'No,' he said shortly.

'And talking of gifts,' Alfie continued, his voice more menacing now, 'did Tommy like those boots? I hear he's got lots of fields to run around in now.'

Alfie had given Tommy some brand-new top-quality football boots for Christmas, but Danny had known it was a bribe, intended to make him feel he owed Delaney something. 'You leave him out of it,' he said. While it was no secret that Tommy had been evacuated to the countryside, he felt uneasy that Alfie was apparently so well informed.

'And how's the lovely Kitty? A little bird told me she's not around at the moment either.'

'What's it to you?' Danny demanded. He'd never liked the way Alfie looked at his sister. Thank God she was safely out of his grasp down in London.

Alfie raised his eyebrows. 'Doing her bit for king and country, is she? Well, I expect she'll have some leave soon. I've always had a soft spot for her and I reckon she likes me 'n' all. I shall look forward to getting reacquainted with her,' he leered.

Danny fought to keep control of his temper. Alfie wasn't fit to lick Kitty's boots. 'Yes, some people do the right thing now there's a war on,' he snapped, knowing that Alfie, for all his bluster and menace, was an utter coward who would do anything to avoid being called up. 'And for your information, no, she isn't coming back any time soon. So if that's all you've come to say, you're wasting your breath.'

'Lucky for you that I'm still in a reserved occupation,' Alfie said, slowly getting to his feet. 'But if I need that favour done sharpish, you can be sure I'll be back. After all, me and Harry Calendar know a few things about you, Danny. Not always so high and mighty, were you? Not always so keen to stay on the right side of the law. When I need you, you'll find it better all round to do as I say.' He buttoned his coat, a luxuriously soft woollen one that must have cost him a fortune – which he wouldn't have managed on a charge hand's wages. 'Give my fondest regards to your sister. Show myself out, shall I? We don't want to upset the invalid now, do we?' With that final dig, he was off, slamming the front door behind him.

Danny put his head in his hands. Suddenly the thought of his sandwich didn't seem so appealing after all.

CHAPTER EIGHT

'Are you sure this is all right?' Kitty said nervously, brushing her hand against the soft silk collar of the dress she was wearing. It was the perfect shade for her, a deep dusky pink, accentuating her rosy cheeks and shiny dark hair. Laura had offered to lend her the dress as soon as she'd confessed she didn't have anything smart. But it made her uneasy – she didn't like borrowing when she couldn't return the favour.

'Of course I'm sure,' Laura said briskly. 'Couldn't have you going out dancing in your overall, now could we? Please, don't even mention it.' She turned around. 'Come on, Marjorie, keep up. We've got to get in the queue as early as possible so we can bag a decent table. We want to be close enough to hear the band and to see everyone who's there. It will be a big crowd tonight, I'll bet you any money.'

Marjorie hurried along the pavement in her peep-toe sandals, which she'd admitted she hadn't worn very often. 'Not sure I like the sound of crowds,' she said uncertainly. 'Really, I'm not used to them.'

Laura looked perplexed. 'I thought you said you came from near Brighton? That's hardly a village, is it?'

'Yes, but I always spent my Saturday evenings studying, or else preparing lessons,' Marjorie explained, nearly tripping over her own feet as she breathlessly drew level with the other two young women. 'This is all a bit much. Why did we have to go so far from our billet? It's taken us ages and we had to change buses.'

'Because the Hammersmith Palais is the place to be, no question about it,' Laura insisted with a knowing air. 'Trust me on this. If you like dancing, there's nowhere to beat it. And if you don't like dancing, well, you're no friend of mine,' she added grandly, sweeping around the corner and joining the back of the queue. 'Well done, girls. We've made it in good time. You won't be disappointed, I swear.'

Kitty glanced around her. There was a tangible air of excitement as the revellers huddled out of the wind, all dressed up in their finery. There might be a war on, but that wasn't stopping this group of young people – and some not so young – from wearing their best and going out with the determination to have a proper night of dancing and enjoyment. She pulled up the collar of her old coat, glad of its meagre protection. There seemed to be a lot of men in uniform, either in groups with the women or in small gatherings of three or four, eyeing the crowd for prospective dance partners, or maybe something more. She squared her shoulders. She was not going to be put off by a few cheeky glances. She'd dealt with worse. She reckoned Laura had too. Marjorie, though – she wasn't so sure.

Slowly the queue shuffled along and they drew ever closer to the big doors to the famous dance hall. Laura was smiling from ear to ear. 'I love this place,' she said. 'I used to come here before the fighting broke out. Of course, once the air raids started, it made coming to London that tiny bit more inconvenient.' She sighed. 'Now relax and remember, just because a chap asks you for a dance, it doesn't give him sole rights over you all evening; there's plenty of us to go round. Here we are. Ready? We can leave our coats in the cloakroom. We don't want to spoil the impression of our lovely frocks with these sensible old things.'

Kitty reflected that Laura's beautiful coat couldn't be called a sensible old thing by any stretch of the imagination, but her new friend had a point. As she handed over her serviceable coat and smoothed down her skirt, Kitty was glad she'd borrowed the lovely pink dress after all. She would have felt completely out of place if she hadn't dressed up.

'This way.' Laura was a woman on a mission, turning down Marjorie's suggestion that they go to brush their hair. 'We can go and freshen up our lipstick in a moment – no, you don't have to if you don't want to, Marjorie, but I intend to. First we stake our claim to a table. Then we can go in turn so we don't lose our place. Here we are, just the ticket. Marjorie, you sit there.'

Kitty was impressed with Laura's choice. They had a view of where the dance band would be and they weren't too far from the dance floor, but they had the perfect angle to view everyone arriving and milling around. And, she had to admit, people would have quite a good view of them too. She knew that Laura, with her air of confidence and stylish hairstyle – and of course beautiful clothes – would attract attention. Maybe she herself wouldn't look too bad either. The pink dress boosted her spirits and looked good with her dark, wavy hair. Not that she was here to find romance – she was going to be totally loyal to Elliott, and his familiar warm face floated before her vision. She knew he wouldn't begrudge her a night out, though, not after her hard weeks of initial training. Soon she hoped to be a fully fledged Wren. She'd write to tell him of their adventure when she got back to the billet.

Marjorie, birdlike, perched restlessly on her seat. She too had borrowed a dress from Laura, with a sweetheart neckline, in a stunning shade of eau de nil. She looked around them, eyes flickering with anxiety. 'Kitty, what are we doing here? I wish we hadn't come. Everyone's staring at us.'

'No they aren't,' Kitty reassured her, almost as a way of reassuring herself. 'Or only as much as everyone's looking at everyone else. Don't worry. You must be accustomed to all your pupils staring at you, aren't you? You'd have to stand there in front of them and demand their attention.' She found it hard to understand why anyone who'd gone so far as to qualify as a teacher could be so nervous, when she herself had so many reasons for feeling uncomfortable among a crowd of people who seemed to have so much more experience of life than she had.

'That's different,' Marjorie said instantly, tossing her hair. 'I know what I'm doing in a classroom. People look at you for a reason. Here, I don't know ... what'll I say if anyone comes over?'

'I suppose you just say what you like,' Kitty grinned. 'Here's your chance to practise – a waiter's coming our way.'

Laura looked up as the smart older man swept over to them. 'What can I get you, ladies?'

'I'll have a cocktail,' Laura said at once. 'Can you do me a gin and tonic? Or as close as you can manage.' She flashed her brilliant smile. 'How about you, Marjorie?'

Marjorie hesitated. 'Oh, just water,' she said.

'You can't have just water on a night out at the Palais!' Laura objected.

'But I don't drink alcohol,' Marjorie protested. 'I wouldn't know how to start, I don't know what I like.'

'Maybe a lemonade?' the waiter suggested diplomatically. Kitty reckoned he'd heard this conversation many times before.

'You've had most of your life to drink lemonade,' Laura interrupted swiftly. 'Time to break away from the schoolroom, Marjorie. How about a martini? She'll have a martini,' she said to the waiter, before Marjorie could contradict her.

The waiter turned to Kitty.

'I'll have a shandy,' she said, feeling very daring. She'd never been one for alcohol either. The memory of her father's drunken rages followed by his moods of abject despair had put her off. But, she reasoned, one glass of shandy wasn't

86

going to turn her into her father. It might even give her a bit of much-needed Dutch courage.

'Right, I'm off to powder my nose.' Laura stood up. 'See you in a minute.'

Kitty watched as plenty of servicemen in uniform turned to observe her sophisticated friend as she made her way across the hall. Several then turned back to see which table Laura might have come from. A few seemed to be interested, and finally two broke ranks and wandered across to them. Marjorie immediately fixed her gaze on the table top. Kitty sighed anxiously. It looked as if it would be up to her to make conversation. She'd have to get a grip and not let nerves overcome her.

The taller of the two men was a corporal in the army by his uniform. Kitty smiled in a friendly way without any flirtatiousness as he drew closer. 'We hate to see you girls sitting on your own,' he said with a grin. 'How about a turn on the dance floor?'

Kitty shook her head, remembering how she had parried the banter in the NAAFI canteen. 'I'm hopeless at dancing, I have to warn you. We're just enjoying ourselves, watching the world go by.'

'And what do you do?' asked the shorter one, whose hair had been slicked back so carefully that it shone brightly, reflecting the lamps dotted around the hall. 'With your looks, you've got to be models. Bet you spend all day getting your pictures taken.' He looked at them hopefully, wondering if his flattery had worked.

Kitty batted it away. 'Now we can't tell you what we do, you know that,' she said. 'Careless talk costs lives; loose lips sink ships. Let's just say it's a bit more useful than modelling.'

The young man's face fell, but his companion's brightened up as Laura returned, her lipstick freshly painted and her hair brushed into shape. 'Who's your friend? I don't suppose you fancy a dance, do you?'

Laura looked him up and down, seeming to assess him as a potential dance partner before cocking her head and saying, 'Well, why not? It's what we've come here for.' Not giving him a chance to change his mind, she boldly took his arm and led him towards where a small crowd was gathering ready for the next dance.

His companion promptly lost his nerve and scuttled back to their group of friends who, by the looks of it, proceeded to mock him roundly for being such a coward.

'Well, Laura doesn't hang around,' Kitty observed, as the waiter came with their drinks. She took a sniff of the cocktail. 'Ugh, she's welcome to that, though. I'll stick to the shandy.' She raised her glass. 'Cheers, Marjorie. To happier days.'

'Ummm.' Marjorie clinked her martini glass against Kitty's and sipped, first cautiously and then with more enthusiasm. 'This is nice, though. It's getting really busy, isn't it? Laura was right to make us arrive early. I wouldn't want to be stuck at the back, or so far forward that everyone trips over you.'

Kitty grinned. It sounded as if Marjorie was beginning to relax and find it not so bad after all. Maybe they'd make it through the evening without embarrassing themselves. 'Did you want to go to brush your hair? I'll keep the table, I don't mind.'

'No, it's all right.' Marjorie patted her hair. 'It'll do. I wouldn't want to leave you on your own.' Her gaze wandered around the room. 'All sorts in here, aren't there? What are those uniforms over there?'

Kitty squinted in the direction her friend was pointing. 'Oh, they're Canadians.'

Marjorie raised her eyebrows. 'How do you know that?' she asked. 'I've never seen them before.'

'We get a lot around Liverpool,' Kitty explained. 'We've always had a lot to do with Canada – we used to get Canadian timber all the time down at the docks where I lived. And there are lots of Canadian servicemen around there now. We even had some come to the canteen where I worked. I liked them. They've come so far from home to fight alongside our boys – you can't help but admire them.'

Marjorie seemed to approve of that and looked at the group with renewed interest. 'I say, they've noticed us.'

Of course they have, thought Kitty, you've been staring at them unabashed for ages, they're bound to realise it. But she didn't say anything, not wanting to bruise her friend's new-found confidence and enjoyment. 'Oh, they're coming over. The one with the light-brown curls looks keen.'

One of the group, a pilot from his uniform, made a beeline for Marjorie, his curls bobbing a little as he rounded the table. Marjorie, far from retreating back into her shell, responded with smiles and

89

nods as he asked her for her name and if she'd been here before. The martini looked as if it had worked its magic and banished her earlier awkwardness. Two of his friends began to chat to Kitty, general questions that didn't require her to think much or give away what she was training as. Although she didn't exactly have access to state secrets, she was always very careful to reveal as little as possible.

The pilot offered Marjorie a dance and, somewhat to Kitty's surprise, she accepted. Marjorie hadn't even said anything about being able to dance, but soon she was on the dance floor, trying her best. Kitty smiled at her friend's obvious pleasure. Then Laura swept by with her partner. She was in a different league; her movements were graceful yet precise, and she'd obviously done this many times. The young man was gamely trying to lead her through the steps but it was clear who was really in charge. Kitty sighed. It would take a brave man to control Laura, on or off the dance floor.

She realised one of the Canadians was still talking to her and she broke off her train of thought to pay attention to him. 'I can't believe you're here without a boyfriend,' he was saying. He seemed to be building up to making his move.

Kitty felt she couldn't let him get his hopes up. 'No, my boyfriend isn't in London,' she explained. 'He's a doctor on Merseyside. He's going to come down to see me soon.' She crossed her fingers as she said this, hoping it was true. Lovely, kind Elliott – and he was a wonderful dancer. She could suggest they come here. Her face brightened at the idea.

'Oh I see.' The young man in front of her seemed to get the picture, and understood that it wasn't him she was smiling about. 'Well, nice meeting you, ma'am. You take care when you've finished your training, now.'

'You too,' Kitty said, and meant it. She knew – as did everyone else – the immense danger all fully trained fighter pilots were in. This young man would be lucky to survive. But nobody said this, of course. She watched as he wove his way back to his friends, wondering what the future had in store for him and the rest of them.

The next dance came to an end and Marjorie and her partner headed back towards Kitty, their faces flushed. He showed her to her seat and then moved off, as Marjorie waved. Over her shoulder, Kitty could see Laura, and the by now somewhat exhausted young corporal also coming their way.

Kitty raised her eyebrows as Marjorie sank back into her chair. 'Not having another dance with him, then? He seemed nice. I thought you two were set for the evening.'

'No, we decided we'd had enough,' said Marjorie, all trace of her earlier anxiety now gone. 'We started talking as we danced and it turns out he's got a steady girlfriend back home in Toronto. He's a very nice young man and I'm not surprised he has a sweetheart, so it's best he goes back to his friends.' She grinned. 'I've surprised myself. He's good looking, isn't he?'

Well, well, thought Kitty, so books aren't Marjorie's sole interest after all. 'Yes, very,' she agreed. 'So now we know what your type is, don't we? We'll have to keep a look-out for others with light-brown curls and pilots' uniforms...' She trailed off as Laura approached and she registered the expression on her face. She looked as if she'd seen a ghost.

'Who ... who was that?' she gasped, her hand to her throat. She could barely force out the words. 'That man dancing with Marjorie – who was that?'

'Laura, whatever's wrong?' Kitty stood up immediately and rushed to her friend, who had frozen to the spot. Gently she guided her to the table and into a seat. 'Here, sip this.' She handed her the cocktail glass. Laura took it and swigged back a mouthful, swallowing hard, almost desperately. 'Steady, now. That smells like strong stuff. Tell me what's happened. One minute you're dancing the night away and wearing out that poor boy, and now you're shaking like a leaf. Whatever is it? Did he say something to you, or what?'

'Oh, my God.' Laura put the drink down and then dropped her head into her hands. 'I'm so sorry. God, what an idiot. What a fool. No, he didn't say anything, it's not him. It's my fault, making a spectacle of myself. Just ignore me.' Her voice broke but she raised her head and was visibly trying to pull herself together.

'Laura, take it easy,' said Marjorie. 'Is it something we've done? Tell us.'

Laura gave a heavy sigh. 'No. Not really.' She gulped. 'It was that young man you were dancing with. I just caught sight of the two of you together when I'd finished my dance and ... for one moment...' She shut her eyes tight and then opened them. 'Well, I thought it was Freddy. Stupidly, I know. It couldn't have been, I know that deep down, but just for a second ... it caught me unawares, I'm so sorry...' She abruptly looked away, biting her lip in a desperate effort not to break down.

Marjorie looked stunned. 'Who?' she mimed, turning to Kitty.

Kitty's heart went out to Laura. 'Her brother,' she whispered. 'He's missing in action.'

'But she never said.' Marjorie's face betrayed her feeling of hurt that she hadn't been told.

'She doesn't. She just spoke about it once, before you all arrived.' Kitty sighed. 'She said they were close. I hadn't realised just how much.'

How hard it must be for Laura, she reflected, suffering in silence, surrounded by young men who must remind her all the time of the uncertainty that hung over her brother's fate, always preparing herself for the worst possible news, never knowing how long she would have to go on in limbo. Kitty recognised that the young woman's devil-may-care attitude was her way of coping, but it only plastered over the wound, it didn't come close to healing it. The confidence – arrogance, almost – masked a deep hurt that could never go away until Freddy's fate was resolved one way or the other.

'You take your time, Laura,' she said. 'You don't have to pretend in front of us. We understand.'

Laura turned back to them both. 'Thanks,' she said, wiping her eyes. 'Oh God. I must look a proper fright.'

'Here, have this.' Kitty retrieved a handkerchief from her sleeve. 'Clear up the worst with this, and then go to put on some more lipstick. I'll come with you if you like.'

'No, no, you stay here.' Laura was recovering now, sounding more like her old self. 'I'll go on my own, I'll be all right. But tell you what.'

'What?' Kitty and Marjorie said together.

'Wave at that nice waiter and get me another one of these. Make it a double.' With that Laura painted on a determined smile and pushed her way to the door of the ladies'.

Kitty twisted around to do as she was asked, catching sight of the waiter and raising her hand. Good for Laura – even though she was in despair about her brother, she wasn't going to let it ruin their evening. And it was an easy mistake to make, Kitty realised. Anyone could do it. For example, there in the corner, among a group of officers in naval uniform, there was a young man with a head of gorgeous blond hair who from this angle was the spitting image of Frank Feeny. But no, she chided herself: that was all past. Her heart was fluttering involuntarily because of all the excitement of the evening – it was nothing more than that...

CHAPTER NINE

'So I'll see you tomorrow morning, then?' Rita got up to go home, even though she'd rather have stayed in her mother's kitchen to carry on the lively conversation. 'Thanks, Violet, you don't know what a relief it is to have your help.'

'Think nothing of it!' Violet insisted, and gave one of her braying laughs, which even after all these months made Rita's ears ring. But she'd happily put up with that for the comfort of knowing the shop wasn't going to be left in Winnie's increasingly incapable hands.

'What about Georgie?' demanded Nancy, pouting at being sidelined yet again. 'I was going to ask you if you could have him overnight and tomorrow morning, then I'd come round to pick him up. Do I have to change my plans?'

'Plans? What plans?' Rita paused on her way out. 'You didn't say anything, Nancy.' Privately she thought for the thousandth time that her younger sister didn't know how lucky she was. She could play with her beautiful, healthy son every day, watching him change and grow before her eyes: he was walking with increasing confidence and beginning to learn their names. Here he was now, just about managing to toddle towards her, holding out his arms, saying 'ri-ri-ri', which was as close as he could get to Rita. She bent down to hug him. He was adorable – why didn't his mother want to look after him? Rita held him close, savouring the smell of his soft hair, which reminded her of her own children when they were that age. She sent up a silent prayer for their safety. Even though she knew they were well and happy, every day without them was like a blow to her heart.

'Oh honestly, I've told you all of this before.' Nancy rolled her eyes. 'You know very well that Gloria's coming home. She's been a big success in London and now she's going on tour. She's coming to Liverpool today and I'm going to go and meet her. They're putting her up at the Adelphi! I'm not going to miss that!'

'Well, that's a change from the Sailor's Rest and no mistake,' observed Dolly, who was fond of Gloria even though she'd got a reputation for being fast. 'I hope she's going to make some time to visit her parents in all of this high life. They won't have seen her for ages.'

'Oh, she's bound to,' Nancy lied. Gloria's parents weren't like Dolly and Pop. Mr and Mrs Arden were more bothered by how well their pub was doing than what their only daughter got up to. 'Mam, you'll take Georgie, won't you? He loves being here, look at him now. It's his favourite place in the world.' She wondered if she was laying it on a bit thick, but she could usually persuade her mother, and it was true that George liked nothing better than to stay at his granny's.

Dolly regarded her most troublesome child with a baleful air, in full knowledge that she was being taken advantage of, but she could never stay cross with her for long. 'Oh, all right then,' she said. 'But make sure you behave yourself, young lady. I won't have you being the talk of the street.' Nancy pursed her lips at her mother but wisely kept any backchat to herself. The business with Stan Hathaway was still a sore spot between them and she didn't want to risk any curtailment of her night out.

'Here, Rita,' Dolly said, 'you get off and give the boy to me. Are you sure you won't take some lettuce? I picked it myself; it's one of the first things that's come up in the victory garden. All

96

thanks to your clever idea of using spare panes of glass from the bomb site to make little green-houses, Violet.'

'That's a good idea. In fact, why don't I drop some off at Danny's?' Rita asked. She knew that Danny would be grateful for the salad, as he would never think to buy it for himself. More-over, letters had begun to arrive at his house from Jack, and she was desperate to hear his news.

'Of course, what a kind idea.' Dolly beamed at her eldest daughter's thoughtfulness. 'There's plenty for both of you.'

'Just make sure you wash it – we wouldn't want Winnie to choke on a slug,' Nancy added.

Rita tucked the precious letter into the waistband of her skirt and buttoned her coat over it to hide any tell-tale bulge. It would be foolish to go to all the trouble of getting the letters sent to her neigh-bour only for Winnie to spot her smuggling one back into the shop to read, and she knew the older woman would take full advantage of any-thing she regarded as stepping out of line. How-ever, even the thought of Winnie's malevolence couldn't dampen Rita's anticipation – she'd waited too long to feel that moment of connection with Jack. Just to see his beloved handwriting made her feel less alone.

Pushing open the door to the living quarters, she was surprised to find Ruby going through to the kitchen. Her startling blonde hair was bright in the early evening sunlight. Ruby jumped, ner-vous as ever.

'Ohhhhh.' Her voice shook. 'It's you, Rita. I'm

... I'm glad it's you.'

'Of course it's me. Who else would it be?' Rita smiled reassuringly as she put down her basket and unpacked it. 'See what I've got from Mam, Ruby. I could make us a nice sandwich. Would you like that? Maybe with some Branston pickle? That's what I'm going to have.' She drew out an enamel colander from one of the cupboards above the sink and began to pull off some lettuce leaves to wash.

Ruby nodded, but didn't seem convinced. Finally she plucked up the courage to say what was on her mind. 'The strange men were back today.' She trembled. 'I hid away. I don't like it when they come; their voices feel funny.'

Rita paused at the sink. 'What men, Ruby? Don't worry, I won't blame you for anything. Tell me what happened.'

The young woman wrung her hands. 'They were angry. They shouted at Winnie. They said bad things. It was loud, I was scared.'

'What things, Ruby? Did they threaten Winnie? Were they the police?'

'They ... maybe not ... a bit like the police, but different uniforms.' Ruby looked helpless. 'They said military police. That was it. They said she had to tell them where he was.'

Rita cast her eyes heavenwards. She had known it almost before Ruby began to speak – it was about Charlie again. Her useless deserting husband still hadn't faced up to his duty and joined up. Now the authorities were after him good and proper. She'd been lucky that they'd come when she was out; despite her hatred of Charlie, the fact that they were all being dragged through the mud along with him was excruciating. She had nothing to hide and had done nothing wrong – but the powerful shame of knowing her husband was a complete and utter coward was enough to drive her to the depths of despair.

'They won't hurt you, Ruby.' She tried to keep her voice level; there was no sense in making Ruby more frightened than she already was. 'They just want to find where Charlie is. And since we don't know, we can't tell them anything useful.'

'Charlie's a bad man!' Ruby suddenly burst out. 'He was mean to me. I don't like him. He took Elsie to the pub all the time, and he shut Michael and Megan away without their supper.'

Rita's heart turned over at the thought of her children going hungry at their father's hands, but she steeled herself. They were better fed now than they'd ever been in their lives. She mustn't let it upset her further. 'You're right, Ruby,' she said. 'He's not a nice man, but he's not here, so we'll be all right. Why don't you pass me the bread and I'll make those sandwiches. You shouldn't let it worry you. After all, it's ages since they last came looking for him.'

Ruby paused as she lifted the loaf from the bread bin. 'It's six weeks and two days,' she said. 'Also, they came at two o'clock last time and this time it was half past three.'

'Really, Ruby?' Rita thought that this was a strange thing to remember, especially as the young woman had been so frightened. 'You've got a good memory. I never know when things have happened or how long ago. I don't think many people do.'

Ruby looked at her seriously. 'Well I do,' she said shortly. 'I see patterns. I know these things. If you need to know then you ask me. I don't forget.'

'All right, Ruby,' said Rita, slicing the bread, feeling slightly startled by the direction this conversation had taken. She berated herself for underestimating the girl; just because she acted strangely didn't necessarily mean she was an idiot, although Elsie and now Winnie treated her as one. 'I'll keep that in mind.'

Ruby beamed as she accepted her sandwich. 'Yes please, Rita,' she said. 'I would like to help you. Michael and Megan are my best friends, so I'll help you. I don't forget anything, ever.'

CHAPTER TEN

'Oh, this is nice!' Nancy flung herself back on the elaborate counterpane of the big double bed and looked at the ornate ceiling. 'They must think a lot of you, putting you up in here. Oh, I could get used to this. Who'd have thought it? If some of those old bags from Empire Street could see you here they'd have a fit. Serve 'em right and all.'

Gloria grinned. 'Believe me, not every hotel's like this. I've stayed in some right fleapits since starting the tour.' She sat down on the velvet stool which stood in front of the mirrored dressing table. It was in the exact shade of the gorgeously thick curtains, which toned with the counterpane

100

– it was all the height of luxury. 'But no, I grant you, this is all right.'

'Just think, all those nights we were downstairs when you were singing, and we didn't know what the bedrooms were like.' Nancy stretched her arms above her head. 'This is the comfiest bed I've ever been on.'

Gloria raised her eyebrows. 'Does that mean you've been trying out a few since we last met? Nancy, you dark horse.'

Nancy gasped, then realised her friend was teasing. 'No, of course not. Don't be like that, Glor. You know I'm not like some girls we could mention.'

'Just as well, I suppose.' Gloria gazed at the wallpaper above the mirror. 'Apart from being on tour, I haven't tried out any either.'

Nancy rolled on to her side and propped her head on her hand to regard her friend. Gloria had always attracted men without any effort – her looks alone guaranteed she would be the centre of attention wherever she went, with her natural platinum-blonde hair and stunning face, but added to that she had the gift of a powerful voice that she used to tug on the heartstrings of anyone listening. In her more honest moments, Nancy admitted she was deeply jealous of her friend, but it had also been useful to stick by her side as she then could bask in the reflected glory and also meet a fair few men herself. But times had changed.

'Your impresario fellow making you work all hours, is he?' she asked. 'You want to stand up for yourself, make sure you get a bit of time off. All work and no play and all that.'

'What do you think this is?' Gloria said, smiling to take the edge off her reply. 'I'm not performing this evening. He knows I can't sing every night, or and move hotels as well. I'll get too tired, and then my voice gets tired and we can't risk that. No, he's good, I've been very lucky. He knows what he's doing. I trust him. No, not like that,' she added, reading the inquisitive expression on Nancy's face. 'I tell you, I'm concentrating on my career now.'

'Really?' Nancy couldn't quite believe it.

Gloria spun round on the delicate little stool to face her friend. 'Yes, really.' She paused and clasped her hands. 'I can't waste my time going out in the evening with men when I've got a chance to really do something with my singing. I can't mess around, this is my one shot at it and I'm not going to waste it.' Her face grew determined. 'I mean it, Nancy. I know we used to have a lot of fun–'

'We did,' Nancy said eagerly.

'And I don't regret it, but things are different now.'

'Don't say "there's a war on",' Nancy said wearily. 'I'm sick and tired of hearing it. Every time I try to liven things up a bit at home, some-one in my family will pipe up to remind me there's a bloody war on. I'm fed up to here of it.' She punched the beautifully soft pillow in exasper-ation.

Gloria laughed indulgently. 'Yes, but your family are all doing their bit, aren't they? This is my way. And talking of family, it's all my mother's fault.'

Nancy looked up, surprised. 'What, has she been writing to you or something? Don't say she's been down to see you, I know she hasn't, I see her around the street every day. Sometimes she says hello, sometimes she doesn't.'

'Don't be daft.' Gloria's voice dripped with contempt. 'She won't bother with you 'cos you're not a regular customer. That's all she cares about. That's my point. She's stuck in that filthy old pub, seeing the same old faces day in day out, watching my dad get drunk with whoever's left after the call-up. But she used to sing, you know.'

'Yeah, I know. Never heard her though.'

'Nobody has. She lost her voice before she had me. She didn't take care of it. She had this talent and she did nothing with it. Well, I'm not going to fall into that trap.' Gloria pursed her immaculately painted lips. 'You've got to seize the chances that come your way, and she didn't. I'm serious about this work. I love it, and also it's helping the war effort. People feel better after hearing me sing. That sounds big-headed, I know, but that's what Romeo Brown says. I don't care if I have to sing "We'll Meet Again" over and over – if that's what they want to hear and if it gives them the will to go on, who am I to say no?'

Nancy looked at her friend with respect. 'You've always had a lovely voice, Glor, but I didn't realise you were so serious about it.'

'Well, I am now.' Gloria sighed. 'After ... well, you know.'

Nancy's face softened. 'You mean Giles?'

Gloria nodded. 'Yes. Giles.' For a moment her voice faltered. 'He was wonderful, Nancy, and I don't think I fully realised it until he was gone. Typical, isn't it?' She shook her head. 'He was kind, and courageous, and he died because he took the blast of that bomb, protecting me. It's taken me ages to even think about it properly. He did that, for me. Everyone used to say that he was just after a good time with a showgirl and that he'd never actually marry me, but he proposed that very night and I know he'd have gone through with it. Then he went and died.' She sighed. 'Well, that was my one chance to marry a pilot and escape the Sailor's Rest that way. I'm not interested in catching another man. The good ones are all in the Forces and then they can die on you. Just like that.' She snapped her fingers. 'One minute you're planning your future, the next – nothing. Well, never again. I'm done with men.' She paused. 'Sorry, listen to me going on. We're here to enjoy ourselves, aren't we? Here, try some of this. I get room service, you know, and I got them to bring us up a little something just before you got here.'

'Oooh, don't mind if I do. What's in that?' Nancy eyed the bottle in the ice bucket on the silver tray greedily. She was disappointed that her evening out looked as if it was going to be spent in Gloria's hotel room – she'd been looking forward to dancing, some music, a bit of harmless flirtation with the servicemen on their night off. Still, at least she didn't have to look at Mrs Kerrigan's curdled features ... and the Adelphi really was lovely. Yes, this was a welcome change all right.

'It's vermouth. I'll make us a cocktail.' Gloria expertly poured the glossy liquid from the bottle and added a little splash of bitters from a smaller bottle, before popping in a twist of lemon and giving it a little stir. 'Here you go. Cheers.'

'Cheers.' Nancy raised the delicate glass and sipped cautiously. 'Ooooh, that's strong.'

'Well, take it easy.' Gloria smiled and raised her own glass. 'It's my treat. I hardly ever drink, and never when I'm singing, it dries the throat. But now and again on my nights off I like something special. Thought you might like it too.'

'Oh, I do,' sighed Nancy, getting into the mood. 'Honestly, Glor, this is the life, isn't it? Just look at us. Two girls from Empire Street, drinking cocktails upstairs at the Adelphi.' She leaned back against the sumptuous pillows.

'Not bad.' Gloria took a small sip. 'But enough about me. What have you been up to, Nancy? It's been so long since I've seen you. It's May already. Tell me everything I've missed.'

'Not very much.' Nancy scowled. 'I'm back living with the dragon, so I don't do anything. I stay in with little Georgie.'

'How is he?' Gloria asked dutifully.

'Oh, he's all right.' Nancy's face broke into a smile. 'No, he's lovely, he's walking and everything. Mam's got him tonight.'

'She's good, your mam.'

'She is,' Nancy acknowledged. 'I'm lucky, I know. She could have refused to help out after that row at Christmas when our Sarah found out about me and Stan. She was furious, of course, but she still takes him when Violet's busy. Well, she's happy to, he's so sweet, he really is.'

Gloria smiled, even though she wasn't really

very keen on babies. She couldn't see the point of them. But Georgie made her friend and her family very happy, so it would be churlish to mention that having him had definitely cramped Nancy's style. 'Any news from Stan?' she asked instead. 'Have you seen him since the row?'

Nancy's face fell. 'He hasn't had leave for ages.' She took a larger swig of the cocktail than she'd intended and spluttered. 'Oh, I must be careful. Hah.' She paused. 'He writes, though, that's something, even if it's no real substitute for having him here. I'll see him the next time he's home – they can't stop me, I'll find a way. Actually I got a letter earlier today and I couldn't get a moment to myself to read it. I have to be very cautious.' She grinned conspiratorially at Gloria.

Gloria smiled indulgently at her friend. She knew that Nancy was in danger of getting her fingers burnt, but Nancy was headstrong and would never be told anything she didn't want to hear. Gloria knew that if word ever got out around Empire Street about what Nancy had been up to, they'd hang her out to dry. It wasn't like the circles that Gloria herself ran in now, amongst the liberal artistic set. They were much more relaxed about things like that. Anyway, this wasn't the moment to burst Nancy's bubble. 'Go on, then, read it now,' Gloria urged her. 'I won't tell, promise.'

Nancy rolled over across the big bed and reached for her handbag, which looked rather battered and out of place in the luxurious bedroom. 'Here we are. Let me see...' Her eyes scanned the single piece of paper. Then she read it again. 'No. That can't be right.' Her hand flew to her mouth. 'No, he can't mean it.' Her face went pale.

'What? What is it?' Gloria rushed across the room. 'Blimey, are you all right, Nance? You've gone as white as a sheet. Whatever's the matter?'

'He's ... he's...' Nancy gulped and then burst into tears. 'He's given me the push, Glor. I can't believe it, he's ... oh no. He ... he says it's not right, me being married and Sid being a prisoner of war. He says it's preying on his conscience.'

'Conscience my arse,' said Gloria pithily. 'Wasn't much sign of his conscience when he was having his way with you before Christmas, was there? How very convenient. What a bastard. Really, Nancy, if that's what he's like, then you're better off without him. Bet he's got a girl or several closer to where he's based, that'll be the truth of it. Conscience, I ask you.' She sat on the bed and went to hug her friend.

'But ... but...' Nancy's tears poured down her cheeks. 'I was going to tell him... I've been so sick, I thought I might...'

Gloria sat back a little. 'What are you saying, Nancy? Spit it out.'

Nancy sobbed bitterly. 'I wasn't sure. You know, this wartime diet and everything, you can't tell ... it's all different now. I lost count.'

'Lost count? What are you on about, Nancy? You're not making sense.'

'My monthlies,' Nancy confessed miserably. 'I lost count of my monthlies. I don't know when I had my last one. But I've lost so much weight. They went haywire anyway, so it might not mean anything. I thought he'd help me, he'd stand by

107

me if I needed him...'

'Nancy, come on, don't upset yourself like this.' Gloria hugged her, trying to calm Nancy's shaking body. 'He's not worth it. Look, if you haven't seen him since Christmas and you've still not put on weight, then you're probably all right, aren't you?'

Nancy screwed up the letter and threw it across the room. 'I don't know, I hope so, I don't know what to think. Oh, Gloria, I've been such an idiot. I was kidding myself he loved me, he was so good-looking and everything, he treated me like I was special...' She gulped again. 'Where's the bathroom? I'm going to be sick.'

'Through there.' Gloria pointed to a narrow door and Nancy hurriedly got up and dashed through it, slamming it behind her. Gloria paced around the bedroom, doing her best to ignore the noises coming from the bathroom, grimly hoping her friend hadn't been caught out. She didn't want to imagine the reception she'd get if the worst happened – Nancy pregnant but Sid still a prisoner of war and everyone knowing it couldn't have been his child. He'd never even seen Georgie, let alone had a chance to father a little brother or sister for him. Nancy's name would be dragged through the mud.

Gloria mixed herself another cocktail, figuring that one more wouldn't hurt and that this was an emergency. She knew she'd been lucky herself – she was no stranger to men, and she'd taken a few risks before the war broke out, although she'd usually been very careful. That was one thing she had to say in favour of being brought up above the Sailor's Rest – you heard everything. So she knew how to take care of herself. Of course, that one time with Giles, there hadn't been a chance to ... but nothing had come of it. In some ways that had saddened her; it would have been the one way of keeping him alive and with her for always. But it wasn't meant to be. She shook herself. Maybe it was just as well. She couldn't have gone on tour with a baby on her hip.

The retching noises had finally stopped and Gloria was just about to knock on the connecting door when there came a terrible groan from inside. Hastily she ran across and barged into the little bathroom. There on the white tiled floor lay Nancy, her hands pressed to her stomach. There was a bright red smear of blood on the thick white towel crumpled up beside her.

'Nancy! Are you hurt? What's...' Then she realised where the blood had come from.

'Sorry, Gloria.' Nancy tried to get up but couldn't. 'I'm so sorry. It's the shock ... or the cocktail ... or both. I didn't mean to make such a mess.'

'Never mind that.' Gloria crouched beside her friend. 'Don't worry about that, they'll have seen worse. No, listen, are you all right? How heavily are you bleeding?'

'I'll be all right. Just give me a minute or two.' Nancy breathed deeply, rubbing her stomach. 'I don't think it's as bad as it looks. It's just cramps now. I don't think it was ... a you-know-what. It's just bad cramps. It was all a bit sudden, that's all it was. That's all,' she repeated, as if to convince herself. 'Nothing to worry about.' But she knew this was more than her monthlies coming late.

She didn't want to admit it, but deep down she'd recognised the symptoms from when she'd fallen with Georgie. Thank God it had happened here and nobody at home would see. If she was careful, nobody would be any the wiser, and she knew Gloria wouldn't say anything.

'Nothing to worry about,' Gloria said soothingly, stroking Nancy's head where the victory roll had come undone, her red hair spilling across her shoulders. 'Come on, then, let's get you up. You can have my bed for the night, I'll have that sofa. Nothing to worry about.'

Slowly, Nancy stood, and Gloria helped her across the expanse of deep-pile carpet back to the bed, carrying more towels with her to mop up any more blood. She wondered if they should call a doctor, but Nancy didn't seem to be feverish or anything. Gloria knew several women from the stage who'd had similar experiences, and they'd said the best thing was to sleep it off and then carry on. Well, so much for a glamorous night of cocktails at the Adelphi, she thought. It wasn't the reunion she'd planned. But then again, if Nancy was no longer pregnant by that good-for-nothing Stan Hathaway, maybe it was a good night after all.

CHAPTER ELEVEN

'It's good of you to give up your afternoon off like this.' Violet paused to wipe the sweat from her forehead and pushed back the faded old scarf she'd tied around her hair to control it in the stiff breeze. 'Honestly, you must be worn out. I know for a fact you are. Yet you still came.'

'Said I would, didn't I?' Rita rested on the handle of her spade. 'I've got to learn how to do this sort of thing. I never tried before, but who knows what we'll have to get used to while this war continues?'

Violet smiled grimly and plunged her spade into the earth. 'It hurts in muscles I didn't even know I had. Still, can't wait around for the men to come home, can we? My Eddy will want some feeding up when he gets back.'

'Can't say the same for Charlie. I bet he's doing all right for himself wherever he is,' Rita said bitterly. She didn't usually even speak about him, she was so mortified at having a deserter for a husband. Somehow with Violet it was different, though; her sister-in-law hadn't known Charlie, hadn't seen what a dance he'd led them all in. It was a relief to be able to vent her frustration. 'Not that we have a clue about that.' Her thoughts flew to Jack, out in the Atlantic, eating who-knew-what rations, and unable to say either exactly what he was doing or when he'd next be home. He'd

111

written that he'd try to give her some notice when he might come back, but realistically she knew that might not be possible.

'We're all having to manage without our men,' Violet said stoically. 'I miss Eddy so much it hurts, but moaning about it won't make it any better. I'm just going to concentrate on learning new and useful things for when he's back. For when we have a house of our own with a garden and I can grow healthy fruit and veg for our children.' She paused. 'Listen to me. Pie in the sky, isn't it? But a girl can dream.' Her face set in determination. 'Here, Rita, pass me that hoe. These weeds between the rows of carrots are little blighters. After all that work of putting down extra protection against the spring frosts, nothing is going to stop these beauties from growing. We'll have our home-grown carrot cake if it kills me.'

'Don't say that.' Rita passed the hoe across. 'Don't even joke about it.' She grinned to take the edge off her comment. 'I don't know how we'd manage without you, and that's the truth.' She wasn't exaggerating. She'd come to rely on Violet in the shop. The customers loved her. Now that they'd got used to her strong Mancunian accent and abrasive laugh, they accepted her – of course it helped that she was married to Eddy, from the popular Feeny family, and everyone knew the risks he was taking every day. But people had warmed to her. She was very good with the older customers, never tutting when they took ages to find their change, or counted it all out in small, carefully hoarded piles of coins, or became confused with their ration books. Mrs Ashby in particular had come to rely on her, as it brightened her lonely day to have such a chatty soul around. Violet jollied them along and left them feeling better for their trip to the corner shop. Unfortunately she was terrible at working the till and often made mistakes – but Rita told herself nobody was good at everything and she couldn't complain. Winnie had almost given up entirely and was a liability rather than an asset when she did help out. God only knows there was little margin for error in the shop's profits – they were hanging on by a fingernail.

'So what shall we take back this evening?' Violet wondered, looking along the neat rows that were now practically weed-free. 'More salad? Everyone likes a fresh lettuce. Gives anything a bit of a crunch.'

'Winnie doesn't,' sighed Rita. 'I don't know why I bother. She looks at it as if I'm trying to poison her. Seriously, if I was going to do that, I'd be a bit more efficient than giving her a lettuce. How about those spring greens? I could use them in a stew. Put them with some barley to bulk it out.'

'Good idea. Georgie will like that.' Violet bent to pick some to put in her trug.

'Have you got Georgie round again?' asked Rita.

'He never left,' said Violet. 'Nancy was taken ill on her night out with Gloria.'

Rita raised her eyebrows in disbelief. 'That's what she calls it nowadays, is it?'

'No, she really was in a bad way.' Violet had no illusions about her younger sister-in-law, but she'd been moved to pity by the girl's white face when she'd eventually got back. 'I felt sorry for her, really I did. She'd been looking forward to her friend coming home for ages and then their big night out never happened. She was lucky to get back; that raid hit the big ship down the docks last night.'

'I know. I'm afraid after the past couple of days we might be in for another big one.' Rita looked grim. 'Come on, let's get these back before it starts to get dark. I don't want to get caught out here in the open.'

Violet began to pack away her tools. 'Yes, and if you come back to ours, I'll show you what I got down at Lewis's. They had some lovely stuff going cheap for once. It fair made my day.'

Rita nodded eagerly. 'You lucky thing. It's ages since I had anything new. Maybe I'll make time to slip down there tomorrow.'

Back in Dolly's cosy kitchen, Rita admired the neat blouse and cardigan in a gorgeous shade of lilac that Violet had found on sale. 'See, there's a tiny bit of stitching gone wrong under the collar, that's why they reduced it,' Violet explained.

'But you can put that right in two shakes,' Dolly said. 'That's a real bargain, that is. Rita, will you stay for some stew? There'll be plenty, thanks to you two and all your hard work today.'

'I'd love to, but I need to get back,' sighed Rita. 'Winnie won't have thought to cook anything and Ruby will need to eat, even if Winnie refuses again. She'll waste away one of these days and I'm not going to stop her. Does that sound awful?'

Dolly shook her head. Winnie was one of the most exasperating women she knew and she

114

wasn't going to waste any sympathy on her. 'No, love, you make sure you look after yourself and Ruby. What Winnie does is up to her; she's old and ugly enough to make up her own mind. Finish your tea, though.'

Rita nodded and lifted her cup. She felt confused and guilty about her mother-in-law, but she was more concerned for Ruby, who didn't seem to have been taught how to cook at all. What if she was delayed getting back from the hospital for any length of time? Winnie wouldn't lift a finger to help Ruby who was, after all, her own unacknowledged daughter. Yet again it was all down to Rita. She didn't even want to contemplate what might happen if Winnie's sordid little secret was blown. People had begun to gossip – it was only natural, and the resemblance between mother and daughter was there for those who cared to look closely. Violet had mentioned more than once that some of the customers had started to speculate why the strange young woman was still there, or why she kept herself in the background so much. It was only a matter of time.

'Thanks, Mam.' She set the cup down again and was just about to reach for her coat when the siren sounded, pushing all other thoughts from her head. 'Not again.'

'Well, I'm not leaving this stew for Hitler to ruin,' Dolly declared. 'Good job we got those big flasks. Come on, Rita, we'll pour as much of it in as we can.'

'I'll bring the biscuits,' said Violet, automatically turning to Georgie and making sure he was safely in his siren suit, which was always at the

115

ready. She caught Rita's glance. They both knew this could be a big raid. It was what they had feared that very afternoon. Last night's damage was still evident, with the big ship that had been hit on nearby Huskisson Dock burning away. Violet shrugged off the old jumper she had been wearing for gardening and pulled on her new cardigan. 'At least I'm going to have some use of this,' she said staunchly. 'Ready, Georgie? Off we go, we'll have singsongs down at the shelter and you'll see everyone you know.' Georgie beamed back up at her. He was used to this, and they all made sure they made it as much fun as possible for him so he wouldn't fret too much.

Swiftly and efficiently, the women packed everything they needed, including the flasks of delicious stew, and made their way down Empire Street to the shelter at the end. Rita looked around anxiously for Ruby, wondering if the young woman could be trusted to find her own way, but there she was, her distinctive, strange hair visible in the gloom. 'Come on, Ruby, walk with us,' she called. Ruby hurried across, anxiety etched on her otherwise baby-smooth face.

'Will we be all right?' She was shaking.

'We'll be safe as houses down there,' Dolly assured her, then realised that might not be of much consolation to the young woman. But she couldn't worry about that. Once she'd got her family to safety, she was going to take up her position as fire-watcher for the street. Something told her she was going to be busy. She sent up a silent prayer for Sarah, on duty down at the docks. There was nothing she could do for her brave youngest child.

116

Then there was Frank, whose digs were towards the centre of the city – although maybe he was safe in his top-secret job in the bunker. She'd wanted him to move home once he was posted back to Merseyside, but he'd protested that there was no room and she'd had to concede he was right. She had no way of knowing where he was right now, and worrying wouldn't make it any better. 'Oh, there's Danny,' she said in relief. 'Danny, you go with them to the shelter and get them all settled.' She handed him her big basket. 'There's plenty there, Rita will sort you out, but I have to go to my post.'

Rita barely had time to say goodbye to her mother when Danny swept them to the door of the shelter and through to comparative safety, escorting them to the back where there was more room. 'There's another letter for you,' he whispered as he came close to her ear. 'I got one too. He's coming home on leave soon.'

'Oh Danny, that's wonderful.' Rita had a burst of hope, even as the anxious crowd surged around her. 'I just hope we survive this raid to see him.'

Sarah shuddered as the siren went on and on. If she was honest, she was exhausted. She'd been on duty last night when the big ship was hit and had worked through the day, helping tend the wounds of the dock workers who'd got too close. To think that until recently she'd only learnt about treating burns from a textbook. Well, she thought grimly, she had plenty of practice now. Trying not to think about her father, who was bound to be on ARP duty, or her mother doing her fire-watching,

Sarah began to roll more bandages in readiness for the casualties that were certain to come.

'Fancy a cuppa, young Sarah?' It was one of the more experienced nurses, Jean, who'd worked full time before she married and gave up her job to have children. Now her skills were needed once more, and the children were being cared for by their grandmothers. She'd confided to Sarah on a quieter night that she felt she should have them evacuated but couldn't bear the thought of separation. Sarah had understood that this was the dilemma so many women faced.

She didn't really want a cup of tea, but then again she had no way of knowing when the next one would come along, so she agreed. Meanwhile she carried on – rolling the bandages, ordering them by size and shape, careful to be exact so that no time would be lost when the station got busy. She had little doubt it would. There wouldn't be much sleep tonight. *Sleep*. She mustn't even think about it. Every cell in her body longed for it but she knew she couldn't give in to the temptation to snatch forty winks. The tea would revive her.

The drone of overhead aircraft filled her with dread.

'Oh boy, now we're for it,' said Jean, looking upwards. 'Sounds like they mean business tonight.'

'Could mean anything,' said Sarah, refusing to think the worst before it actually happened.

'No, I feel it in my waters,' Jean insisted. 'You see if I'm right. They'll be doing their damnedest to destroy Liverpool tonight.'

Sarah wanted to block out her colleague's gloomy prediction – it did no good to assume disaster. 'We might be lucky. You never know.'

'Well, I'm just going to stick my head outside to see if there are many people heading our way,' Jean said.

'Wait, your tea will go cold,' said Sarah alarmed now. 'Don't go outside if the planes are so close. The wounded will find us soon enough.'

'I'd rather know what we're in for.' There was no stopping Jean now. She put down her chipped old mug, drew her nurse's cloak around her and hurried out of the door, leaving it ajar and letting the cold night air through.

Sarah turned to go to shut it, but she never got there. Suddenly an explosion far, far louder than anything she'd ever heard before in her life sounded from what felt like directly outside. The shock waves crashed into her and she fell, momentarily disorientated. Her ears rang and she couldn't tell up from down, she was so dizzy. She held on to what some faint internal voice told her must be the leg of the table on which she'd been sorting her bandages and somehow she rolled underneath it. She could hear crashes but couldn't tell if they came from inside the nurses' station or not. There were screams, high and piercing, but she couldn't do anything about them; she couldn't stand, couldn't think straight. The noise and con-fusion seemed to go on for ever. There was dust in the air and the horrible smell of burning – scorched wood, and something else more earthy.

She had no idea for how long she lay under the table, but gradually the confusion lessened and the air began to clear. The dim light bulb hadn't gone out – she had thought everything had gone

119

dark but maybe she'd hit her head and it had just seemed like that. Now she could make out that the explosion had dislodged items from the shelves around the walls, but the small station was still basically intact. Jean's chipped mug had fallen nearby and smashed to pieces. Distractedly, Sarah pushed the shards out of the way; they were sharp and shouldn't be stood on, but they could be cleared away properly later. Groaning, she rolled over on to her hands and knees and crawled from under the table. She slowly got to her feet, almost laughing to see her neat rows of bandages still in place. How could everything around be falling apart but those be so straight and orderly? Then she shook her head. Get yourself together, she thought. Tidy this place up and get ready for the onslaught. A banged head and dizzy spell is no excuse for shirking your duty.

Still shaking, she quickly set about restoring order, and then it hit her that the screams had stopped. Gingerly she made her way to the door and stepped out. The sky was bright with the light of blazing fires, and the smell was over-powering. She gazed upwards, bemused by the orange glow, shuddering at what it might mean – for the city, for the docks, for the houses around. Where were her family? Were they safe? She bit her lip. If they weren't, there was nothing she could do about it now. She mustn't think about it or it would overwhelm her.

Not far ahead of her, along the street, some-thing dark lay on the pavement. With a growing horror filling her, she ran to it and crouched down. The familiar dark material of a nurse's cloak was easily recognisable even in these conditions. 'Jean, Jean, are you all right? It's me. Listen, I'll help you up.' Sarah reached out to the older woman and gave her a little shake. There was no response. Carefully Sarah pulled back the cloak, and then sat back on her heels with a gasp of horror. Jean's face was intact but her head was at the wrong angle, and there was blood across the upper half of her body, pouring from an unseen wound. Cautiously Sarah felt the woman's neck and then reached for her wrist but she knew it was futile. Jean was dead.

'No, Jean, no, you can't die. We need you.' A desperate sob rose in Sarah's throat. She didn't want to be on duty alone; she now felt desperately afraid and unable to cope, and swamped with sorrow for her colleague, who had been chatting and drinking tea only a matter of minutes ago. And her children – she had two children. Sarah's head dropped to her chest as she cried for her fallen comrade.

'Come now, nurse, this is no place for you.' The voice of the ARP warden rang out. It was not Pop, but his colleague who patrolled this area. 'What have we here? No, I'm afraid you can do no good by staying with her. Friend of yours, was she? We'll get her taken care of, don't you worry, but you can't stay here. There've been a lot of fires at the docks. We've got to expect injuries from all the flying debris.'

Dimly Sarah recalled that the docks had suffered an onslaught yesterday as well. She shook her head but allowed the man to help her to her feet.

The ARP warden noticed how young this nurse

was, how pale her face in the light from the fires all around, but he knew that showing sympathy now would be of no avail. It would help nobody if she broke down. So he took her firmly by the arm and walked her back to the nurses' station along the road, talking to her all the while. 'That's right, you're doing well. I'll get reinforcements sent across to help you, but you are needed at your post. Plenty of places near here have taken a battering and that's only what we have heard of so far. I'm sorry about your friend but you have to prepare for a busy night, nurse.'

Sarah nodded, wearily wiping her eyes. Her breath was returning to normal. She couldn't let herself fall apart or Jean would have died for nothing. Whatever happened, she had to keep the nurses' station open and functioning – people's lives depended on it. She brushed the charred smuts from her sleeves and straightened up.

'I'll be all right,' she assured the warden.

'That's the spirit.' They had reached the door of the station. Already they could make out the shape of an ambulance racing down the street. 'Chin up, nurse. We're relying on you.'

Danny looked around at the mostly familiar faces crowded into the shelter. Rita had fallen asleep, her head resting on Violet's shoulder, while Violet had nodded off with her head bent over little Georgie, safely wedged on her lap. He'd been fractious to start with but had soon calmed down, with his devoted aunts playing with him and soothing him. Rita had assured them all that Nancy would have gone with her detested mother-in-law to the shelter nearest her house, so there was no need to worry on that score. Ruby, that strange young woman who nobody knew much about, had remained awake for ages, cautiously taking note of everything around her, but had finally dropped off about ten minutes ago, sitting bolt upright as if ready to flee at any moment.

Danny sighed, wondering if Sarah was all right. She was so brave, taking on so much work at such a young age. She got it from Pop and Dolly, of course. It made him all the more frustrated not to be helping in any significant way. He'd gone back to work on the docks but was restricted to light duties, which mainly meant going round with a clipboard counting crates. All right, some-one had to do it, but it didn't have to be him. Tommy could have done it, it was so simple and repetitive. It exercised neither his body nor his mind, and he was bored stiff. Come to think of it, Tommy would have been as well. He was better off where he was, chasing the goats and causing cheerful mayhem on the farm.

Danny's irritation at the world in general was keeping him awake, although he reasoned he could do his job half-asleep anyway. Still, he was finally beginning to doze off, wondering in a confused way what Jack was up to at that moment and what he'd like to do on his leave, when he was jolted back to consciousness by an earth-shatter-ing detonation. Immediately Georgie started cry-ing, and he wasn't the only one. The shelter shook with the reverberations.

'Keep calm, everyone, keep calm, we're all right in here,' he said loudly. He hoped it was true; that

123

explosion had sounded terribly close. Even though he wasn't in uniform, he had been surprised to find people listened to him these days. They didn't consider him the young tearaway any more; after they'd learned he had been a hero in the fire that had nearly cost him his life, he'd earned a new respect on the streets around the Dock Road. Now he realised it was his job to contain the situation here. There simply wasn't room for a mass panic.

Slowly he moved around the over-full shelter, trying not to step on anyone, offering reassurance that all would be well as long as everyone stayed put and didn't try to rush outside or have a screaming fit here. He looked in alarm at Ruby, who seemed on the verge of losing control, but Rita had woken fully and was now with her, gently talking to her. Violet was shushing Georgie, who'd been yelling at the top of his lungs in sheer terror at the loud explosion. Danny shook his head. You and me both, pal, he thought. There's times I feel like letting go like that too. But now was not the time or place.

Keeping his steady smile fixed to his face, he made his way back to his narrow space on the bench at the back. There was now nothing to be done but wait until the all-clear. But what would they find when they finally emerged from their shelter on this most terrible of nights for their beloved city?

CHAPTER TWELVE

Frank Feeny struggled to adjust to the bright glare of daylight after the relative dimness of the bunker, where he'd been on duty all night. It was a fine May morning, but all about him were signs of destruction. The centre of the city he thought he knew so well had been transformed. Carefully making his way over the remains of shattered buildings, he stared around him in horrified disbelief. Of course they'd known from their underground offices that there had been a severe raid taking place above ground, but knowing it in theory and seeing it in practice were two very different things. Now the grim reality hit him.

He found many of the roads were closed and he had to divert when and where possible. He had no plan in mind, but felt compelled to see as much of it for himself as he could before he attempted to get back to his billet – if it was still standing. He thought of the landlady, strict and severe. He hadn't bothered making the effort to become friends; in fact their paths rarely crossed as his shifts were so irregular. But he didn't wish her ill. While it could never be called home, his Spartan small room served a useful purpose and he could do with falling into the narrow bed right now. But he had to see for himself what the night's raids had done.

Picking his way through rubble and shattered

glass, he found himself in front of one of the city centre's biggest and most popular shops: Lewis's. Or rather, what was left of it. He gasped at the scale of the damage. Not that he or his family had made a habit of shopping there; usually they made do with the goods in the local markets. But Kitty always talked about it as somewhere she'd buy her clothes if she could, and he'd often vowed to himself he would give her something nice from there – just as a token of friendship; of course there could be nothing else to it now that he was so badly injured. He grimaced. Getting around on his artificial leg on all the uneven pavements was more of a problem than he'd ever admit to anyone.

'Frank! Frank Feeny!'

A bright female voice jolted him out of the uncharacteristic moment of self-pity. Glancing down the street he caught sight of a figure with striking platinum-blonde hair, wrapped in what looked to be a very expensive long coat. There was only one person it could be.

'Gloria! I didn't know you were back in town,' he called as she approached him. Impulsively he stepped forwards and gave her a hug. He'd known her since she was a toddler, and now her presence here brought him back down to earth.

Gloria gave a wry smile. 'Picked the right time to pay a visit, didn't I? Nice of Hitler to send a welcoming committee.' She shook her head. 'Look at this place. And to think I was planning to go shopping there later. Don't suppose they'll be open today.'

'Not for a while, if ever, I'd say.' Frank gazed at

126

the once impressive frontage of the tall building, now all but destroyed. 'You'll have to get your glad rags elsewhere, Gloria.'

'Maybe I won't bother.' Gloria flashed him her brilliant smile. 'Suddenly I'm not in the mood for shopping.'

Frank raised an eyebrow. The Gloria he remembered of old was clothes-mad, which was just one of the reasons she got on so well with his sister Nancy. But war changed everyone. 'Up here for work, are you?'

Gloria nodded. 'Can you believe I was singing last night at the Adelphi when this all began? We tried to carry on but it was no good. Usually I'm quite happy to keep on singing for as long as there's an audience to listen, but this lot got a bit close for comfort. Have you seen much of it?'

Frank shrugged. 'I came straight from my night shift down in Derby House. I've been wandering round ever since. Fancy joining me for a while? I don't know why, but I feel that as I'm here, in the middle of it all, I need to see with my own eyes what's happened.'

Gloria nodded. 'I know what you mean. Yes, I'd be happy to – that's if you're all right?' She automatically glanced down towards his leg.

Frank bristled. He couldn't bear to be thought of as anything other than the fully fit young man he had been until so recently. 'Of course.'

'I just meant, you must be tired if you've just come off duty,' Gloria said hurriedly.

Frank nodded in acknowledgement. 'Not so tired that I can't walk. I can sleep later. Now I need to see what's happened around here.'

As if in mutual understanding, they turned and began to head down towards the Mersey. For a while the devastation was so shocking they fell silent, just staring around them, taking it all in. The streets where they and their friends and families had strolled so often were utterly changed, many transformed into wasteland overnight. Every now and then Gloria gasped and pointed at one more familiar landmark now ruined. She swayed on her high heels.

'Not the best choice of footwear,' she said sadly. 'I didn't think of that when I packed – shoes for performing, yes. Shoes for picking my way through rubble, no. Forgot that.'

'Bad planning,' said Frank grimly, and gave a heartfelt sigh. 'You've been in London, haven't you? So what was it like down there?'

'Oh, destruction follows me wherever I go,' Gloria said lightly, not wanting to go into details of the overcrowded shelters and Tube platforms used whenever there was a raid on the capital. 'I just keep on singing until they tell me to stop. Isn't Kitty down there now? Nancy was saying she'd joined the Wrens and left them all behind.'

'I believe so,' said Frank shortly. 'We don't write.'

'Oh.' Gloria realised she'd touched on a sensitive topic, and hastily attempted to put things right. 'Well, I'm sure she's doing well. She'll be safe, I should think; they wouldn't put trainee Wrens in danger.'

'I should hope not,' said Frank, trying hard to keep his voice level and show no fear for Kitty's safety. They were all exposed to risks, wherever they were – and, after all, she was nothing special to him, he told himself firmly. 'Let's turn down here, see if we can get through to the river. It looks as if there's plenty of damage down here too.'

Gloria gasped inadvertently when she saw the devastation before them. The road had opened out and now they had a clear view looking along the waterfront, all the way down to the docks. She put her hand to her throat. 'Oh Frank, I hope everyone is all right out in Bootle. Maybe I should try to get back to see Mam and Dad. It doesn't look good that way, does it?' She shivered in sudden fear.

Frank took hold of her arm. 'Don't think about it. There's nothing you can do one way or the other. I considered going there as well, but we'd only be in the way. They'll still be clearing up any damage, there won't be any transport for the likes of us, and we'd be better off staying out of it. Sorry, that sounds harsh, but it's true.'

Gloria gulped. 'You're right, of course. It would be selfish to put extra strain on the emergency services by adding to the crowd.' She wobbled again on her high heels. 'Sorry. I don't know what came over me just then.' She shook her hair in the breeze that was coming off the river. Then she pivoted around and pointed. 'Look, Frank. Look up there.'

'What?' For a moment he couldn't see what she meant. Then he followed the line of her index finger and the penny dropped.

Despite the devastation all around, there, on top of the Royal Liver Building, were the famous statues of the Liver Birds, standing guard over the city, undamaged and intact. Gloria tugged on his arm, and he could see there were tears in her eyes.

'They're still there, Frank. Somehow Hitler didn't get them. They're still there.'

Silently, he nodded.

'It's an omen, isn't it?' she said, staring in wonder. 'I know it sounds stupid but I really feel it is. They are up there; it's almost as if they are protecting us. It shows we won't be beaten. Hitler can drop all the bombs he likes, but the people of Merseyside will come through. It's a miracle how they haven't been destroyed but they are still there.'

Frank blinked hard. It was miraculous that the graceful creatures hadn't been toppled in the overwhelming force of the raid. Maybe Gloria was right. Part of him said it was superstitious nonsense, but the other part of him agreed wholeheartedly that these, the very symbol of the city, were a source of strength and hope for all who saw them.

'We will come through,' he assured her. 'It'll take more than nights of bombing to defeat us. One way or another, we will come through this.'

CHAPTER THIRTEEN

Kitty snatched up the letter from her pigeonhole, recognising the writing. She decided to take it back to her dormitory and read it in peace so that she could savour it. Then she could put her feet up at the same time – a welcome break, as they were being worked harder and harder, the sessions of cramming in the various training establishments growing longer.

Other letters she'd received recently weren't so welcome. There had been no definite news about the destruction of her home city in the newspapers or on the radio, just reports that somewhere in the northwest had been targeted. But rumours soon flew about, and she had realised with a sinking heart that Merseyside had taken a pasting. Then came the letters from home.

Rita wrote to her sadly that old Mrs Ashby had been killed in the big raid. She'd been too frail to make it out of her house, and Dolly had found her, had tried to get her out, but it had been too late. A piece of burning debris must have landed near her back window and set fire to the flaking wooden frame, as Dolly reckoned it had been smoke inhalation that had done the damage, though the whole house was now uninhabitable. Rita reported that Violet had been the most upset of anyone, even though she'd known the old lady for less time than the rest of them. Apparently they'd become quite close when Violet had helped her with the shopping. Kitty sighed in sorrow. She'd been fond of her old neighbour, and Empire Street wouldn't be the same without her. Nancy and Mrs Kerrigan had had a very narrow escape getting to the shelter, and Mrs Kerrigan had hurt her leg, and was now going round on crutches claiming to be a victim of the war just like her poor imprisoned son. Nancy was consequently spending even more time at her parents' as she couldn't stand her mother-in-law's moaning.

Sarah had been a heroine, running the nurses' station single-handedly for a while before they got reinforcements to her after her colleague was killed. 'I can't believe she's only seventeen,' Rita had written. Yes, thought Kitty, but war meant Sarah's last years of girlhood had been taken from her. She'd had to bear responsibilities nobody could have dreamt of. Yet again Kitty thanked her lucky stars that Tommy was safe out on the farm. Otherwise he'd have no doubt tried to be in the thick of it, collecting shrapnel souvenirs as the docks burnt about him.

Now Kitty hurried along the corridor, careful not to be seen running, and rushed up the stairs to her sanctuary. She had a precious couple of hours free, and she was going to relish the chance to read her letter at leisure for once. Even more unusually, the dormitory was empty. She flung herself on her bunk and ripped open the envelope.

Elliott's slanted handwriting stared up at her, beautifully neat by most people's standards, but she knew it well enough by now to realise that he'd written this in a hurry. Time was always tight for him. During the week of raids at the beginning of May he'd worked virtually non-stop, snatching brief bouts of sleep at the hospital, never making it back to his billet. She gave a whoop of joy as she read the first paragraph. His devotion in that week had been recognised and he was being given leave. Would she like it if he came to London?

'Whatever's got into you?' asked Laura, sweeping through the door. 'Oh, you lucky thing, you've got a letter. Good news, by the looks of it.'

'I'll say!' exclaimed Kitty, quickly skimming the

132

rest of the single page. 'Elliott's finally going to visit. I was so worried for him, in the thick of all the bombing, and he must have seen some dreadful things.'

'All the more reason to show him a good time then.' Laura threw herself on to the bed beside Kitty. 'Budge up. That's better. When's he coming?'

'Let me check.' Kitty scanned the letter again. 'I'll have to work it out, it's taken a while to get here ... oh, that's soon! This Friday!' She paused, her old insecurities rising to the surface. 'Laura, I've got to get my hair done and I've nothing to wear...'

'Calm down,' Laura said at once. 'We've always sorted you out before, haven't we? I shall go through my extensive wardrobe,' she nodded towards the narrow cupboard containing her clothes, 'and if there's nothing suitable we'll see what the shops can do. Don't look like that, Kitty, you must have some wages saved up – you never spend anything on yourself. Don't you fret, we'll get you looking just the ticket for when the glamorous doctor comes to town.'

Kitty laughed. 'Don't get your hopes up. He's not exactly glamorous.' She smiled warmly as she thought of his kind face. 'But I do want to look right for him. He's used to mixing with girls who really dress up. That's not me and he knows it, but I don't want to let him down.'

'You won't, I won't let you,' declared Laura decisively.

Kitty took one look at her friend and knew she meant it. The weeks that had passed since their initial training had taught her, if there had ever been any doubt about it, that when Laura set her mind to something, she fully intended it to happen. It was sheer good luck that the two of them plus Marjorie were still in the same dormitory, in the same old school building. Many of the young women who'd arrived at the same time had been sent elsewhere to continue their training, once it had been decided what their specialism would be. Laura's future had been decided almost at once, when the senior officers discovered that she could drive. They had been even happier to find she didn't mind what sort or size of vehicle she was given. Therefore she was currently scaring unwitting bystanders in north London, who would glance up at the noise of a large lorry approaching, only to see a striking young blonde woman at the wheel. Laura had been particularly delighted when a very smart City gentleman had almost fallen backwards off the pavement at the sight. That had made her day.

Marjorie had stood out for her academic abilities, and there had been some debate as how best to use them. It turned out she had a flair for languages, so she was currently on a crammer course in German and French in central London, commuting to and fro each day. Sometimes this was easy if the buses and Tubes were working; other days it involved a lot of walking. She didn't mind. She was being given free rein to use her brain and she took to it like a duck to water. Unfortunately Laura and Kitty were no good to practise on.

Kitty herself had caused them some problems to start with. She had no obvious qualifications, other than having run a home from the age of eleven. For a dreadful few days she had thought she was going to be stuck cooking again. It wasn't that she didn't like cooking – but she'd already proved she could do it, and wanted something new. Then it became clearer that she was extremely organised and logical. So now she was being trained as a telephone operator, as everyone knew how vital communications might become if the war lasted for a long time. She knew the job could change and develop as time went on, and might take her anywhere. She didn't mind. She liked the sense of freedom that brought. At present she was based in a commandeered college on the northern edge of the city, easy to reach when the Northern Line was working, and tricky to reach by bus if it wasn't.

Now she stretched back on the unforgiving mattress and sighed with pleasure. 'I can't wait. It seems like years since I saw Elliott, although it's only been a matter of weeks.' She counted back. 'Well, a couple of months or so. A bit more. Anyway, no time at all really, yet we've done so much. And he's been through the horror of that awful week at home.' Her expression grew serious as she remembered the sad details in Rita's letters.

'Well, my girl, it is therefore your patriotic duty to take his mind off all of that,' said Laura grinning wickedly. 'Look upon it as an order, for king, country and our hard-working medical staff.'

'In that case I will,' Kitty smiled back.

Rita washed her hands, making sure she'd been thorough, before hurrying back to the nurses' station. She knew better than to run; as a sister she'd had to tell off many a less experienced junior for doing such a thing. However, there was no time to waste, as usual. Her ward was crowded with casualties, mostly as a result of the raids in the first week of May. Once the immediate damage had been assessed and the injured allocated to beds around the city, they were once again full to capacity in Linacre Lane Hospital. Many of the badly hurt had been caught up in the massive explosion when the SS *Malakand* had gone up in flames in Huskisson Dock. It had happened after the all-clear had been sounded, so people had been walking home from the shelters in the false belief that the danger was over.

She stopped by one of the beds. 'How are you feeling today, Mr Pryce?' She positioned herself where the elderly man could see her, as he was unable to turn his head. He'd taken a bad blow to the forehead and had been confused for days, believing she was his daughter and that he was back in Cardiff, where he'd grown up.

'Sister.' He gave a weak smile and his eyes crinkled at the sight of her.

Rita bent forward and gave his chilly hand a squeeze. 'That's right, Mr Pryce. Any better today? Do you recognise where you are now?'

The old man coughed but when he spoke he seemed perfectly lucid. 'Hospital, Sister. Stands to reason. You there in your uniform. Where else would I be? Unless I've died and gone to Heaven and the angels are all done up like nurses.' He laughed at his own weak joke and began to cough again.

136

Rita was pleased to find him so improved. 'You could do a lot worse,' she said, mock sternly. 'Here, let me give you some water.'

Mr Pryce shuffled so that he could sit up and gratefully slurped from the glass Rita held for him. 'Thank you.' He blinked slowly. 'Sister, has my daughter been in? I don't rightly remember but I don't think I've seen her. She'll be worried about me, she will.'

Rita tried not to grimace. As far as she knew, there had been no visitors for the confused old fellow. That could mean that he and his family didn't get on but, judging from the way he spoke, she didn't think that was the case here. Or, which wouldn't be uncommon, his family had been caught up in the bombings, and were themselves too injured to come – or worse. She couldn't let that suspicion show on her face, though. Bad enough to have to break the news if they had confirmation. 'I'm afraid I don't know,' she said honestly. 'I've only just started my shift. I could check with the nurses from this morning if you like.'

The old man turned his rheumy eyes to hers, moving slowly so as not to dislodge the bandage on his head. 'If you could, Sister. I don't want to be no trouble, but I'd be ever so grateful.'

'Of course.' Rita squeezed his wrinkled hand once more and stood up properly, setting down the glass of water where he could see it and reach it. As she made to go, there was a flurry of activity at the door of the ward. One of her more officious colleagues was trying to prevent a younger woman from coming through.

'I must ask you to respect the regulations,' the

137

nurse was barking. 'You may see for yourself, visiting hours are clearly displayed in the entrance. You must not disturb the patients outside those times.'

Rita hurried across the well-mopped floor. 'What's the problem here, Nurse Maxted?' She knew she must nip any trouble in the bud. The wounded and sick in this ward needed all the rest they could get, and any unexpected noise would upset them.

The younger woman pulled her threadbare jacket more tightly around her body, as if she was cold, but she looked to be in no mood to cave in. 'I believe my father might be here,' she said breathlessly. 'I've come all the way from Wavertree. One of the porters said as it might be him. I've been all over looking for him; haven't seen him since the beginning of the month. We're beside ourselves with worry. I've got to know if he's here.'

Nurse Maxted drew herself up to her full height, and she made an imposing figure. Not many people had the nerve to say no to her. Rita knew she had a quick decision to make. Either she let her colleague quote chapter and verse, which might result in a scene, or she could intervene and sort this out herself. While she didn't really have the time, it might be the quickest thing to do in the long run.

'I'll see to this, Nurse,' she said firmly. 'You will be needed back on your ward.'

Maxted looked as if she would argue, but even she didn't dare contradict the word of her direct superior. She gave Rita a glance that spoke volumes but merely said, 'Very well, Sister,' and swept out, stately as a galleon.

Rita faced the anxious young woman. She could see now that she likely hadn't slept properly for days, although she'd made the effort to appear respectable, with her hair in a tight knot and matching belt and handbag, neither of which were new. Her eyes were full of exhaustion, and apprehension. 'So, Miss...'

'Goulden. Eileen Goulden. I'm looking for my father.' She took out a handkerchief from her patch pocket and began to twist it. 'I am sorry to land on you this way, but it's like I said, we've been searching for him for days, and when my neighbour's son said he thought he'd seen his name on a list up here ... well, I came as soon as I could. I didn't wait to read your visiting hours.'

'I'm not sure we have a Mr Goulden,' Rita said, trying to estimate the woman's age. Older than herself, she guessed. So her father might be any-thing from fifty onwards, maybe–

'Oh no, his name isn't Goulden.' The woman interrupted her train of thought. 'Sorry, I should have said, that's my married name. He's called Pryce. Ernest Pryce.' Her tired eyes were at once full of hope and brimming with tears. Rita could see she was not far from collapse. 'Have you got him here? Or ... don't tell me, he's not died here, has he? We just don't know.'

Rita reached across to the sturdy oak desk that stood at the centre of the ward, between the two rows of beds. Quickly she scanned the notes and checked old Mr Pryce's name. There it was. Ern-est. Next of kin – an address in Wavertree. Bingo.

She took the woman by the arm. 'My colleague was quite right, we are outside visiting hours,' she said quietly, 'but under the circumstances I believe we can exercise a little discretion. Promise me you won't make much noise and that you'll only be a minute.' She drew her along to where the old man was lying back against his pillows once more, his eyes shut. Wordlessly the woman looked at him, then at her, and nodded.

Rita tactfully withdrew, but not before she heard the woman gasp, 'Dad. Oh, Dad.'

Sometimes, she thought, she really loved her job.

Frank carefully stacked the papers from that morning's meeting as quietly as he could while the senior officers of Derby House continued their conversation as if he wasn't there. The commander in chief, Sir Percy Noble himself, was joining in. Frank did his best to listen without appearing to do so. It wasn't often that he was privy to the deepest concerns of these men.

'It's simply unrealistic to say that we haven't been affected by the casualties of the first week of May,' one began. 'Obviously that information doesn't go beyond these walls, but we have to admit that some of our vital personnel are no longer with us. We can keep them safe while they're on duty, but if they're above ground then they are as vulnerable as the rest of the population in their homes or out on the streets.'

Frank paused briefly, thinking of the flirtatious young woman on the telephones who had been making eyes at him for a few weeks. She was one of the ones who had not made it through the May raids. She had been twenty-four. What a tragic waste.

'But you can't just employ any Tom, Dick or Harry,' another protested. 'These positions require a certain sort of brain. Most will have had specialist training for years, on top of an inherent aptitude. We won't find those wandering around on the street.'

'Then maybe we target those with aptitude and train them fast.' Sir Percy took charge of the discussion, his face etched with lines reflecting his many years of experience at the highest level of command. 'Correct me if I'm wrong, but we have plenty of people who've undergone years of training but who aren't quite up to the mark. You can train someone all you like, but if they don't have the razor-sharp mind to start with, then they'll never make the grade. We must change our way of thinking to reflect the needs of the moment.'

There was some muttering, and then the first man spoke again. 'Reminds me of something Johnny Forrester was saying to me the other day. Remember him? Old chap but one of the best. He's down south now, but was in hospital up here a few months ago, got taken sick when visiting family. Said he'd been incarcerated in this dull ward, and the one bit of entertainment he had was showing this young fellow how to do crosswords. Turned out the man had never even thought of trying them before, but within a few days he was solving them like a natural. Think he said the fellow had wanted to join the services but had a dicky heart. Couldn't even carry on working on the docks. Strikes me that's just the sort of young blood we need. Someone who's keen, has the intelligence, but who's been overlooked.

141

Think of everyone who's been turned away for flat feet. I don't care what their feet are like if their brains are in full working order.'

'That's all very well,' said the second man. 'Firstly, I don't imagine it would be in the public interest to intensively train up someone who's about to pop their clogs. Secondly, how are we meant to find this young man you're speaking of, even if we wanted to? Seems to me the hospitals round here will have had one hell of a lot of young male casualties through their doors recently.'

Frank stood motionless. He told himself this was pure coincidence and that it could be anybody. All the same, it would fit with what he'd heard the last time he went back to Empire Street, which he'd felt obliged to do after the raids had died down, to assess the extent of the damage.

'Very well, make contact with Forrester for a start,' snapped Sir Percy. 'Seems like a round-about way of proceeding, though. I need quick results, not ages spent chasing after one young man. We'd better try every available avenue to get as many suitable minds as we can.'

Frank gathered his courage and cleared his throat. 'Excuse me, sir.'

They all turned round, with expressions that might as well have said 'You're still here, are you?'

'Warrant Officer Feeny, sir. I think I might have a quicker way of reaching the young man in question.'

'Really?' barked the first officer. He didn't need to add 'seems highly unlikely': his face did it for him.

'Are we talking about the Royal Infirmary, sir?'

'I believe so, yes.' The officer's expression didn't soften.

'Then I suspect the man you want is called Daniel Callaghan,' said Frank, aware that he was making an almighty leap in the dark, and yet utterly certain that he was correct. It matched exactly with what Danny had told him, and also with the completed crosswords in the newspapers that he'd seen scattered around the Callaghans' kitchen. 'And I know exactly where to find him.'

CHAPTER FOURTEEN

'Winnie, have you seen the corned beef?' Rita was searching through the boxes in the storeroom, trying not to breathe in the dust. She knew she'd seen the box recently, but now it was nowhere to be found.

Winnie stood in the doorway, leaning on the frame. It was the middle of the morning and Rita wasn't due at the hospital until the afternoon. Winnie, nevertheless, was unsteady on her feet and her hands shook a little. She seemed distracted.

'I said, have you seen the corned beef?' Rita repeated, her patience fraying. 'It was definitely here before the weekend. I took out three tins – two for the shelves and one for Mrs Mawdsley. She wanted it for her Saturday tea.'

Winnie's eyes became focused and gleamed with spite. 'Oh, her. No better than she should be, that one.'

Rita raised her eyebrows at the insult to one of her mother's friends, but said nothing. At least she seemed to have got Winnie's attention now. 'Yes, so that's how I know there was a box of it here. So where can it have gone?'

Winnie tutted. 'You want to ask that Ruby. She's probably gone off with it; she's not right in the head. Or that Violet woman you think so much of. We don't know anything about her really – she could be anybody, coming in here. Stealing our stuff.'

'Honestly, Winnie, what a thing to say.' Rita wanted to scream in frustration. 'You know darn well that this shop would have ground to a halt if it wasn't for Violet. She keeps the place together so you can lie in your bed.'

'Well, you should be working here, not gallivanting off,' Winnie protested, going back to her favourite theme of the past eighteen months or so.

'Hardly gallivanting.' Rita wiped her hands on her faded cotton printed apron. 'Right, I can't spend any more time looking for it. I'll try again later. Excuse me, I'm going back to the shop.' She had to brush against Winnie, who was slow to move from the doorway, and caught the unmistakable smell of sherry on the old woman's breath. Involuntarily she gasped and drew back, it was so unpleasant. She'd suspected for some time that Winnie had been hitting the bottle, but never had she smelt it so strongly.

'What?' demanded Winnie belligerently.

Rita turned to face her. 'You need to go steady on that sherry, Winnie. It's not even lunchtime.'

144

'Don't know what you're talking about,' Winnie insisted, straightening up, but still holding on to the doorframe. 'Don't you go spreading rumours about me. I won't have it.'

As if, thought Rita. What would be the point? Still, she couldn't help wondering where Winnie was getting the extra money. In the old days she'd have been selling her black-market goods to her specially selected group of customers, but that had all changed now. Or had she found some way of palming off the corned beef in exchange for sherry? Rita shook her head. She was being ridiculous. Violet would have noticed something if that had been the case. There had to be another explanation.

'Why don't you go back upstairs and have a nice wash, Winnie?' she suggested, unable to stop herself wrinkling her nose.

Winnie glared at her malevolently through red-veined eyes. 'Don't you imply anything about me, young lady,' she hissed. 'I shall go upstairs, but only because I don't care to be in the same room as you. That's all.' She tottered unsteadily along the dim corridor and headed up the steps.

Rita stared after her for a moment but then forced her mind back to the job in hand, restocking the shelves so that Violet wouldn't have to. Violet would forget to record which items had been moved from the storeroom to the shop itself, and then the whole system would break down. It was precarious enough at the best of times as more and more goods became hard to obtain, but Rita made an effort to keep some semblance of order. They needed to keep the shop going; her nurse's wages weren't enough to get by on. There had still been no word from Charlie, let alone any money, and now it looked as if they had Winnie's sherry habit to support as well.

A noise from the living quarters made her turn. Ruby was there, smiling shyly. 'Would you like a cup of tea, Rita? I can boil the kettle.'

Rita smiled back. 'I'd love one.' It was only recently that Ruby had plucked up the courage to do this, even though it was coming up for six months since she'd arrived. Rita hadn't wanted to let her near the kettle or anything hot to begin with, as she seemed completely incapable of working out what was dangerous and what wasn't. It was a slow process, getting her to adjust to normal life – or as normal as it got these days. For the hundredth time Rita wondered what Ruby's existence had been like before she came here. Now she nodded encouragingly as the young woman brought through a tray with a teapot, two cups and saucers and a small jug of milk.

'There you are,' she said seriously, setting them on the counter. 'See, I know how to do this now.'

Rita grinned in gratitude. 'And very welcome it is, Ruby. Tell you what. Do you mind standing here behind the counter while I take out the empty cardboard boxes? I'm going to keep them in the back yard until Mam can collect them. She can tear them up and put them on the victory garden compost heap.'

'What ... what if someone comes in?' Ruby asked nervously.

'Then you ask them nicely to wait a minute and call me,' explained Rita. 'I won't be a moment.'

146

Ruby's face became determined. 'All right.'

'Good girl,' said Rita, thinking that although Ruby was only a few years younger than herself, the age difference seemed much greater. Still, the girl was improving. She would never have agreed to mind the shop until recently. Rita went to the corner where she'd left the boxes, bent to pick them up and pushed through the back door to the tiny courtyard. She'd propped up a makeshift roof of old galvanised metal across the corner of two walls, so that she could stack the cardboard out of the way where it could keep dry until Dolly could fetch it.

Rita noticed with a groan that the back wall could do with repairing. It must have been all the explosions shaking it; several bricks had been dislodged. She didn't have time to do anything about it now, but she'd add it to her list of chores. Maybe Pop or Danny could help her, or at least ask someone who was handy. She wouldn't know how to start.

Turning from her improvised shelter, she felt a prickling at the back of her neck, as if she was being watched. She straightened up and gazed around, but there was nothing out of the ordinary, just the same old back yard. Don't be daft, she told herself. It must have been a breeze. That, or you've spooked yourself by thinking of what Winnie is doing to get her sherry money. Don't let yourself imagine something when there isn't anything there.

She was about to go back inside when she heard a faint noise, a slight scuffling, maybe like a stone being struck along the paving. Again she turned anxiously and gazed around.

Suddenly there was a flash of movement to her left and she wheeled about, catching sight of the culprit. It was a tortoiseshell cat, leaping from the side wall on to the galvanised roof. Insolently it came to a halt and sat there, watching her intently with its big hazel eyes.

Rita breathed out heavily. It was the creature that usually hung around the end of the road by the Sailor's Rest. Obviously it had decided to broaden its territory. Well, not a lot she could do about that, and as long as it didn't try to get into the dustbins or come inside after scraps it wasn't really doing any harm. 'Go on with you, puss,' she said half-heartedly, clapping her hands at it. It didn't move, and then stretched before settling down in a patch of sunlight.

It's all right for some, muttered Rita to herself, returning to the shop to relieve Ruby. What I wouldn't give for a nice morning nap in the warmth. Fat chance of that.

Danny groaned as his supervisor down at the Gladstone Dock gave him yet another tedious list of crates to check. He'd done nothing but check crates in the warehouse all week. No matter how hard he tried to convince himself that this was vital for the war effort, he was bored out of his mind. The supervisor didn't help. The man had done the same job for years and was self-important and petty. Nothing was ever right for him. Even if Danny completed his latest task in double-quick time, the man would find fault with the exact angle of his ticks on the form.

148

Gritting his teeth, he picked up the detested clipboard and made his way to the doorway of the warehouse to begin at the first aisle.

'All right, Dan?'

Danny spun round and saw a figure silhouetted against the brightness of the sun's glare. For a moment he struggled to make out who it was, but it didn't take long to work it out.

'What do you want, Alfie?' he asked wearily. 'I'm working, as you can see.'

'So am I, Dan, so am I,' Alfie said easily, taking a long drag on his cigarette. 'Just thought I'd pop by and see how you were getting along. A little bird told me you were back at work. Does that mean you're feeling better? Not too much better, I hope. That'd spoil our little arrangement.'

'Thanks for your concern, Alfie,' Danny said, his voice heavy with sarcasm, 'but, as you damn well know, we have no arrangement, little or otherwise. So you can sling your hook and get back to wherever you're pretending to work.'

'Danny, Danny.' Alfie held up his hands in mock surrender. 'That's no way to treat an old friend. I was just enquiring after your health. And making sure exactly where you were.'

'What's it to you?'

'So I know how to find you if I need to,' said Alfie. 'Just in case anything urgent should arise, if you know what I mean.' He ground his cigarette butt into the ground with precise aggression.

Danny briefly shut his eyes. As long as he worked on the docks, Alfie would have an excuse to come and find him at any time. Was there to be no escape from the man?

'Oh aye, here comes trouble,' Alfie said brightly. 'That's your boss, isn't it? Looks as if someone's shoved a bee up his arse, I've never seen him move so fast. What you been up to then, Dan? He's got a face like thunder. And look over there, that's top brass, that is. Oh Danny, have you been a naughty boy? Time I wasn't here.' He turned lightly on his foot and sped off, not waiting to see what the supervisor wanted.

Danny drew himself up straight. He couldn't imagine what this might be about, but it must be serious. He squinted towards the uniformed man in the distance, and could make out a gleam of gold on his jacket. Not your average naval officer, then.

'Mr Callaghan, come with me,' the supervisor ordered, slightly out of breath and red in the face. His face betrayed controlled fury. 'I don't know what you've been doing but you've been summoned to go immediately with Lieutenant Commander Sykes here. You've left me in the lurch good and proper, and you'd better come back with a bloody marvellous excuse.' He held out his hand. 'Give me that clipboard.'

Utterly baffled, Danny did as he was asked. His heart sank. Had Alfie set him up? What on earth was going on?

CHAPTER FIFTEEN

'Kitty, you look lovelier than ever.' Elliott's warm eyes met Kitty's as they came to a halt outside the famous old pub near Hampstead Heath. The sun had just set over the treeline and the last of the birds were calling their cries at dusk. The warmth rose off the pavement and it seemed for an instant that all was at peace with the world.

'Elliott! You do say some funny things.' But Kitty was pleased. She had almost surprised herself at how happy she'd been to see the doctor, who'd turned up at her billet to escort her out for the evening. Kitty had worried that she didn't know anywhere smart to go, or that he'd expect a night of dancing in the West End, but he hadn't. He confessed he'd had to work right up to the time he'd had to leave to catch his train, and then had had to stand most of the way, so even his enthusiasm for dancing had been curbed. 'Tomorrow, maybe,' he'd said when she'd voiced her anxiety. 'But for tonight, may I take you to somewhere where I used to go when I was a student? It's near my parents' house in Hampstead. I think you'll like it. Don't worry, it's not too far from where you are, and of course I'll see you home.'

Kitty had never doubted that he would; he was the perfect gentleman in every way. She felt shy as he pushed open the heavy old door and held it for her as she stepped inside, worrying that everyone would recognise him and stare at her, but people carried on their conversations without a pause. There were plenty of young men and women in uniform, as well as those in civvies, marking the start of the weekend or simply taking advantage of a night without an air raid.

'Shall I get you a glass of wine?' he offered.

Kitty hesitated. When they had gone out together at home, to the prestigious New Year's Dance at the Town Hall, he had brought her wine and she had sipped it, but honestly hadn't enjoyed it. Then, she'd felt too unsure of herself to admit it. The pressure of being among so many elegant, wealthy people had rendered her almost speechless. But here it was different. She didn't have to pretend, to avoid hurting his feelings.

'If you don't mind, I'll just have shandy,' she said.

'Shandy? Is that what the newly trained Wren about town has these days?' he asked with a broad grin. 'Very refreshing, a good choice. Here, you sit down and I'll fetch it for you.' He pulled out a comfortable-looking chair by a small table and gestured for her to sit down on its faded velvet cushion. It was next to a window; she could see the Heath beyond, gathering its shadows in the fading light.

Kitty laughed inwardly at the idea she was an 'anything' about town; she hadn't dared venture too far yet, except for a few forays with Laura and Marjorie into the city centre to go to the cinema. There simply hadn't been the time, or they were too tired even when they did have evenings off. But it was fun to think Elliott imagined that's what she was.

'Here you are,' he said, pushing his way through a group of young men in RAF uniform. 'I decided I'd join you in a shandy. Cheers.' He sat down opposite her and they clinked glasses. 'I don't mind telling you, I'm glad to sit down. And in such beautiful company.'

'Elliott, you can't mean that,' Kitty protested, aware she was blushing and wishing she wasn't. 'And you must be exhausted. It's good of you to have come out, and to have fetched me on top of that. You must have wanted nothing other than to curl up at home with your mother's good cooking.'

'Actually I had some of that before I left,' he smiled. 'They'd love to meet you, you know.'

Kitty leant back in her seat, her face falling. 'Oh no, I couldn't do that. I wouldn't know what to say.'

Elliott's expression grew concerned. 'I'm so sorry, that was very presumptuous of me, wasn't it? I don't want to rush you, Kitty. That was a silly thing to say. It's just that I told them I was meeting a very lovely young Wren and they were delighted.'

Kitty fidgeted nervously. 'It's not that ... well, that's not all it is,' she said hesitantly. 'All right, I hope you don't mind me saying ... I'd feel that I was being compared to your fiancée. That's what it is.'

'Oh, Kitty.' Elliott's eyes were bright. 'I do understand. I can't pretend I wasn't devastated when Penelope died, and yes, my parents were very fond of her. But I have put all that behind me now. It happened before the war broke out, before

I moved to Liverpool. Life has changed tremendously in every way. I was sad for a long time, but,' he reached across the table for her hand, 'now I've met you. I'm not going to jump to any conclusions, and we haven't known each other for long, but they can see I'm happy. Therefore they're happy. One day, when the time is right, it would be wonderful if you would like to meet them – but there's no hurry.' He squeezed her hand tenderly. 'As long as you're happy too, Kitty. That's the most important thing.'

Kitty squeezed his hand back. She knew she'd moved on too. She was no longer the uncertain young woman on the verge of leaving home. She was in the heart of things, absorbing her demanding training, mastering the technicalities and making new friends. It didn't matter that she'd had a drunkard for a father who'd driven her mother to an early grave, or that she'd had to miss out on much of her schooling to help bring up Tommy. She'd thought she was stupid; now she knew she wasn't. She had a friend who had a teaching certificate, another who could drive a big lorry and hold her cocktails with the best of them. And she was holding hands with a doctor who thought she was beautiful.

'I am, Elliott,' she said, her eyes shining in the light from the many lamps adorned with pretty chintz shades. 'It's lovely here, isn't it? I'm so glad we didn't go dancing; it gives us a chance to talk properly. I love to get your letters but it isn't quite the same.'

'I'll say.' Elliott raised his glass and took a sip. 'Every time I read yours, I imagine you writing it, and can't wait until I see you again. Now we're here. I've missed you, Kitty.'

'I think about you too,' Kitty said. 'I know you don't have much time to write, so that makes your letters extra-special. I'm so glad to get them.' Their eyes met, and for a moment she thought he was going to lean forward and kiss her. Then from the bar came a roar from the RAF men, and a figure emerged from behind their group.

'Fitzgerald! You never said you were coming back, how sly!' A man of Elliott's age with fair skin and red hair came up to their table. 'I saw your folks the other day and they didn't say a dickie bird. Good to see you, old chap.'

Elliott rose and shook the man's hand warmly. 'Smedley, I had no idea you were still here.'

'I'm at the Royal Free these days, specialist unit,' the man said. 'Didn't you go up north? Up to the wilds somewhere?'

Kitty tried not to flinch; she was getting used to all southerners assuming civilisation didn't reach very far past London.

'Hardly the wilds,' said Elliott. 'But we've had a bit of a rum do up there recently, you could say. We've been kept busy, no doubt about it.' He turned to include Kitty in the conversation. 'Kitty, may I introduce you to Dr Bill Smedley, scourge of the operating theatre and my very good friend from when we trained at Barts. Bill, this is Kitty Callaghan of the WRNS.'

'Very pleased to meet you,' the red-haired man said, shaking her hand easily. 'Elliott, you lucky man. A Wren, eh? And how do you like London, Miss Callaghan?'

155

Kitty brought herself back down to earth after the uncertainty of not knowing if Elliott was going to kiss her or not, but soon fell into relaxed conversation with the man. He obviously thought a lot of Elliott, and she found herself glowing with pride for him. She'd known he was a good doctor from his time treating Tommy and Danny – and besides, Rita always knew what the nurses thought of the doctors, and the ones who were all mouth got little sympathy from them. But to hear it from an old friend was immensely satisfying. It wasn't until he'd made his way back to his friends – 'Mustn't outstay my welcome', but said with a wink – that she took a moment to realise that she was actually sitting in a pub in the capital city making conversation with two doctors, neither of whom were looking down on her. In fact, one was looking at her in a very special way indeed.

'Maybe you'd like to go dancing tomorrow, though, Kitty?' Elliott asked, a tender but hopeful look on his face. 'I could show you my favourite spot in the West End. I'm sure you'd like it.'

Kitty felt excitement well up in her. Elliott was a very skilful dancer – he'd once confessed he had been a champion, back in his student days – and she suddenly remembered the way he'd held her round the waist on New Year's Eve, which she'd found herself enjoying far more than she would have imagined, despite all her nervous insecurity at the time. She decided she would very much like him to hold her that way again, with his warm hands pressing against the silky fabric of her dress. 'Oh yes please,' she said. 'That would be wonderful.'

'It would be my pleasure, indeed, my honour,' he said with a grin to show her he meant it but wouldn't take it too seriously. 'Would you like to ask your friends to come too?' Marjorie and Laura had met him briefly when he'd come to collect her earlier; they'd been extremely keen to meet the fabled author of the letters which Kitty anticipated so keenly. 'I wouldn't neglect you, I just thought you might enjoy having them with us.'

For a moment Kitty fought off the sensation of inadequacy. Part of her wanted to keep Elliott all to herself on their brief weekend together. She'd have to compete with Laura to be seen as someone who fitted in with the London nightlife, who knew how to dress, dance and behave in such a sophisticated set. Then she berated herself. He hadn't asked Laura out – he'd asked her. 'That's so kind of you to think of that,' she said. 'I'll ask them.'

'But they won't hold a candle to you, Kitty,' Elliott assured her. Then he leant forward and, in the middle of the crowded pub, softly planted a kiss on her lips. He drew back before she could be embarrassed. 'That's just on account,' he smiled. 'But I couldn't resist you, Kitty Callaghan.'

She had to stop herself from gasping aloud. He'd done that – him, a doctor, and her just plain Kitty Callaghan from Empire Street. It was all too much to take in. Across the room she caught sight of a young woman with slightly tousled dark hair, eyes bright, cheeks slightly flushed, and immediately alongside her the back view of a well-set man in an immaculately cut jacket. It took her a moment to register it was a mirror and the man was Elliott,

157

the young woman was her. Everything was happening so fast and she could feel herself changing along with the pace of the times. Where would it all lead? She had to gather her courage and see where this new life might take her.

Rita stared at the letter, her heart hammering furiously. She'd known this would happen but it was still a horrible shock to see it in black and white. One of the main suppliers to the shop was demanding immediate payment for its goods or it would suspend trading with her. Rita knew she needed this firm; they'd done business for ages and it would be well nigh impossible to sign up with anyone else. They'd take one look at the slowly failing shop and turn her down without a backward glance. She also knew she didn't have the money. Wild ideas came into her head. Should she ask Danny to see what fell off the back of a lorry down at the docks? But she couldn't go down that route – that was Winnie's way, but it wasn't hers. Even when her back was against the wall, Rita knew she couldn't be dishonest. She wouldn't be able to face herself in the mirror in the morning if she did that. Damn Charlie – he'd treated her like a punchbag, brought disgrace upon the family, and scarpered off without a care in the world, leaving her with this mess, which she'd never asked for in the first place.

Was there another way of balancing the books? Had she done the sums right? Had Violet made any obvious mistakes and Rita been too tired to see them? Damn Charlie for causing his mother to go into such a tailspin. Rita also wondered if some customers were staying away on principle, knowing he was a deserter. She wouldn't put it past them. She could understand all too well how they might feel. She hated cowardice, and resented being tarred with the same brush as her faithless husband. How different it would have been if he'd turned out to be the man she was hoping for: someone she and the children could have relied on, someone she could have shared her troubles with. At least they were safely out of it, happy and well, although achingly far away. When it came down to it she was on her own. Violet was kind and never said no to working late, but she didn't really understand the business, for all her outgoing cheerfulness. Rita still had little idea of what went on in Ruby's head and certainly wouldn't dream of burdening her with the realities of the shop. And as for Winnie ... well, she was just Winnie.

Rita sighed heavily as she checked the blackout blinds were properly fastened across the shop window. Dusk had fallen and she needed to turn on the lights, though she dreaded the extra expense. Maybe she could negotiate. Perhaps she could offer to pay an extra amount per week or per month – she'd have to find it somehow, but it was better than doing nothing. She had to keep the shop going, there were no two ways about it. Shivering, although it was a warm evening, she turned to go back to the living quarters.

There was a soft knock on the shop door, and she jumped. Fear shot through her that it was someone from the suppliers, come to demand their money in person. She hesitated, not wanting whoever it was to be heard in the street; she couldn't have borne the shame of a public confrontation. Her name was in tatters already, and she couldn't risk putting off even more customers.

'Rita, Rita,' called a male voice, 'are you in there? Are you going to let me in?'

Rita gasped as she recognised the voice, barely able to believe that it was who she knew it to be. Her knees went treacherously weak. Then she made her way across the shop floor to the door, hastily opening it, fearful that the light would be visible and the ARP warden would notice. If it wasn't Pop, it could mean even more trouble for her. But she couldn't wait to see her caller.

For a moment neither of them spoke as they absorbed the sight of one another. It had been long, long months since they had last been together. Then she could hold back no longer.

'Jack, Jack, you've made it home!' Despite herself she flung her arms around his beloved broad shoulders, but then jumped back. 'Oh no, how's your injury? Have I hurt it?'

'Don't be daft.' Jack hugged her tightly, knowing she was the most precious woman in the world. But he would go no further. While he was in no doubt he loved her with all his heart and soul, she was still a married woman, even if in name only.

'Oh, Jack.' Rita breathed deeply, inhaling the magical scent of him, the essence of a strong, good man. How she would have loved it if she could only let him take care of her, lift all the worries that had been besetting her since Charlie disappeared – and, in truth, long before that. But she couldn't.

It wasn't fair on him. She was still tied to Charlie: devious, vindictive Charlie. She broke away, as she knew she must. Jack was her very good friend, the very best friend she could ever have, in fact, but he could be nothing more.

Jack stood back and regarded her. Even in the meagre light from the sallow overhead bulb she was radiantly beautiful. 'You know what, Reet?' he said softly. 'You're a proper sight for sore eyes and no mistake.'

'Jack.' Rita forced herself to break away, and held him at arm's length, taking in the sight of his familiar features. 'Oh Jack, I'm so glad to see you. When you wrote to say your leave had been delayed, I didn't know what to think. I thought you'd been posted somewhere far away and I'd never see you again.'

'Reet, don't say that, you know I can't tell you where I've been or where I'm going. That's if I even know, which often I don't. But I'll always come back. You know that.' Jack's eyes glowed in the half-light as he drank in the sight of her.

'I know. Well, I hope so.' She still couldn't quite take in that he was here in front of her; she was conscious that the clock was already ticking and the precious time they would have together would be short. 'How long have you got this time?'

'A couple more days.' He drew a finger around the collar of his uniform jacket. 'I stopped by your parents' house before coming here to check you weren't on shift. Your dad says I can have the cart tomorrow and that it's your day off.' His eyes were dancing. 'Fancy a trip out to Freshfield?'

'Oh yes, Jack. That would be marvellous.' All

161

thoughts of money worries fell away at the prospect of seeing her children again – and the thought that Jack was Michael's unacknowledged father made it all the more special. 'I'd like that better than anything.'

CHAPTER SIXTEEN

Danny stared at the piece of paper in front of him. He couldn't quite believe what had happened. He felt like pinching himself to check if he was dreaming or not, but the stern face of the naval officer who'd summoned him from the warehouse stared down at him. Danny didn't think he was the sort of person who'd take kindly to any form of joke.

They were in a small office in one of the buildings in the city centre that had managed to avoid being damaged by the blitz at the beginning of May. The smart black car had brought them here and Danny had gasped as they had gone through the familiar streets, many now almost unrecognisable. He hadn't left Bootle since the raids and, even though he'd heard what the centre had suffered, it was still a shock to see it for himself. The cathedral had taken a hit and St Luke's Church was all but a ruin. What made it worse was he still hadn't been told what all this was about. He felt as if he was headed for his doom, with destruction all around him.

Then they had pulled up at a nondescript door,

which gave no clues as to what was inside or what firm or organisation owned the premises. The officer had shown his ID to a guard inside the door – there was an air of secrecy to the whole procedure. Danny was shown to a seating area and told to await further instructions. It reminded him of being hauled before the headmaster, when you knew something bad was coming but the waiting made it worse. He paced around, too restless to sit on one of the worn old leather office chairs arranged around the walls. There were no notices on the walls to give a clue what this place was for. His earlier fears that Alfie Delaney was somehow behind this began to be replaced by something much worse.

Eventually, after he'd been kicking his heels for what felt like hours, a young woman in smart WAAF uniform approached. 'Commander Stephens will see you now,' she said, watching him calmly with her grey eyes, 'so follow me.'

Danny did as he was told, still more puzzled by the young woman. She led him briskly down a series of bland corridors before knocking sharply on a plain brown door. 'Mr Daniel Callaghan for you, sir.' She pushed open the door and left him to face whatever was coming. By now he was fearful and curious in equal measure.

A man in naval officer's uniform stood up and offered his hand for Danny to shake. 'Mr Callaghan – Commander Stephens. Good of you to come.' Danny was baffled. Good had nothing to do with it. He hadn't exactly been given a choice.

'You'll no doubt be wondering what all this is about,' Stephens went on, giving Danny a genial smile. 'Sorry about all the subterfuge, but you'll understand when I explain.'

Danny had to bite his lip to keep his temper. He could tell no good would come of losing it, but he was by now extremely fed up with how he was being treated. 'I'd appreciate that,' he said bluntly. 'I don't know why I'm here, but I'm not in the navy and so am not answerable to you. And that young woman was a WAAF. I'm not in the air force either. Not for want of trying,' he concluded bitterly. If things had been different that could've been him in the smart dark uniform – although possibly without so much gold on his sleeves.

'Excellent observation,' Stephens said, his smile not faltering at the challenge. 'So, yes, where you are now is rather unusual. As you have seen for yourself, it involves close co-operation between the air force and the navy, and the Royal Marines as well, as a matter of fact.'

Danny looked at the man's face for any sign of a threat but found none. He decided he was telling the truth. In which case there was only one place he could be talking about. 'You mean Western Approaches Command,' he said. 'That's the only place I can think of where that happens. But we aren't in Derby House now.'

Commander Stephens smiled even more. 'Spot on, young man. No, we aren't in Derby House, as everyone there has to have security clearance. But we're sometimes allowed the use of some neighbouring offices.' He sat back down. 'Do have a seat and I'll try to fill you in.'

Danny would have preferred to stand as he still felt too restless to keep still, but it would have been rude to refuse. Besides, he needed to hear what the commander had to say.

'Let me be totally straight with you,' the officer began. 'We are looking to recruit people with very particular talents for our operation, and we have received word that you might be just the sort of person who would be suitable.'

Danny's jaw would have hit the floor if he hadn't been biting his lip so hard. Whatever he'd expected the man to say, it most definitely wasn't that. 'But,' he finally managed to reply, 'I can't. I've applied to every one of the armed forces and been turned down by the lot. I'm useless for the war effort. I've got a damaged heart.'

'We know all about that, Mr Callaghan,' Commander Stephens said reassuringly. 'It is most commendable that you tried so hard to join up. That's one of the things that drew our attention to you. The other, believe it or not,' he flicked at an invisible piece of lint on his sleeve, 'is your heart condition.'

'What?' Danny blurted. This was getting ridiculous.

'Or rather, your stay in hospital. The Royal Infirmary, wasn't it?' the man amended. 'Where you met Captain Jonathan Forrester.'

Danny searched his memory and drew a blank. He and his fellow patients hadn't exactly swapped ranks on the ward.

'The man who introduced you to cryptic crosswords,' the commander prompted.

Suddenly the pieces fell into place in Danny's mind. 'Yes, I know who you mean now. But I didn't know he was a captain in the navy. We didn't talk about such things. I knew he'd been a high-ranking officer of some kind, but that was as far as it got. I just called him Jonny.'

The commander smiled again. 'Yes, he really is a very informal chap. But he happened to mention to one of our team that he'd come across a young fellow who had a natural aptitude for solving tricky puzzles, who in a short time had picked up enough to tackle the most fiendish ones – all without any former background in such things. That's pretty rare, you know.' His expression changed. 'I must ask you to keep all of this absolutely to yourself. What I am about to propose needs to be treated as top secret. It is nothing short of being at the heart of what we do here at Western Approaches Command.'

Danny was taken aback at the change of direction. 'Of course,' he said. Who exactly was he going to tell, anyway?

'We need you to take a short test,' the commander went on briskly. 'Nothing too bad; certainly nothing to someone like you if Forrester was right – and I'd trust him with my life.' He rose and ushered Danny towards the door. 'Through here. Lieutenant Commander Sykes will supervise you.'

They were in another small, anonymous room, but there was the man who had summoned Danny earlier that day, looking as though he wished he were somewhere else. He indicated a desk, on which there was a single piece of paper. 'Do sit, Mr Callaghan,' he said, his tone making it clear this was not a request. 'After Commander Stephens has left the room you will work your way through these questions and then hand the

166

answers to me. I am here to oversee you and not to help, so please do not direct any questions to me.' He saluted as Stephens made to leave.

'Good luck, Mr Callaghan,' the commander said cheerily on his way out.

Danny glanced up at the wall but there was no clock. So he figured he might as well get on with the task in hand. Warily he skimmed the page. Well, those were easy; they were obviously anagrams. Those looked like some kind of verbal logic. There were a couple of numerical sequences he thought he'd be all right at; the final ones were some kind of maths he hadn't come across. He'd worry about them later. He picked up the pen they had provided and set to it.

In what felt like no time at all, he looked up and met Sykes's steady, unwelcoming gaze. 'Finished,' he said. 'Or as finished as I can be.' He hadn't been able to do the final questions; they went beyond the simple arithmetic and geometry he'd done at school, which he'd been all too keen to get away from. He figured that was hardly his fault. No doubt most of the people they tested had gone to private schools, and quite likely university too. He'd done his best, and if that wasn't good enough, then too bad. He was expecting to fail. He didn't dare think about what this could lead to; there was no point, he wouldn't make the grade.

'Wait there, Mr Callaghan.' Sykes took the paper and vanished through the door, leaving Danny on his own yet again.

Danny stretched his arms over his head and leant back in the chair. Well, it beat counting crates

167

in the warehouse. Now the test was over he realised he'd enjoyed it, or at least the puzzle aspect of
it. He wasn't so sure about being shut in a small
room with Sykes; he could tell the lieutenant
commander thought all of this was an enormous
waste of time. He could sense the friction between
him and the commander, who presumably was his
superior officer, and wondered if by some miracle
he did pass, whether he'd end up being caught
between the two of them. Still, he probably
wouldn't see any more of these men after today.

He stared at the ceiling. There was only one
person who could be behind this: Frank Feeny.
All of Empire Street knew he had come back to
work in Derby House on some vital but hush-
hush project. Quite how he had heard about
Jonny, or Captain Forrester as he now knew him
to be, Danny couldn't work out, but he intended
to ask him the next time he saw him. Frank was
a good bloke and hadn't deserved his injury – but
then, as Danny knew all too well, fate had a habit
of flinging unwelcome hardships at you.

A noise from the corridor brought an abrupt
end to his thoughts, and he hurriedly stood as
Stephens and Sykes re-entered the small room,
which was stuffy with all three of them in there.

'Well done, Mr Callaghan,' said Stephens with
his smile as wide as ever. 'Now I notice you had
some trouble with the final questions.'

So that was that, thought Danny. He'd failed.
Still, nothing ventured. 'That's right,' he said. 'I
have never seen anything like them, so didn't
know where to start.'

'Very well, I understand,' said Stephens. 'But I

168

have to say you were one hundred per cent on everything else. And in a very quick time, too. We were most impressed, weren't we?'

Sykes nodded slightly and gave a noncommittal grunt.

'All the more so as I understand you left school at fourteen and would have had no chance to experiment with any of the puzzles here other than those directly related to solving crosswords.'

Blimey, thought Danny, they have done their homework. It felt slightly alarming that they'd been checking up on him already. But he supposed they could simply have asked Frank.

'We would therefore like to ask you to join us,' Stephens continued. 'You will be trained in all forms of code breaking. There can be no more vital task for a young man of your, what I have to say are quite exceptional abilities.' He met Danny's eye. 'So you will have worked out that Warrant Officer Feeny has been involved in all of this and he vouches for your character and integrity. As he is highly thought of by those in command here, that is recommendation indeed. We propose that you are brought in as part of the Royal Navy, initially at midshipman level. What do you say?'

Danny thought he caught Sykes muttering, 'Highly irregular.' But he didn't care. He was going to be part of the armed forces after all, and in an elite position. Even more surprising, he'd been secretly selected. He almost laughed. If his headmaster could have seen him now...

'I say yes, sir,' he said, and shook Stephens' offered hand. 'Yes, with all my heart.'

CHAPTER SEVENTEEN

'We're making a habit of this,' Jack laughed, as Pop's cart made its way along the road to Fresh-field. He held tightly to the reins, but would have preferred to have his arms around Rita. Still, she was snuggled up beside him on the narrow front seat – there wasn't much room for two, but he wasn't going to complain if it brought the woman he loved close to his side.

'I wish we were, all right,' Rita said wistfully. The countryside was opening out and was green and lush in the first burst of summer. 'It was more than six months ago we brought the children to the farm, can you believe it? But they're so happy there – well, you'll soon see for yourself.'

Jack nodded. 'I know you torment yourself about it all the time, Rita, and you miss them, but it's the right place for them.'

Rita turned to face him, her eyes shining. 'It's hard to explain, Jack. Even though I know what you say is true, there's not a day goes by without me feeling I'm missing a limb. They're such a part of me. Everything I do is for them. I hate for them to be away from me. I know it isn't far really, and compared to what some families are going through, it's nothing at all, but to be separated is agony.'

Jack shut his eyes briefly and then focused on the road ahead, which was slowly narrowing to a lane. 'I understand, Rita, I honestly do. I know what it's like to miss someone, to want to be with them every minute of the day and night, but to know it's impossible.' He paused. 'That's how I feel about you, Rita. What keeps me going is the thought that one day we could be together.'

Rita gave a little gasp. It was as if he was voicing her own innermost desires. 'And I feel like that too, Jack. It would mean more than anything in the world to me, but we'd be foolish to even think about it. You're a free agent but I'm not – I'm still shackled to Charlie whether we like it or not, and there's nothing we can do about it.' She tossed her hair, which she'd tied back for the journey. 'I wish things were different, but they're not.' Her heart was heavy with regret. But for a moment of chance, she'd have married Jack instead, and they'd be together with their son.

Jack wondered if this was the right time to bring up something that had been on his mind for some while. He knew she might not like it, but he'd never get a better time. If she got upset there was no one to see, and there was nobody around to hear. 'Rita, listen,' he began. 'The fact is, Charlie has deserted you. Not only is he a deserter for failing to enlist when he got his call-up papers, he's left you and taken up with another woman. So what right has he got over you?'

'He's still my husband, Jack,' Rita pointed out. 'Whatever he's done, wherever he is, he's still my legal husband. I don't love him, I realise now I never really did, but I tried so hard to make it work, and now he's upped sticks and gone off with that Elsie Lowe. Yet we're still married. I

171

can't change that.'

'There might be a way, Rita.' Jack gathered his courage to make his suggestion.

'You could get a divorce.'

Rita sat bolt upright and stared at him. 'What are you saying, Jack? A divorce? But that's impossible. Marriage is for life, you know that.' She got out her handkerchief and twisted it in her hands, hardly knowing she was doing it. 'We married in sight of the Lord and that's all there is to it. That can't be ended with a divorce. Anyway, you know that divorce isn't for the likes of us. It would be shameful, and my family would be shamed along with me. Think of what that would do to the children. No, I can't even imagine such a thing.'

Jack swallowed guiltily, recognising that she had a point. He ought to have guessed – Rita had never been one to run away from anything, however difficult. 'Please, Rita, don't upset yourself,' he said, switching the reins to one hand for a moment and gently touching her fingers. 'I didn't mean to distress you. But think, Rita. Times are changing. This war is going to make it all different, you see if it doesn't. The likes of you and me are going to be able to do all sorts of things we didn't think were possible. Charlie has deserted you and he never deserved you to start with – the world is becoming a different place and people like Charlie can't get away with things like they used to. We can do something about it – together. I'd never let you down when you needed me.'

Rita hesitated before replying, and tried to keep her voice steady. 'I know you wouldn't, Jack, and I am grateful, really I am. But it doesn't change anything. I might not get to church as often as I used to, what with all the different shifts and being too tired to stand let alone get down the road to Mass, but it doesn't alter how I was raised – and you too. Marriage can't be set aside so lightly. Whatever we might want doesn't alter that.'

Jack sighed. 'I was afraid you'd say that. But I had to bring it up, you see that, don't you? I want you to be free, I want for us to make a life together. We have to have hope.'

'I know, Jack.' Looking at Jack, seeing his open and honest face, and the adoration for her she found there, regret filled Rita once again, and inside her she felt the deep, persistent longing for this good man that was never far from the surface. 'I want that too. But this isn't the way. We've got to make the best of what we've got, and our time together. Please, Jack, let's not spoil today.' She dashed away the unbidden tears that were threatening to overwhelm her. Rita didn't want to arrive at the farm with red-rimmed eyes or it would upset Michael and Megan, which was the last thing she intended to do.

'You're right,' he said heavily. Then he drew himself upright. 'Let's make today a good one. The sun's shining on us, we're out in the countryside and we're going to see the children.'

'And Joan will have baked a cake, if I know her,' said Rita, desperately trying to lighten the atmosphere.

'And will it be as good as one of Kitty's?' Jack asked.

'Oh, I don't know about that. Kitty's cakes would knock anyone else's into a cocked hat.' Rita smiled but her heart was heavy, knowing that Jack's words could now never be unsaid. He'd laid his cards on the table. He was good man, the best man, and he was offering her a way out, but deep down she knew it was one she could never, ever take. But if this way was closed to them, then where was their hope for the future? Charlie would never give her up, she knew that, so how on God's earth would they ever be together?

There was nothing in the world as precious as the first hugs from her children after such a long separation, and Rita treasured every moment. As Michael and Megan ran to meet her, she knew that this time it was extra-special thanks to Jack's presence. She could see the pleasure in Jack's face as he took in the sight of his true son, Michael, who, like Megan and Tommy, was positively thriving. Luckily, Jack was being kept busy by Tommy, who couldn't wait to quiz his big brother about life at sea. 'And have you shot many Germans?' he demanded. 'What was the most exciting moment? Have you brought me any bullet cases? Have you capsized or anything?'

'Tommy, Tommy, one thing at a time,' Jack said, bending down and swinging his little brother around. 'Blimey, I won't be able to do that for much longer. Look at the size of you. What are you feeding him?' he asked, catching sight of Joan and Seth.

The kindly farming couple had kept their distance, not wanting to interrupt the reunions. Now Joan stepped forward. 'Come and see for yourselves,' she said, shaking Rita's and Jack's hands.

'Oh, it's good to see you back here. Welcome to the farm. We thought you might be hungry after such a long journey.'

Rita felt a warm glow as she followed them towards the farmhouse, reassured that all was well in this part of the world, even if everywhere else was under threat. She held Megan's hand and the little girl gripped her tightly, smiling radiantly.

'Did you help collect the eggs for Auntie Joan this morning?' Rita asked. Megan had written to her that this was now her job. Rita had felt her heart swell with pride at that – her little girl was getting up early before school to help around the place with the chores, and also that she'd managed to write about it. There had been a time when Megan was so unhappy that it seemed she was going to be slow at her lessons, but now she was obviously flourishing.

'There were only eight today,' Megan said seriously. 'Sometimes there are twelve or more. Auntie Joan says baker's dozen then. But I think the hens at the far end of the shed are unhappy and they aren't laying as much.'

'Really?' Rita crinkled her eyes in amusement. 'What could make hens unhappy, pet? Do you think they can smell a fox?'

Megan tutted. 'We have a big fence to keep out the fox. You have to dig it in very deep, Uncle Seth showed me. No, I don't think there can be a fox anywhere near them.' She swung her hand so that Rita's arm went to and fro as well. 'No, I think it was the shadow man.'

Michael turned around to face his sister, from where he had been walking ahead. 'Don't be silly.

175

There's no such thing as the shadow man. He's all in your imagination. Remember what Uncle Seth said about that.'

Megan looked mutinous. 'Don't call me silly. It's true. There's a shadow man.'

Rita stooped in her tracks and turned to face her little daughter. She crouched down so she was at the same level. 'What's this, Megan? Who's the shadow man?'

Megan pushed back her hair, grown long now. 'When I go out when it's getting dark I sometimes feel there's someone there. But when I go to look all I see is shadows. So I say it's the shadow man. I'm not making it up.'

Rita gazed at her daughter and saw she was not telling lies, but that didn't mean there was anything there. 'Sometimes we all feel like that, Megan. When it's getting dark you can see all sorts of shapes that aren't there in the daytime, but it's nothing to be afraid of. It'll just be trees or something like that.'

'Oh, I'm not afraid,' said Megan, setting off towards the farmhouse door. 'Come on, Mam, let's have some of the cake Auntie Joan made. You'll like it, I did the decoration.'

'You put some bits of old nuts on it, you mean,' teased Michael, running past them, followed by Tommy. Megan broke free and chased them inside the house, whooping as she went.

Rita watched her, thinking how she'd blossomed from the terrified, tongue-tied child she had been at Christmas when she and Jack had rescued them from Charlie and brought them to the farm. Now Megan seemed perfectly happy to imagine a creature in the shadows and yet not be worried about it. Rita reassured herself that all children dreamed up monsters and ghosts and all manner of things and were none the worse for it. She did her best to push to the back of her mind the incident in the shop yard when she could have sworn someone had been watching her. That had been the cat, nothing more. It was her intense concern for her children, combined with the never-ending way she missed them so much, that made her fear the same person, thing, whatever it was, was also targeting Megan. Stop it; you're making something out of nothing, she told herself.

Gratefully she stepped inside the kitchen and gasped in delight at the spread Joan had laid on: pies, tarts, sandwiches and, in pride of place, a beautiful fruit cake, topped with carefully arranged, very slightly askew, nuts in a circle.

'Do you like it?' Megan asked, suddenly shy.

Rita hugged her daughter tightly. 'I can't imagine anything better.' And it was true, she thought, gazing around. Here she was with her beloved children, where they were safe, and here was Jack with them. Michael was pointing out to him which sandwiches he'd helped to cut, and Jack was solemnly inspecting them. If only he was able to admit he was the boy's real father – what a wonderful role model he would be. Michael obviously thought he was the bee's knees. Charlie would never have bothered with such a small domestic detail, but she could see how Michael swelled with pride under Jack's approval. This was how it should be. She would hold on to these moments, and that would help her to face whatever the future might bring.

'It's frightfully good of you to ask us along,' Laura said, touching Elliott's arm briefly as they pushed their way out of the busy Tube station. Crowds were milling about, around the entrance, along the street, and in Leicester Square in the distance. 'I thought you two lovebirds might want some time alone.' She turned her full-beam smile on him and shook her lustrous blonde hair.

Kitty silently reflected that her friend might well be right – it was a kind offer of Elliott's to all go out together, but he was going back to Liverpool tomorrow and every moment was precious. She told herself not to be mean. It wasn't often that Laura and Marjorie would have the chance to be escorted to the West End by a handsome young doctor – especially one who'd promised to take them to one of his favourite haunts. They all deserved a night out – for the three young women to have a weekend evening off together was rare, as they worked so hard, and even when they planned a trip to the cinema, the odds were that a raid would prevent them from going.

Laura gazed around. 'So where are we headed for? I can't believe you know of a club around here that I haven't been to.'

Elliott looked as if he was having the time of his life, surrounded by three young Wrens all done up to the nines. Kitty and Marjorie had ended up borrowing more of Laura's clothes, as there hadn't been time to go shopping or make anything new. Marjorie had a puff-sleeve dress in lemon yellow, while Kitty wore a more dramatic deep-blue frock

178

with a nipped-in waist. It was too hot for their coats, although Kitty had insisted they carried cardigans in case the temperature dropped later. She had slung her own cream knitted bolero around her shoulders. She clutched the sleeves as she asked, 'Yes, where are we going, Elliott? Do we need to make our way through these crowds?'

Marjorie looked around apprehensively. 'It's terribly busy. I do hope there isn't an air raid. We'd never all fit in the shelter if there was.'

Elliott turned to her. 'Don't worry, I'm going to take care of you all.' He indicated a narrow side road leading them away from the bustling main street. 'It's just down here.' He brought them to a corner of a small alley, deep in shade, and came to a halt in front of a dark-brown door.

'Is this it?' Laura looked at it askance. 'It's a good job we trust you, Elliott, or I'd be seriously wondering if this was another kind of club entirely.'

'It's one of those places you just have to know about; it doesn't advertise its presence. It'll be worth it, you mark my words.' He knocked sharply on the door and a dark-haired man stuck his head outside, breaking into a broad grin when he saw who it was.

'Fitzgerald! You old dog. Haven't seen you for months. Nobody told me you were coming. And with such gorgeous girls, too. Come on in, you'll love the band we have on tonight.'

He disappeared back inside and they all followed him, down a dimly lit staircase into a basement. Kitty began to have second thoughts. This was a whole new side of Elliott – he clearly had rakish friends who ran secret nightspots and who knew

what else? She was struck by a wave of apprehension. Laura was in her element and surely
Kitty wasn't imagining that her friend was being
flirtatious? She knew that was often Laura's way,
putting on a show of being outgoing and out-
rageous, but it still didn't take much for all her old
insecurities to re-emerge.

The stairs turned right at the bottom and Kitty
gave a gasp. They were in a vast basement room,
with a brightly lit stage at one end, a gleaming
dance floor in front of it and a long bar down one
side. The rest of the room was filled with elegant
small tables, each with its own lamp, and slender
chairs. People of all ages, some in uniform and
others not, gathered at the tables and along the
bar. Kitty had never seen anywhere quite like it.

'I say, I'm impressed,' Laura exclaimed. 'How
clever of you, Elliott, to discover a place like this.
Can't think how I missed it.'

'Oh, some of the chaps from Barts introduced
me to it,' he said. 'I like to come here whenever
I'm in town. What can I get you ladies? The band
will come on in a minute and then the place will
be packed. Here, you take this table.' He reached
across and took an extra chair so there would be
room for all of them.

'Cocktail please!' said Laura at once. 'I don't
mind which, surprise me.'

'Lemonade for me,' said Marjorie, but then
shook her head. 'Oh, what the heck. A martini.'

'A shandy,' said Kitty, sticking to what had
become her favourite. Elliott even talked differently when he was with Laura, she thought. It was
as if they shared a common language, that of the

180

wealthy, who were accustomed to nights out in the capital city. She felt left out. She didn't like it at all. It brought up all her anxieties about him – why had he chosen her, when he could have had anyone of his own class? Last night it hadn't seemed to matter and she had revelled in his company and fitting in with his circle. Now she felt all that shatter. Her fragile new-found confidence evaporated. Laura was his type and she wasn't, that was all there was to it.

'Penny for 'em,' Laura said to her now. 'I say, Elliott's a dark horse, isn't he? You never said he could get us into places like this.'

'I didn't know,' said Kitty, wondering if her doubts were evident in her voice. But Laura didn't seem to notice.

'I can't wait for the band to come on,' her friend continued. 'I bet the dancing here will be tremendous. Do you think he might give me a spin?'

'I'm sure he will,' said Kitty, certain that Elliott would like nothing better than to take to the dance floor with the glamorous Laura. They would look perfect together. Even her hair would make the ideal contrast with his, which Kitty's own didn't. She had been an idiot to imagine they'd come out and he'd want to stay at her side all evening. She would just have to steel herself against the inevitable disappointment. She wouldn't show how she felt; she wouldn't spoil everyone else's evening by making a scene.

'Kitty, are you all right?' Elliott had returned from the bar with the drinks and sat down beside her. He gazed at her with concern. 'You seem very quiet. Here, have some of this. Doctor's orders.'

181

He smiled warmly at her as he set the half of shandy on the little table with its spindly metal legs.

'Thank you,' said Kitty, obediently taking a sip. It didn't taste as good as it usually did. She realised he was waiting for an answer. 'Oh, it's nothing, I'm just a bit hot, that's all.'

She was saved from saying more by the arrival of the band on the stage, smart in sharply pressed suits, their instruments gleaming. A cheer went up around the room and several couples rushed to take their places on the dance floor.

'Well, if you're hot, maybe Elliott wouldn't mind if I borrowed him?' Laura asked, clearly desperate to be one of the first to dance. 'Sorry, Elliott, you'll think me dreadfully forward.'

Yes, exactly, said Kitty sadly to herself, keeping her thoughts from her face with some difficulty.

'Not at all,' said Elliott gallantly, rising to his feet. 'If you're sure you don't mind, Kitty?'

'Of course not,' said Kitty. She looked down at her drink so they wouldn't see her expression.

The music began and the dancers started to move, some ineptly but most with assured rhythm, making it all seem effortless. The musicians were top class, filling the room with an infectious tune, and everyone began to tap their feet. Elliott was in his element, spinning Laura around at exactly the right moment, and Kitty remembered the wonderful sensation of being in his arms, seeming to float as he skilfully led her through the moves. He had made her feel as if she too was a dance champion – that was the skill of the true expert. With a sinking heart she acknowledged that Laura was a wonderful dancer and the combination of the two of them was well nigh flawless.

'They're awfully good, aren't they,' breathed Marjorie. 'I knew Laura was, of course, but when she's got a proper partner, she's like something out of a film.'

'You're right,' said Kitty, struggling to get the words out.

'You never said Elliott was such a good dancer,' Marjorie went on, oblivious to her friend's distress.

'He was a champion when he was a medical student,' Kitty told her. 'Him and his fiancée.'

'Oh, was he engaged?' Marjorie asked, curious. 'What happened? Was it the war?'

'No, she died before it began,' said Kitty, twisting the sleeve of her bolero on her lap. 'She was his professor's daughter.' The sort of girl he should be with, she thought despondently. One who could keep up with him on the dance floor and in any conceivable social situation. Not like her. She gulped down the rest of her drink, suddenly wishing she were anywhere but here.

Marjorie finally took the hint and didn't press her with any more questions. After what seemed like an eternity, the tune ended and some of the couples broke away and returned to their seats. Laura led Elliott back to the table, but was claimed by a tall man in a naval uniform before she could sit down.

'Would you care for a dance? I noticed you were rather good on your feet...'

Laura looked at him briefly, making one of her instant assessments, and accepted. She raised her eyebrows at Kitty and Marjorie over her shoulder as she returned to the fray.

'How are you now, Kitty?' Elliott glanced at her glass. 'Gosh, you really must have been hot. Shall I get you another?'

'No, don't bother,' Kitty said hurriedly. She made a fuss of refolding her bolero as a man in army uniform came shyly across and spoke to Marjorie. Marjorie exchanged a few words with him and then rose to take his hand and head for the dance floor too.

Elliott turned to face Kitty and rested his arm along the back of her chair. 'Kitty, what is it? You aren't yourself this evening. We had a lovely walk this afternoon and you were all right then, but now you've gone terribly quiet. Are you ill? You should have said, we didn't have to come out.'

Kitty wouldn't meet his gaze. 'It's nothing, honestly.' She would rather have died than admit how she felt. What sort of person resented their friends having a good time? She must face up to the fact that Laura was so much more suitable for Elliott in every way and get used to the idea.

'Kitty, look at me.' Elliott was insistent. 'Listen, we can go home if you'd rather. I don't want you to put up with a stuffy club just for me. I don't want you to be unhappy.'

Suddenly it was all too much and Kitty gave a stifled sob.

'My darling girl, whatever is it?' Elliott's arms were round her in a second. 'Has something happened? Was it when I went home to my parents to change – did you get a letter or something?'

All at once his warm reassurance worked its

184

magic and Kitty felt her fears fade away. She hastened to set him right. 'No, no, nothing like that.' She sighed and rested her head on his broad shoulder. 'It was something really silly. I saw the way you and Laura were dancing and I thought ... well, I thought ... just how good you looked together. Better than I look with you. I'm sorry, I don't want to make a fuss.'

Elliott rocked her gently. 'My darling girl, don't be worried. Yes, your friend Laura is a marvellous dancer, but she's not a patch on you. She's fast and she's funny and you're lucky to have a good friend like that – I feel safer for knowing you have such lively and interesting companions when we're so many miles apart. But you dance with your heart, Kitty. Just because you aren't as polished as she is doesn't mean you're any worse. I love dancing with you – it's another excuse to hold you close. Don't worry about Laura, you silly sausage. She can't hold a candle to you.' He pulled back and gazed at her face. 'My beautiful Kitty.'

Kitty gave a final sniff and shook her head. 'Don't listen to me, I'm being ridiculous. I know that now. It's because ... well, I love dancing with you too. We've had such a lovely time this weekend, please do forget me spoiling it like this. I don't want to ruin your leave, it's too precious.'

Elliott brushed her cheek with one gentle finger. 'You could never spoil anything for me, Kitty. I'm privileged to have spent my weekend with you, I mean it. I can't remember being so happy.'

'Really?' Her eyes shone with delight and just a little relief.

'Really. I wouldn't lie to you – I'm a doctor, remember?' She laughed at the familiar joke as one tune ended and another began. 'And now, Miss Callaghan, may I have the honour of the next dance?'

Kitty rose to her feet, her anxieties thrust aside like the foolish notions they were. 'You may, Dr Fitzgerald, I would be honoured.'

Together they made their way on to the crowded dance floor and began to move, holding one another tight, in perfect rhythm, oblivious to the many envious glances all around them.

CHAPTER EIGHTEEN

'I can't bear to think you have to go back tomorrow, Jack.' Rita found it hard to believe that the all-too-brief hours of his leave were almost over. They had had such a wonderful day on the farm and the children had been all over him, begging him not to go when they'd finally set off in the cart to return home to Empire Street. Rita had kept smiling, even though she felt exactly the same way. Michael had clearly thought that if he hugged Jack hard enough he wouldn't need to leave. Rita only wished that were true. Now they were standing in the little back yard of the shop. Jack had managed to do the much-needed repairs to the damaged wall in the last of the fading daylight.

'You know I'd rather be here, even if I can't be with you,' he said, laying down his trowel and wiping his hands on the old rag she'd found for him. 'But those ships won't defend themselves without the Fleet Air Arm, you know that. We've all got to do our duty.'

'I'm proud of you, Jack.' Rita looked at him longingly. 'There won't be a day I won't think about you.'

'It's knowing that that keeps me going,' he said, staring at her intently. 'And you know it.'

Rita looked away reluctantly, not wanting to break eye contact, but unable to bear the longing she saw there, which so mirrored her own. 'I do know, Jack. Stay safe for me, won't you? That's all I ask.'

He reached out a warm hand and tenderly caressed her arm. 'Hadn't I better go now? Or your lovely mother-in-law will be on the warpath.'

Rita shook her head. 'No, for once she's got Mrs Delaney round and they're sitting in a room which faces the other way. As long as you leave via the back alley, nobody will be any the wiser. You'd better not go out of the shop door or everyone will know about it – it's just the time that people head for the Sailor's Rest.'

'How's the shop doing, Reet?' he asked suddenly. 'Only I couldn't help noticing when I was there that the shelves aren't as full as they used to be. Is that because folk can't afford to buy as much these days – or are you in trouble?'

'Oh, Jack.' Rita had wanted to forget about her money problems for an evening. Now even Jack seemed to have cottoned on to the parlous state of the business. 'Don't let that worry you. I'll deal with it. Yes, things are going through a rough

187

patch, but I'll think of something.'

He gave her a straight look. 'Reet, you can't go on carrying this place all on your own. I'm not daft, I can see what's going on. You'll wear yourself out, I know what you're like.'

'Really, it's all right,' Rita insisted. She had her pride. She wouldn't beg for help, not from this wonderful man who'd already made it clear he wanted to give her so much.

'Reet, come on.' He shook his head in mock exasperation. 'Look, if you're short of money I can lend you a bit. There aren't that many places to spend my earnings out on the ocean wave. They pay me all right too. I might even get a promotion soon.'

'Jack, that would be wonderful and you deserve it.' Her hand flew to her mouth. 'But you can't give me your money. I won't take it. It's not right. I know you mean well but I couldn't do it. Don't ask me again, it'll only cause hurt between us, and I can't bear that on top of seeing you go.' Her eyes were bright with tears. He stepped towards her and enveloped her in an embrace.

'Well, don't be afraid to ask me if you need to – that or anything else,' he said softly into her wonderful thick hair. 'There's not much I wouldn't do for you, Reet. Anything you want, you only have to ask.'

'I know.' She looked up at him, his dear, familiar face, now leaner than before, and showing signs of the difficulties she knew he must be facing day in, day out. 'It means a lot to me to hear you say it. Even though I can't accept.' A sudden noise from the direction of the back alley made her start.

'What was that?'

Jack shrugged. 'Probably nothing, a stone or something blowing in the wind.'

Rita frowned. It wasn't even breezy, so that couldn't be it. Then she remembered again the cat from the Sailor's Rest, and told Jack about that incident. 'Silly creature's probably looking for somewhere more peaceful than the pub on a Saturday night,' she said. 'I'm just glad it was nobody looking at us. I'm not ashamed to be with you, but it wouldn't do any good if people round here started talking. You know what it can be like.'

'I do, Reet. I wouldn't do anything to tarnish your good name,' he assured her. 'And nobody can see over that wall now I've mended it good and proper, so don't you worry yourself about that. It'll withstand anything that Jerry throws at it from now on.'

'I hope it doesn't get put to the test,' breathed Rita, meaning it with all her heart. 'I've had enough of those damn raids to last a lifetime. And my name is mud already, thanks to Charlie taking off like that, and now everyone knows he's done a runner and is a coward on top of that. So I don't need anything else to set off even more gossip. I'm sorry we have to be so cloak and dagger.'

'I understand,' said Jack. 'It won't always be like this, Reet. We'll find a way. I respect you for not wanting to divorce him, even though it means we'll have to wait longer to be together. But that's all it is. We'll manage it, one day. I promise you.'

'Will we, Jack?' Her face was full of longing. 'That day can't come fast enough. Sometimes I can hardly get up in the morning, wondering what dreadful things are about to happen, here or at the hospital. But it's defeatist to talk like that, isn't it? If I've got a lifetime with you to look forward to, I'll get through all this somehow. No matter what they say about me, as long as I know you love me, I'll be all right.'

'And I do love you, Reet, more than I can say.' Jack gazed at her and pulled her close to him once more in a heartfelt embrace.

Rita couldn't resist. It was what she wanted more than anything and she melted into his arms, marvelling at the way he was so gentle and yet so strong. At last, someone to take care of her – even if he would be gone tomorrow. Tomorrow would just have to take care of itself.

Later, as she slowly undressed in her bedroom, she went over and over the events of the day, particularly those final moments. Jack was the man for her and always had been – what a pity she hadn't realised it sooner or been in a position to do something about it. How different sharing a bed with him would be. She hardly dared let herself imagine. He'd care for her, treating her well, loving her properly, nothing like the harsh brutality of Charlie. She shuddered involuntarily at the memory. Her husband had taken no notice of what she wanted or when, satisfying his own urges no matter what, and sometimes worse than that too. Then of course he'd taken himself off elsewhere, and at first she hadn't known whether to be disappointed and humiliated or relieved. It was a dire state of affairs whichever way you looked at it. But with Jack ... she sighed. That would be another thing entirely. Dare she dream that it would happen, one day? She slid beneath the cool sheets and wished with all her heart that somehow, one day, they would be together.

Over the back wall, in the alley just beginning to be lit by moonlight, a quiet figure slunk away from where it had been standing, listening to the whole conversation and then watching the silhouette of Rita through the thin fabric of the bedroom curtains. How he hated her. How he'd make her pay for chatting up her fancy man. He could show her a few things she wouldn't forget in a hurry. She might think her war hero was going to rescue her, but he'd remind her of what a real man could do first. Then she'd be very, very sorry.

PART TWO

CHAPTER NINETEEN

Late summer 1941

'Blast, I've broken another nail.' Gloomily Laura examined her hand. She'd managed to acquire a light tan and it suited her, making her still more glamorous, if that were possible. 'Can't think how I've done it as the wretched captain makes me wear white gloves every time I drive him anywhere. White gloves! In this heat! I notice that whenever he's not in the public eye, he takes off as many layers as possible. I've even seen him in shirtsleeves in the back seat, when there's absolutely no chance of anyone noticing he's not in full regalia. But when I asked him if I could take off my gloves and my hat, which, as you can see, flattens my poor hair in a most unattractive way, he practically bit my head off. He's really got it in for me, and I can't think why. I wish I was back driving the lorries.'

The three Wrens were sitting in their canteen by an open window to try to catch the slightest breeze. North London was shimmering in a heat haze – it was even baking hot in their billet up on the hill – and they were all suffering as a result. What had once been the school gardens, or what was left of them under the numerous vehicles parked along the front and sides of the building, were parched and looking sorry for themselves.

195

But it was better than the dormitory, which, being on a higher floor, caught the full force of the sun and was stifling as a consequence.

'At least you manage to get out and about,' Marjorie said. 'I'm sick of being stuck in one room. As soon as I think I'm getting the hang of signals in one language, they switch to something more difficult. Now they're talking about springing another language on those of us daft enough to show we were good at French and German. My money's on Dutch. I can't begin to think how I'll get my teeth around those sounds.'

'Dutch? Like those dishy men we met in Soho that time?' Laura brightened up. 'You could always practise on them. I could go along and show how useless I am at languages and make you look good in comparison. What do you say?'

'Laura, you are impossible,' groaned Marjorie.

'Anyway, they're probably back fighting by now,' Kitty pointed out. 'They were only in London for a long weekend. It was so brave of them to join up with foreign forces. I'm not sure about going to that club without Elliott though.'

Laura grinned mischievously. 'And how is the lovely Elliott, the dashing doctor? Is he coming to see you again soon?'

Kitty sighed and pushed a curl back behind her ear. 'I don't know. I hope so. It was lucky he made it down a few times over the summer as the raids haven't been anything like as bad back home as in May. But if it all starts up again, he can't leave the hospital – you know that, he told us.' Elliott had visited as often as he could and had willingly taken on the job of squiring Laura

196

and Marjorie around town to all the places he knew of that were still open for business. They'd all enjoyed themselves enormously, and Kitty had finally got over her fear that someone like Laura would be far better suited to him. In a way she understood that Laura regarded him as a surrogate brother – someone to tease and have adventures with – but nothing more. They could all see that Elliott only had eyes for Kitty.

At one point over the summer he'd floated the idea of her coming back to visit her family and friends. Kitty had had to explain that she didn't think she'd get enough leave to make the long journey, although she missed everyone badly. She was still grappling with the finer points of working the complex system of telephones, but Tommy was never far from her thoughts, even though they wrote to each other as often as they could. She guiltily wondered how Rita was managing; Elliott had reported the nurse was increasingly tired when they were on the same ward, and often short-tempered, which wasn't in her character at all, although living with Winnie would try the patience of a saint.

'That's a shame,' said Laura, digging around in her bag until she found a nail file. 'He's a proper tonic. Well, we shall have to find something else to do the next time we all have the same day off. That's if I don't get called back on duty like last Friday. Honestly, when I found out I was going to be a driver, this wasn't what I thought I'd be doing.' She pulled a face at the memory. They'd been getting ready for a visit to Lyons Corner House in the West End when the summons had

197

come from Captain Cavendish for Laura to chauffeur him to a meeting near Whitehall. Laura had been obliged to go, but she did so with very bad grace.

'That was an exception,' Marjorie pointed out.

'Was it?' Laura filed the corner of her broken nail with furious energy. 'I'm not so sure. He could have got anyone on duty to do it; it didn't need special skill or detailed knowledge of that part of town. But no, he had to insist on it being me. I swear he knows when I've got a treat planned and goes all out to ruin it.'

'Why on earth would he do that?' Kitty couldn't see the logic.

'Who knows?' Laura regarded her handiwork with vexation. 'I've made the damn thing worse, it'll have to be trimmed off, it's too bad. No, I think he might well be one of those officers who can't accept women drivers. There's a lot, you know. You'd have thought they would have got used to it by now, but some take extra delight in giving you impossible routes or claiming you've made a mistake when you haven't. You should have seen the space Cavendish wanted me to park in! I could tell he thought I'd mess it up.'

'But you didn't,' guessed Marjorie.

'Of course I didn't. I angled it in perfectly, not a scratch on it, all in reverse, and there wasn't a thing he could say. Bet that ruined his meeting,' Laura replied forcefully. 'Oh God, it's too hot to be cross. We're going to expire from heat on this very spot if we aren't careful.'

Kitty shook her head. 'He sometimes comes into our sessions to speak to our officers and he seems all right to me. Very smart, and you can tell he's clever. Quite good looking in fact,' she joked, raising her eyebrows at her friend.

'Oh honestly, Kitty Callaghan, you've no idea what you're talking about,' Laura exclaimed. 'I'm sure on first appearances he is perfectly civilised. It's just when you can see his eyes in the rear-view mirror all day, calculating how else to make your journey hell, and knowing that he's staring at the back of your head, it puts one right off.'

'Keep your hair on,' said Marjorie lightly. 'I've seen him around, I don't think he's bad looking at all. It's all right for Kitty, she's got Elliott. But you can't blame a girl for wondering.'

Kitty reflected that Marjorie had completely come out of her shell. She would never have made a comment like that when they'd first arrived. 'So what are we going to do this evening?' she said, trying to focus her friends on the task in hand. 'We could go to the cinema. Let's just try the local one, then we won't have to worry about transport being disrupted again. I read in the paper that *Major Barbara* is on, and I'd love to see that. It's got that Rex Harrison in it.'

Marjorie nodded. 'His hair's a little like Elliott's, isn't it? Bit on the dark side for me. I've decided I prefer fair-haired men. But he's a super actor.'

Laura looked up, animated at the prospect. 'He is, and I've already seen the play it's based on, and that's jolly good.' But before she could say more, the canteen door opened and a petty officer stood there, ramrod straight and no trace of humour on her face. She briskly strode across to their table.

'Which of you is Fawcett?'

Kitty and Marjorie looked at Laura, whose face had fallen. She stood wearily.

'You're wanted urgently. Kindly see to it that you pick up Captain Cavendish outside the officers' mess in fifteen minutes. Look sharp.' And she turned on her regulation low heel and left again.

Kitty realised they'd all been holding their breath, waiting to see if Laura would explode in frustration. She managed to say nothing until the petty officer had shut the door behind her. Then she threw down her bag in annoyance.

'You see? This is typical. He probably knows I was going out this evening and he's done it deliberately to spoil my fun.'

'Laura, we'd only just decided to go to the pictures,' Kitty pointed out.

But Laura was having none of it. 'Well, obviously I shall have to go to see what he wants. But I'll get my own back on him, you see if I don't,' she said, picking up her bag and striding from the room.

Danny wasn't usually one to sit in a pub by himself, but tonight he reckoned he'd earned a drink. His head was spinning. He'd never worked so hard in his life, even though he knew his old mates down on the docks would have laughed at him for saying so. He'd barely moved from his desk, so it wasn't exactly tough physical graft. But the amount of information he was expected to take in was vast, and then he had to show he understood it and could do something with it. That was on top of the incessant puzzle solving. Even though he knew he was good at them, he had to get to grips with ever more fiendish versions, variations on sorts he knew along with completely new challenges. When he tried to sleep at night he saw numbers and letters revolving round in a wheel, threatening to drive him crazy. But it was all in aid of the war effort, to try to understand the enemy signals when they were intercepted. Eventually he'd be assigned to do it in reality, so that German planned attacks could be pre-empted.

Now he'd been told he'd passed the first part of the training and he was walking on air. Who'd have thought it, he asked himself, shutting his front door. He still lived at home, cycling to and from the centre of Liverpool. No point in having digs when there was a perfectly good house not that far away, and he wanted to keep it for when Jack, Kitty or Tommy returned. So he'd decided to pop down to the Sailor's Rest.

'Danny! Haven't seen you for ages! And look at you, in uniform now.' Sarah Feeny was coming out of her own front door, not in her own uniform for once, but wearing a bright print summer's dress. Danny always had to pinch himself when he saw her these days – the girl he'd spent his boyhood thinking of as a kid sister had long gone. She was a young woman now, and, he realised not for the first time, an increasingly good-looking one. But she was still almost family, he told himself.

Yet something made him say, 'What are you up to this evening then, Sarah?' He thought she was looking at him a little differently, as plenty of people were starting to do now he was recognisably part of the navy.

She shrugged her shoulders, nonchalantly. 'I
201

fancied a bit of fresh air. Who knows how long this weather'll last?'

'You probably deserve it,' he said warmly. 'Word is you've been the backbone of the nurses' station.'

'Nonsense.' But she looked pleased, he thought.

'Don't suppose you fancy joining me for a quick drink, Sar?' he asked impetuously.

'Oh, I don't know.' Sarah wasn't used to going into pubs. She wasn't quite eighteen and had no interest in mixing with the men who were seen walking in and staggering out of the Sailor's Rest or Bent Nose Jake's down at Canada Dock. But she didn't see much of Danny any more as he was so busy with his new job. She liked his company and still felt rather protective of him, knowing more about his health than most. 'Don't tell Mam, will you? She'll only worry,' she said, her unease mixing with her pleasure at the thought of spending time with Danny.

'I don't want to worry your mam,' Danny assured her. 'We'll see if the bench out in their back yard is free; we can sit out there, catch the sun's rays and cool down over a beer – or a lemonade if you'd prefer,' he added, catching sight of her expression. 'If there's no room out there, then we'll just go for a wander.'

'Then that would be lovely. Danny Callaghan, I accept.' Sarah fell into step beside him and they made their way down the street, which bore signs of the Luftwaffe's visits: boarded-up windows, sandbags around front doors, and old Mrs Ashby's house standing forlorn and empty, still marked by the damage from the smoke that had killed her. There was dust everywhere, baked dry

202

by the heat of the day. Remnants of the damaged houses were still blocking up the gutters.

They were in luck. The Sailor's Rest was yet to fill up at the end of the week with the dock workers who hadn't joined up, and the crooked wooden bench propped up in the back yard was free. Cyril Arden, Gloria's father, was polishing the pumps, his sleeves rolled up to his elbows. Nobody was playing the piano in the corner, and the few early drinkers were chatting peaceably over their pints. No one paid any attention to them as they entered via the sturdy porch and Danny made sure Sarah was settled before buying the drinks. He had just elbowed the back door open and was halfway through when he heard a voice. He almost dropped the glasses.

'Evening, Cyril,' came the brash tones of Alfie Delaney.

Danny cursed under his breath. He hadn't seen the man since the day down at the warehouses when he'd thought Alfie had set him up. Now Danny no longer worked on the docks their paths hadn't crossed, which was yet another reason he was pleased with his new position. He would be happy if he never saw the bumptious, malicious coward ever again. Now it seemed his luck had turned. He placed himself so that he could hear the goings-on and see some of the bar, but Delaney couldn't see him.

Sarah looked up and mouthed 'what?' Danny carefully set down the drinks and put his finger to his lips.

They could hear the background low-level noise in the half-empty bar die down as Alfie went on to order a pint.

Danny squinted for a view between the edge of the door and its frame. He could just make out the figures through the narrow gap.

Cyril laid down his polishing cloth and turned to his latest customer. Although far from in the prime of his youth, he wasn't a man to be messed with. He'd run this pub for over twenty years and prided himself on needing no outside protection to keep troublemakers from his door. Now his brow creased. 'I don't think so,' he said firmly.

'What d'you mean, Cyril?' Alfie was taken aback.

'I mean what I say,' said Cyril. 'You'll get no more pints from here, Delaney. Now sling your hook. I don't want to see you on my premises again. If you've got any sense, you'll stay away from the whole area. That would be best for you and best for me.' He glared hard at the young man.

Alfie's expression turned sour and he ran his finger around the inside of his collar. He was still in his dock worker's clothes although, as Danny knew all too well, he never did much work unless he was forced to. 'You threatening me, Cyril?' he said, and laughed mirthlessly. 'You think you can tell me to keep away, when my own mother lives round the corner? Pull the other one. Remember who I know, and count your lucky stars I haven't clocked you one yet.'

Cyril shook his head but didn't back down. 'It's no good, Alfie. We know what was in that last batch of goods you touted round here. It's bad enough when you said you had chocolate for the kiddies and it turned out to be laxatives. Now we

204

find that you've been selling poisoned food. Several people round here have been took bad. That was after you came in here last week with what you said was fresh pork. Weren't no such thing. We reckon it had been condemned. Good job nobody died of it – you'd have been wanted by the coppers then.'

'You're lying,' said Alfie, his eyes cold. 'Don't you go spreading tales about me. I could get your pub done over just by clicking my fingers.' He moved closer to the bar.

Danny stiffened. If this was going to get nasty, he wouldn't let Cyril face Alfie alone. Sarah crept forward, having heard it all and knowing what he was like. 'Stay back, Danny. You can't get involved. You can't exert yourself if it comes to a fight,' she whispered.

Danny bridled, knowing she was right but furious that his heart condition meant he couldn't even defend his local publican. What Alfie had done was despicable. Sure, he himself had benefited from the occasional slightly dodgy deal down at the warehouses, but to take condemned pork and sell it as fresh was something only the lowest of the low would do. Everyone knew good meat was hard to come by round here nowadays, and he wouldn't blame anyone for jumping at the chance to feed their families with it. It sounded as if they'd all paid the price. Then, someone else spoke.

It was one of the older men, husband to one of Dolly's friends, still in his overalls. 'He's right,' the man said, 'you told us it was ideal for the Sunday roast and my missus was sick for days. I thought it was going to be the end of her. We don't want your sort round here.'

Alfie laughed again, amazed that two middle-aged men would dare to stand up to him. 'She probably got the flu or something. There's all sorts going round.'

A figure from the other side of the bar stood and came over: Mr Mawdsley, in his clerk's clothing. He allowed himself one half of stout every Friday, and no more. He was a mild-mannered man, usually happy to let his extrovert wife do the talking. Now he was precise and calm.

'I'm afraid that's not true, Mr Delaney. Some of my wife's friends were in the same position and they'd all eaten your contaminated meat.' He regarded the young man steadily. 'Of course I can always report this to the authorities if you'd prefer. It's up to you. But my word carries some weight in those circles. I doubt you'd be willing to take the risk.'

Alfie was at heart a coward, and he began to falter. Despite the fact that each of the men before him was over twice his age, he didn't fancy taking the three of them on – and now the rest of the customers were watching him carefully, too. None was under forty, but they were for the most part dock workers – still fit and strong, able to handle themselves. Cyril was making as if to come out from behind the bar. Alfie glanced behind him and made his decision.

'This isn't the last you'll hear of this,' he growled as he backed away towards the leaded glass door. 'You know who I'm going to tell. He won't be frightened off by a load of old men.'

Yes, but you are, Danny thought, holding his

breath and standing still.

'Tell who you like, son,' Cyril said confidently. He had known Alfie Delaney since he was a boy and was certain he'd be too embarrassed to tell Harry Calendar, his gangland boss, what had happened. 'Just get out and keep it that way, then we can all be happy. The door's right there behind you.'

With a final sneer, Alfie was gone. Cyril went back to polishing the pumps as if nothing had happened.

'Blimey,' Danny said, turning to face Sarah in the sunny back yard. 'Never thought I'd see the day. Well, I can't say I'm sorry. He won't be able to bother me now.'

Sarah looked at him over the rim of her lemonade, her face concerned. 'Bother you, Danny? What's he been doing?'

Danny could have slapped himself. He'd never breathed a word of Alfie's threats, and here was the last person he wanted to burden with the knowledge.

'Oh, just his daft schemes down the warehouse,' he said vaguely, hoping she wouldn't press him.

Sarah looked at him keenly. She was getting used to telling when he was holding something back. But it was Friday evening, the sun was out, and they both deserved a quiet drink in peace. So she would say nothing more about it unless she had to. But it was one more reason that she resolved to keep an eye on Danny; after all, there was no one left nearby from his own family to do so. She wouldn't mind doing that at all.

CHAPTER TWENTY

Violet put down the trug of tomatoes on the kitchen table. 'There you are! Aren't they beauties?'

Dolly beamed. She'd been impressed with her daughter-in-law's skill at gardening and this was the best crop yet. 'What a lovely smell they have as well. We'll have to bottle some of them to make them last through the winter. Make sure we have our vitamins, like the government says.' She picked one up to admire it. 'Is this the last of them? Surely they won't go on for much longer.'

Violet wiped her hands on her pinafore, which bore traces of the victory garden all over it. 'Well, we deliberately chose some late-cropping varieties. Old Mr James from the allotments told me how to do that. So they should keep going a bit longer yet, as long as we have enough sun to ripen them. I'll make sure Rita has some to sell in the shop.'

'What's that?' The door opened and Rita came in, catching her own name as she did so. 'What am I going to do?'

'Sell some of these,' Dolly said, automatically reaching for the kettle so that her hard-working eldest daughter could have a welcome cup of tea. 'You sit yourself down, love. Let me fetch you something to eat, you look as if you need feeding up.' She regarded Rita critically, aware of how much weight she'd lost over the past few months.

'You'll be wasting away to nothing and we can't have that.'

Wearily, Rita sank into a chair. She hadn't got the energy to argue. She'd been run off her feet at the hospital yet again, even though there had been no major bombing incidents for weeks. That meant more patients were being transferred to them to recuperate, at the same time as emergency nurses were being sent to areas where they were most needed, leaving her ward short of staff. She knew in many ways it was sensible, and yet for her it made a difficult task nearly impossible.

Georgie ran towards her. 'Reet!' he shouted joyfully, and Rita bent over to pick him up. She kept to herself how much she missed the only other person to call her by that name. He hadn't had any leave all summer, and from his letters she couldn't work out where he was – which was only right, but it meant she worried at any news of convoys being struck, fearing that Jack might be among the injured. She buried her face in her nephew's hair to hide her fears, and the action reminded her – as it always did – of how much she missed her own children.

'Look what Auntie Violet has brought us,' said Dolly, showing the little boy the tomato. 'Shall I make you a sandwich?' Georgie jumped off Rita's lap and held on to his grandmother's skirt, looking up at her with devotion. 'Mmmmmm,' he said.

Dolly turned to find the breadboard. 'We could do with more butter,' she said cheerfully. 'Don't suppose you've got any trips planned to the farm, Rita? Pop can take you next time if you like.'

Rita shrugged. 'I'm not sure when I can go

next. They'll welcome us at any time so that's not a problem, but we can't spare anyone from the ward at the moment. I'd love nothing more but I'll have to see.' She picked at the frayed edge of her cardigan. 'This is coming undone again. It seems like no time at all since I last sewed it up.'

Dolly considered the colour. 'I've probably got something like that in my make-do-and-mend basket. Let me finish doing this for Georgie and I'll fetch it.'

Rita sat back and for a moment closed her eyes, letting the comfort of being in her mother's kitchen wash over her. How tempting it was just to stay here. Then another voice shook her out of her reverie. Nancy swung into the room, calling out to Georgie. 'Oooh, what have you got there? Did Grannie make it for you? Why don't you let Mummy have a bite?'

Typical, thought Rita, without rancour. Taking food from her own child's mouth. That was enough to beat the band, but Nancy could get away with anything.

Dolly didn't rise to it. 'Sit down, Nancy, and leave the poor boy be. I'll make you one of your own. There's plenty of tomatoes to go round. Salt and pepper?'

Nancy nodded eagerly, her beautifully styled rolls of hair bobbing. 'I missed lunch, I'd love one. Here, Georgie, have it back and finish it up like a good boy.'

'Missed lunch?' asked Violet. 'Were you busy?'

'I was! You'll never guess,' said Nancy. 'I'm going to help with the WVS. They've got a canteen in the city centre doing refreshments for

210

visiting servicemen. They need all the help they can get, you know, posted in a strange town and sometimes in a strange country. I'm going to be really doing my bit from now on, so you can't tell me I'm not contributing any more.' She gave Rita a glare before taking a huge bite of her sandwich.

'Well, now, that is a surprise,' said Dolly, who'd spent the past two years or thereabouts trying to get Nancy to join the local branch of which she herself was such a mainstay. 'Are you sure you have to go all that way, pet? You could come along with me and then you wouldn't be away from Georgie so much.'

Nancy nodded vigorously. 'I appreciate your concern, Mam, but they said they were really short-handed and so I don't mind making the sacrifice, I really don't.'

Rita bit her lip. Trust Nancy to get the position where she'd be in the prime place to be chatted up by all the troops, and also right near the shops that remained open. She could spot her sister's ulterior motives a mile off, though her mother often seemed to have a blind spot where Nancy was concerned.

'That's very good of you, Nancy,' said Violet, knowing full well that it would be her and Dolly who'd be looking after Georgie in his mother's place. But she didn't mind in the slightest. It would be good practice for when she and Eddy had their own children – whenever that might be. He hadn't been home for months, and often she went without a letter for weeks at a time – and then several would arrive at once. She knew she mustn't grumble; there were so many worse off than herself.

Rita got to her feet, unable to put up with Nancy's brazen behaviour a moment longer. 'I'd better be off. Thanks for the tea, Mam.'

'You know you don't have to thank me,' said Dolly, giving her eldest girl a hug. 'You're all skin and bones, Rita, my goodness me, whatever are you eating? Not enough to feed a bird. You want to take care of yourself, we don't want Michael and Megan to have a skeleton for a mother.'

Rita tried to raise a smile. She was too tired to eat half of the time, even if she could grab a moment for a proper meal.

'Wait, let me give you those tomatoes,' said Violet, hurrying to separate some of them into a tin. 'You take these. Shall I bring some more over tomorrow when I come to work?'

'Only if you can spare them,' said Rita. 'I'd love to have them, they're very popular.' She took the tin and left, grimly thinking that there was less and less to sell in the shop, popular or not.

Ruby was waiting for her when she went through the door to the shop, which had been closed since teatime. This wasn't unusual these days, but Rita was brought up short by the sight of all the account books spread over the counter. She set down the tin and stared at them.

'What are you doing, Ruby?' She couldn't believe that the young woman would be able to make any sense of them. They were complicated, with figures all over the place; she'd struggled to understand the system herself when she'd first encountered it.

Ruby looked up, her expression solemn. 'There

212

you are, Rita.' She paused, as if summoning her nerve to continue. 'Rita – the shop isn't making enough money, is it?'

Rita gasped in surprise. 'Whatever makes you say that, Ruby? We're fine, we're absolutely fine,' she hurried to reassure her.

Ruby shook her head. 'We aren't, Rita. Look at these sums. We're losing money and it's all draining away. You should have said something before.'

Rita stared at her in amazement. 'But how can you tell, Ruby? Those sums are very difficult. I've been doing them for ages now and I still get confused. You shouldn't worry, you've probably not understood, but I can't say I blame you.' She couldn't bear to think that Ruby was worried. The young woman needed protecting from a world that had treated her cruelly and in which she struggled to cope – the last thing she needed was to face the reality of the business's finances.

Ruby stood her ground. 'You don't have to pretend to me, Rita. I don't want you to pretend any more. It's making you worried, isn't it? But I can help.'

'Ruby, Ruby.' Rita felt despair wash over her. It was so kind of the girl to offer, but she could have no idea of the complexities of running the place. It would be far, far beyond her limited understanding of how the world worked. 'You don't know what you're saying. It's generous of you to say it. But really, don't worry.'

Ruby came around the counter and put her hand on Rita's arm. Her large pale eyes were steady and determined. 'I told you ages ago, Rita. I can see patterns. It's not a lie.'

'No, no, I never thought you were a liar,' Rita said hastily. 'That's not what I meant. But this isn't like playing snap or something like that.'

'It's patterns in numbers,' Ruby insisted. 'I can see them, I don't know how. I can see them in these books. I can help. You must trust me, Rita. Don't you trust me?'

'Yes, but...'

'See here,' said Ruby. 'This is where you have paid extra all summer, isn't it? You pay a bit more money to this person, and they are meant to put it towards the big sum you owe.'

Rita stared in astonishment. It was the only way she'd been able to keep supplies coming in, even though it was chipping away at what slender reserves she had. She'd had to include those figures in the overall totals, but how anyone other than herself could have noticed it was beyond her. 'Well done,' she breathed. 'Yes, that is what those numbers mean.'

Ruby looked at her sadly. 'But here is what you still owe,' she said. 'It isn't changing like it should. If you meant to make the big sum smaller, it isn't working.'

Rita stared even harder. That was a fact she hadn't wanted to face. It had been eating away at her, but as she hadn't known what else to do, she was carrying on as if all was going to plan. How come Ruby had spotted it?

'What do you suggest, then?' she asked, scarcely able to believe she was saying this to Ruby of all people. Jack, yes – he was clever with numbers. Or Danny; everyone knew that he'd got his new job because he was smarter than anyone realised. But she had far too much pride to ask them, even if Jack were here or Danny had the time. She would be too ashamed to admit she had failed to keep the shop in profit.

'I think I should take these books and read them very carefully,' said Ruby slowly. 'I don't want to talk to the people you owe, I don't think that would do any good. But if I check all the sums, then I could tell you what you could manage to pay to make a proper difference. I could do that. That might help, mightn't it?'

Rita gazed at the young woman almost as if she were a stranger. This unexpected new turn of events was unlike anything she could have predicted. Ruby certainly didn't talk like an accountant, and her huge eyes made her look like a child as usual; but she might be on to something. Rita felt a little flutter of something she hadn't known for a long time: hope. Well, why not give Ruby a chance? It couldn't do any harm, and it might just help them all turn the corner.

'Ruby, thank you,' she said, giving the strange young woman a hug. 'Thank you. I would love it if you could help.'

CHAPTER TWENTY-ONE

Frank stood before his commanding officer, wondering what the problem was this time. It was what he loved about his job and what he dreaded – never knowing what was going to come next.

215

The pressures they were all under not to make a single mistake in their vital job of co-ordinating the defence of the Western Approaches were draining; it was their collective responsibility to ensure the supply routes from North America stayed open, and to outwit the many U-boats whose job it was to sink those all-important cargo ships. The strategic value of the North Atlantic could not be overestimated; Britain completely relied on it for important supplies. Although Frank did his utmost to maintain the necessary highest standards, he could never be completely sure that one tiny error hadn't crept through. Was this what the summons was about?

He gazed steadily straight ahead, noticing the rudimentary comforts that Commander Stephens had introduced to the small underground office, where every inch of space was precious: a small tapestry cushion on the back of the desk chair, a slim photo frame on the desk – although he couldn't tell what was in it from where he stood. He liked his commanding officer – he was a fair man, even when demanding the seemingly impossible. These little human touches reminded Frank that Commander Stephens had a home life too; something he was fighting for, something that kept him going as well as his patriotic duty. He forced his own thoughts not to go down that path.

'Well, Warrant Officer Feeny, I dare say you are wondering why I've called you in here.' The commander looked at him with interest but gave nothing away.

'Yes, sir.' Frank thought there was no point in saying anything more. If he was in for a dressing down, he wasn't going to give away any ammunition.

'Let me reassure you, it is nothing to worry about. You may stand at ease,' the commander went on. 'It has come to the notice of the higher authorities that you have been performing above and beyond your current remit, Feeny. Your work leading to the detection of the location of the *Bismarck* back in May was exceptional, and I don't have to tell you how vital that was to the overall war effort, or what effect its sinking had on morale. Well done, Feeny.'

'Thank you, sir.' Frank struggled not to breathe out heavily in relief. He'd only done what he was asked to do, and many personnel had been involved in the sinking of the vast German battleship, pride of the fleet, which had been deployed to disrupt the Atlantic shipping routes so important to Britain's survival. But it was satisfying to hear that his careful plotting and detailed documentation of the results had been recognised. He'd stayed up through the night on more than one occasion, even when on day shift, his eyes itching and his temples throbbing as he'd pored over the reams of information to spot the relevant figures. On a few occasions he'd even been known to loosen his false leg, as it wasn't designed to be used for twenty-four hours at a stretch. He'd been prepared for sharp glances or offended looks but none had come. People simply accepted it as part and parcel of a dedicated serviceman who would go the extra mile to perform his duty. Yet anyone else in his position would have done the same – and plenty had.

'You've also helped us to recruit one of our most successful new members of staff,' the commander continued. 'As you are probably aware, opinion was divided as to whether we should take on personnel from outside the service and bring them into such a sensitive operation. It is fair to say that opinion was even further divided when it came to your suggestion of Mr Daniel Callaghan. But he has surpassed all our hopes, and his being here is entirely down to you, Feeny.'

'He's a good man, sir.' What else could he say? If Frank thought about it, it was very strange to be talking about his childhood friend in this way. But Danny had proved himself, against a fair weight of opposition from above. That was typical Danny – when it came down to it, he didn't really care what other people thought of him. If he was interested in something, he would throw himself into it. Now all his deep frustration at being unable to fight for his country was being channelled into puzzle solving and pattern detecting for the unit, and everyone was astonished at the results. He was a natural. It was a long way from being a wide boy down at the docks.

'He is indeed, Feeny. You have demonstrated that you have an eye for spotting particular talent even in unconventional circumstances.' The man nodded sagely. 'Which is why I have called you here today. We feel that in addition to your current role, you should take on more training of new recruits. Your manner towards your juniors is calm and encouraging and I have seen the effect for myself. I am convinced you would be an asset in this area. You will therefore be promoted to acting sublieutenant for the time being, and then we shall see how far you can progress beyond that.'

Frank almost gasped aloud. It was less than a year since he'd been made a warrant officer. Now he was being offered the chance to rise further in the ranks, and it was down to his own hard work. He had thought at first when his leg was amputated that his career would be over, that he'd be thrown on the scrapheap and his participation in the war would be finished. He'd loved his life in active service and fighting in the boxing ring, and hadn't been able to imagine being of any use once all that was closed to him. His heart swelled in pride.

'Thank you, sir. I would love to train more new recruits. It's one of the aspects of this post that I enjoy the most,' he managed to say, when he wanted to dance with joy on the spot.

'I'm glad to hear it, Feeny,' said the commander, although they both knew that the decision had been made and – like it or not – that was what Frank would be doing from now on. He had no doubt that this young man would be a credit to him and flourish in the new position. What had happened to him would have broken a lesser man, but Feeny had overcome his physical limitations and never let his disability affect his work. He was just the sort of young officer who needed to be entrusted with such a task. 'I shall inform my superiors and the process will commence as of tomorrow. Well done. You are dismissed.'

'Sir.'

Frank saluted sharply and turned to leave. His thoughts were whirring as he made his way down

219

the dim corridor. What would this new position bring? Would he be up to the job? No point in wondering, he told himself firmly; if they didn't think he could do it, then they wouldn't have asked. There were many others who would have given their eyeteeth for such a chance. All right, it was still a desk job, and some would say it was a soft option, but it was as good as he was going to get. He'd be a sublieutenant, and that would mean extra money coming in too. He was so lost in his reverie that he almost crashed into a figure emerging from a side door – and saw it was Danny Callaghan.

'Frank!' Danny grinned and then forced his face to be more solemn. 'Sir!' He saluted his old mate with a cheeky smile. 'Haven't seen you for ages. Do you have a minute, or are you on your way somewhere important?'

'Midshipman Callaghan.' Frank attempted to be formal, and knew he should go straight back to his desk, but couldn't resist sharing his news. After all, if he couldn't tell Danny, then who could he tell? And who else would be in a better position to appreciate it? He hurried to describe what had just happened.

'Blimey! Sublieutenant Feeny!' Danny teased. 'Seriously, mate, that is good news. An officer from Empire Street – that'll show 'em.' He shook his friend's hand. 'It's not a secret, is it? I can write and tell our Jack and our Kitty? They'll be made up.'

'No, it's not a secret. It'll be public any day now – certainly before any letters reach them.' Frank's heart beat painfully in his chest at the thought of

220

Kitty getting the news. In different circumstances he would have loved to have rushed to tell her himself, to share the joy of well-earned promotion with such a special girl. But that was not to be. 'How are they doing?' he forced himself to ask.

If Danny noticed any awkwardness in the question, he didn't acknowledge it. 'Jack was back earlier in the summer, of course, but we don't know where he is now, although from his last letter he seems to be fine. He's hoping for a spot more leave soon. Kitty's doing well, living it up in London.'

'Is she still friends with that doctor?' Frank asked, his cheeks flaming, certain that Danny would know he was forcing himself to sound casual.

Danny nodded. 'Yes, it's Elliott this and Elliott that these days. He goes down to see her whenever he can, apparently. She says she hopes to meet his parents soon, as they don't live that far away from her billet.'

'And she never comes home to visit?' Frank asked. 'Not even to see Dr Elliott?' He tried not to sound too obviously jealous.

Danny gave his friend a careful look but didn't ask any questions. It was none of his business. 'No, not since she left in March,' he said. 'She never gets much leave and I reckon they are working them hard down there. You know how it is, it's the same here, the women are doing men's jobs and have to make sure they are as good as or better than the men they are replacing. From her letters I don't think she has a lot of spare time, and I don't blame her for spending it getting to

221

know London. Good for her. Shall I say you were asking after her?'

Frank swallowed. 'Yes, do give her my best.' Inwardly he blanched. He knew that sounded stuffy and formal, but what could he say? Kitty was clearly getting on with her own life. 'Well, I must be going, Danny – or should I say Midshipman Callaghan? See you around.'

Danny saluted again with a broad grin. 'See you then, Sublieutenant Feeny-to-be.'

Frank grinned back, and then ploughed on down the corridor, as always making the extra effort not to limp. He couldn't bear anyone to glance at him with pity. Pulling back his shoulders, he told himself not to let the encounter ruin the enormity of what had happened in the commander's office. He was to be promoted; his efforts had been recognised – he should be on top of the world. And yet, it would have been so much sweeter if he had had someone special to share it with – and in his heart that someone special was always Kitty. He recalled the way her hair curled, the spark in her bright eyes, the way she had always teased him as they grew up together, and then how he had realised his feelings for her were changing, growing into something more profound, more tender. That was before he'd lost his leg. Now she could not be expected to be interested in him – or not in that way, not romantically, not physically. He simply was not the man he used to be. He should feel glad she had found happiness with this doctor fellow. He should be man enough to wish them good luck and all the best, for heaven only knew it was tough going to find time for love in the middle of a devastating war. Nonetheless, he had to acknowledge that what he actually felt towards Elliott was bitter jealousy, for winning the heart of the woman he ached to confess that he loved.

'So you see, Mrs Kerrigan, we always keep the urn topped up, and then you can fill the kettles from here.' Mrs Delia Moyes, veteran of the WVS, demonstrated how the system worked, eyeing her latest recruit with some apprehension. Young Mrs Kerrigan didn't somehow seem the type to be able to lift large amounts of boiling water around in a confined space. Still, she would be a tonic for the exhausted men in uniform, and that was a fact. Her hair was swept up in the latest style, she wore peep-toe sandals even though there was an autumnal chill in the air, and from her nipped-in waist it was scarcely believable that she was mother to a little boy. Her presence would brighten the utilitarian canteen, sandwiched as it was between bomb-damaged buildings right in the centre of Liverpool. Despite the salvage teams' best efforts, the place often filled with dust. Nancy Kerrigan would help to ensure the hard-working servicemen's rare moments of leisure were as pleasant as possible. What the equally exhausted servicewomen would make of her was another matter entirely, but Mrs Moyes reckoned you couldn't please everyone at once, and it was best to concentrate on one thing at a time. 'Do you think you have got the hang of it, Mrs Kerrigan?'
Nancy nodded vigorously, even though she was by no means sure. She hadn't joined the volunteer

staff here to heft around heavy equipment; she could have done that back in Bootle, but that would have meant working under the sharp eyes of her mother and sister-in-law. Pushing back a stray strand of her vivid Titian-red hair, she told herself that if she had dealt with tricky customers at George Henry Lee, the big department store where she'd worked before she'd had Georgie, then she could easily manage this.

Nancy had signed up to the WVS on a whim, partly to get out of her mother-in-law's gloomy house, where it got more depressing by the day. Sid's mother had never exactly been the life and soul of the party, but she'd taken to the role of suffering martyr with a vengeance. Never had sorrow been so loudly and consistently proclaimed. Nancy screwed up her eyes at the very thought of it. All right, so Sid had been a POW almost since the fighting had started, but he was still alive, he was receiving Red Cross parcels and was probably a damned sight safer than most of them were, she told herself crossly. He hadn't had to endure the Liverpool Blitz for a start and, even though the raids had almost stopped for the time being, who knew when they might begin again? Hitler hadn't managed to destroy the docks, though not for want of trying, and so they would still be a magnet for the Luftwaffe's attentions. Sid might be in a cell somewhere – truly Nancy had little idea where he was or what the living conditions might be like – but he wasn't forced to share a stinking, overcrowded cellar with a load of neighbours he couldn't stand.

Nancy had retreated into her shell immediately

after the hideous events in the Adelphi Hotel, when she'd ended up lying in a pool of blood on the elegant bathroom floor instead of living it up with Gloria. The shame and disappointment had been bad enough, but then she had been utterly drained after the miscarriage. She'd tried to tell herself it hadn't happened, but her body told her otherwise, and she'd been weak and shaky for longer than she wanted to admit.

She would rather have died than tell her mother-in-law what had happened, knowing the reaction she would have faced if Mrs Kerrigan had known that the young woman living under her roof had been having a sneaky affair. It would have been even worse to have confessed to her own mother what had been going on, as Dolly had very strict views on the sanctity of marriage, even if one half of that marriage wasn't around. Rita wouldn't have been much better. Reluctantly, Nancy had had to admit that the Adelphi had been the best place for it to have happened. There would have been no chance of her passing off the baby as legitimate, and she had to convince herself that everything had worked out all right in the end – even if in her quieter moments she wondered what the child would have been like. There was no point in thinking about that, though – what had happened had happened.

At least it was all but impossible to shock Gloria. How she missed her best friend and wished she were still around. But Gloria had gone back down south after the rest of her highly successful singing tour, and her latest letter had said she'd been approached by ENSA, the Entertainments National

Service Association, which had been set up to entertain the troops. Nancy sighed with envy. How she would have loved to see the world, doing nothing more than wearing beautiful dresses and singing every night, before being taken to dinner in the most glamorous hotels. She blithely ignored the less exciting parts of the job which Gloria had told her about: the weariness that came from living out of a suitcase, always having to smile and maintain the professional front, shaking hands with the most odious and pompous officials, living in fear of the voice giving out.

Now Nancy felt fully recovered and ready to try something new. She knew very well what her family thought of her choice and why they suspected she'd picked this particular canteen, but she didn't care. Of course it would be lovely to be back in the centre of the city, even if much of it had been blown to smithereens by Hitler's bombs. It was important to show that the people of Liverpool weren't afraid, for a start. She didn't intend to be cowed. It would take more than a few nights of utter destruction to stop her going shopping, searching out where was still open and what bargains were to be had. It wasn't impossible, just much more difficult than before, but that made the hunt all the more satisfying. Besides, she reasoned, none of her family would turn down the offer of a bolt of new fabric, even if it was a little fire-damaged. That was exactly the sort of thing she'd be best placed to find.

She also felt starved of male company. She was only twenty-one; she didn't want to be cooped up indoors, missing out on the best days of her life.

She liked dressing up and the admiring glances she got when she did so. Stan Hathaway didn't know when he was on to a good thing, she thought grimly, tossing her head a little at the memory of him, his warm hands, his intimate suggestions. He'd proved to be a faithless heart-breaker, but at least she'd had fun. While she wasn't going to rush to make that sort of mistake again, it wouldn't do any harm to meet a few men her own age. They needed cheering up: everyone said so.

'If you're sure you know what we'll be doing, I'll open up,' Mrs Moyes said now, wiping her hands on her sensible print overall. She handed her latest recruit a pinafore to tie around her slim waist. 'Take this, Mrs Kerrigan. We don't want to ruin your pretty dress, now do we?'

'Thank you, Mrs Moyes,' said Nancy dutifully, knotting the pinafore's fabric at the back, mindful that she wouldn't easily replace her frock if it did get damaged. It was from 1939, but she'd carefully mended it and sewn on new buttons at the neck to bring it as up to date as she could, and she didn't want that effort to be for nothing. Now that clothes rationing had come in, it was all the more important to make the most of what she already had.

Mrs Moyes was ushering a group of young men across the room to the counter where Nancy stood waiting. 'Now here are some gentlemen just arrived from America,' she beamed. 'I expect they're thirsty, aren't you, boys?' Her tone was motherly and comforting.

Nancy perked up at once. America was officially

227

neutral but, thanks to the Lend Lease Agreement, under which the United States had promised to supply the Allies with equipment and other help, more and more service personnel were arriving in Britain. Some people complained about them, saying they were too loud and brash, but Nancy intended to give them the benefit of the doubt.

'Hello,' she said, her eyes gleaming. 'Now, how exactly can I help you?' She peeped up at them from under her hair in its victory roll and her voice was anything but motherly. From the reactions she could observe, she immediately knew she'd made the right decision in coming here.

CHAPTER TWENTY-TWO

Rita hurried along what had once been a bustling shopping street at the heart of Bootle, although it was barely recognisable after the bombings of earlier in the year. She couldn't imagine that it would ever thrive again. So many of the landmarks of her childhood had gone or been severely damaged: churches, the street market, the Town Hall, the theatre, the boys' school. Once this war is over, she thought, where are people going to earn their keep? There's no more dye works and the Bryant and May match factory has taken a pasting. Not that she would have chosen to take a job there. She wouldn't want to be around the sulphur all day. She remembered all too well being frightened as a child when she'd seen women with phossy jaw caused by the white phosphorus used to make the matches, whose victims had to have their jawbones removed; even though times had changed, it still sent a shiver through her.

Rita loved nursing, and on a day like today she thanked her lucky stars she could do the job she felt she was born forand serve her country while doing so. She was good at it, she knew. Her patients responded to her and her colleagues valued her highly. It wasn't being big-headed to recognise this. She hummed to herself. Now that things had calmed down and the pace of work was steadier, she was back to being happy at the hospital. She'd even found time to speak to Dr Fitzgerald, who she knew had seen a lot of Kitty over the summer. He had talked of her friend with such animation that she could tell he was deeply smitten. Rita was pleased for Kitty. She'd made her break and it was working out well for her.

Rita knew she had other reasons to be happy too. Only yesterday, when she'd popped round to Danny's to check if he needed anything from his ration book in case his shifts prevented him from going to the shop, he'd passed her a new letter from Jack. Rita glowed at the thought. Jack had written that he hoped his promised leave would be soon. 'With luck it'll be for a decent amount of time,' he'd said. 'You know I can't tell you precisely when it'll be, as we don't know from one day to the next when and where we'll be needed, but I'm hanging on for the day when I can see you again. You are the most important person in my life and I can hardly wait to be there with you.'

Rita was grateful to him for not repeating his

idea that she should divorce Charlie. She allowed that he had been right to raise it as a possibility, and that plenty of women in her situation would have agreed to take that step, but she couldn't bring herself to do so. Not only would it be deeply shocking to her family and friends, it went against her most profound beliefs. It tore her apart, but not even with the promise of Jack's love and his strong comforting arms around her would she cross that line. It would bring her what she longed for most in the world, and yet she would be betraying herself in doing so. It would taint their future. She hoped he would not mention it again when he came home. She screwed up her eyes for a moment. She didn't know how she could bear the waiting, the intense craving to see him again.

The upside was that she wouldn't have to worry about his offer to lend her money now. It was hard to credit it, and yet the spring in her step was partly due to what had happened when she'd come off shift that afternoon. She'd arranged to meet her main supplier for the shop and, as his office was closer to the hospital than to Empire Street, she had gone to see him there. She had been armed with a fresh set of figures that Ruby had compiled. The young woman hadn't been wrong – she really did have a talent for spotting patterns in the complex columns of income and expenditure that Rita so dreaded. There was no way on this earth that Ruby would have met the supplier in person, but her suggestions had done the trick. She'd come up with an amount that Rita could afford to pay and that the supplier was able to accept. After all, Rita reasoned, it wasn't in his interests for her to go out of business; this way they both benefited. Ruby had proved herself, and Rita could rest easy for once, on this score at least. She wondered if she could buy Ruby something special to celebrate. She had had so few treats in her young life, and she surely deserved a little present. What a shame the main shopping street was in such a state, even after the salvage teams' efforts to clear it.

Maybe she could ask Nancy to find something in the city centre. Her sister would like nothing more than a reason to go bargain hunting, Rita was pretty certain of that. Or perhaps she would offer to take Ruby to the farm to visit the children? Ruby often spoke about them, and Rita made sure she shared Michael and Megan's letters with her. Yes, that would be perfect. She would speak to Pop about it. In fact, thought Rita, she could do that now, as he wouldn't be on ARP duty for a few hours yet. Rounding the corner near her parents' house, she thought she could hear the sound of him practising his accordion.

She tried to remember the last time she'd heard him play. Before the war, he'd loved to keep them entertained at home, or to join in if anyone was on the piano down at the Sailor's Rest. Recently he'd been so busy with his ARP work that he'd scarcely had a moment to go back to his favourite old hobby. She hoped he'd decided to take it up again – she loved to listen to him and sing along to the choruses of the songs they all knew.

'Rita.' She stopped dead in her tracks, her reverie shattered. A cold shiver ran down her neck. Who was that? Did somebody whisper her name? Or had she been mistaken?

Carefully she looked round. It was still daylight but the shadows were long, casting the pavement into darkness, making it indistinct. There was nothing to be seen. The gutters were filling with the first of the falling leaves and the remains of the rubble from the houses that had taken a battering all around. She couldn't make out any human form. Don't be daft, she said to herself, you've been thinking about Jack and now you've gone and conjured up that noise you thought you heard in the back yard that time. There wasn't anything there then and there's nothing there now.

A noise came again and she swung around sharply. Was it her name, or was it a piece of scrap metal rolling over in a gust of wind? There was a slight movement towards the edge of her vision and she turned her head, but it was a rag caught on a rusty nail poking out from a gateway in the wall. Then came a shuffling, but again there was no sign of anybody.

I could kill that cat, Rita swore. That's what it'll be. I've a good mind to go down to the Sailor's Rest, find out who actually owns it and tell them to feed it properly. It's always hanging around this end of the street, trying to beg scraps. Well, I'm not having it.

The sound of the accordion had stopped and now the door to her parents' house swung open and Pop stepped out, his silver hair vivid against the dark brickwork. With a huge rush of relief, Rita ran across to him, waving eagerly. 'Pop! I was just coming to see you.'

He looked up with a big smile on his face and

held out his arms. He'd never been shy of showing affection to his daughters, and Rita, with her courage and steadfastness, held a special place in his heart. 'Coming to see your old dad, were you?' he grinned, giving her a hug. 'How can I help you?' He took a closer look at her face. 'Is everything all right?'

'Yes, everything's fine.' Then she stopped herself. 'I'm being silly and imagining things. I thought for a moment someone called my name back there, but there's nobody about.'

Pop looked at her with affection. 'You're probably just tired,' he said. 'We all know how hard you work. You hold everything together, don't think we can't see what effort it all takes.' And that feckless husband of yours hasn't helped, he thought to himself, but didn't say out loud. At least when the man wasn't here, he couldn't mistreat his beloved eldest daughter. 'What can I do for you today?'

Rita could feel herself relaxing from her moment of fear. 'I was just wondering about when I could go to the farm next...'

Pop put his strong arm around her shoulder and ushered her through the front door. Behind the opposite wall, a figure let out an exasperated breath and swore softly.

'I call it the Curse of Cavendish.' Laura strode angrily across the dormitory and glared out of the window at the fading skyline. 'Do we see any enemy aircraft? No. Any ack-ack guns? No. Any burning buildings, even? No. Not a trace. And yet it's an emergency, and yet again I am to give up my precious evening off for Captain Blooming

Cavendish and his ever-insistent desire to be ferried across our capital city.'

Kitty sighed in sympathy for her friend. 'It's rotten luck, Laura, but you can't do anything about it. That's the lot of being a driver. He must rate you highly, if he asks for you specifically so often.' Sometimes she envied Laura her job – she got to see the world outside, different things every day. But in truth she wouldn't have swapped. She prided herself that she had got the hang of being a telephone operator now, keeping calm under pressure to connect heavy loads of calls, knowing how to prioritise the urgent ones, and always remaining cool and polite, no matter what the parties on the other end of the line demanded – and being discreet if the calls were of a confidential nature connected with important war business, which made her feel trusted and in a position of responsibility. Also, even though her shifts were long, she knew she was highly unlikely to get called back in when she'd planned an evening off – not like her friend.

Laura shook her head and her blonde hair swung about in the light from the low-watt bulb that dangled from the ceiling. 'Can't get anyone else fool enough to do it, more like,' she snapped. 'The rest must be better at avoiding the summons. It's always me, always.'

'You'd better pin back that blackout blind,' Kitty pointed out. 'Otherwise we'll have the ARP complaining, and then it'll be even worse for us.'

Laura muttered under her breath but tucked the harsh black fabric back into position. 'There. I'm only doing it for you, mind, because I don't

234

want to get you into trouble. If I got taken away by the ARP warden, then Captain Killjoy would have to find somebody else, wouldn't he?'

'For me, and because you really don't want the building to get blown up by a passing bomber,' Kitty said cheerfully. There had been no raids for what felt like ages, and she was cautiously optimistic that this would continue. 'Maybe he wants to go to see his girlfriend. That would count as an emergency.'

'Girlfriend!' Laura snorted. 'No, because that would mean he'd have to have a heart. He hasn't, believe me. He has no normal feelings. It's all work, work, work, and the blessed call of duty. Don't look at me like that, I know there's a war on, but this man is something else. He never lets up, and doesn't understand that not everyone else is like him.'

Kitty shrugged. 'I'm sorry but he really doesn't seem so bad. Pretty handsome, in fact. Look on the bright side – he could be one of those grizzled old chaps. You must be doing something right if you're in such high demand, so serve you right for being good at reversing into small spaces. Anyway, you'd better be off. Wear something warm, the evenings are getting chilly.'

She shivered for effect, but she felt deliciously warm inside. Elliott's latest letter had said he was planning to come to London again towards the end of October, and he would love to introduce her to his parents. They were so keen to meet the woman who had stolen his heart and brought joy to his life after the death of his fiancée. Kitty had held out all summer when he'd suggested it, fearing it was still too soon, but now she knew how he felt about her, she was ready to take the next step. It filled her with trepidation and yet she was excited too. She wasn't afraid of making a fool of herself any more, or that they would look down on her for not being out of society's top drawer. Now she was confident she could hold her own, as the valuable work she was training to do placed her at the centre of the war effort, and she knew she was as good as anybody else. All right, some people still saw things differently, imagining they were superior and automatically worthy of deference from the likes of her, but she was sure Elliott's parents would not be like that. They couldn't be, having produced somebody as kind and generously supportive as he was.

'Marvellous,' snapped Laura, rooting around in her drawer before pulling out a scarf. 'This should do it. It's not regulation, but he can't seriously expect me to freeze to death while he's out saving the nation single-handedly once again. Do you like it? It was a present from Freddy actually.'

Kitty started; it had been ages since Laura had mentioned her missing brother. She'd never let her guard down since that day many months ago, although Kitty was aware that the sorrow was never far away, bubbling beneath Laura's bright surface. 'It's beautiful,' she said, gazing at the length of green-and-cream fabric. 'Is that cashmere?'

'Certainly is,' Laura replied, jauntily wrapping it around her neck. 'Let's see if the captain dares complain about it.' She pulled on her uniform jacket. 'Rightio, best be off. Don't wait up.'

'Hope he doesn't keep you out too late,' Kitty

said, meaning it, and yet perversely glad that she would have an evening alone in which to reply to Elliott. She'd tell him how much she looked forward to meeting his family, in the full knowledge of how much that would mean to him.

Laura fumed silently as she expertly guided the captain's car through the nearly empty streets, accustomed as she was by now to driving in the blackout. She was surprised there weren't more incidents. When the blackout had first been imposed, more people had died in accidents than in enemy attacks. Now most people avoided travelling around if they could do so. That was all very well for those who had the option, but she couldn't exactly say no when faced with a direct order. At least Captain Cavendish hadn't commented directly on her non-uniform scarf, which was still wrapped very deliberately around her neck, and a fine job it was doing of keeping her warm too. He'd raised his eyes when he first saw it, but then just barked, 'Reform Club, Fawcett,' and made no further remarks as she'd taken him to Pall Mall.

She was quietly furious. So he was off on some social jaunt to meet a stuffy old friend, probably someone as supercilious as he was. Reluctantly she conceded that Kitty and Marjorie might have a point, he was actually pretty good looking, but that was of small comfort to her as she had been stuck outside the club in the cold and dark, while he no doubt enjoyed himself inside – if he was capable of doing anything so frivolous. He'd kept her waiting for half an hour and then had emerged, shaking hands with someone she could tell – even from a distance and in the brief glimpse of light from the open doorway – was in the uniform of a very high-ranking naval officer indeed.

He'd offered no explanations when he'd got into the back seat, but she thought she detected a change in his expression, from anxious – although he'd tried hard to hide it – to satisfied. 'Return to where we started, sir?' she'd queried and, instead of biting her head off for stating the obvious, he'd simply nodded and said, 'Much as I'd love to think the world was our oyster, Fawcett, pressure of work dictates that you convey me to my billet as swiftly as possible. Within safe limits, naturally.'

'Very well, sir,' Laura had said, thinking this was as close to skittish as she'd heard him. She caught his eye in the rear-view mirror, registering that he looked positively light-hearted, but looked away as his eye caught hers – and held it for a touch longer than she felt comfortable with. Was that the beginning of a smile on his lips? Whoever the gold-braid-covered superior officer had been, he'd put the usually curt captain in an uncharacteristically good mood. She briefly wondered which way to go, and then decided to head through the residential back streets of Camden, as direct a route as she could follow back to the northern reaches of the capital. She zigzagged neatly through the deserted roads while the captain retreated into his usual taciturn silence.

Some fifteen minutes later she was privately congratulating herself on a good job when the dull beam of a shaded torch waved at her and she realised somebody was flagging her down. She wound down the window and looked up at the shadowy figure, his armband marking him out as an ARP warden. 'Can't go down there, miss,' he said. 'The UXB boys are seeing to a little present Jerry left behind. Best to double back on yourself and keep a wide berth.' His voice was calm but she could tell he was deadly serious. She shivered involuntarily. Those service personnel who dealt with unexploded bombs had the shortest life expectancy of anyone in uniform, fighter pilots included, and faced the prospect of death at every call-out. She shifted the gear stick into reverse and began to back into the narrow mouth of an alley to turn around.

'Good show, Fawcett,' muttered the captain, and Laura almost smiled to herself as she'd imagined him falling asleep after his successful meeting. But then, before she could complete the manoeuvre, there was an immense explosion and the ground beneath them shook.

For a moment she lost her sense of where she was, and wondered if there had been an earthquake. Lights were flashing and there was a smell of burning, of brick dust, and something sharper. Oh no, those poor bomb disposal boys, she groaned, as the realisation struck her of what must have happened. Her hand flew to her mouth and only then did she realise she'd spoken the words aloud. Swiftly she tried to marshal her thoughts and check if the car was intact, that the windows hadn't broken in the shock wave from the blast.

'You all right, Fawcett?' She couldn't tell if the captain's tone was perfunctory or concerned.

'Perfectly all right, sir.' She hoped that was true.

Then, in the light of the fierce blaze, she saw that debris had fallen across the road, blocking their way. 'Bit of a problem with the route back, though. We might have to walk.'

'Good thinking, Fawcett.' The captain didn't sound shaken at all. She supposed he'd been through much worse on active service. 'Let's get on with it before something else goes up. Not much we can do here. They're bound to have evacuated the residential buildings already.'

They got out of the car and Laura drew her scarf across her nose to try to block out the smell and the smoke that was now billowing down the street between the tall terraced houses on either side. Some of them had lost their windows and glass cracked underfoot. She almost fell on some and Captain Cavendish automatically slipped a hand under her elbow to steady her. 'Careful, Fawcett. No sense in adding to the casualty total.'

'No indeed, sir.' She couldn't tell if he was trying to make light of the situation or not, but she registered that his hand was very strong and could sense the warmth of it against her arm, which she hoped wasn't shaking. For a moment she thought he was going to keep it there. Then he dropped it.

They edged around the debris and could make out a clear path to the next street, but then a scream pierced the air. A woman was running towards them, her distress plain to see in the firelight. She was pointing at one of the houses at the other end of the row, closer to the fire.

'My baby!' She was beside herself in grief, in panic. She pushed past them as Laura tried to

240

reach out to calm her. 'Let me through, my baby's in there!' She broke free and ran towards the building, just as they saw the roof begin to catch fire. Sparks were flying all around now, and Laura instantly hit one that landed on her sleeve.

'Stop!' cried the captain. 'The authorities have cleared the buildings, your baby will be safe.'

The woman turned and screamed in anguish. 'He isn't, they didn't know he was there. My neighbour was watching my kids and the older ones are with her, but they left the baby, they left him ... she thought I'd taken him with me but I hadn't, he's in there still. I'm going to get him.'

Cavendish didn't hesitate. 'You hold her back, Fawcett. She'll do no good in that state. I'll go in and check. Which floor?' he shouted at the woman, who was now half collapsed and clinging to Laura.

'T ... t ... top floor,' wailed the woman, almost incoherent through fear and despair.

The captain ran faster than Laura could ever have imagined, and plunged through the door of the building, the windows of which were smashed. Laura thought she could hear a wailing from inside, but the noise of all the spreading fires and breaking glass was so great she couldn't have. She had no time to fear for the captain; all her attentions had to be on keeping the mother out of the way and as calm as possible.

'Now there's no need to worry,' she began, though her teeth had started to chatter with stress, 'Captain Cavendish is the best there is and he'll get your baby out. We must get you to the nearest ARP post. Do you know where that is? Is it behind

241

us?' She dreaded to think what had happened to the kindly warden who'd spoken to them what must have been only a few minutes before, but he ought to have colleagues somewhere.

The woman was whimpering and Laura couldn't make out what she was saying. She asked her again, and finally worked out where to head for, half carrying the anguished mother, who was dragging her feet in the shards of glass. Laura was finding it harder and harder to breathe through the combination of exertion and smoke, and had never been so thankful to see a policeman rushing towards them. Quickly she explained what had happened.

'I'll take care of this,' he said. 'Madam, you must come with me. You too, Miss.'

Laura was about to follow his suggestion, when she realised she could not leave the captain to his task alone. Who else would know exactly where he had gone? It was her duty to return to ensure he emerged safely with the baby, and tell him where the mother could be found. 'I must find my superior officer,' she told the policeman quickly and then, before he could stop her, she turned and sprinted back down the street. More roofs had caught fire, and now she was surrounded by blazing buildings, the smoke thicker than ever, the glass crunching beneath every footstep, but she didn't halt until she got to the woman's house. Her face was streaming with sweat and her throat was sore as she shouted 'Sir?' as loudly as she could. She hoped against hope he had found the child and got to a lower floor, as the flames were licking the shattered windows of the topmost, and nobody, not even the athletic Captain Cavendish, could survive there. 'Sir?' she shouted again, desperately listening for any kind of response. 'Sir! I'm out on the street right in front of the house! Can you hear me?' But all she could hear was the roar of the fire and the crash of collapsing buildings and the sound of breaking glass. She swatted at falling sparks and strained every nerve to catch a trace of him, but the fire drowned everything out.

'Sir!' she tried again. 'Captain Cavendish! Can you hear me?' She racked her brain to remember his first name. She knew she'd seen it written down somewhere, although of course she would have been forbidden to use it to his face. What was it? Something from the Bible. Matthew, Mark ... Peter, that was it. 'Peter!' she shouted desperately, ignoring the searing pain in her throat. 'Peter, are you in there?'

Then, just above her, in the window of what might have been the ground-floor flat's living room, she saw a shape and it was him, pushing aside what remained of the glazing, then turning and bending down. The next moment he was there again with a small bundle in his arms. 'Fawcett!' he bellowed, his voice hoarse but still strong, 'Fawcett, is that you? Are you out there?'

'Sir! Peter! I'm right here, just beneath you!' A gust of wind briefly blew the smoke clear, and they could see each other, lit in the bright orange of the searing flames that were getting ever closer by the second.

'I'm going to pass you the baby!' he shouted. 'Stand just beneath me and stretch up your arms.

243

Can you reach? Not quite? Well, I hope you are good at catching. I'm going to drop him into your arms. On the count of three.'

Laura didn't hesitate but got as close as she could to the burning building, ignoring the first-floor windowsill now alight and dropping splinters of burning wood on to her. 'Sir!'

'One. Two.' Another, larger, piece of burning wood crashed down and almost hit her. 'Three.' He dropped the bundle and she struggled to hold it, the weight more than she had counted on, but somehow she grasped it and held it to her chest, unable to tell if it was alive or dead. The flames were playing about the top of the ground-floor window now, the frame smouldering, the sparks coming thick and fast.

'Sir! Get out! Peter, don't wait, jump!' she cried, backing away so that the precious bundle wouldn't catch fire as well. 'Do it now!' For a terrible moment she thought he hadn't heard, as he seemed frozen to the spot in the window, the flames now burning erratically around the top of the frame. Then he sprang into action, his blond hair bright in the ghastly orange light, climbing on to the sill, pausing for balance, and then leaping through the smoke and fire to land heavily at her feet. His uniform jacket was undone and his shirt, she noticed, was torn. There was a bloodstain down the front, too, but he was alive. Hefting the bundle on to one shoulder, she reached a hand down to help him up.

Grimacing, he took it and hauled himself up. 'Better make ourselves scarce, Fawcett,' he said and then broke into a grin. 'I don't think this is

244

the best place to be hanging around. Do you mind if I lean on you – I've ricked my ankle.'

'Of course, Peter. Sorry, sir.' Laura shifted the bundle once more and it emitted a tiny wail. She felt it tug at her heartstrings, but now was not the time to think about it. They had to get back down the length of the burning street before they were safe, and then find the ARP post. If she allowed herself to, she would begin sobbing, in a mixture of relief for the child and fear for the peril that still faced them, but there wasn't a moment to waste on that right now.

Cavendish swatted at a stray spark which was singeing her uniform jacket, but it was no good. 'Fawcett. Get your coat off at once. Here, we'll shelter under mine.' He threw her jacket aside just as it burst into flames, and held his own much larger one over the pair of them and shielding the baby. As fast as they could, him limping and leaning on her, her twisting to support him but still protecting the baby, they got themselves down the street and to the shelter of the corner, where there was a break in the buildings that the fires hadn't crossed. The light of the flames revealed the baby's blanket was singed and damaged, and it was beginning to give off smoke.

'Throw that rag away before the smoke chokes the poor creature,' he ordered gruffly, and Laura swiftly unwound the remains of what once had been a pretty wool blanket, embroidered with teddy bears, and flung it into the gutter. 'Here,' she said, unwrapping her scarf, 'we'll put this around him.' Gently she tucked it around his wriggling body, as he wailed some more. 'That's right, you have a good cry,' she said, 'and let's hope that means your lungs are all right. Come, his mother is this way.' Slowing now, and realising just how exhausted she was, Laura led Cavendish along the side street towards the blessed sight of the ARP post and help.

Laura sipped her tea, which had the luxurious addition of a generous dollop of sugar. They were in the local police station, and she was wearing a Red Cross blanket around her shoulders in place of her ruined uniform jacket. If she'd been the sort of young woman given to embarrassment, she might have blushed at the knowledge that her very much non-regulation underwear was on show. Everyone was busy milling around, but all she could do was huddle on the wooden bench and warm her unaccountably cold hands against the mug. Shock, she supposed.

The baby had been reunited with his tearful mother, and both had been taken away by a Red Cross nurse to be assessed for any injuries or smoke inhalation. Judging from the ever-louder cries of the little child, he was going to recover well – maybe sooner than his distraught mother. She had, however, managed to thank Laura and Captain Cavendish, telling everyone that they were heroes and the baby would have been dead had it not been for their swift action. Laura screwed up her eyes at the thought. The woman was probably right. Now that the rush of adrenaline was over she was shaky, almost unable to believe what they had done. The heat, the fear, the urgency – and worst of all that moment when she'd thought the captain wasn't going to make it. Her heart had turned over then – but he had made it, he had jumped to safety. He was now getting patched up somewhere in the police station. She knew he'd damaged his ankle in that final desperate leap but she couldn't help thinking about the blood down his shirt. Was he badly hurt? What had happened in the burning top-floor flat to give him such an injury? Frantically she looked around, trying to see if there was anyone to ask, but everyone seemed to be too busy. She supposed the evacuation of the local streets had caused chaos on top of the regular disruption of war.

Pull yourself together, she muttered. Your job is to buck up and be ready for when Captain Cavendish is fit to leave. You'll be no use to him or anyone else in this state. She forced herself to sit more upright, though her shoulders had begun to ache from the force of catching the falling child. Her mind was in turmoil. She hadn't been prepared for the touch of the captain's hand on her arm, still less the sensation of holding him as he valiantly tried to walk on his injured ankle. It was as if he was a different person – no longer the demanding taskmaster who required her to jump to his bidding, but a human being, one who was vulnerable and who had been prepared to risk his own life for that of a child he didn't know. Also, a small voice said in her head, one who was very good looking. She didn't know what she'd do if it turned out he was badly hurt. That blood could have come from a deep wound caused by breaking glass, or a blow from falling debris, or–

'Fawcett, there you are.' His familiar form

247

limped around the sergeant's desk and sat down beside her. 'Bearing up?'

Laura looked at him and gasped. He was wearing what must be a borrowed, ill-fitting shirt, and she could see a bandage had been applied underneath. 'You're injured, P ... sir. Are you all right?'

'Right enough,' he said with a grimace. He took in her expression. 'Yes, I admit, it's not only the ankle that's bothering me, but they've cleaned me up and I'll be as good as new once I've had a proper night's sleep. I've asked one of the police officers to telephone base and they're sending another car and driver to fetch us.'

'Really?' Laura was surprised but delighted. She'd been dreading having to walk, and wondering how on earth the captain would manage.

'Under the circumstances there was no quibbling,' he assured her. He met her eyes directly. 'I understand you disobeyed the policeman earlier, Fawcett, when he instructed you to accompany him to the ARP station.'

Laura gazed at the floor. Surely she wasn't going to be in trouble for that? She'd completely forgotten that moment, but now he reminded her it was true. 'Yes, sir.'

He waited until she looked up. 'I'm damned glad you did, Fawcett. I'd have been a goner back there – and the baby too.' He cleared his throat. 'Thank you, Fawcett, and well done. That took guts to go back down the burning street when you could have got to safety.' He seemed embarrassed, something she'd never have thought he could ever be. His eyes were a warm brown, somewhere between chestnut and honey. She couldn't look away. 'You might just have saved my life – and the baby's – tonight. So yes, you are getting a ride back in the admiral's limo. Even *I* couldn't insist that you drive after an evening like this.' His face creased with good humour and she found herself smiling back.

'Glad to hear it, sir.' She felt her old good spirits returning. 'Not sure that my reversing would be up to its usual standard – I might have pulled a muscle in my shoulder somewhere. But if that's all, then I've got off lightly.' She grew serious. 'Really, are you going to be all right? I ... I saw the blood before. There wasn't time to ask but I did wonder how deeply you'd been cut.'

He sighed, and doing so seemed to cause him pain, which he immediately tried to mask. 'It was just some flying glass. I barely noticed at the time. But, put it this way, I shan't be carrying any heavy weights for a while. Don't make a fuss, Fawcett, it will heal perfectly, they've assured me.'

'Very well, P ... sir.' She was relieved and didn't know why.

His warm eyes flashed. 'You called me Peter, back there.'

'Sorry, sir.'

'Best not let it happen again.'

'Of course not.' She could feel the blush rise in her cheeks. So he had heard her shouting out to him.

'Dreadful name. I've got a twin brother called Paul, which makes it worse. Don't know what our parents were thinking of.'

'Must have been tricky, sir.' Laura couldn't believe she was joking with the man she'd thought of as Captain Killjoy, while stuck in a dismal corner of an overcrowded police station, both of them stinking of smoke. She reflected she must be feeling better, as in her earlier state of shock she hadn't even noticed such a detail. She took a final sip of her sweet tea, not wanting to waste it; she didn't know when she'd have such a treat again. Then her hand went to her throat. Of course – the scarf had gone, she'd used it to keep the baby warm when his own little blanket caught fire. One more memento of Freddy lost. Still, it was to a good cause. She wouldn't think about him now or she might break down and cry after all.

'Something wrong, Fawcett?' The captain leant closer, concern on his face, worry in his bright eyes.

Should she tell him? No, she couldn't. He was a captain, and after tonight she would be back to being his driver, one of many, and there would be nothing between them but the usual back of the driver's seat. She forced herself to smile. 'No, sir. Just got a tea leaf stuck in my throat, that's all.' She held the smile confidently, knowing she'd put on a happy face ever since the terrible news about Freddy had come through. That would stand her in good stead – she could act the part of cheerful, competent Wren Fawcett now, and evade the searching look the captain was giving her. She had to convince him. She couldn't trust him with her secrets; this moment of intimacy would not come again and she couldn't bear to think of him barking orders at her and yet knowing about her poor missing brother. 'I'm getting better by the minute, sir. I'll be right as rain by the time we're back at base.' Her smile grew bigger, and she willed him to believe her.

'As you wish, Fawcett.' He looked at her askance but didn't press the point. 'But just one thing.'

'Sir?'

'You might wish to visit what passes for the powder room around here before the car arrives.' He leant even closer and astonishingly touched her nose. 'You've a smudge, Fawcett.' Gently he stroked the tip of her nose, and then dropped his hand as a big grin broke across his face.

CHAPTER TWENTY-THREE

'So, would you like to do that, Ruby?' Rita's eyes danced with pleasure at seeing the delight on the young woman's face. She'd waited until she knew when Pop would be free to take them to the farm on his wagon, rather than get Ruby's hopes up only to find Pop was on extra duties and they couldn't go. Yesterday he'd told her he had a definite day of leave, or as definite as anything could be in wartime, and she felt confident that she could broach the idea. Now she was glad that she had. She felt she owed it to Ruby; the young woman had helped more and more around the place, even though she still hated talking to anyone in the shop. Rita had attempted to make her look more like her age by giving her some of Sarah's cast-offs, but it had been only partially successful. Ruby still held herself as if she was afraid of the world for most of the time. Now, though, her expression was transformed.

'Really, Rita? Really? I can go to see Michael and Megan? Oh, I'd love to. I've missed them so much.' Ruby clasped her hands to her chest. 'They'll have grown tall, won't they? I can't wait. You're too kind to me, honest you are.' Her lip began to tremble and for a moment Rita feared she might cry.

Rita moved around the shop counter and put her arm out to Ruby. 'Not a bit, Ruby. You've been such a help. I'd never have thought of that way to sort things out with our supplier. You're an asset to the business, that's what you are.'

Ruby glowed. She'd had more praise this morning than she could ever remember. Finding her way through the complexities of the account books hadn't been any trouble at all; arrangements of figures made complete sense to her. It was talking about them afterwards that was the problem, because whenever she'd tried to mention money to mean Elsie Lowe in her previous life, there had been a row. Ruby hated rows. They scared her – one of many things that scared her. Now, though, she was getting the best reward she could have wanted. She loved Michael and Megan and felt deeply protective of them. It was one of the reasons she'd felt so safe with Rita all those months ago when she'd been rescued by her – she could tell Rita would defend her children as fiercely as was necessary. You had to trust somebody like that.

She pushed back a wisp of blonde hair that had escaped one of her few precious kirby grips and decided to raise something else she'd found. She'd never get a better moment. It was just the two of them in the shop; the early rush of customers had gone, and Violet wasn't due until after lunch, to take over when Rita went on her nursing shift. 'I was counting boxes,' she began.

'Boxes?'

'Yes, in the storeroom. They should match what you paid for, but some are missing.'

'Yes, that's the idea,' said Rita, 'but you know, Ruby, it doesn't always work exactly like that. Things get lost, or misplaced, or now and again something isn't available but we get sent a replacement. It's never completely accurate, I wish it was.' Privately Rita knew another reason for the discrepancies was that Violet never could quite manage to keep a proper tally of what came in, what went on the shelves and what substitute goods arrived. She'd carry on talking to the customers instead of breaking off to make a note, and then forget the details later, if she wrote them down at all. It was the price Rita paid for having the help of her gregarious and generous sister-in-law.

'I know,' Ruby said solemnly. 'But certain things go missing regular.'

'It wouldn't be sherry, would it?' Rita grinned. They both knew who'd be responsible for that. Rita had decided the easiest course was to turn a blind eye to Winnie's pilfering. After all, it was technically her shop still, even if she'd shown no interest for months on end, and rarely ventured downstairs any more. In the end it made Rita's life easier.

Ruby shook her head seriously. 'Not sherry. It's food, tinned food. Luncheon meat, or beans, things like that. It's mostly once a fortnight. I've been counting.'

Rita remembered being unable to find a delivery of Spam a while back, but hadn't noticed such a thing since. 'Black market, do you mean? Is Winnie up to her old tricks, I wonder?' she said, thinking aloud. Ruby looked blank. Of course she wouldn't be aware of the goings-on at the shop in the early part of the war, with Winnie holding back choice goods for her favoured group of friends, or taking secret deliveries from the docks. The shady world of the black market was one of the things that Ruby would find hard to understand. She liked everything to be straightforward, not full of secrecy, hints, nudges and lies.

'Doesn't sound like it, though,' Rita went on. 'Beans and luncheon meat – it's not as if it's luxury produce. Yes, they can be scarce, but there's so much more you'd make a bigger profit on. It doesn't make sense.' She sighed. 'Leave it with me, Ruby. I'll think about it. If you reckon you know exactly when things go missing, maybe we can keep a special eye out the next time we guess it might happen.'

Ruby nodded, although she didn't want to be the one to keep an eye out. There might be shouting and she couldn't bear that. Still, she couldn't refuse to help. 'All right,' she said. 'I'll go and look at the kitchen calendar now and see when might be next.' She disappeared through the internal door just as the main shop door bell rang.

In came Nancy, wearing a coat Rita hadn't seen

before. It was of good-quality wool in a lovely dark green and had a tight belt, showing off her younger sister's neat figure and emphasising her curves. Rita felt a pang of envy. Once she too had had curves to be proud of, but those days were long gone.

'Morning,' she said, trying to keep the emotion from showing in her voice. 'That's a fine coat you have there, Nancy. Where did it come from?'

'Fire damaged, can you believe it?' Nancy pirouetted on the spot. 'You can't tell but the lining is scorched in places. I'm going to replace it when I have a moment. Honestly, Rita, I'm rushed off my feet now.'

Rita raised her eyebrows but said nothing. When it came to being rushed off her feet, she was the expert. She didn't need Nancy making a show about it.

'It's all these American engineers arriving in the city,' Nancy continued. 'You've no idea how many are over here now. And they all need taking care of – after all, it's our duty, isn't it? Even though they are from a neutral country, they are still helping us out in the fight against Hitler. I feel for them being so far from home, I really do. I wish I could do more for them than just give them a cup of tea.'

'Nancy, you're a married woman,' Rita began, but Nancy let out a delighted yelp of laughter.

'Oh, listen to me, what have I said? I didn't mean that. No, but they're used to better food and everything, and all we can give them is a biscuit if they're lucky. Still, mustn't grumble. I do feel I should make an effort though, you know – cheer them up by adding a bit of glamour to their lives.' She brushed her sleeve. 'Don't suppose you have any nice soap in? I always feel more like myself if I have a decent bar of soap.'

'We've got Lifebuoy,' Rita said bluntly.

Nancy's face fell. 'Is that it? Are you sure? I was hoping you'd have some Pears. I love that, it's so delicate.'

Rita shook her head firmly, thinking how her own fair skin had suffered without the softer brands of soap. 'No, Nancy, it's Lifebuoy or nothing.'

Nancy came closer to the counter. 'You wouldn't have any round the back, by any chance? I know that Winnie...'

Rita sighed in exasperation. 'No, Nancy, we don't. We don't do sales from round the back any more. If we had some Pears I'd be delighted to sell you some and I'd use it myself, but we don't.'

'Oh well, worth a shot.' Nancy didn't seem too disappointed. 'I'll see if there's any in Lewis's warehouse. I'm just around the corner from there, it's so convenient.' And with that she breezed back through the door, forgetting to close it properly.

Rita followed her and resisted the urge to slam the door, thinking how lovely it would be to have something more fragrant than the carbolic she usually made do with nowadays. But until the war ended, that seemed about as likely as finding out where all the tins of beans were vanishing.

Laura listlessly picked up a tray in the mess queue and wondered what the options would be today. As Wrens, they were being fed adequately, as everyone knew you had to make sure service personnel had proper sustenance, but none of them actually looked forward to meal times any more. Kitty had regaled them with tales of corners they'd been forced to cut when she was in the NAAFI canteen back home, and that was before the rationing got so bad. Now the choice was Spam fritters or a meat pie. Laura could guess that the contents of the pie would only be very slightly laced with meat, and the rest would be made up of oats or some other cereal to eke out the precious flavour. At least there were plenty of potatoes. She sighed for the days when they would have come slathered with butter, but butter was very strictly rationed now and was definitely counted as a luxury. She thought of all the farms near her family home, and wondered if Cook had managed to come to an arrangement with them. Her parents would be sitting down to a delicious lunch right now, with fresh eggs, maybe a chicken... Laura could feel her mouth watering at the idea. Maybe she should try to go home on her next leave – and yet she didn't feel inclined to do so.

Wearily she chose the pie and nodded when the kind woman behind the counter offered her an especially large helping of potatoes. Word had got around that Laura had performed a heroic action and saved a child, and suddenly everyone was bending over backwards to be nice to her. She knew she should be grateful. People were making an extra effort in recognition of what she'd done, and yet she couldn't rise to the occasion and appreciate it. She didn't know what was wrong with her.

Laura carried her laden tray across to the tables.

A group of Wrens she barely knew were gathered at the closest one. All of them smiled, and a dark-haired young woman moved her chair so there would be room for one more person to sit down. Laura smiled back but shook her head. She really didn't feel like company, certainly not that of people she barely knew. She'd have to explain to them what had happened, and she'd already told the story what felt like a thousand times. She'd made sure to keep her account as basic as possible, resisting the urge to embroider it, leaving out some of the more gruesome details, if anything, not wanting to horrify her listeners. She briefly squeezed her eyes shut. The noise of the burning buildings, the breaking glass, the over-whelming heat: how could she possibly convey this to anyone who hadn't been there? She made her way to a small corner table that was far from the rest of the staff, not wanting to be drawn into conversations or to have to listen in to whatever the others were discussing.

It had been a week now since the night of the fire, and she hadn't seen or heard from Captain Cavendish in all that time. She didn't know what to make of it. She couldn't remember when there had been so long a gap without seeing him, not since she'd first met him when she'd had to take him to a meeting not long after she'd qualified as an official driver. Of course she'd spent most of that time cursing her luck and wishing him elsewhere. Now she had to admit it was strange – it was more than strange. If she was completely honest with herself, she missed him – his constant demands, the way he made her attempt the

258

impossible on a daily basis. Then, of course, there had been those extraordinary moments in the police station when he had gazed into her eyes and touched the tip of her nose. What did he mean by that? Was it just a warning to look smart before leaving the station, or was there something else behind it? For a brief flash she could have sworn there was, but now he must be avoiding her. Was he embarrassed? That seemed unlikely. Did he regret letting his guard down? Had he found a better driver? Her professional pride bristled at that. She was good, she knew it. So what was going on? She was also increasingly annoyed that she was unable to stop going over and over the same thoughts. Really, she told herself, she should snap out of it.

Laura had had plenty of contact with men her own age, as her brother had always brought friends back from school or university, and she'd often gone along with them to whatever entertainments were available back home. Then there had been the frequent visits to London, which had served her well in her quest for fun, now they were stationed within reach of the city centre. She loved dancing and flirting, and considered herself an old hand at both.

Not one of the men she had danced or flirted with had ever got close to her heart, though. They were for amusement, nothing more. She didn't take them seriously, and she knew full well most of them didn't take her seriously either. If anyone ever hinted that he was becoming keen, she would drop him like a stone, not wanting anything to get in the way of light-hearted fun. They were boys, that was all. If she wanted serious masculine conversation, there had always been Freddy.

Now she had to face the fact that this was something different. Somehow the captain had got under her skin, riling her most of the time, but making her react in a way she had never done before. She had thought she'd hated him. But when she believed he was going to die in that blazing house, she had desperately wanted him to escape, to be safe, to be alive and with her. He had held her and his touch had been strong and reassuring, even when he'd been hurt. He'd stroked her nose, an astonishingly intimate gesture, totally unexpected, and somehow more special than if he'd tried to kiss her or hold her hand or something more usual. Then, after the powerful experience of getting through that evening of danger, he'd vanished off the scene. She just didn't know what to think or what to do. Common sense told her to forget the whole thing – and yet she couldn't.

There was a clattering behind her as someone pushed a chair aside and Marjorie arrived, carrying a tray of Spam fritters and a much smaller portion of potatoes than Laura had been given. 'Room for two more?' she smiled. Laura nodded. She didn't mind Marjorie – at least she wouldn't ply her with intrusive questions about the fire, or weigh her down with congratulations she didn't feel she deserved.

'I swear these helpings are shrinking,' Marjorie complained, setting down her plate. 'I know my waistline is, and I didn't have much of one before. It's a conspiracy to save material when we have any new uniforms, I tell you.'

'You may be right,' Laura said, feeling a little guilty about her own big helping. She hadn't come close to finishing it, and Marjorie had obviously noticed. 'Here, you have some of mine,' Laura added hurriedly.

'Don't mind if I do, if you're sure,' Marjorie said eagerly, sitting down and adjusting her chair so that she could see the rest of the room. There was Kitty, picking up her own tray and coming across. 'I almost didn't notice you here, tucked away. Gosh, you wouldn't think it was possible to get so hungry just sitting still all day but, I tell you, I could eat a horse.'

'Sadly there don't seem to be many of those roaming the streets of north London,' Laura said, attempting some of her old humour. She heard the words come out flat and heavy, but Marjorie didn't seem to care. She tucked into the potatoes with gusto and only paused when half of them were gone. Kitty pulled up the other chair and made a face at the size of the portion she'd seen Laura give to Marjorie. Hers was far smaller.

'Suppose you got these because of the other night,' Kitty said without rancour. 'I think you should get more than a few potatoes, though, Laura. They should give you a medal or something.'

'Don't be daft,' Laura said quickly. 'People do this sort of thing every night of the week. When I think about that poor ARP warden, or the policeman that came to escort us, or the bomb disposal teams … what we did was nothing.'

Marjorie crushed the last of the potatoes into the remains of the thin juice from the fritter. 'Ah.

261

That's better. Still, they should reward you for bravery. You aren't one of the teams meant to deal with these things; you were just passing by and stayed to help. I reckon that counts for something. What does Captain Cavendish say?'

Laura kept her expression calm with some effort. 'Oh, I've no idea. I haven't seen him since, actually.'

'Of course not.' Marjorie glanced up at her friend. 'Stupid me, I'd forgotten.'

Laura put down the fork she'd been playing with to hide her agitation. 'Forgotten? Forgotten what?'

Marjorie shrugged. 'Why, that he wouldn't be going off to meetings in his condition, sending you all over the place and annoying you to pieces as usual.'

'In his condition?' Kitty echoed. 'What condition?'

Marjorie gaped. 'Don't you know? It's all over the language groups, so I thought someone would have told you, of all people.'

Laura stared at her. 'No, nobody's told me anything. What's all over the language groups? What's happened?' She did her best not to sound over-anxious.

'Well, that he was hurt in the fire, of course,' said Marjorie. 'You were there, you must have seen it all.'

'I know he hurt his ankle, I told you about that,' Laura said. 'I even had to practically carry him along the street. You've never seen anything so funny, him so much taller than me. Thank God nobody we knew was there to watch it. And yes, he did have a cut, as there was blood on his shirt.

He said they'd cleaned him up at the police station and there would be no problem.'

Marjorie pushed away her plate. 'That's not what people are saying now. I heard he'd been rushed to hospital, something about a wound being infected. He's been really ill. I can't believe you haven't heard.'

Laura stared at her. So that was why she hadn't seen him or been summoned to drive him anywhere. He hadn't been avoiding her – he'd been in hospital. Her mind flashed back to that evening and the blood on the shirt and then the large, very obvious bandage he'd been wearing on the journey home. She should have guessed that was no flesh wound. 'Is he in danger, do you know?' she forced herself to ask.

Marjorie shrugged. 'I don't really know. You know what it's like, the rumours spread like wildfire and they grow out of all proportion. The stories range from he's being held in for bed rest, to he's hanging on to life by a fingernail.'

Laura couldn't stop her exclamation of distress. 'But that's terrible. He seemed so sure it would all be well when I last saw him. I've got to go to see for myself. I can't believe nobody told me.'

'Maybe they only told his family and his immediate team,' Marjorie pointed out. 'Just because you were there with him doesn't mean they'd think of you. You know how it is: careless talk costs lives. If you were his girlfriend, I suppose they'd have said, but you were only his most regular driver, and as it doesn't affect your work, they'd say there was no reason for you to know. I say, are you all right?' She finally noticed that her friend was uncharacteristically silent.

Laura pulled herself together. 'Yes, of course, totally. It was just a bit of a shock. Here was I thinking he hadn't sent for me because I'd done something wrong, and all the while he was fighting for his life in hospital. After everything he's been through – it doesn't seem right.' Inwardly she was screaming, but she wasn't going to admit that, not even to Kitty and Marjorie.

'If you want to go to see him, I'll come with you,' Kitty offered. 'I don't have any more shifts until tomorrow.'

'Thank you,' Laura said hurriedly. 'I'd like that. Do you know where he is?'

'I can find out,' Marjorie said. 'Don't you have to be on duty this afternoon?'

'I'll tell them I had a relapse,' said Laura. 'How could they not tell me? When I was there right beside him? I damned well deserve some time off to check him for myself.' Suddenly all her old energy returned. 'Right. Let's get going. I won't rest until I see him for myself and find out just how bad he is.'

CHAPTER TWENTY-FOUR

It was always disorienting to emerge from the bunker of Derby House into the daylight, Frank thought. No matter how many times he did it, the contrast in the light levels, the temperature, the sense of being released into the fresh air always hit him. Today the air was chilly, autumn beginning to set in, and as ever the atmosphere was full of dust from shattered buildings mixed with the sharp tang of the nearby river Mersey and the sea beyond. He could hear the cry of gulls overhead.

'Thank you for that lecture, sir.' One of the new recruits he'd been detailed to oversee walked up and fell into step with him. 'It's taken me ages to get the hang of co-ordinates. It's good to have a refresher.'

Frank looked at her. She was in Wren uniform and was probably in her early twenties, and he couldn't help noticing she had shiny black curls, tumbling in an unruly fashion from beneath her cap. He recognised her from the talk he'd given earlier that morning. She'd been sitting in the second row and his eye had been drawn to her then, he had to admit. Perhaps it was the curls.

'Glad you found it of value … I'm sorry, I don't recall your name. It's always difficult in the larger groups,' he said apologetically.

'Hemsley, sir. Sylvia Hemsley.' She smiled up at him and he could see she had bright-blue eyes and a smattering of freckles left over from the summer across the bridge of her turned-up nose.

'Of course.' Frank found himself smiling broadly at the young woman, who gave the impression of infectious energy. More often than not he found an excuse to cut off any of the recruits who tried to make conversation outside the classroom, but now he decided not to be so churlish. It wouldn't hurt to make a bit of an effort. 'How are you finding Liverpool, then?' Even from their brief exchange, he could tell she wasn't from the local area. Her accent placed her to the north, he thought.

'I love it, sir,' she said enthusiastically. 'Even though everyone says I should have seen it before the war, it's so friendly. People talk to you and nobody minds giving you directions if you get lost. I did my basic training down south and some people there look at you as if you're some kind of alien if you ask for help. I didn't take to it at all.'

'Yes, I know what you mean,' Frank said. He'd been based in Southampton before being posted back to Merseyside and, though he'd enjoyed it, some of his colleagues had had similar experiences. 'So where are you from originally then, Hemsley?'

'The Lakes, sir. Not too far from Penrith,' she said, her eyes lighting up at the thought of her home. 'It's beautiful there and I miss it, but there's so much more to do in a city like Liverpool. I don't have to wear Wellingtons to get down the lane, for starters.'

Frank laughed, despite the caution around women he'd adopted since he'd lost his leg, and made to turn to answer, but the sharp movement caused him to stumble a little. Damn, whenever he let down his guard, his leg betrayed him.

'You all right, sir?' Hemsley's face showed her concern.

'Yes, nothing to worry about,' he said hastily. So she didn't know. He had imagined that it was the first thing anyone learnt about him, and that they all talked about it behind his back: the fact that he had only one leg. But perhaps that was his paranoia running wild and they had better things to gossip about. He decided to get it over and done with. Then she could tell the rest of the recruits if she felt like it. 'Actually, it's because I lost a leg in action a while back, and now use a false one. Every now and again it plays up. Right as rain now.'

'Sorry to hear that, sir,' said the young woman, taking the news in her stride. 'Does that mean you don't go to the Grafton dance hall very often, then? Bet that wouldn't stop Douglas Bader.'

Frank could have laughed out loud. Was this recruit trying to chat him up? He decided to play along. 'I wasn't the best dancer in the world before it happened, to tell you the truth,' he said. 'I leave that sort of thing to my younger sister. She was always out, often down the Adelphi. They used to have some wonderful music there before the war broke out. Still do, now and again,' he added, remembering Gloria's visit as Hemsley fell into step beside him.

As they rounded the corner, he could see Danny heading towards them, ready for his shift. He stopped to say hello. Frank felt obliged to do the introductions, and couldn't help registering how Danny looked at the Wren with appreciation.

'Good to meet you, Hemsley,' he said with his infectious grin. 'Frank, sorry, Sublieutenant Feeny, I'll see you later.' He hurried off, close to being late as usual.

The Wren gazed after him for a moment and then turned her attention back to Frank. 'I've seen him around, haven't I? They say he's one of the best trainee code breakers. Whoops, have I said something I shouldn't?'

'Actually yes,' said Frank, 'so you want to be

267

careful who's around when you talk about such things. Best kept for in the bunker if you want to be certain nobody can overhear. We need to keep what goes on in there a secret from the outside world as much as we can. It wouldn't do for half of Liverpool to know what Danny Callaghan does for a living – he's too valuable an asset to have his work made public.'

Hemsley nodded, her eyes widening. 'I'll be more careful,' she said. 'I wouldn't want to put anyone at risk. He seems nice, though.'

Frank shot a look at her. So, she was like many of the women of his acquaintance – impressed by just a minute's worth of Danny Callaghan's company. Well, he couldn't blame her; Danny was a good-looking young man, highly rated in his work, and footloose and fancy-free. Despite his looks, he'd never taken advantage of them when it came to women, as far as Frank could remember. Now of course there was the issue of his enlarged heart, but that wasn't Frank's secret to tell.

He remembered his own days before the accident, when he'd never been short of female attention. While he hadn't played the field over-much, he'd certainly made the most of it, and had never been backward in coming forward. Everything had changed since then – or, no, he told himself: strictly it had been just before that when he'd noticed how Danny's sister Kitty had transformed from a child into a very beautiful young woman. But there was no way she would have been interested in him once he'd lost his leg, and now she had Dr Elliott Fitzgerald, and they all said he was crazy about her. Good for him. What excellent taste he must have. Nevertheless, this young woman before him now had something of Kitty about her: the bouncing curls, the blue eyes, although they weren't as dark. She was bolder than Kitty had been, for sure, but then again he had no way of knowing what Kitty was like now, six months into her own training and living far away in London. More importantly, Wren Sylvia Hemsley was here in front of him, not all those miles away and, even if she was impressed by Danny, she also seemed to be showing signs of interest in Frank. Why not pursue it for once? Live a little, he told himself. You've come close to death once; what harm can a little encouragement do?

'So what have you seen of the city so far?' he said now. 'I'm afraid you've missed the chance of visiting our cathedral or St Luke's Church, or even our best department stores. Hitler decided we had too many beautiful buildings and set about destroying them. But you must have seen the Liver Birds at least.'

Sylvia laughed, a little shame-faced. 'Do you know, I haven't been down there yet. Everyone says I must see them – that they're the symbol of the city, and as long as they are there then Liverpool will never be defeated. But I've been so busy settling into my billet and starting at Derby House that I haven't had a moment.'

The sun came out from behind a cloud and shone down on them, turning Frank's hair the colour of warm molasses sugar. Sylvia smiled up at him and he couldn't resist taking the next step.

'Well then, Wren Hemsley,' he said, 'would you let me have the honour of escorting you to see our

269

fine birds? You can't really say you've been to Liverpool without that sight. It's not far, just down there and across to the river. Can I persuade you to accompany me?' Until recently he would have added, 'If you don't mind being seen with a cripple with one leg.' But he held his tongue – it was her who had approached him to begin with, after all.

She looked up directly into his eyes and smiled with pleasure. 'Thank you very much, sir. I'd be delighted.' A sunbeam caught on her shining curls and he smiled back. The sharp poignancy of his thoughts about Kitty eased a little. He decided Wren Sylvia Hemsley was somebody well worth getting to know.

Laura and Kitty walked swiftly down one corridor after another in the almost silent hospital, attempting to find the right ward from the directions a nervous receptionist had given them. Laura hadn't exactly lied to get them past the front door, but she'd let the young woman assume that they were family. She made sure her accent was at its cut-glass best, had instructed Kitty to let her do the talking, and was behaving according to one of her brother's favourite maxims: act like you belong and nobody questions your right to be there. She didn't know how far this would get them, but she was going to give it her best shot.

'This must be it. She told us to look out for the big painting of Winston Churchill.' Kitty pointed to a portrait in a heavily carved gold frame. 'It'll be one of the doors at the end.'

Laura looked to where her friend meant. French

windows at the far end of the corridor gave on to a rose garden, by the looks of it, and she thought what a beautiful sight that would have been under different circumstances. She couldn't dwell on that now, though. Every minute counted, as they could be turned back at any moment. She began to march smartly towards the doors near the full-length windows, but before she'd got far, two people emerged from one of the doorways, one in a matron's uniform and one clearly extremely senior in the navy. His gold braid shone in the light from the French windows and Laura was momentarily dazzled.

The matron did not look best pleased. She didn't shout, presumably so that her patients would not be disturbed, but she swept towards Laura and Kitty with a look of ill-disguised fury on her face. 'What do you think you are doing here?' she demanded. 'This area is not open to the public and you need security clearance to be anywhere remotely close to this corridor. You must leave here at once.'

Laura refused to be intimidated by the angry nurse. She drew herself up to her full height and made sure her shoulders were back. She didn't intend to leave the premises without finding out what had happened to Peter. 'We are here to see Captain Cavendish,' she said, steadily but utterly firmly. 'Please tell him that Wren Laura Fawcett is here.' She could sense Kitty's nervousness but she would not back down.

'You will do no such thing,' the matron replied immediately. 'Captain Cavendish is in no state for visits, and certainly not from the likes of chits

271

like you.' She pointed back the way they had come. 'Now leave this instant, or I shall report you to your commanding officer.'

Laura had expected that but she still wasn't going to turn around. She was more desperate than ever to discover what had happened to the captain. What would Freddy have done in such a situation? He'd have brazened it out, probably used his considerable charm to win the furious matron over. Laura knew she would stand little chance of that, but it didn't mean she couldn't try with the naval officer – an admiral no less, she realised, as she noticed the detail of his uniform. Well, nothing like going straight to the top.

'I wonder if you can tell me how he's doing, sir?' she said, as winsomely as she could.

The man had deep lines etched into his brow and he regarded her with the utmost seriousness. For a moment Laura thought he was going to echo the matron's command for them to leave. Then his expression changed a fraction. 'My dear young lady, did you say your name was Fawcett?' he asked.

'That's right, sir.' Laura saluted smartly.

The admiral turned to the matron. 'While it is highly irregular, and usually I would concur that this is a breach of security, I can vouch for this young lady,' he said with a sigh. 'You were Captain Cavendish's driver on the fateful evening of the UXB blast, were you not?' Laura nodded, not trusting herself to speak. 'Then I must thank you for saving my nephew's life.' The man paused and drew breath, and before he could go on Laura leapt into the gap.

'So he is still alive?' she said, hoping against hope that this was what he meant.

Wearily the admiral drew her down the corridor, the impatient matron at his side, Kitty following in consternation. When they were well out of listening distance of the far doors, he halted.

'Yes, at the moment he is still alive,' he said slowly. 'He has been gravely ill, however, and has been unconscious for some days now. Even I have been permitted to see him only for short bursts at a time, and only from a distance. I am afraid there is no question of you being allowed to visit him. He wouldn't know you were there–'

'Absolutely not,' the matron broke in. 'We cannot risk transmission of any further infections. He has enough to cope with as things stand.' She bit her lip, as if she had given away more than she intended to.

'Is he not out of danger?' Laura asked, controlling her voice with difficulty. She knew she must not reveal her true feelings, or they would tell her nothing.

The admiral's face took on an expression of deep sadness. 'I'm afraid not, my dear. All we can do is wait, and trust in the fact that before the fire he was a very healthy young man with everything to live for. Often that is what helps cases such as this pull through – that, and excellent nursing,' he added, turning to the matron. 'I appreciate you coming here. I feel all of this is rather my fault, you see. It was I who summoned him to an urgent meeting that night, and I know that meant you were forced to forgo your free evening to drive him there and back.'

Laura realised that this was the figure she had caught sight of from a distance in the doorway of the Reform Club. So the admiral was Peter's uncle, and from the tone of his voice it hadn't been a family gathering but something far more important. Had Peter had time to act upon the information he'd been given that night? How tragic if he'd been given a special mission and was now unable to complete it, all because she had chosen that particular route back to base.

'If I hadn't gone via Camden...' she began, horrified as the significance began to hit her.

'Hush, my dear.' The admiral laid his hand on her arm. 'It will do you no good to think like that. You did what you considered best, and by doing so you saved a small child. You are to be praised, not blamed. You and my nephew acted selflessly and with the utmost bravery, which cannot be wrong under any circumstances. He would have it no other way. Please do not tell yourself that you are at fault.'

Laura stared at her feet in their sensible uniform shoes, unable to meet his eyes. She'd clung to the idea that she'd be able to come to the hospital and find that all the rumours had been exaggerated, that Peter would be sitting up in bed, fit as a fiddle, and that they'd share a joke about the whole thing – how everyone was making a fuss over nothing and mollycoddling him. Now it seemed that was far from the case. She didn't think she could bear it – to lose him just as she was beginning to discover what he meant to her. First Freddy, now Peter. She gulped and held back the tears that threatened to overwhelm her.

The matron had softened slightly but was still keen for them to leave. 'Come,' she said, 'you can't stand around here. There are patients all about and we can't have them caused additional distress. Now you know what the situation is, you must go back to your base.'

Kitty stepped forward and took Laura's arm. 'Let's go,' she whispered. 'We're doing no good here. At least we know now.'

Every cell in Laura's body urged her to stay, to be close to Peter in his hour of need, but she knew that would be impossible. She couldn't even tell anyone how she felt – she barely knew herself. All she knew for certain was that she didn't want him to die. She didn't care if he barked at her to reverse in unfeasibly narrow alleys, to drive him for hours in the middle of the night, to take him to ridiculously out-of-the-way locations and back again while scarcely uttering a word. All that mattered was that he recovered.

'Would you like to be kept informed of his progress, my dear?' asked the admiral. 'I can arrange it if that is what you want.'

Laura gave herself a mental shake, recognising that this was a considerable kindness. Of course the admiral didn't know what she was thinking, but he must assume she had a keen professional interest at least.

'Yes, sir. Thank you,' she breathed. 'I would appreciate that very much. All manner of rumours have been going round and one can't help but imagine the worst.' She attempted a smile.

'Indeed. Never listen to the rumour mill, that's my advice.' He held out his hand. 'Goodbye,

Wren Fawcett, and good show.' He nodded to her and to Kitty. It was a clear dismissal, and this time they did as they were bid, making their way back through the labyrinth of silent corridors until they were out in the autumnal sunshine and dry leaves blew about their feet.

'We can get the bus,' Kitty suggested, then stopped as she saw how wretched Laura was looking. 'Are you all right, Laura? You look a bit pale. Would you rather try to find somewhere that's open where we can have a cup of tea?'

Laura shook her head. 'I think I need something a little stronger than tea, to tell the truth.' She kicked at the leaves, despair and frustration filling her heart. 'Oh Kitty, there were scores of routes I could have taken that night and I go and pick the one that could have got us killed, and now he's in there and we don't know if he'll make it.'

Impulsively Kitty gave her friend a tight hug. 'You can't blame yourself, Laura. You heard what the admiral said – gosh, imagine Killjoy Cavendish having an uncle who's an admiral. After all, if you hadn't been there, then that baby would have died – and maybe the mother too, if she was going to go back in after it like you told us. You're both heroes. Captain Cavendish would have known the risk he was taking. He's probably done all sorts of training for that sort of thing.'

'Probably,' Laura agreed, but she knew it had been an instinctive reaction that had driven him into that burning building. All the training in the world wouldn't have changed the essential facts. The image of him throwing the baby to her and then how he teetered for those awful few seconds on the windowsill came back into her mind and she could have screamed. She'd thought that was when he was in greatest danger, but she'd been wrong. Now he was in that silent wing of the hospital with the formidable matron, no doubt receiving the best possible care, but fighting for his life all the same. She remembered how he had touched her nose, and a groan rose to her throat. Now she would never know what was behind his expression when he'd done that; if it was a joke, or if he'd sensed some deeper, more vital connection between them. Had she imagined it? The prospect of going through the rest of her life not knowing would be unbearable. Yet that was what she was faced with. She didn't know if she could do it.

'Come on, then,' Kitty urged her, breaking away and then linking her arm through her friend's. 'We should be back at base in time for tea. Let's not hang about. At least now we can put anyone right about the captain. We should tell Marjorie; she'll want to know. She rather liked him.'

'Likes him,' said Laura fiercely. 'Not liked. He's not dead yet.'

'Likes him,' Kitty corrected herself, not reacting to her friend's abruptness. 'Anyway, she'll want to hear what we've been up to. Funny that you feel this way now, considering he was your very worst passenger, isn't it? It's such a coincidence that both of you were in the car when the bomb went off. Anyway, it makes a change from you always complaining about him.'

Laura felt her heart contract with sorrow. Kitty had no way of knowing how her words were twisting the knife, and there was little point in confessing why it hurt so much. 'Yes, that's right,' she said instead. 'It's all I ever did. He was a confounded nuisance and made my life hell day in day out, but I don't want him to die. I really, really don't.'

CHAPTER TWENTY-FIVE

'There's absolutely nothing in it, Winnie, and nobody will convince me any different,' Vera Delaney assured her friend as she drained her cup of tea. 'I just thought you should know what folk are saying so you can be prepared next time you go out and bump into them. Some people will do anything to spread a bit of gossip, you know that.'

Winnie nodded glumly.

'Not that you've been out and about much recently,' Vera added, snapping shut her battered handbag and getting up to leave Winnie's cramped table. 'Not that I blame you. I always tell them as says you're hiding away from them that you've got enough on your plate what with managing a shop when there's a war on and taking in that girl out of the goodness of your heart. Just because she was left homeless when the house where your Charlie was staying got bombed. They should be praising you for doing a good deed, not casting aspersions about you and her.' She stopped to snatch a breath. 'Talking of which,' she said slyly, 'heard anything from him lately, have you? Your Charlie?' She turned her gimlet eyes on her friend. 'Only my Alfie was asking about him. Alfie's working ever so hard down the docks now half of the men have joined up, and it's wearing him out; sometimes I hardly see him from one end of the week to the next. It's no soft option having a reserved occupation, no matter what anyone says to the contrary. He's doing his bit for king and country and almost dropping dead of exhaustion, and I won't hear a word said against him. Do let Charlie know he was asking after him if you hear from him, won't you?' She waited eagerly for an answer. She'd give her ration book to know the whereabouts of Charlie Kennedy. Alfie had dropped several hints that his associates – Vera didn't question him too closely about who they might be – would love to find him, and might even be prepared to give a reward to anyone who could say where he was likely to be. Then of course the military police were after him as a deserter – plenty of people had seen them come knocking more than once on Winnie's door, for all that she denied it.

Winnie made a noise that could have meant anything, and then got to her feet. 'Don't let me keep you, Vera,' she said, a touch of the old firmness in her voice. 'I know how busy you are, what with your boy still being at home.' She waited until the other woman had left and then sank back on to her favourite seat in the breakfast room behind the shop. She could imagine Vera walking down the street, head held high, turning to look around her, no doubt keeping an eye out for anyone else she could pass her malicious tales on to.

The sound of the door to the back yard made her jump. 'Rita? Is that you?'

Rita poked her head around the breakfast room door. 'I thought you still had company or I'd have come in,' she said. She was in her nurse's cloak, ready to go out. 'Vera's gone, has she?'

'Good riddance to bad rubbish,' said Winnie viciously, with more energy than Rita had heard from her for ages. 'No, don't go, I want a word with you.'

Rita obliged, wondering what it was this time. It had been so long since Winnie had used that tone of voice with her that she'd almost forgotten how unpleasant the old woman could be. 'Can you make it quick, Winnie? Only I'm running late already.'

'Late for that hospital where you never should have got a job in the first place, do you mean?' Winnie spat, her long-held grudge resurfacing. 'Let them wait for once. I need looking after too, you know.'

'You're fitter than many your age,' Rita began firmly, but that wasn't what Winnie was after.

'Who've you been talking to?' she demanded. 'Vera said people know about Ruby, where she came from. They're all out there saying she's my bastard and it can only have come from you. What do you mean by it, blackening my good name like that?'

Rita had to stop the reply that first came into her mind, that it wasn't blackening Winnie's name to repeat what was simply the truth: she was Ruby's biological mother, and had conceived the child out of wedlock and then palmed her off on the

280

loathsome Elsie Lowe. But that wouldn't help the situation, and besides, she hadn't breathed a word since the night they'd found Winnie's secret box of documents during the raid. It suited Winnie to blame Rita, when really it was as clear as the nose on her face to anyone that Ruby was related to her. Winnie's sullen silence on the matter had fanned the flames of the local tittle-tattlers and she only had herself to blame. However, Rita didn't want to become entangled in an argument when her patients were waiting. Instead she took a deep breath and replied calmly.

'Why would I tell anyone that, Winnie? It does nobody any good to make that public.'

'Because you are always looking for a chance to tell lies about me!' raged Winnie, her face going an unhealthy colour as her temper rose. 'First you say all sorts of evil nonsense about my Charlie, and now you're out spreading gossip about me and that useless girl who hangs around the house doing nothing. Well, you can stop it, and kindly tell your excuses for friends that they've got it wrong.'

'That will only add fuel to the fire,' Rita pointed out. 'I don't have time for this now, Winnie. I'm sorry to hear the news has got out but, before you say anything more, I'll tell you straight, it's only because it'll upset Ruby if she thinks folk are talking about her and branding her a bastard. She's the sweetest girl alive, which you'd know for yourself if you ever bothered talking to her or tried to get to know her. She's also been a big help in keeping the shop going – not that you'd know that either, as a fat lot of use you've been since she got here. We'd have gone under if it wasn't for her, so put that in your pipe and smoke it.' She wheeled around. 'Now I'm off. Don't worry, I'm not going to say anything. But you might manage a kind word to her, if you've got it in you, rather than running her down all the time.' She slammed the outside door behind her before she said anything else she might regret.

Walking swiftly along the main road, hoping to catch a bus now they were running more regularly, she wondered what this might mean. Maybe Winnie was coming out of her shell again, ready for a fight. That wasn't good news, whichever way she looked at it. But perhaps it was inevitable; Rita wasn't sure that she'd have wanted her mother-in-law to quietly drink herself to death, no matter how much she disliked her. Meanwhile Ruby would need looking after, and it was such a shame, as the girl had been gaining confidence recently and was even going out on her own. Perhaps that was what had started it; people would have begun to speculate who she was and why Winnie, not famous for her charity, had taken her in.

Rita knew that none of her own family, who were among the very few who knew the truth, would have spread the news deliberately. But Empire Street was such a close-knit community; they were all living cheek by jowl in the terraced houses, and the walls were shakier than ever after all the bombing. There was no such thing as soundproofing and everyone knew everyone else's business. It was perfectly possible that Dolly or Violet or Sarah had been overheard through an open window or door, and all it would have taken was one sentence and the word would have got round. Rita swore under her breath as she reached the bus stop. She didn't want Ruby to be upset – she was becoming genuinely fond of the girl and knew that Michael and Megan thought the world of her. When they'd recently gone to the farm on Pop's cart, the children had been beside themselves with delight to see her, and hadn't wanted her to go. They'd only managed to leave when Pop and Rita had promised to bring her back again soon.

A further reason to keep Ruby happy was her clever way of analysing the figures and the stock. She'd worked out when it was going missing and when it was likely to happen again if the pattern continued. Rita prayed the girl was right and they could do something about it. She broke off her train of thought as a bus drew up and she nodded to the conductor before sinking on to the un-accustomed luxury of a seat to herself. She looked out of the window as they passed the war-ravaged buildings, the shops and houses ruined by the May blitz. She counted forward in her mind to the next likely dates. If all went well, then one of them would be during Jack's forthcoming leave. She sighed from the depths of her heart. If only she'd married Jack and not Charlie. If only Jack were here to help her with the incessant problems that beset her at every turn. How she needed him, what a comfort his loving arms would be. But she couldn't have him. Her longing was suddenly so intense that she could hardly stand up to get off at her stop near the hospital. Enough of that, my girl, she told herself sternly. You made your bed, now you have to lie in it. But oh how she wished things had been different.

For once the shift passed swiftly and without major incident, and Rita was reminded once again just how much she enjoyed her job. Even better, today she was on the same shift as her favourite colleague, Maeve Kerrigan. Maeve had a temper as fiery as her hair, but she'd learned to tame both, and was now a highly competent nurse. Rita could relax when she was around, knowing there would be no mistakes and everything that needed to be done would be done, and far more besides. Maeve took no nonsense from anybody, patients or staff, irrespective of their rank. Occasionally this annoyed those who didn't know her well, particularly those of middle rank who felt they deserved respect purely because of their position. Maeve didn't care. The lowliest private got the same diligent attention from her as a major general.

'I reckon we've earned a few minutes to put our feet up,' Maeve said, stacking the last of her reports in a neat pile ready to hand over to the next shift. 'Wait till you see what I've brought with me.'

Rita watched as Maeve reached into her locker and took out a tin. It was brightly coloured, if a little scratched. She opened it with a flourish. 'Ta da! Seed cake!'

'Ooh, where did you get that?' Rita breathed. She hadn't had any cake since she'd been to the farm. It was just too hard to get hold of sugar, eggs and butter. Things had been different when Kitty lived over the road, as she always seemed able to get a few ingredients and was famed for making something out of nothing. This was a rare treat.

'My neighbour got it at a WVS sale, and then she got toothache and felt she shouldn't risk it,' Maeve said with delight. She found a knife and set about cutting them generous slices. 'She likes me because I cleaned up some minor cuts she got from broken glass in a raid. One good turn deserves another, I'd say.'

Rita nodded in agreement, but she couldn't answer as her mouth was too full. It was a taste of heaven, and all the more welcome after the busy shift.

'Have you heard anything from our Sid recently?' Maeve went on. Sid, Nancy's husband, was Maeve's cousin. It had been a surprise to find that she was working alongside his sister-in-law, Rita. It meant that she sometimes had news of him to pass back to her family over in Ireland, who found Maeve a more reliable source of information than Sid's morose mother.

Rita brushed a crumb from her top lip. 'Not really. Nancy got a letter via the Red Cross about a week ago, but there's nothing new to say. He's alive, he's not being treated too badly, he wishes he could see Georgie. That's about it.'

'And how's Nancy?' Maeve wanted to know.

'Oh, you know Nancy,' Rita said with a laugh. 'She's carrying on much as normal. She's still living with your auntie, but you wouldn't know it from the amount of time she spends at Mam's, and she's always leaving Georgie there. Not that Mam or Violet object to that, of course. Still, Nancy's living it up now. She's only gone and got herself a volunteering position at the WVS station in the city centre. She's quite an expert in showing visiting servicemen the ropes. She was telling me she's offered to give them guided tours, particularly the US engineers who are over here because of the Lend Lease Agreement. She says it helps them to feel at home.'

'Nice work if you can get it,' said Maeve.

'They seem to appreciate it, that's for sure. If the amount of nylons she gets given are any measure of it, anyway,' Rita added. 'I can't remember when I last had a new pair.'

'Me neither,' said Maeve, looking down at her sensible lisle stockings. 'Not that I have any occasion to wear them. They'd be wasted around here, for a start.'

'You're right there.' Rita sighed. 'Sometimes I almost forget what it was like to get all dolled up and go out dancing. Not that I ever did much of that on account of having Michael so young.'

'Your day might yet come,' Maeve told her encouragingly. 'Just think, when this war is over, your children might be almost old enough to look after themselves. They'll probably be quite independent after being evacuated. Then you'll have time to go out and enjoy yourself – think of that.'

Rita laughed and shook her head. 'I don't think so. Well, yes, they're learning heaps on the farm that they'd never have been able to at home, and Megan's finally speaking up for herself. She's beginning to write short letters, and she sends pictures – you should have seen the one she did of a dead chicken. Apparently a fox got it. She really went to town with all the blood everywhere.' Rita felt anxious suddenly, remembering Megan's words about the shadow man. Surely that couldn't

286

have anything to do with the dead bird? She tried to shake off her unease. 'They're spoilt rotten, though. Anyway, who would I go dancing with? If Charlie ever dares to show his face again, we won't be going down the Grafton, that's for certain.'

'No news from Jack, then?'

Rita sometimes wondered if it had been wise to have admitted to Maeve that she was still in contact with Jack, fearing that word could somehow get back to Empire Street and reach Winnie's ears. But things were complicated enough as they were, without adding another layer of subterfuge. So she'd poured her heart out one time when they were on night shift, confessing how she felt and the impossibility of it all – but she'd left out the fact that Jack was actually Michael's real father. That was a secret she would keep until Michael himself was ready to be told – if that ever happened. It certainly wouldn't be while she was still married to Charlie, and she could see no way out of that which didn't involve betraying every value she held dear.

Now she pulled a wry face. 'He's due leave later this month. He's told me the dates but we all know these things can change; it'll all depend on what's happening to the convoys in the Atlantic.' She knew Jack would always put his duty as an experienced member of the Fleet Air Arm before anything else, and she would have it no other way. Then the sound of footsteps silenced her, as she had no intention of letting anyone else overhear their conversation. Jack's precious letters were too sacred a secret to share any further.

'Hello, hello, what's all this?' A warm voice

came from the figure who had rounded the corner into the nurses' welfare area.

'Dr Fitzgerald!' Maeve said. 'I didn't realise you were on duty or I'd have let you know in advance what I've brought in with me. Come and join us.' Many nurses wouldn't have dared to be so informal with any of the doctors, but Maeve wasn't going to stand on ceremony. Besides, everyone knew that he was sweet on Rita's friend Kitty. 'Pull up a chair.'

'Don't mind if I do,' said Elliott, happily accepting a slice of seed cake. 'I'm due on shift in half an hour, but this will set me up properly. Much appreciated, I'm sure.'

Rita put down her own plate with a sigh of satisfaction. 'Good to see you, Doctor. It seems like ages since we were on the same shift. What have you been up to?'

Elliott beamed. 'Well, I've been covering lots of nights and putting in some extra hours so that I can have a long weekend and go away to London. I'll be staying with my parents and, as I'm sure you know already, Nurse Kennedy, I intend to introduce them to Kitty. I'm certain they will love her.'

'Of course they will!' Rita couldn't imagine anybody not loving her friend. 'She sounds as if she's doing so well, from her letters. To think that this time last year she was running the canteen, and now she's living the high life ... well, when she's not on yet another training course.'

'They work them hard all right,' Elliott agreed. 'But that's typical Kitty, throwing herself into everything, making the most of every opportunity.

I'm so proud of her.' His warm eyes shone, and for a moment Rita wished she had somebody like Elliott to be proud of her like that. He was clearly very serious about Kitty. To begin with, she had wondered if he would last the course, or if he was just toying with her friend until someone of his own social class came along, but obviously she'd got that all wrong. He was genuinely thrilled to be introducing her to his parents. Also, he didn't begrudge that she was living her own life far away from Liverpool, and approved of it thoroughly. Lucky Kitty.

'Well, must be getting on,' he said now. 'There are some scheduled operations to attend to, so I'd better get scrubbed up. Thank you for the delicious cake. Tell you what, I'll return the favour once I'm back from London, and then I can give you all Kitty's news at the same time. How about that?'

'It's a deal,' Rita assured him, thinking again that Kitty was a very fortunate girl. Elliott was not only kind and fun to have around, she had to admit he was good looking too, and plenty of nurses' noses had been put out of joint when he'd chosen Kitty above any of them. But there was no doubt about it – Kitty was the only girl for him. That look in his eyes when he spoke of her couldn't be faked. Even if her own life was lacking in love, Rita thought, things were going right for her friend at last.

CHAPTER TWENTY-SIX

It had been a week since they'd talked their way into the hospital, and it felt like the longest seven days of Laura's life. She didn't count waiting for news of Freddy – that was a constant background ache that she could do nothing about. With Peter it was knowing that he was only a few miles away and, no matter what anyone said, he was in that hospital partly because of her. She couldn't shake the guilt, the weight of it pressing her down with every step she took. People still came up to her and congratulated her for saving the baby, and it was agony to answer politely, thanking them and giving them a short version of what had happened. Even her usually brusque commanding officer had praised her, suggesting that Laura might be able to have half a day of extra leave in recognition of what she had done.

Laura had refused as civilly as she could, but she had wanted to shout back at the very idea. The only thing that was keeping her going was being on duty. When she was driving she had to concentrate so hard to avoid potholes or roads closed for no reason, or cope with the lack of street signs and the poor-to-non-existent lighting that she had no time to think of anything else. Plenty of other officers demanded that she be their driver, keen to boast that they'd been ferried about by the heroine of the hour. Some had wanted to make conversation, some wanted to flirt, but Laura didn't react. Not that she would have done so anyway – flirting was strictly for when she was off duty. Now, though, she just didn't have it in her to respond to any such overtures. The light-hearted banter and joking that she used to enjoy so much now seemed stupid and shallow.

She had come to dread her free time. Whereas before she'd always been the one to organise trips to the cinema or Lyons Corner House, now she didn't want to stray far from base in case she missed a phone call, or the admiral trying to get word to her by some other means. On the other hand, she couldn't sit still, and would pace around the dormitory, canteen or common room with restless energy. It was making her a nervous wreck. It was making her bad-tempered with everyone, biting the head off anyone who tried to make light conversation, but everybody assumed it was a de-layed reaction to the night of the fire and didn't take offence. Laura wished someone would – a good old blazing row might help vent her mount-ing frustration. Yet all the people around her – from the canteen staff to her superior officers – just smiled and said they understood.

The awful thing was of course that nobody did understand what was at the root of it all, not even her closest friends. She'd allowed them to carry on thinking that Peter was nothing special, that she was so upset because she'd chosen that particular route – and to some extent that was true. But underneath it all was the agony of not knowing what that expression had meant when he'd reached out to touch her, and the idea that he

291

might die without her having the chance to find out. She had to know, she had to. Even if it was just a joke on his part, she would rather know. Yet it was likely that she never would. The longer the silence went on with no news from the hospital, the more the cold hand of dread closed around her heart. The infection must have taken hold and he must be fighting it. How long could he go on doing that? Even if he was extremely fit to start with, wouldn't the body have to give up sooner or later?

Angrily she pushed a chair out of the way and almost ran down the corridor, desperate suddenly for fresh air. She would walk around the grounds, and then she could get rid of some of this useless energy that fizzed through her veins, but she'd be within reach when the vital message finally arrived. If it ever did.

'Laura! Wait a minute!' Kitty was hurrying after her. 'Where are you off to in such a hurry?'

Laura sighed and waited for her friend. 'Oh, nowhere. Thought I'd take a stroll around the block, stretch my legs. Make the most of it being a fine day. What are you doing here? Have you finished early?'

Kitty looked at Laura with concern. There were shadows under her eyes, and her hair, usually so glossy, hung lank around her gaunt face. 'Yes, we're meant to be learning about the most up-to-date telephone system, but the demonstration material got delayed and won't be here until tomorrow, so they let us go. I thought they might make us do extra square bashing, but for once they didn't.'

'Good thing too,' said Laura, trying to act normally. 'We're all pretty expert at bashing those squares by now.'

'We are,' Kitty agreed. 'I'll come with you if you don't mind. I've been inside nearly all day and could do with some fresh air.' She buttoned her uniform jacket, which she hadn't had time to take off, and linked her arm through her friend's. 'I've been meaning to ask you,' she said as they stepped outside and the keen breeze hit their faces, 'would I be able to borrow another frock? You said before you wouldn't mind.'

Laura nodded. 'Of course. Ah, has the dashing doctor got leave, then? That's the only thing that gets you all dressed up, if I'm not much mistaken.'

Kitty laughed. 'You've got it in one. Yes, he's got his dates confirmed and he's going to come for a long weekend. He'll stay with his parents, and I'm going to meet them this time. He's asked before, of course, but I thought it was too soon. Now, though, it feels right. I thought I should look my best though.'

'Oh, you don't scrub up so badly when it comes to it,' Laura said, trying to be happy for her friend. 'You'll look wonderful, Kitty, and he'll be proud of you. I shall make it my mission to have you as near to perfect as can be.'

'Thanks, Laura,' said Kitty warmly. Even though she was far more confident about the meeting these days, it would be a huge boost to have Laura's lovely clothes and the power of her expert eye to ensure she looked the part of a rising young doctor's girlfriend. 'I really hope he doesn't have to cancel for any reason. There have been hardly any raids over Merseyside for ages now, though. He says it's been much quieter, so he thinks it will be all right.'

Laura squeezed Kitty's arm. 'Of course it will. He won't cancel; he'll be far too keen to get down here to see you.'

Kitty nodded, knowing it was true – he really did want to be here with her, and this time she was bubbling with excitement at the thought of seeing him again. But she had to put her excitement to one side and find out what was wrong with her friend. She wasn't fooled by Laura's light tone for an instant. She'd come to recognise how clever Laura could be at putting up a brave front, but she knew she wasn't sleeping – she was restless nearly all night. It was most unlike her to want to mooch about in the grounds when there were more exciting things to do only a short bus ride away.

She wondered how best to broach the subject. Laura had been touchy – to say the least – over the past few days; downright rude sometimes. But she mustn't let that deter her. Finally she decided to come straight out with it.

They came to a halt under a tree that was rapidly losing the last of its leaves. 'Laura, hang on a minute.' Kitty faced her squarely. 'You aren't acting yourself,' she told her friend. 'I know the night of the fire was pretty bad, but is that all that's wrong? Why aren't you sleeping properly?'

Laura fought the instant desire to fling herself away, to say it was none of Kitty's business. She'd come out here to try to escape her whirling thoughts, not to have to explain them. But Kitty had that determined look about her, and Laura knew she couldn't avoid her easily for long. But how was she to begin when she didn't fully understand herself?

'Oh, I don't know.' She clenched her fists. 'It's hard to say, it's such a muddle.'

'Try, Laura.'

'Well, it's complicated. I'm probably imagining the whole thing. Yes, it's to do with the night of the fire, of course it is. But it's not just the fire.' She paused to gather her words, to try to make sense of the conflicting emotions raging within her. 'It's Peter being in hospital. It feels like partly that's my fault.'

'Yes, I know, you said. But it isn't really. Remember what they said at the hospital – you know deep down it's not because of you. The pair of you could have turned away but you didn't and you saved the child.'

'There's more, or maybe there isn't,' Laura groaned. 'It was being in that fire with Peter. I thought he wasn't going to make it, but sort of didn't have a second to think about it properly at the time ... we just had to get the baby and then get out. Then I helped him to walk because he was injured, and suddenly I didn't hate him any more. It was like ... I don't know. As if we fitted together. I thought he'd be furious but he wasn't. Then, at the police station, he was so kind and funny. Now I look back, he must have been in agony, but he didn't say, he was just human for once. It's so hard to describe, I couldn't even put it into words before.'

'And you realised you didn't hate him after all,' Kitty prompted.

'Something like that,' Laura admitted. 'It wasn't as if he said much, it was just somehow completely different between us. Or I thought so, anyway. Something changed, something that felt terribly important. But now he's fighting for his life and I might never know.'

'Oh, Laura.' Kitty reached out and gave her friend a hug. 'That's bitterly unfair, isn't it? And you can't even see him to find out.'

'That's about it,' said Laura, feeling slightly better now that her torment of a secret was out at last. 'It's crazy; you hear all the time of how people find each other in the intensity of danger, and look how some of that turns out. I don't want to jump to conclusions, I just want to *know*.' She fought down a sob. 'And I don't want him to die. He's such a brave man. I know he can be annoying and rude and standoffish, but when it came down to it, he didn't hesitate.'

'Neither did you,' Kitty pointed out loyally. 'He would have known that. He would have seen how courageous you were.'

Laura nodded slowly. She hadn't thought of that. Perhaps that was what some of the sense of connection had been about – mutual respect. What a terrible waste if he should die and they couldn't see where that took them. But she had to face it.

'He might die, Kitty, and then I'll never know,' she said tiredly.

'No,' said Kitty, 'but you'll always know you both did the right thing.' She paused. There was nothing else she could say to ease her friend's agony, as any reassurances she could give would be false and they both knew it. What a cruel twist of fate. 'I'm glad you told me,' she added. 'We were worried about you, you know. Look, I suppose we should go back in. You could try to get some rest before we go to the canteen.'

She took Laura's arm and began to lead the way back to the main building. Laura patted her face. 'Do I look a fright?' she asked. 'I know I've let myself go a bit this week.'

'Don't worry,' Kitty said, but before she could go on, a smartly uniformed leading Wren came out of a side door and marched towards them.

'Wren Fawcett? I've been looking for you everywhere,' she barked sternly. 'Telephone call from the admiral's office. I don't know what you've been doing but it's urgent.'

Laura's eyes grew wide and her step faltered.

'Did they say what it was?' Kitty asked hurriedly.

The senior Wren glared at her. 'Obviously not. You are wanted immediately, Fawcett. Look sharp.'

CHAPTER TWENTY-SEVEN

'Not again.' Sarah sighed wearily as the air-raid siren sounded out its wailing cry, and Georgie instantly joined in. She had just come off shift from her post down near the docks and wanted nothing more than a quiet night in. She hadn't even had time for a cup of tea, although the kettle was always warm in Dolly's kitchen.

It had been so long since they'd had a raid over Bootle that Sarah had come to believe they'd be spared from now on. She struggled to remember what to do, what to bring to the shelter. There should be a bag somewhere with all the essentials in it, but had they topped it up since last time?

Dolly swept in from the back yard, all purpose and organisation. 'Don't just stand there, our Sarah, but fetch me down that tin from the top shelf. I've got some emergency biscuits put by. Then make a flask of tea, quick. Georgie, don't worry, we've done this before, haven't we? Go to Auntie Violet, she's in the parlour, she'll sort you out.'

Georgie looked up at his grandmother, his big eyes uncertain; but once reassured by her comforting tone, he ran into the front room as he was told.

'Oh Mam, I can't face the thought of that shelter,' said Sarah, exhausted from running around all day. She took down the tin and passed it to Dolly, before pulling on her worn-out coat over the cardigan she'd knitted from old wool that had been unravelled from one of Pop's ancient jumpers. It wasn't a colour she'd have picked out herself, but beggars couldn't be choosers. 'I thought all of that was over.'

Dolly looked steadily at her youngest child, registering how tired she seemed, but now wasn't the time for defeatist attitudes. 'Come on, love,' she said briskly. 'That's not like you. We need you to help get everyone sorted out and to safety. Here's the flask, look – you get that filled while I pack the blankets. Where's the big torch? Let me

298

just check the batteries are all right. Violet will get Georgie into his siren suit. Thank goodness I'm not on fire-watching duty tonight, I can help out with him.'

Sarah poured the hot water for the tea, carefully closing the stopper on the enamel flask. The last thing they wanted was anyone getting burnt from it. 'Where's Rita, Mam? Has she stopped by to-day?'

Dolly shook her head. 'She's on lates, she'll be at the hospital now. We'll just have to keep our fingers crossed they are all right over there.' She sent up a quick prayer for her eldest daughter, who she knew full well would put the safety of her patients above her own. 'Well, that means one of us should go and check that Ruby knows what to do. I can't see Winnie doing anything to help her.'

Sarah groaned. She avoided going to the shop if she could, partly because Violet always brought back whatever they needed, but also because she couldn't stand Winnie. But now Violet was busy and she knew that Rita would want somebody to do it. She didn't have a choice.

'All right, I'll go.' She put the flask of tea into Dolly's capacious bag. 'I'll see you down at the shelter.'

Swiftly she crossed the alley over to the corner shop, and went round to the back door. She tapped on it. 'Ruby! Are you there?'

The door swung open and Winnie glared at her. 'What do you want? Come round to get more fuel for your gossiping lies, have you?'

Sarah noticed how the old woman had lost weight since she'd last seen her, her skin sagging from prominent cheekbones, her jaw slack but her eyes bright with spite. 'No, I've come to see Ruby to the shelter,' Sarah replied firmly, drawing on her nurse's training to remain calm under threat. She'd faced far worse than a vindictive neighbour over the last few months and couldn't let this encounter rattle her. 'Will you come too, Mrs Kennedy?' She thought it best to ask, even though she could guess the answer.

'Down to that fleapit? They let anybody in there,' snarled Winnie. 'You wouldn't catch me dead in there.' Sarah didn't say that she might well wind up dead if she didn't go. She could tell it would be pointless. 'I'll be perfectly safe in my own cellar, thank you very much.'

Sarah didn't try to persuade her otherwise – she could see the old woman's mind was made up. But she still had to find the younger woman. 'Is Ruby in there? She needs to come with me.'

Winnie tutted loudly, but Sarah could see Ruby's shock of white-blonde hair in the dimness of the kitchen doorway. She was loitering shyly, not wanting to provoke Winnie when she was in a temper. Sarah coaxed her forward. 'Come on, Ruby, you have to get to the shelter. Have you got some warm things to wear? We've got tea and biscuits so you won't go hungry.' Sarah thought it was ironic – here was Ruby living above the gold-mine of Winnie's hoard, which probably contained enough biscuits to feed the whole of Bootle, and here she was offering the girl her own.

Ruby edged closer. She reached to take what looked like a shapeless jersey off a hook, and emerged into the dim light of the yard. 'Thank you,' she said quietly. 'Did Rita send you?'

'Rita's at the hospital, I'll look after you,' Sarah said hurriedly. She didn't want to be caught in Winnie's back yard if the bombs started falling. 'She'll be safe there, but she would want you to come with me.'

Ruby shot a look at Winnie, but the old woman turned away. 'All right, if Rita says so,' Ruby said uncertainly.

'And Violet will be at the shelter with Georgie,' Sarah went on. 'Are you ready? Right then, let's go.' She didn't want to wait any longer. She took the young woman's arm and led her away, with Winnie still glaring at them from the back door. 'Quick, Ruby, let's not hang about.'

The pair of them hurried down Empire Street, as neighbours emerged from their doorways from both sides. Sarah spotted Danny ahead of them and called out. 'Danny! Wait for us!'

He turned and waved, and if he was surprised to see Ruby hanging on to Sarah's arm, he didn't say so.

Sarah could feel that Ruby was nervous but she couldn't do much about it. 'You know Danny,' she said as they drew level with him. 'He'll look after us both, you'll see.' She flashed Danny a grateful smile. She felt safer when he was around, knowing he wouldn't let her come to any harm if he could possibly avert it.

'Hurry up, ladies,' he said now, seemingly relaxed. 'It's probably nothing, but we'd better get to that shelter as fast as we can.' He offered to take Sarah's satchel, which she'd hurriedly slung around her shoulder. 'What's in there, Sarah? All your precious bits and pieces?' he joked.

'Yes, exactly,' said Sarah smartly, to let Ruby know he was teasing. 'My most precious possession ever – my first-aid kit. I'm never seen out without it, I'll have you know.'

'Glad to hear it.' Danny was about to gently tease her some more when one of the neighbours, Mrs Pinkerton, stopped by the gutter and pointed.

'Well, look who it is.' Her face was a mixture of delight and malice. 'Winnie Kennedy's illegitimate daughter! Where do you think you're going? This is a shelter for respectable folk and space is limited, I'll have you know.'

Ruby froze to the spot in shock, gazing at the woman in horror.

'Cat got your tongue, has it?' the woman went on, seizing on her target's weakness. 'I should think so; you can't have anything good to say for yourself. I wonder you have the nerve to walk down our street, bastard that you are.'

Sarah gasped at the woman's crass rudeness. Rita had warned her that the news had got out, but she hadn't thought anything about it in the urgency to help the girl to the shelter. Now the angry woman was blocking their way, her shoulders drawn back in self-righteousness. What Sarah didn't know, because Rita hadn't known either, was if any of the gossip had reached Ruby's ears. Had she realised the old woman with whom she shared a house, who treated her with such contempt, was actually her mother? From Ruby's reaction now, Sarah would have guessed not.

'What?' she breathed, her face white in the remaining light. 'What is she saying, Sarah?'

'Don't you listen to her, we need to get to the shelter,' Sarah said firmly, linking her arm more tightly around Ruby's. 'She's just making trouble because she's got nothing better to do.' She stared straight at Mrs Pinkerton, as if daring her to interfere any further.

Danny stepped in, using all his charm. 'Now then, Mrs Pinkerton, we all need to get to the end of the street, so how's about you turn around and come with us. Let's not be having any more of these silly rumours.' He could see the woman had the potential to cause a whole lot of trouble, which was the last thing they needed at the moment.

'Don't you soft-soap me, Danny Callaghan.' Mrs Pinkerton was having none of it. 'You might use that voice on all them silly young girls to get them to drop their knickers, but I can tell you it won't wash with me.'

Danny closed his eyes in momentary horror at the image. He'd never used his looks or voice to seduce girls, although he could have if he'd wanted to. He certainly didn't want to use them on Mrs Pinkerton. 'Now then, let's not say any-thing we might regret,' he began, trying to pour oil on troubled waters. 'If you'd just step aside...'

'I'll do no such thing.' The woman was getting more and more enraged, oblivious to the danger they were all now in. 'She's not coming into the shelter and that's all there is to it. I'm amazed she has the gall to walk down the street. We don't want your sort here,' she turned her rage from Danny to Ruby, 'so you can bloody well find somewhere else to hide. You're a disgrace, and your mother is no better, putting on all those airs and graces for years, pretending she was better than everyone, looking down her nose at her customers. Well, it's not going to work any more.'

Sarah was just beginning to realise that half the problem was that Mrs Pinkerton hadn't been one of Winnie's cronies; she would have missed out on all the black-market luxury goods available only to the select few, so was using this as an excuse to blacken Winnie's name. But there wasn't time to dwell on this, because she felt Ruby's hand break free, and to her horror the girl began to run in the opposite direction to the shelter, down the dock road. Frantically Sarah turned and ran after her, shouting, but Ruby was fast and they could hear her terrified cries of 'no, no, no...'

'And good riddance!' Mrs Pinkerton shouted in triumph, before heading into the shelter and slamming the big door shut.

Danny sped after the two young women, regardless of what such a pace would do to his damaged heart, and caught up with them just as the all-too-familiar drone of enemy aircraft began. 'Come on,' he said urgently. 'Don't mind her, Ruby, she's just a poisonous old bag with nothing better to do. We've got to get to safety, we can't stand around out here – we're sitting targets if we do that.'

Sarah looked into the evening sky and could see the lights from the ground defences sweeping the edges of the clouds. The ack-ack guns would start any minute. Danny was right, they couldn't stay out here. She shivered in apprehension.

'Ruby, come on, don't be daft. She's talking nonsense. We have to get inside.'

Ruby trembled uncontrollably. 'She hates me

and I don't know why. What does she mean about Winnie? What's going on?'

'She doesn't hate you, she doesn't even know you,' Sarah said insistently, taking the girl's arm once more and beginning to lead her back along the dock road. 'You have to ignore what she said, or she'll have won; she'll have got her way and stopped you getting to safety. That's right. Come with us. Danny, you take her other arm, look, we're nearly there.'

Suddenly there was an enormous explosion and everywhere lit up, the docks illuminated in the orange glow as sparks flew and fires took hold.

Oh no, thought Sarah, we're too late. She struggled to stand, shifting her treasured satchel so she could support Ruby. Danny glanced anxiously at her.

'You all right, Sar?'

'Right as rain,' Sarah said staunchly, though she felt anything but. 'Come on, let's get to the shelter door.'

Ruby was moaning now – not in the way she had before, full of terror and incomprehension, but in what Sarah recognised as pain.

'Ruby, what ... oh no.' Sarah looked down and saw blood, a bright stream of it along the pavement, shiny in the orange light. 'Ruby, what is it, can you walk?' There was glass all around, jagged edges reflecting the sparks and the fire from the ack-ack guns. The smell of burning drifted towards them.

Ruby didn't reply but just gasped.

'Come on, we'll carry her to the shelter.' Danny didn't hesitate, but picked up the girl as if she weighed no more than a bag of sugar, and half ran with her the short remaining distance to the shelter door. He banged on it and shouted, 'Let us in! It's Sarah Feeny and Danny Callaghan! We've got a wounded woman with us!'

For a moment they couldn't hear a reply as the noise all around was so loud, of glass shattering and buildings collapsing. Then came a firm voice. 'We're full. You'll have to go elsewhere.'

'Mam!' cried Sarah, panicking now. 'Mam, make them let us in!' But if Dolly had heard them, they couldn't tell, as more and more thunderous noises joined the cacophony, explosion following explosion. Bootle yet again was taking a pounding from the Luftwaffe, and there could be little hope for anyone directly caught out.

'Sar, it's no good.' Danny knew he had to keep his head and improvise now if they weren't going to get into the shelter. 'Look, we have to get Ruby somewhere where she can keep still. How about over there?' He pointed to the large porch of the Sailor's Rest. Its solid pillars had withstood all the bombings of the May blitz and, although there was some broken glass by the steps, the basic structure still seemed undamaged. 'It'll do for now. Come on.'

Knowing that hesitation could kill them, Sarah agreed, and they half carried Ruby, now moaning and semi-conscious, to the porch. Danny hurriedly swept debris aside with his foot and they all collapsed on to the cold stone, huddling as close as they could to the wooden bar-room doors.

'That's it, that's it,' Sarah said as calmly as she could, pushing aside her remaining panic. She tried to breathe deeply, pretending she was on duty and knowing that people's lives depended on her. 'Danny, take my torch from my satchel and I'll have a look.' Gently she examined Ruby's injured leg. 'That's it, that's where you've been hurt.' She gave a small prayer of thanks that it wasn't an internal injury, which she could have done little about. Then she set about cleaning the deep cut as best she could, deftly removing shards of glass with her nurse's tweezers, sluicing out the wound with her precious disinfectant, and finally, when she was as satisfied as she could be that she'd got it all out, she covered the wound with gauze and bandaged it into place. She tried to remember her training. If she was right, the glass had missed a major artery by a fraction. It was a nasty wound and would have to be seen tomorrow by a doctor as there would be a risk of infection, but it could have been so very much worse.

'Settle down, Ruby, we'll look after you,' she said softly. It was getting cold, and she was hungry – Dolly had all the food and drink with her, shut inside the shelter. There was nothing for it but to make the best of things. Gratefully she sank against Danny, who drew his big coat around her, but she barely noticed as, finally exhausted beyond measure, she fell asleep.

Elliott put away his white coat in his locker and drew out his warm jacket. Another shift ended, and hours after he'd intended to leave the hospital. Glancing out of the window he saw it had gone dark. The October nights were drawing in, no doubt about it. Pulling his old college scarf from his pocket, he tied it tightly around his neck, knowing it would be chilly outside. A couple of nurses coming on shift nodded to him as he pushed open the door to the outside world, but he didn't want to stop to make small talk. He had to sort out his thoughts. Turning on to the pavement, he decided to walk for a while rather than wait for a bus to his billet. Walking was always a good way to think things through.

Only a few more days and he would be on his way to see Kitty. He didn't resent working late if it meant he could leave on time on Thursday and get that train. He was delighted that she'd finally agreed to meet his parents. It had been stupid of him to have suggested it so soon in their relationship – no wonder she'd felt overwhelmed at the idea. He kept forgetting that she would have reservations, as all he saw was a beautiful, talented young woman who had no reason to feel inferior to anybody. Now they were all to meet on Saturday. He couldn't help feeling this marked a major development and he wondered where it might lead.

He wouldn't rush her. He realised now that to do so always produced the opposite result to the one he'd intended. He'd see how they all got on, how at home she felt. He was certain his parents would adore her. They knew she made him truly happy, and how could anyone fail to love Kitty? He broke into a small smile at the thought of her face, with those magnetising dark-blue eyes, and that dark, wavy hair he loved to run his hands through. She was truly special, and he hoped he wasn't fooling himself when he admitted that he wanted them to have a future together. He'd take it slowly, but he knew this was no casual wartime romance.

He was so lost in thought that for a moment he didn't register the sound of the air-raid warning. Damn, there hadn't been much in the way of raids for ages – well, one last week, but that wasn't over the Bootle docks, more towards the other side of the city. He looked around but wasn't sure where the nearest shelter was. Never mind. He felt lucky. He'd chance it and carry on walking. He would see Kitty soon and nothing, not even the Luftwaffe, could dampen his spirits.

CHAPTER TWENTY-EIGHT

The war-ravaged streets of London sped past the window of the car, but Laura scarcely noticed. Her mind was racing, her heart hammering in her chest. The admiral had seen to it that a car had been sent for her to bring her to the hospital where Peter lay fighting for his life. What did it mean? The message had been abrupt and gave nothing away, but surely she wouldn't have been summoned if he was still in grave danger. She tapped her fingers against her scratchy uniform skirt in impatience. It was only a short ride away, but seemed to go on for hours – and of course the most direct route was impossible as a building had collapsed and all the traffic had to take a detour. So many small things, unimportant on their own, added up to this war taking its toll in so many ways.

The driver had barely acknowledged her, and she wondered if the woman, in the uniform of a Wren of her own rank, knew what any of this was about. It was strange to be driven about, to sit in the back seat as Peter had done so many times in the past few months. Laura thought it was as if she was cocooned, safe from the dangers outside on the streets, the bombs, the injured people, the food shortages. Even so, she couldn't wait for the journey to end.

At last they pulled up in the driveway in front of the hospital's front door. This time there was no problem getting in. A nurse was waiting for her. 'Miss Fawcett? This way please.'

Laura glanced around, half expecting the formidable matron to descend upon them, although common sense told her that such a senior nurse would have far better things to do. 'How is Captain Cavendish?' Laura breathed, desperate to know and yet fearful of learning the truth.

The nurse escorting her along the corridor didn't break her stride. 'Oh, haven't they told you?' she asked cheerfully. 'Well, I expect they wanted the captain to tell you himself.'

Laura wanted to stand still and take that in, but the nurse walked briskly on and she had to keep up. 'So he's conscious?' she asked.

'You'll soon see for yourself,' the nurse said in her no-nonsense way. 'Right, do you know where you are now? Just at the end of the corridor, the door on the left. Better make the most of it, you won't have long.' She pointed along to the familiar set of French windows. Laura nodded her thanks and made her way down the corridor, her footsteps echoing on the immaculately clean floor. There was a faint scent of disinfectant.

She hesitated outside the door. Already she was flooded with relief that he was alive, and must be well enough for visitors, but now she didn't know what she would find when she saw him. Was he going to be angry with her for that near-fatal choice of route? Would he be his usual aloof self, or would she see that other side to him, the one she'd only known so briefly that desperate night?

There was only one way to find out. She tapped on the wooden panel of the door, and waited.

'Come in.' It was Peter's voice – weaker than usual but definitely his. She turned the brightly polished doorknob and walked in.

He lay propped up in bed, three or four pillows behind him, bright white sheets tucking him in tightly. A large bandage was visible at the neck of his pyjamas and his skin was nearly as pale as the sheet, although no doubt Marjorie and Kitty would still have called him rather good looking. Laura found that thought simultaneously irritating and only too true. Then his face broke into a smile. 'Fawcett. You came.'

Laura wanted to exclaim in relief, but understood that wouldn't be of any help to anyone. So instead she said, 'Of course, sir. I always obey orders, you know that.'

His eyes crinkled. 'I think we both know that isn't the case. Such as when you are explicitly told to leave the scene of a major fire and you go and do the very opposite.'

311

Laura shrugged. 'Just the one time then, sir.'

'Come, sit down,' he said, indicating the ladder-back chair to one side of the bed. Obediently Laura perched on it. 'That's better. I don't have to look up at you now. Well, I understand that you and a friend tried to visit me before but I was otherwise occupied. Most kind of you, I'm sure. I hear you've met my uncle. He told me you were most determined and you almost caused a security incident by bluffing your way in.'

Laura shuffled uneasily. 'Not quite that bad, surely. I just thought I should come to see how you were. Everyone was saying different things, you know how it is, like Chinese whispers, so I thought it best to find out for myself. I didn't realise...' she broke off, swallowed hastily and then continued, '...didn't realise quite how ill you were. I was very sorry to hear that.' She gazed at him, trying to gauge how he felt.

'Oh, it's been a bit of a nuisance,' he said lightly. 'This dratted wound to the chest got infected. They told me, if it had been in a limb they'd have cut it off. As it was, they just had to clean it up and hope for the best.'

Laura gasped at that, she couldn't help herself. 'And is it better now?' she demanded.

'On its way,' he assured her. 'It must be, as I've been stone cold out of it for the best part of a week, so they tell me. But do you know, at one point I could have sworn I heard your voice.'

'Well, I did make it nearly as far as your door,' Laura admitted. 'Then I bumped into your uncle and the matron and, er, got turned back.'

'Quite something, that matron,' he said. 'I

wouldn't fancy Hitler's chances against her. She'd give him one of her quelling looks and he'd turn back in a trice.'

Laura gave a small smile. 'Your uncle seems a decent sort.'

'Oh, he is.' Peter grinned, but winced in pain. 'Sorry, it's still giving me gip. Yes, anyway, he's pretty good and has been coming here as often as possible, even though he's an admiral with one or two other things on his plate. But he's based in central London and he knows his sister, my mother, would expect it – and you don't argue with my mother. She's worse than the matron.'

'Gosh, sir.' Laura didn't know what to say.

'Well, he seems to have taken a shine to you,' Peter went on. 'Probably on account of you saving my life like that. I expect that had something to do with it.' His eyes sparkled and she remembered how they were a rich honey brown.

Suddenly she couldn't keep up the light banter. 'But if I hadn't taken that route then you wouldn't have been there to start with,' she burst out. 'You'd never have been in danger in the first place. We wouldn't have been anywhere near the fire.'

Peter shook his head a little. 'And if my uncle hadn't summoned me to that meeting then both of us would have been safely in our billets the whole evening,' he said. 'And if Hitler hadn't started this war, we wouldn't have been here at all. Fawcett, you can't think like that. You'll end up going around in circles and that's no good to anyone. I've spent a lot of time thinking whilst I've been stuck here, but that idea had never occurred to me.'

'Really?' Laura stared into his face, searching for clues as to whether he meant it or not. 'You haven't been lying here blaming me? You don't hate me?'

'Honestly, Fawcett.' He shook his head. 'Don't be a fool. I never took you for a fool. Of course I don't hate you. You saved my life, and helped save that baby. Why would I hate you? In fact ... come a little closer.'

Heart in her mouth, Laura did so. He reached out his hand and touched her nose. 'At least you got rid of that smudge I see, Fawcett.' His eyes blazed into hers.

'Of course. Like I said, I always obey orders.' Her tone was light but the expression on her face was anything but. Then there was a noise from the corridor and the door swung open. Laura hurriedly leant back in her chair. The young nurse came in.

'Visiting time is up,' she said pleasantly. 'You mustn't tire the captain, he still needs plenty of rest.'

'Yes, I do understand.' Laura stood, having little option. 'Very well. I'm glad to see that you are on the mend, sir.'

Peter nodded. 'Still a way to go yet, Fawcett. I expect I shall be in need of plenty of visits, if you could see to that.' His eyes danced.

Laura broke into a delighted smile. 'I'd be happy to oblige, sir. And please do give my regards to your uncle.'

'He'll be happy to have them,' Peter assured her.

But before he could say anything else to delay Laura's departure, the nurse intervened.

'That's enough now, Captain. You know you aren't to get overexcited. Come with me, Miss Fawcett, and I will let you know the schedule of visiting hours so that you may attend when you aren't on duty.' The nurse gave them both a knowing smile, but she was still firm in ushering Laura out with her.

Laura turned as they went through the door, catching a last precious glance of Peter as he lay back against the mound of pillows. It was true, he did look terribly tired. She wondered with a pang if she had set back his recovery by staying too long. Then he caught her eye and unmistakably gave her a wink.

CHAPTER TWENTY-NINE

'How long is he down for, Kitty?' Marjorie asked. She had just come off duty and was getting changed in the dormitory. Kitty was almost dancing with anticipation along the narrow gap between the two long rows of beds.

'A whole long weekend. I can't remember when we spent this long together. Not since I was posted down here. In fact, we never have, as one of us was always on duty when we both worked in Merseyside.' She couldn't hide her excitement. Laura had made good on her promise to lend Kitty another of her frocks, and this one was in a deep coral pink with a delicate print of flowers and leaves. It brought out the roses in Kitty's cheeks.

'And when are you meeting his parents?' Marjorie wanted to know. 'Are you nervous? I would be.'

Kitty shook her head with determination. 'A little bit, of course. But if they are anything like Elliott, then it's going to be all right. As long as I don't say anything too stupid. We're having lunch with them on Saturday. That gives me two whole evenings of his company first.'

'I bet he'll be very reassuring,' Marjorie said with a glint in her eye, and laughed.

'Oh, he will.' Kitty twirled around and the wide skirt of the beautiful frock whirled around her shapely legs. 'He's taking me out tonight and is picking me up here first. Even the dragons on the door love him; he could charm anyone. I hope his train doesn't take too long. They can be awfully crowded these days and he'll have done a shift at the hospital earlier – that's how he could manage so many days off together.' She knew there would be members of all the armed services trying to get from one end of the country to the other, many prepared to sit on their kitbags or stand for the entire journey, and she knew that if Elliott had a seat but saw anyone struggling, he would immediately have given it up. She could just imagine him standing the whole way, gazing out of the corridor window of the train, squashed against young men in uniform, tired but refusing to show it. Her heart went out to him, for going through the uncomfortable journey just to see her. Yet she knew he would think it was worth it. This was the first time, Kitty realised, that she and Elliott had planned to see each other and she hadn't felt real nerves or trepidation about fitting in. Maybe she was finally starting to enjoy herself.

'Shall we go to the common room and wait for him there?' Marjorie asked.

Kitty hesitated. She'd been thinking about checking her hair one more time. She wanted to look as good as possible so that Elliott would be proud of her on his arm.

'You look lovely, Kitty,' Marjorie said, guessing what was on her friend's mind. 'Come away from that mirror and have a cup of tea downstairs. You're making me feel tired just watching you. Anyway, if you're downstairs you won't have so far to go when the message comes that he's here.'

Kitty could see the sense of that. 'All right. Just let me clip back this curl.' She adjusted her hair one more time and then picked up her coat. By a miracle she had managed to get a new one, a lovely warm tweed, from a shop that was shutting down because the family who ran it had decided to leave London for somewhere safer. It had taken a chunk of her savings and coupons, but she knew it was a sound investment.

'I expect Laura's down there,' Marjorie said. 'She was going to visit Captain Cavendish when she came off duty, but visiting hours will be over by now.'

'She's certainly changed her view about him since the fire,' Kitty observed as they made their way along the corridor and down the wide stairs. 'Funny how she's gone from hating the very mention of his name to following every detail of his recovery. But if you've gone through an experience like that, I suppose it brings you together no matter how you started out.' She didn't want to betray Laura's confidence about her real feelings for the captain; it wasn't her secret to tell.

'Well, I dare say she'll fill us in with all the latest news,' Marjorie predicted.

An hour and a half later and the common room was becoming crowded, as more and more Wrens and trainees finished their different shifts. Kitty, Marjorie and Laura had commandeered a group of worn but comfortable chairs in the corner, from where they could see the door, so that they would know as soon as Elliott arrived. Meanwhile Laura was describing every inch of progress in Captain Cavendish's road to recovery, to the extent that Kitty thought even Rita, with all her years of nursing experience, couldn't have done it better. Maybe Laura had missed her calling. But she couldn't blame her friend. Whatever had gone on between her and the captain, it must have been heartbreaking to think he might die, and so soon after his act of selfless bravery.

Anxiously she stole a glance at her watch. Even though she knew the train was unlikely to be on time, it was getting late now. She smoothed the beautiful fabric of the frock against her knees so that it wouldn't be too creased before Elliott saw her in it. She was growing more jumpy by the minute. It was probably last-minute nerves about meeting his parents. Even though deep down she was sure that Elliott would make certain it all went well, she couldn't help the old habit of doubt. He was a doctor, so far above her in station. His late fiancée had been his professor's daughter. They came from utterly different backgrounds. And yet she knew the world was changing around them, and she herself was now a trained Wren, with acknowledged skills, and far more social ability and polish than when she had left home just months before. She could hold her own, she just had to steel herself not to crumble. Above all she was lucky to have Elliott. He believed in her. Where was he?

'So they think he might be allowed out of bed some time next week,' Laura was saying. 'He can sit up straight now without so much pain, and that's a very good sign.' She glanced across at Kitty. 'I say, are you all right? You're miles away, I can tell.'

'No, no, really,' Kitty said quickly. 'Just wondering when Elliott will get here. Honestly I'm very pleased the captain's on the mend.'

Laura nodded, understanding Kitty's anxiety. 'He'll be here soon, you know as well as I do what it's like on those trains at the moment. It's annoying, isn't it, when you're all dressed up and ready to go and then there's a delay. But don't worry, it doesn't mean he's any less keen to see you.'

'Oh, I know that, I'm not worried like that,' Kitty reassured her hastily. Her concerns for a curtailed evening were as nothing compared to what Laura had gone through when she thought Peter was going to die. She must make more of an effort. After all, Elliott hadn't been injured and would be whirling her round the dance floor tomorrow. That was a long way off for Laura and the captain – if they even decided to go that far.

Yet she couldn't concentrate on what her friends

were saying. Marjorie was describing an incident in one of her language classes, but it felt as if it had nothing to do with her. She'd waited so long to see Elliott again, any extra delay was twice as agonising. Every precious minute counted, and she resented those that were being stolen from them.

Marjorie broke off to suggest they all got another cup of tea, which they agreed was a good idea, and it wasn't until they'd nearly finished their drinks that a fellow Wren came to the common room door and called, 'Callaghan?'

Kitty looked up, and something in the woman's expression caused her to spill the last of her tea, narrowly missing the skirt of the beautiful frock.

'I say, steady on,' Laura said, but her tone was joking.

Kitty frowned. Well, maybe this was one of the dragons who wasn't charmed by Elliott. Even he wasn't infallible, she supposed. She set down her cup and walked as calmly as she could across to the messenger. The other two followed. 'Might as well come and say hello,' Laura remarked, 'seeing as you two lovebirds will want to have the rest of your weekend on your own.'

The messenger nodded to Kitty. 'There's a gentleman come to see you, says he's a doctor.'

Kitty sighed with relief. How silly she had been to be worried. Everything was going to be all right now he was here. What had she been so anxious about – could it be, she wondered, that he might even propose this weekend? How would she feel if he did? Of course if she was to be sensible it was too soon, and they were in the middle of a war. If she added up the hours they had spent together it wasn't actually very long, not compared to how a courtship would have been in peacetime. Still, she was lucky to have someone like Elliott who felt so strongly about her...

'Look sharp, Callaghan,' said the messenger, her face still unremittingly grim. 'He's waiting at the front door.'

Kitty nodded. Of course men weren't allowed in the Wrens' billet. Heaven knew plenty had tried, but it was a strictly adhered-to rule. She hurried along to the entrance lobby, her feet light at the prospect of being reunited with Elliott at last.

Except it wasn't Elliott. The man had deep-red hair, not warm-brown. It was Elliott's friend and former colleague, Bill Smedley. Kitty halted, trying to understand what it could mean. He must have driven to the station in his car to give Elliott a lift, and Elliott would be waiting outside, that was it.

The look on his face told her that wasn't right, but she held on to the hope even while her heart was full of misgiving.

'Kitty.' Dr Smedley stepped towards her. 'Kitty, I'm so sorry, I'm so desperately sorry.'

Kitty couldn't form the words to ask what he was talking about. She just stared at him, registering that any of her female friends would have loved to have his hair; that his tie was crooked, that he had lines on his face she didn't remember seeing before.

'Sorry about what? Whatever is it?' Laura, direct as ever, came forward and took her arm. She'd have known Bill from the occasional night out earlier in the summer when he'd met their group for drinks, Kitty recalled. As if it mattered.

'Kitty...' He met her gaze and his eyes were full of deep pity. 'I ... I have to tell you that Elliott won't be coming this weekend. He's...' The doctor took a quick breath. 'Kitty, he's dead.'

Kitty just stared.

'What do you mean, he's dead? He can't be.' Laura again asked the question that Kitty couldn't.

Dr Smedley shut his eyes for a brief moment, collected himself and forced the words out. 'There was a raid on Bootle on Monday. It was the heaviest since the blitz. Quite a few people were injured; some were killed. I'm so sorry, Kitty. Elliott was one of them.'

'Monday?' gasped Laura, almost as if getting the details straight would change the outcome. 'But that was days ago.'

Dr Smedley didn't back down in the face of her fierce questioning. 'Yes, Monday evening. It took a while for them to identify everyone, and then they had to inform the next of kin – Elliott's parents, of course.' He glanced at Kitty in apology. 'They wanted to get hold of you but didn't know how. They telephoned me to break the news – I've known them for years. They asked me if I knew where you were stationed and to come and tell you in person.'

'How ... how...' Still Kitty couldn't speak properly. Her mouth wouldn't let the words come out. It was going at a different speed to her brain. This couldn't be happening. Elliott was still on a train, it had been held up, he was going to come to see her and introduce her to his parents. He

322

couldn't be dead – he was full of life, full of energy, full of love. He wasn't old enough to die. He had so many plans.

'He was walking home after coming off shift, that's what they said,' Bill went on. 'There were some direct hits on Bootle – he wouldn't have suffered,' he assured her. 'He was right in the middle of it all – he wouldn't have known. Kitty, if there's anything I can do…'

Kitty felt her knees go weak and sensed Laura on one side, Marjorie now on the other, holding her up. But the entrance lobby was beginning to swim as her vision grew blurry. She could hear Bill's voice but it was getting further and further away. She gasped as the truth of it hit her, the finality, and she could stand up no longer. Then she was gripped by a pain in her heart, a sharp, stabbing pain as she took in the news that he was gone for ever. Now she would never know what could be, what would have happened in the future they'd only just begun to talk about, full of possibilities. A future that he had worked so hard to secure, that he would have grasped with both hands. How could someone so loving and kind and full of compassion for the world around him be snatched away like this? And what about her own feelings – was this true love, this grown-up sensation of being so comfortable with someone and knowing you could trust them with absolutely anything? Right now, she couldn't answer that, but she knew there was a big empty, gaping hole inside her; and one that she wasn't sure would ever heal. As the awful reality of the war hit home, Kitty knew that things would never be the same again.

CHAPTER THIRTY

'It's all right, Ruby, they say maybe you can go home tomorrow.' Rita smoothed the pillowcase made of starched hospital linen. It had come as a tremendous shock to her to find the young woman admitted to the ward, even though it wasn't the one where she was working herself. The sister in charge had expressed her concern, as Ruby hadn't said a word since she'd arrived, on the morning after the worst raid for ages. They'd been able to treat her leg, which turned out to be broken as well as cut to ribbons by shattered glass, but the sister was worried that she might have taken a blow to the head, as she seemed unable to speak.

Rita was pretty sure it was shock rather than a physical blow that had silenced Ruby. Sarah had explained what had happened – the encounter with the vicious old neighbour, being denied entry to the shelter, Ruby running in terror along the dock road as the raid blazed all around them. Then Danny, Sarah and Ruby had spent the best part of the night huddled in the porch of the Sailor's Rest, barely safer than if they'd been out in the street. It was no wonder Ruby's senses were reeling. She must have been in agony – Sarah's efforts to clean the wounds had staved off infection, but they hadn't known about the broken bone. Now Ruby's leg was in a cast, but as for what her mind had endured, that was a different matter.

She was vulnerable and sensitive at the best of times; how would she cope with being called a bastard in public? Rita wasn't even sure if Ruby knew what it meant, but her heart went out to the frightened young woman, whose pale-blonde hair was spread like a halo over the pristine pillow.

Rita herself had spent the night of the raid on a makeshift bed in the nurses' welfare area, curled under a table and wrapped in a spare blanket. The casualties had been high and she'd been able to snatch only a few hours' sleep. She'd worked extra shifts and had hardly been back to Empire Street since it happened. She'd forced herself to focus on her work, to be professional and caring while keeping all emotion at bay, or else she knew she'd simply collapse. It was too much: the sheer numbers of injured people, what had happened to Ruby, and on top of it all the news about Elliott dying. She couldn't take it in. He was so desperately needed at the hospital, for his calm kindness, his steadiness under pressure, his deep medical knowledge which he'd never vaunted. As for what Kitty must be feeling ... no, Rita couldn't let herself even imagine it.

Now she sat in the uncomfortable visitor's chair and wondered if Ruby would ever come back to them. The young woman's skin was paler than ever, her smooth face making her seem once again more like a child than somebody of twenty-one years of age. Her eyes were shut. Rita prayed that her mind was undamaged, and that all the improvements of the past few months hadn't been destroyed by one night of horror. If only Mrs Pinkerton hadn't chosen that very moment to go to the shelter. If only Dolly had been with them. If only Rita hadn't been on duty. Yet she couldn't change what had happened, and now she had to face the grim fact that Ruby might not recover.

Maeve came past, her arms full of folded towels. 'Any change?' She stopped behind Rita, her eyes full of concern. 'Has she woken up yet?'

Rita shook her head. 'The sister said she's opened her eyes for a while but still hasn't said a word. I think she's sleeping now but it's hard to tell.'

'Maybe that's the best thing for her,' Maeve said comfortingly. 'After what she's been through, it's the natural way for the body and mind to repair itself. You can't beat a good sleep.'

'True.' Rita tried to remember the last time she'd had such a thing. 'But it's been days now. I can't help worrying. What will become of her? Oh, I could just kill that neighbour with her big old mouth.'

'Don't say it,' Maeve replied. 'I know what you mean though – fancy coming out with such a thing and then not letting them in the shelter. After all your family do for the street and every-one around it. That's sheer ingratitude, on top of being monstrously cruel.'

Rita sighed. 'Mam was beside herself when she found out. She'd got Violet and Georgie settled at the far end of the shelter and didn't hear a thing, what with all the bombing and ack-ack gunfire. They assumed Sarah and Ruby were safe some-where else. She went round to Mrs Pinkerton's and tore her off a strip once she found out about it, but the damage has been done. And Ruby's suffering the consequences.' Again she smoothed the pillowcase, wanting to reach out to the girl who'd arrived as a stranger but who was now close to her heart. She couldn't come to permanent harm. How would she explain it to Michael and Megan? They'd be heartbroken if anything happened to their companion. While the adult world condemned her for being different, the children had taken to her instantly, recognising a kind soul. They would never understand the viciousness of the attack on her, the self-righteous snobbery that lay behind it. Now Ruby, who was blameless in the whole affair, lay still in her hospital bed.

'Shall I fetch you something?' Maeve asked, knowing that Rita had been on her feet all day and had barely stopped for a break since she started her shift. 'How about a nice cuppa? I'll bring it over, Sister won't mind.'

Rita realised she was parched. 'That's good of you, Maeve, I'd love one.' She turned to her friend in gratitude.

'I'll be right back.' Maeve hurried off, still balancing the heavy towels. She disappeared round a corner. Rita stared after her absent-mindedly, wondering how long her Irish colleague had been working today, knowing it was an extra effort to bring the cup of tea, but relieved that she'd offered, for Rita wanted only to sit at Ruby's bedside. Maeve had extraordinary reserves of energy, but even she must be feeling the strain after the week they had all had. It was like the May blitz all over again – every bed full, all medical staff pushed to their limits. It never ceased to amaze Rita how everyone pulled together at such times of crisis to ensure the best possible treatment for the victims of the raids. Only, she reminded herself sadly, Ruby hadn't needed to be a victim. If it hadn't been for that interfering gossip of a neighbour, she would have been safe in the shelter.

She was so lost in her thoughts that for a moment she didn't notice the slight stirring in the bed beside her. Ruby was trying to move. Her hands traced the sheet folded tightly over the blanket. Rita turned to her and gently touched the back of one hand. 'Hush now, Ruby. Don't you fret. You're going to be fine.'

Ruby's head twisted slowly from side to side and her eyelids fluttered. 'Rita?' she whispered. 'Is that you?'

'Ruby! You're awake!' Rita brought her head close to that of her friend, afraid she would miss the barely audible voice.

'Rita, I thought I could hear you.' Ruby's eyes opened further. 'You were talking, I knew it was you.'

'Of course. I wanted to see how you were. Do you know where you are?' Rita regarded her closely, trying not to let her own anxiety show in her expression or her words.

'Hospital. It smells like hospital,' Ruby said, her voice stronger now. 'It smells clean.'

'It is, it's very clean,' Rita assured her, knowing that she and Maeve had spent many a long hour working to make certain the whole place was as germ-free as possible. 'Yes, you are in hospital. It's the one where I work so I have been coming to see you every day. You hurt your leg. Do you remember?'

Ruby's forehead creased in a frown. 'It feels strange, I can't move it.'

'It's in a cast. You broke your leg so they've had to set it to keep it straight. It will feel heavy. But don't worry, you can get around on crutches. I'll show you how. It will be as good as new when they take the cast off.' Rita hoped this was right. But Ruby had youth on her side and, thanks to Sarah, there was little risk of infection. The chances were that her leg would heal completely; it was everything else that Rita was worried about. 'Do you remember how you broke it?'

Ruby shifted her body. 'There were planes, and bombs. We were in the doorway. Sarah and Danny looked after me.'

'That's right,' Rita said encouragingly. 'Sarah told me all about it. You were very brave.'

'No, I was afraid,' Ruby said suddenly, trying to sit up. 'There was shouting, but I can't think what it was about.'

Good, thought Rita. Maybe that's for the best.

'You weren't there,' Ruby went on. 'You were at work. I was going to tell you something when you got back.'

'Well, never mind,' said Rita. 'You'll have plenty of time to think about that now you're getting better. Your leg is doing so well that the doctors say you can come home tomorrow. How about that?'

Ruby twisted as best she could under the firm hold of the starched sheet. 'But have I been here long?'

'A day or two,' said Rita. She didn't want to

worry Ruby more than necessary.

'Days,' muttered Ruby. She looked as if she was struggling with a difficult thought. 'So ... is it next week yet?'

'No, we're at the end of the same week,' Rita said. 'The raid was on Monday evening and you came in here on Tuesday. Don't worry, you haven't been asleep for ages, you haven't missed much.' She kept her tone cheerful, though the thought of next week brought her further misery. That was when Jack should have come home on leave, but he'd written to say it was going to be cancelled after all. Her hopes of seeing him were dashed yet again.

Ruby's face grew determined. 'Next week is important. It's the pattern. I was going to tell you but there's still time.'

'What pattern?' Rita asked gently. She didn't want Ruby straining herself, working out something complicated when she'd only just recovered consciousness. 'Really, Ruby, all in good time, you need to rest, you've had a bad injury and that's going to make you feel very tired. You don't need to tell me about it now.'

'But I do,' said Ruby stubbornly. 'It matters. It's when things go missing. You know, you told me before.'

Rita nodded. In all the activity of the bombing, the vanishing cases of stock had completely slipped her mind. It didn't seem terribly important when set beside Ruby's ordeal and the death of Elliott. But obviously Ruby was anxious to explain. 'Yes, I remember now.'

'It will be next Wednesday,' Ruby predicted,

totally serious. 'That's when it will happen again. If I'm home by then I can help.'

'If you're at home on crutches you will do no such thing,' Rita said forcefully. 'You leave all that up to me. You are to have complete rest when you get back. You have been through a lot.' She gave silent thanks that Ruby didn't seem to recall the details of the row that had caused her to be outside when the explosions happened. 'If you won't let me tell you as a friend, then let me do so as a nurse. Total rest, and that's an order.' She smiled to take the edge off her words.

'I want to help,' Ruby said, her big eyes gazing at Rita. 'But I trust you. You are good at sorting things out. As long as you know it will be Wednesday.'

'All right, I'll be extra-vigilant on Wednesday,' Rita promised, figuring that Ruby wouldn't settle unless she agreed. 'Now you stop worrying and lie down and make yourself comfortable. That's better. And look, here's Maeve, come to see if you've woken up.'

The Irish nurse beamed in delight as she arrived with two cups of tea. 'Well, will you look at that. Our patient is better. Will I get you a cup of tea as well, Ruby? Wouldn't you like that?'

Ruby shook her head. 'No, thank you very much,' she said politely. 'I want to go back to sleep now.'

'You do that,' Rita said, relieved that Ruby seemed calmer now she had remembered her piece of vital information. 'We'll go and leave you in peace. I'll see you tomorrow, and with luck you'll be coming home.' She bent and planted a small kiss on Ruby's head, then quietly followed Maeve away from the ward and along to the welfare area. Well, that was one less thing to worry about: Ruby seemed fundamentally unshaken by the events of Monday night. As for the suggestion that something was about to happen on Wednesday, Rita would deal with that when the time came. There was only so much a person could cope with at any one moment – and she had just about reached her limit.

'Oh, this is nice!'

Sylvia Hemsley looked up at the curves of the building above the ornate main door to the pub where Frank had taken her. She'd never seen anything like it. The windows were mullioned and there were domes right at the top. It was beautiful and impressive both at the same time.

'Do you like it?' Frank grinned. He'd guessed she'd be surprised by the place. While the Philharmonic Dining Rooms wasn't where he would usually choose to come, being too far from Derby House and his billet, he knew it would be somewhere she would appreciate. 'Well, wait till you see inside.'

He pushed open the heavy door, careful to keep his balance. He'd managed to walk all the way from the bunker to the pub, even though some of it was uphill, and he didn't want to spoil things now. He was doing his very best to move as normally as possible. Sylvia hadn't known him before his injury, of course, but neither had she seen him when it had been new and raw, before he'd got the hang of his false leg. She was judging him by how he was now, and this was as good as he was likely to get. So he didn't want to mess it up.

Sylvia's cheeks were rosy from the cold but also, he realised, from anticipation. They hadn't gone for a drink together before, or at least not as a couple, on their own. She'd been amusing company when he'd shown her the waterfront, admiring the Liver Birds as they guarded the city from on high, taking in the expanse of the Mersey as it flowed northwards past the docks and his home. He'd seen her around at work several times since and they'd had tea or cocoa at breaks between shifts, but always with other colleagues around as well. Now he had grasped the nettle and asked her to come for a drink, half expecting her to say no or to make an excuse. But she hadn't. She had accepted at once, her bright eyes dancing with mischief, apparently glad to be with him and to learn more about him. For the first time in a long while, Frank had felt optimistic.

'Don't tell me this is your local,' she said now, as he led her to a corner with plush seating, from where she could appreciate the elaborate décor of the place.

'Not exactly,' admitted Frank, thinking of how different this was to the Sailor's Rest, or even Bent-nose Jake's down at Canada Dock. 'I'm not sure I'd take you there, to be honest. I used to come here before the war, though, if I was out in town.'

'If you wanted to impress a girl,' Sylvia guessed, and from his reaction she could tell she'd been right. 'I can see why. It's splendid, isn't it? All ... what do you call it?'

'Art Nouveau,' Frank told her, hoping he'd said it right and not adding that he'd never heard the term back in those days – when he'd played the field without a care in the world, before he'd lost a leg. 'What would you like to drink?'

Sylvia slipped off her warm coat with its fake fur collar, which she'd bought second-hand especially for their date. She was glad she'd made the effort. All around people seemed to have done the same, making the best of what wartime Liverpool could offer, splashes of vibrant colour amid the uniforms of the servicemen and -women enjoying time off. Frank was still in his; she was proud of the way he looked in his navy jacket, now bearing the insignia of a sublieutenant. She tried to work out what other women her age were drinking, but it was beyond her, so she played it safe. 'A lemonade, please.'

Frank nodded and set off for the bar. She watched him, aware of how much effort he was making not to limp or reveal in any way that he used a false leg. If he was doing so for her, he needn't have worried. Everyone at Derby House knew about it and that he'd been injured in the war, which made him a hero in her book. She'd never been bothered by it. Plenty of people had war wounds and, if she wasn't mistaken, there would be a whole lot more before it all finished. You couldn't go around discounting anyone for that reason. She liked Frank for who he was – good company, funny, sharp, always interesting, with opinions on all manner of subjects. He was just the sort of person she'd hoped to meet when she'd signed up. She loved her home and the

334

majesty of the great hills and lakes, but she wanted more.

He returned with the lemonade for her and a pint of bitter for him, which he set steadily on the highly polished table. Really, if you hadn't known, you couldn't have spotted the injury, she thought. He was good – and that was after the walk, when he'd gently held her arm and made her feel special and protected. She'd feared it would be too much for him but not a bit of it.

'Thank you.' Sylvia grinned up at Frank, enjoying how his eyes sparkled in the lights of the colourful bar.

For a moment Frank's mind flashed back to his rushed visit to Empire Street; he'd wanted to check for himself that everyone was all right. There were broken windows everywhere, loose or missing tiles on many roofs, and what had remained of old Mrs Ashby's house was in a sorry state. His mother had regaled him with what had happened at the shelter and the fate of poor Ruby, which had offended his innate sense of justice, but fundamentally they were all in one piece. Then Dolly had told him about Elliott.

He had gone through a swift mixture of emotions at the news. He was hugely saddened to learn that the gifted young doctor had died; he knew as well as anyone that his skills had been desperately in demand and that he would be dearly missed. He knew too from his sister Rita that the man had been widely liked as well as admired. Most of all he could scarcely bring himself to imagine what it must have been like for Kitty to hear about the tragedy. Who would be looking after her now, far away at her training centre in London? Part of him wanted to leap on a train and comfort her. Then again, he had enough self-knowledge to admit that comfort wasn't all he was thinking of. Kitty was free now. She would be emotionally available once more.

He'd told himself to stop considering any such idea. He would write, as an old friend, with condolences, which would be the most suitable thing to do. She'd made her break from Empire Street, and the very fact that she hadn't once been back to visit told him where her priorities lay. He was no longer the man she had known; she would inevitably judge him by what he had been like before, everything he had been able to do that his impaired mobility now prevented. She too would be different now – more sophisticated, more educated. He must put aside all romantic thoughts of her, no matter how it cut him to the quick to do so. As he'd struggled through the bomb-ravaged streets between Bootle and the centre of the city, he'd resolved to forget about her. She belonged to his past, not his future. If she had dreamed of a future with her doctor, then she would see her life heading in a very different direction and it would not feature Frank Feeny. He had to be strong and turn his back on his dreams.

Sylvia was untainted by memories of his past. They shared a close bond in the present, through their secret war work, which was demanding, exhausting, and yet deeply fulfilling too. Now she was sitting opposite him in The Phil, her expression bright and keen. Frank smiled back and felt himself relaxing a little at last as he sank into his comfortably padded seat. For a moment he could almost believe the war wasn't happening. Here he was, in this friendly and beautiful historic pub, with a good-looking young woman who seemed to want to spend her precious time off with him. He sipped his beer with relish. He was going to make the most of this evening. They both deserved it; it had been one hell of a week.

She could be his future, if he dared to think that far. Sylvia, not Kitty. He raised his glass to her and she raised hers in acknowledgement. 'To happier times,' he said.

CHAPTER THIRTY-ONE

Kitty went through the next days in a trance. She hardly noticed if she ate or drank and wanted only to sleep. However, when she tried to do so she would jerk awake again and sit up in confusion, knowing that something was wrong but not what it was. Then she would remember and the whole nightmare would begin again.

This would usually wake Laura, who still had the top bunk above Kitty. Mindful of how caring her friend had been when she'd confessed about her brother, and also when Peter had been so ill, Laura would slip down from her bed and rescue Kitty, walking her up and down the corridor outside the darkened canteen, letting her sit and cry if she needed to. There was little she could say. Nothing would alter the facts. The wonderful

Elliott was gone, and there would be no more trips to exclusive Soho nightclubs for them all. Laura knew that Kitty had begun to hope that there would be so much more to come in their future together; she would never have agreed to meet his parents if this had been a flash in the pan. Now that had all been taken away from her.

Laura couldn't help but feel a little guilty, as Peter was visibly improving every time she managed to go to see him, which was almost every other day. She knew Kitty wouldn't begrudge her this, but it was such a contrast to how they had been just a short time before. Now their positions were totally reversed. Kitty was devastated, trying to come to terms with her loss, knowing that Elliott had died in an unforgivably cruel way and that everyone thought he was a hero. Peter had survived the crisis and was coming on in leaps and bounds. Whether they would have any sort of future together, Laura still didn't know; she wasn't going to force the issue while he was still bedridden. But they had moved far beyond distant captain and reluctant driver. They had a connection nobody else could understand as they had been through the fire together, an experience that she knew had changed her and suspected had changed him too. Now she was content to see where this led them – but at least she would have the chance to find out.

Wearily she trod the familiar path up and down the corridor, letting Kitty lean on her. 'Do you want to sit down for a bit?' she suggested finally. 'We could try the canteen; it'll be empty and there are loads of chairs.'

Kitty shrugged as if she didn't mind either way. Laura cautiously tried the door and it swung open, revealing the large room in darkness, except for at one end where the blackout blind had been removed to let light in for the early shift and the moonlight streamed in. She led them to where the silvery beam picked out the shapes of the functional chairs and tables and sat down, letting Kitty take her place opposite.

Kitty sighed and rested her head in her hands. Then she looked up. 'Do you think I should go to the funeral?' she asked abruptly.

Laura thought for a moment. 'Do you want to?' she asked.

'I don't think so,' said Kitty at once. Then she softened. 'I'm not really sure. His parents have written to ask me, you see. It's going to be at their parish church in Hampstead. It will be all his family and whoever is left in London from when he did his training. It's going to be everyone who knew him from before, from when he was engaged to the professor's daughter. I'd have to ask for special leave.'

'What about Bill? He'll be going,' Laura pointed out.

Kitty gave a long sigh. 'I know, he's bound to. But it won't feel like anything to do with me. Do you reckon they'll think badly of me if I don't go?'

'None of their business,' Laura said robustly. 'You have to do what you think is right. I'm sure nobody will blame you. If you feel you want to go, or that you should go, I'll come too. I bet Marjorie will as well. After all, we knew him. But if you'd rather not, then don't.'

'I don't think I could bear to,' Kitty said, trying to explain her feelings when she wasn't really sure of them herself. 'I mean, what a way to meet his parents. After all our plans for the weekend, when it was going to be like a celebration. It's too much. I don't think I can stand there and shake their hands and have them looking at me wondering what I'm like. Not without him there too.'

Laura nodded slowly. 'Well, you don't have to make up your mind tonight. Think about it and let me know if you'd like me to come. It might help. You know. Make it seem more final and all that.'

'It feels final all right,' Kitty said disconsolately. 'It's sunk in now and there's nothing I can do to change it. It's as if I've been hollowed out from inside somehow. Some major part of me is missing. I can't shift the feeling.'

'Early days yet,' Laura said, reaching for her hand. 'Don't be so hard on yourself. It would be stranger if you felt all right, if you were running around as usual. It's perfectly normal to be like this – you've lost your chap and he was a wonderful man, no doubt about it. It's not fair, but life isn't, is it? When you think of all the cads and the spivs, or the cowards, it's not right that one of the good ones has to die. I'm so sorry.'

Kitty suddenly thought of Alfie Delaney and Charlie Kennedy, two of the most despicable men she knew, still to the best of her knowledge alive and well and taking advantage of everyone back home. She shook her head. 'He was one of the good ones, wasn't he?' she said quietly. 'Everyone knew it. He never lost his temper; always had something nice to say about everyone; never

340

avoided his duty, no matter how tired he was, he just kept on going. Till that bomb got him.' She let out a sob. 'Oh Laura, I feel so heartbroken, but the funny thing is, I'm not sure I was in love with Elliott, though I was so fond of him, and if we'd had the chance I think I might have fallen for him properly, but I was too busy worrying about whether I was good enough for him – I wasted that short time we had together fretting.'

'Oh Kitty, feelings are funny things. Falling in love doesn't always happen immediately. Everyone who knew you both could see that you adored each other,' Laura reminded her.

'Elliott was so good to me. He showed me that I could be somebody different ... that there was more out there in the world for me if I was brave enough to look for it ... and now he's gone and I'm not sure I'll ever get over it.'

'There, there, Kitty, there's no point trying to predict the future.' Laura was anxious for her friend. Kitty was such a gentle and kind soul, who felt things deeply. She cursed the war and that blasted Hitler who had thrown so much pain and heartache their way. 'Come on, let's go back to the dormitory. See if you can sleep a bit now.'

Kitty dragged herself to her feet. 'Thanks, Laura,' she said, tired but meaning it. 'I know I shouldn't rush into any decisions now about the funeral. Heaven knows there are plenty of other people in the same boat as me – and worse, in fact. I'll go where the navy needs me now. That's the best thing I can do to honour Elliott's memory – to do my duty too, wherever I'm called to go.'

'Come on then, Kitty. There's no way you can

do your duty if you haven't slept,' Laura urged her gently and, taking her friend's arm, she led her back up the stairs to the dormitory.

Rita held open the door to the kitchen as Ruby carefully tried to manoeuvre her way inside, uncertain of her balance on the crutches. The small space was crowded enough when there was more than one person in the room, but with somebody on crutches it was twice as tricky. Eventually Ruby managed to get to the table and slowly sat down on one of the hard chairs.

'There. You did it.' Rita had been endlessly encouraging in the few days since Ruby had come home. It was going to be a long process, but she couldn't let the young woman down, or she would retreat into her shell once more. Rita was determined that would not happen. Ruby had spent so many years cowering and afraid, being told she was good for nothing. She couldn't let this horrible incident set her back.

'Now, look what the postman brought,' Rita said. 'A letter from the farm – how's that for a welcome home present? I haven't even opened it; I knew you'd want to see it too.'

Ruby's face broke into a smile. 'Yes please.'

Hastily Rita opened the envelope, carefully saving it to use later – she never threw anything away any more if she could help it. Her heart soared at the thought of news from her precious children, whom she still missed painfully every day. But thank God they hadn't been here during the latest raid. As ever, she told herself they were in the best place and in the safest hands. She unfolded the sheets of paper and was delighted to see one was from Michael and the other from Megan. Rita could guess that Joan or Seth must be helping her, as she was only seven, but her handwriting was improving each time. Rita's sense of pride in her children welled up. If she wasn't careful she could easily shed a tear, but she knew she must keep herself under control or it would upset Ruby. 'Let's see what they have to say.' She scanned the first page. 'Michael's been chosen for the football team at school. Fancy that. He always loved kicking a ball around in the street but I couldn't tell if he was any good or not. Maybe Seth has been teaching him.'

Her heart constricted at the thought that Charlie had never bothered to do anything like that. He'd avoided the children whenever he could and Winnie had simply complained that they were too noisy. What sort of upbringing was that? She fervently hoped that Seth was showing Michael how to be a good man, a good husband, in a way that Charlie never could have done. Of course, if it had been Jack at the head of the household, everything would have been different. What a fine example he would have set, and he'd have been out there playing football at every opportunity. But fate had decided differently – and in any case he would still be away serving his country, of that she had no doubt. How she had longed to see him this week, counting the days until his leave, but she would have to wait.

'Michael's been helping with Bessie the goat, who was sick but is better now. Joan has made rosehip syrup and tells them to have some every day – that's good for their vitamins, Ruby – and he's got new shoes because the others were too small.' She stopped again, saddened that she was not there to see how her son was growing. He was a proper boy now, not the little child she sometimes automatically thought of. 'Here, you can read it for yourself while I look at Megan's.' She passed Michael's letter across to Ruby.

Megan's letter was much shorter and the writing was larger, with the letters still separate and not joined up. But they were clearly formed and even-sized, which made Rita very proud. To think Megan had once been thought of as slow. She wasn't at all.

'I helped with the eggs,' she read. 'Now there are not many ... oh, no, that's strange.' She didn't want to alarm Ruby, but Megan had described the return of the shadow man. Again she didn't seem afraid but mentioned it as if he was a fact of life, like the hens stopping laying for the winter. The fences had been broken and the hay bales thrown around so they wouldn't be any good to use. The milk pail had gone missing. Was it the little girl's overactive imagination, or was there some peril lurking in the apparently safe lanes and fields of the farm? Rita shuddered at the very idea. No, surely not. Seth and Joan would guard her precious children. They had none of their own and had taken to her two and Tommy as if they were family. To all intents and purposes, that's exactly what they were. They would not let them come to harm. The fences must have been broken in the wind, and maybe a cow had knocked over the hay bales. Anyone could mislay a pail. It didn't mean

344

that there was some malevolent force around. Children's imaginations were bound to run riot as the nights drew in and the shadows grew darker, yet that unease she'd felt before when Megan had written to her about the dead bird still persisted... She might write to the couple just to check, and she wouldn't let Ruby read this in case it worried her.

'I expect you're hungry,' she said now. 'Why don't I make us something to eat – we could have some Spam sandwiches with a bit of Branston pickle.'

Ruby looked up from Michael's letter. 'Yes please.' She paused. 'How is Megan? Is she all right?' Her eyes were keen.

Rita cursed herself for forgetting how much Ruby loved her daughter – clearly she had picked up that there was something wrong. 'She says the hens aren't laying as much,' she replied brightly, refusing to let any fear enter her voice. 'She doesn't say much else, not nearly as much as Michael. Here, pass me that plate.'

She noticed with relief that her diversionary tactic had worked and Ruby let the subject lie. But Rita couldn't quell a growing sense of unease, as if someone, somewhere, was a potential threat to her children.

CHAPTER THIRTY-TWO

On Wednesday morning Rita was singing to herself. The day had dawned cold but fine, with a breeze coming in off the Mersey, and she decided to make the most of her morning off by getting stuck into the pile of washing that needed to be done. Now she had lifted the heavy laundry basket full of dripping clothes into the back yard. All she needed to do was put up the washing line and then she could peg them all out. The yard was too small to keep the line up all the time – she'd risk running into it when she put the boxes out. So she took the looped end and strung it diagonally across the cramped space, stood on a few broken bricks to reach the sturdy nail in the wall, and hung it taut.

She fastened the old canvas peg bag around her waist and picked up the first of the wet clothes, a worn-out blouse she had had since Megan was a baby. Its polka-dot pattern had faded over the years, but it fitted her properly again now she'd lost so much weight. She couldn't afford to throw it out; it would be difficult to replace. It would do for another year or two yet if she was careful. She gave it a gentle wring, twisting it firmly, and feeling her chapped hands protest at the action. Then she shook out the creases and pegged it on to the line.

Next came a dowdy skirt that Ruby had brought

when she'd arrived last Christmas. Already that was nine months ago. Heaven knew how old it was, and Rita couldn't remember when that style had been fashionable, if it ever had been. It was a dull brown and she wouldn't have chosen it in a month of Sundays. Ruby however didn't seem to mind what she wore, as happy with this as Sarah's castoffs, and at least it would be warm. Its stiff fabric was hard to twist and so it was still dripping all over Rita as she reached to hang it up.

One by one she lifted the clothes and strung them along the old rope line, hoping that today wouldn't be the day it finally chose to break. It was fraying in several places but she'd never found the time to replace it. She would have to do it soon, and before the real winter took hold, as they would all be wearing heavier clothes, which held the water more and weighed down the line. Wiping her chilly hands on the peg bag, she turned to fetch the long wooden pole with which she propped the line up higher. It was leaning against her makeshift roof, which sheltered the flattened cardboard boxes. As she did so she thought she heard a noise but didn't bother to look, assuming it was the stiff breeze dislodging the little pile of broken bricks in the opposite corner.

She hadn't intended to take today off, but the hospital had recognised that she had worked so many extra hours after the recent bombing that she deserved to swap a shift. She was delighted – she hadn't done it for the reward, but it was good to know that her work had been noticed and appreciated. Maybe she would go into the city centre later and see if Nancy wanted to go shopping. They could look for something for Megan, to keep her warm in the winter. Rita sighed. She never had time to make her daughter anything, but Dolly had promised to knit her a scarf from some wool she'd come by in one of her make-do-and-mend classes, and if there was enough left over she might manage a little hat as well. Rita chuckled to herself as she imagined her daughter's happy face when she saw her presents.

Suddenly she was aware of somebody behind her and, before she could think of who it could be, she felt something cold and sharp at her throat. Then she was being dragged backwards. A hand was over her mouth so she couldn't scream, although she was so shocked by the abruptness of what was happening that she hadn't even thought to call for help.

'Don't try anything funny, Rita,' said a voice against her ear, and her heart sank. Charlie, back after all that time. 'This isn't a joke. Don't try anything clever, or this blade goes straight in.'

Rita gave a little whimper of fright but it was muffled by his hand.

'You stay quiet and maybe you won't get hurt,' he said, almost at the open back door now. 'You and me are going inside. I've got unfinished business here today and you've made the mistake of staying around where you're not wanted.' He dragged her over the threshold, bruising her heels on the step, and shoved her violently to the floor, standing over her waving the knife. 'You should've gone running off to your little hospital as usual, do-gooder that you are.' He spat in contempt.

At first she was too frightened even to look at

him, but when she did she saw he was much thinner than when she'd last seen him, back in December when she'd rescued the children after he'd taken them away from her. He was unkempt, his thinning hair ragged, the horrible moustache of which he'd been so proud now untrimmed and his chin stubbly. Gone were his dapper clothes. Now he looked filthy. He was almost unrecognisable from the suave insurance salesman he'd been before the war, who had treated her so cruelly and then left her high and dry. She tried to think how to persuade him to leave her alone, but there was a frantic energy about him and she didn't want him to lose control, not with that sharp blade so close to her face.

Somehow she had to try, although she was almost too scared to think straight. 'Charlie,' she began in barely more than a whisper. 'Charlie,' she tried again, her voice stronger this time. 'Look, you don't have to use that knife. Just tell me what you want, I'll help you if I can.'

'Help? Since when were you any help?' His voice was full of bitter sarcasm. 'You were a useless wife and mother. If you'd been any good, I wouldn't be where I am now, so don't bother offering.'

Rita knew she had to keep going, keep him talking. She remembered how violent he could be, the times he'd hit her, the marks she'd had to hide. 'So why are you back now? Are you home for good?'

'Oh you'd love that, wouldn't you.' He gave a mirthless laugh. 'Welcome me back with open arms, would you? I don't think so. I can do better than you any time. Just because that cow Elsie did the dirty on me doesn't mean I have to come back to you. It's not as if you were ever a loving little wife, is it?' He leered at her and she drew back against the floor, the cold of the tiles seeping into her bones.

'I always tried to be a good wife to you,' she gasped. 'I wanted our marriage to work, you know I did.'

He crouched down to her and nicked the blade against her leg almost playfully, catching her woollen stocking and cutting a slice through it. 'A good wife,' he mocked. 'Well, let me tell you something. I've seen what you get up to in the back yard, whore that you are. And I don't spend all my time around Bootle, I like to roam around a bit. Guess where I go.'

'Wh-where?' She could hardly form the word.

'I get this overwhelming urge to go to the country sometimes,' he went on, in a horrible parody of a singsong, storytelling voice. 'I go out to Lancashire, little place called Freshfield.'

She shut her eyes.

'Look at me, Rita. Like a good little wife.' He drew the blade along her leg, deeper this time. She flinched at the pain. 'There's a farm out there, all wholesome it is. They let the kids run wild there, all hours of the day and night, no supervision at all. Sometimes I stay to watch them.'

Rita gasped. The shadow man. Charlie was the shadow man. He'd been spying on the children and doing it for months.

'I'd say that little girl is the spitting image of her dad,' he went on.

'Megan's your daughter, Charlie,' Rita couldn't resist snapping back, more wounded by his refusal to use her name than by the mounting agony in her leg.

'But the boy doesn't look like me one bit,' he continued. 'Funny that, isn't it? I used to wonder sometimes when he was little, but now he's getting bigger it's clear as daylight. Looks like his mother, there's no doubt about that. But who's his father? That's what I'd like to know. Now I've seen what a whore you are as well. If anything happened to that boy, who'd be sorry?'

'What do you mean?' Rita gasped, frantic he would make good on his threat and hurt Michael. 'Charlie, don't be daft, you're imagining things. Michael looks like me and Megan looks like you, that's how it's always been.'

'That's what I'm saying, Rita, only you don't seem to be listening. What do I have to do to make you listen?' He slashed at her leg again, faster this time, and blood began to pool on the old tiles, catching in the grouting where it was uneven because she'd scrubbed it so often.

'I'm listening, Charlie, I'm listening,' she breathed, pale with pain and terror.

'I don't think you are, Rita. You've made a fool of me all these years.' His eyes were wild. 'You and that cow Elsie, and now you've got that daft idiot she used to have following her round living here. Where's that creature? Am I going to have to take care of her too?' He waved the knife at her throat once more.

'N ... no. Leave Ruby out of it,' Rita insisted, fear for her friend lending her the energy to fight back. 'She's upstairs, she can't get around, she's got a broken leg. She can't get down the stairs on her own.'

'Good.' He shifted position from his crouch to a low stoop. 'Well now, what am I going to do with you? Still want to be a good wife, do you?' Suddenly he reached forward and shoved his hand down her jumper, twisting her breast, causing her to scream in pain. 'What, don't you like it? You used to. Not such a willing wife now after all, are you?' He twisted again and she screamed once more.

'What's going on?' The inside door to the shop opened and Winnie came through; she'd been minding the premises while Rita had hung out the washing.

Charlie swung around and got to his feet as Rita tried to rearrange her clothing, wincing in agony. 'What's she doing here? You said she always worked on Wednesdays?' He glared at his mother. 'How can I collect the stuff if she's hanging around?'

Winnie didn't even bother to glance at Rita huddled on the floor with the blood spreading around her. 'I put up that sign we agreed so you'd know not to come. My old red vase on the windowsill. You should have waited.'

'I came in round the back – you should have put the vase in the window round there,' he snarled. 'Now look what I've got to sort out.' He stood over Rita and lashed out with a kick, making her double up and groan.

'Leave her and just take the food,' said Winnie bluntly. 'The longer you're here, the riskier it is.' She tottered a little, unsteady on her thin legs.

'Yes, but how do we know she'll stay quiet?'

Charlie glared at his wife, who was trying not to make any more noise, but who couldn't help whimpering at the pain.

'Shut her in the cellar then,' Winnie said brutally. 'That'll give you time to get away.'

'I ... I won't say anything,' Rita gasped.

'You'd better not. If you do I'll be back here to cut your throat,' Charlie hissed, watching Rita's face, enjoying the look of fear in her eyes that she couldn't hide. 'Or maybe I'll do something to hurt you even more. How about if I went out to Freshfield and showed those kids what I can do with my knife? How would you like that? If I got rid of that boy who you said was my son, who I've paid for all his life, when he was just a bastard and nothing to do with me at all? How would you like that, eh? Then you'd know him being killed was all your fault and you'd have to live with that for the rest of your life.' He smiled at the idea. 'That would hurt, wouldn't it?'

'You wouldn't!' Rita sat up in horror, despite the agony in her leg, stomach and breast. 'You wouldn't hurt Michael!'

'Wouldn't I?' He leered at her, loving her fear. 'I've nothing to lose. He's not mine, I know it, and nothing you can say will persuade me different. He's nothing to me, I wouldn't miss him. You would, though, wouldn't you, Rita? You always loved those brats more than you loved me. Obvious from day one, that was. Well now you can miss him good and proper, because if you say one word he'll be gone for ever and I'll make sure it hurts him as well.'

'No!' Rita almost screamed it. 'Don't hurt

Michael! He's only a little boy; he's done nothing wrong. I won't say anything, of course I won't. I'll help you, I can make sure you get away without anyone knowing, I'll give you food...'

'You'll help all right.' His expression changed as he thought of another idea. He turned to Winnie. 'Get me the stuff, will you?'

Winnie didn't question him but walked unsteadily to the storeroom. She smelled strongly of sherry.

'Right, you and me are going upstairs.' Charlie spat the words in Rita's ear. 'You're still my wife, I can do what I like with you. If you don't scream out and let me do what I need to do, then I might just leave the boy alone this time. You understand me? You said you wanted to be a good wife, well now I'm claiming my rights as a husband, and if you dare to cry out or try to stop me I'm off to that farm. So you better be good. Spread your legs like you used to and pretend to enjoy it, though I don't think you ever did, that was just more of your lies. You were spreading them all the time for that Jack, weren't you, just having me on you loved me. So now it's my turn and I'll enjoy it all the more knowing you wished it was him.'

'I ... I...' Rita's stomach turned over at the idea of him touching her. He was filthy and smelled of sweat and fear, and his fingernails were black. She had tried to enjoy sex with him when they'd been living under the same roof, wanting to make the marriage work and keep the family together, but now the thought of it was deeply repulsive. However, she had no choice. She couldn't risk Charlie harming Michael, and from the manic look of him

354

she didn't doubt he would do it. It was no empty threat. She had to get this over with for the sake of her son. Desperately she tried to think of anything that would make the ordeal more bearable. She knew she had to be strong and get through it, endure the next few minutes, or however long he decided it would take. Surely it wouldn't be long – he'd want to get away. It might be no worse than it used to be, when he'd hurt her for his own pleasure in the knowledge that she wouldn't cry out in case it woke the children. Perhaps it wouldn't be so bad. After all, he was Megan's father, and if she'd never met him then she wouldn't have Megan, the joy of her life. She could do this. She could force herself to look as if she was enjoying it just so her children would be safe. It would be nothing really. She could manage this, she had to.

Looking at Charlie again, she found she pitied him. This was a man who had had everything: a fiercely protective mother, a decent home, a reliable job, a willing wife and two adorable children. Yet he'd lost it all, through his own cowardice and greed, thinking he could have any woman he wanted, bearing no responsibility for his family. Winnie had ruined him, spoiling him, making him think he was above everyone in Empire Street, as she had portrayed herself. It had done neither of them any good. Now she was a pathetic drunk, hardly able to get around her own shop, just her spite left to keep her going. She'd been able to siphon off some foodstuffs to feed her son, but she couldn't help him now he was on the run. He'd brought that on himself – and yet he would never have had the backbone to knuckle down to army discipline. He was a desperately sorry creature. Maybe if she thought of him that way it would make what he was about to force her to do more bearable. She got to her feet, bracing herself against the pain.

Charlie lunged at her and groped her breasts under the jumper. 'Let's get a feel of what I'll be having,' he said, his voice uneven, his breath short. She could smell the foulness of it. 'You've lost weight, Rita, it doesn't suit you. You used to give me a nice handful, now there's hardly anything there. Like that all over, are you? I shall have to check.'

She forced herself not to push him away, though his hands were hard and rough. She turned her face away from the stench of his breath, but he caught the movement and wrenched her head around, jerking her neck violently. 'Look at me, Rita. I know you don't want to but you're my wife, you don't turn your back on me. Not unless that's how I want it,' he added, with a grim snigger. She thought she would be sick but she looked at him steadily, this wreck of a man who had somehow fathered the most beautiful little girl. He was pushing her towards the stairs and she briefly shut her eyes at the thought of being in their old bedroom together, bringing back the painful memories of all she had endured there.

'Don't shut your eyes, I told you to look at me.' He slapped her hard and the noise rang out like a gunshot. She staggered but didn't fall as he had his cruel hands on her under her clothes, pawing mercilessly, twisting and pinching her flesh.

'Up you go. Come on, I'm in a hurry.' She

could feel his body against hers and he was growing hard at the idea of causing her pain.

Just as she made herself climb the first step, there was a noise from the shop, several voices shouting at once.

Winnie emerged from the storeroom, a big cloth bag in her hands, which she was struggling to lift. 'What was that?'

Charlie swung around, releasing Rita so swiftly that she fell into the wall. 'You bitch, have you set me up?' he snarled frantically, grabbing the bag from his mother. 'Come on, we're leaving.' He took his mother's elbow and shoved her towards the door to the back yard. 'You'll be sorry for this, Rita, I'll make you pay. You won't see Michael again – until he's lying in his coffin.'

'I didn't do anything, I don't know anything!' Rita cried in desperation, but it was too late, the door slammed shut behind a fleeing Charlie and Winnie.

Before she could tug her jumper properly back into place, three men in military police uniform burst through the internal shop door. 'Where is he?' the first one demanded sharply, then softened his tone as he took in the state of Rita, leaning against the wall, her clothes crooked, bleeding from the leg and a vivid red weal across her cheek. 'Where is Charles Kennedy? We know he is here.'

Wordlessly she pointed to the back door and two of the men ran through it. The final police-man stayed to question her. 'And what is your name?'

Rita shuddered as she told him. 'If you don't catch him, he's going to kill my son,' she added,

357

her mind racing in fear, while trying to work out what had happened. 'Why are you here? How did you know? I had no idea he would come, I haven't seen him since before Christmas.'

'We had a tip-off,' said the man. He had kind eyes but they were sharp with determination. 'Somebody got in touch to say your husband, a deserter, would be on these premises at ten o'clock today. So it wasn't you?'

'No, I don't know anything about it. It's just chance I was here. I should have been at work but I swapped shifts... I was just going about my housework...' Rita gave a sob, the shock of the morning's events beginning to hit her, but she knew she had to hold herself together and find out where Charlie had gone. She wouldn't be safe until she knew he'd been apprehended.

'Then I must follow my colleagues. We will probably need to question you further later on, Mrs Kennedy.' The man made for the back door. Rita followed him, still bleeding, but more concerned to learn Charlie's fate than for her own injury. That would have to wait. She urgently had to know if Michael was going to be safe or not.

The policeman crossed the back yard, bending to avoid the washing flying in the breeze, and went through the gate. He seemed uncertain which way to go, but Rita pulled him around the corner and out on to the top end of Empire Street, as she could hear that something was going on further down. Sure enough a small crowd had gathered in front of the ruined façade of what had been Mrs Ashby's house. She half ran, half limped the short distance to where they stood, while the man hurriedly went to join his colleagues, who were standing outside the remains of the front door.

One of them stepped forward and called through the broken door. 'Come out, Mr Kennedy. There is no point you hiding in there – we know where you are. You must come with us.'

Rita stared in horror as Charlie's face briefly appeared through the shattered panes of one of the upstairs windows. He must have dragged Winnie in there too, although maybe she wasn't fully aware of what was going on if she'd been on the sherry since breakfast. Still, they couldn't hide away in there for long. The houses on that side of the street had no back alley, so the only way out was via the front.

The first policeman banged on the doorframe to emphasise his point, and immediately there was a sound of something falling, a clattering, from inside.

'It's not safe!' cried Rita, pushing to the front. 'That house got damaged in the air raids, it caught fire round the back. It's not safe.'

The policeman with the kind eyes turned to her. 'All the more reason for you to stand back, Mrs Kennedy,' he said firmly. 'Your husband and mother-in-law are in there, but we must get them out before they come to serious harm. We don't want you added to the casualty list – any more than you already are.'

Rita had all but forgotten her own pain now. She was filled with foreboding, the sense that a tragedy was about to unfold before their eyes. She had to try to stop it somehow. She hadn't loved

Charlie, and she'd hated what he'd done to her, how he'd threatened her and the children, but she didn't want his life to end here in the dereliction of a bombed-out house. 'Tell your colleague not to bang on the doorframe–' she began, but before she could finish there was a deafening crash from inside the house and dust billowed from the gaps in the broken door and shattered windows. Then the remains of the door fell in and everyone could see what had happened. The upper floor had given way, and everything from the bedrooms had crashed to the ground floor – the burnt furniture, the bricks and plaster, an odd assortment of Mrs Ashby's pathetically old personal possessions, and, underneath all of this, two bodies.

'Stand back!' shouted the first policeman, urging the crowd away, but Rita broke free of the group and ran inside. 'Mrs Kennedy, leave the premises at once!'

'I can help, I'm a nurse,' she called back, as she began to scrabble through the rubble, hoping she could somehow pull Charlie and Winnie clear. Ignoring the pain in her leg, she worked as fast as she could, joined now by two of the police while the third stood guard at the door. Rita hoped the sherry had dulled the impact for the old woman; that she hadn't been fully aware of what was going on. Gradually they threw aside the debris and uncovered the faces of mother and son, lying silent and still on their bed of plaster and bricks. There was no sign of life in either of them.

'Come now, Mrs Kennedy,' said one of the policemen. 'Your nursing skills won't be any use here. They're beyond your help.'

Rita gulped, but even though she could see what he said was probably true, she couldn't quite believe it. Wordlessly she reached for Winnie's wrist, brushing the coating of dust from her dry skin. There was no pulse. Rita shut her eyes, remembering what her mother-in-law had been like – carping, manipulative, overly proud. Yet she had also worked hard for years in the shop, and had a good business brain, until the combination of Charlie's desertion and Ruby's arrival had taken away her standing. She'd been largely the architect of her own downfall, but without her there would have been no Megan. Rita's heart contracted in sorrow for the old woman. Nobody deserved to die like this.

As for Charlie, she was filled with a turbulent mixture of contradictory feelings: pity for the needless waste of a life, sadness that he hadn't realised how lucky he had been, but also relief that he would no longer be able to hurt her or the children. Michael would be safe. He and Megan need never know about the threats and the danger they were in. She would tell them Charlie and their grandmother had died in an accident, but not why they came to be in that house in the first place. Maybe when the children were older she would have to explain, but for now she would spare them all but the most basic details.

Poor Charlie. Now he'd never have the privilege of seeing the children grow up into the fine people they would undoubtedly be. Rita knew they were her reason for living and yet Charlie had turned his back on them, had failed to recognise the glorious potential of his own little daughter. He'd done many mean, wicked, selfish things, but to ignore the promise of his own flesh and blood – that was beyond her comprehension. The sad thing was, neither child was likely to miss him. Charlie had forfeited the right to their love when he'd walked out on Rita, and now their lives would continue much the same as before.

'Come away, Mrs Kennedy.' The policeman was insistent now. 'This house clearly isn't safe. You can do no more for your husband and his mother, you've seen that for yourself. We need to get you seen to. You've got a nasty wound there by the looks of it.'

As he escorted her out through the damaged doorway, Rita realised her leg was still bleeding copiously and that it hurt a lot. Now the urgency of the situation had receded, the pain hit her like a wave, and she sank to the pavement as soon as she was outside. She knew the wound needed to be cleaned up at the very least, and maybe she'd have to have stitches as well, but the only person she could think of who could help was Sarah, and she'd be at work. Gritting her teeth against the agony, she looked around as the small crowd dispersed. None of her family was there. Her father would be at work, Dolly and Violet were most likely down at the victory garden. She couldn't exactly ask Ruby for help – the young woman would still be marooned upstairs over the shop, hampered by having to rely on crutches. Poor Ruby – she'd lost her mother without really ever having had her. She was more alone than ever now.

Rita screwed her eyes against the bright daylight, wondering if the pain was making her see things, or if by some huge coincidence there was another person on crutches. For coming down the short length of Empire Street towards her was a young woman with blonde hair, swinging herself unsteadily along but managing to cover the distance. Yet how could this be Ruby? Yesterday she'd hardly been able to get to the bathroom.

'Rita! Are you hurt?' There was no mistake, it was Ruby, and now she was trying to bend down to see how Rita was.

'Ruby! What are you doing out?' Rita's first thought was concern for her friend. 'Oh Ruby, the most dreadful thing has happened...'

'Did the military police come?' Ruby asked. 'I told them when they should be there. I went all the way to the ARP station and told them to pass on the message. Is that why they are outside Mrs Ashby's house?'

'Oh Ruby, you've been really brave and clever,' sighed Rita. 'I need help, but if you could ask one of them to get me to the shop then you could fetch me the first-aid box and I can look after my leg. Then I'll tell you what happened.'

Ruby looked along the street. 'You need somebody to lift you.'

'Well, there isn't anyone, so we'll have to make do as best we can,' said Rita, her determination returning.

'Yes there is,' said Ruby, a big smile spreading across her face. 'I told him to come too. Look, here he is.'

For the second time, Rita thought she must be seeing things as a beloved and familiar figure came towards her along the street, breaking into a run as

363

he realised she was injured. 'Jack!' she cried, unable to believe her eyes. 'Jack – is that really you?'

Jack took in the scene with one glance and didn't bother to reply. Instead he scooped her into his arms and lifted her as easily as if she were a child, hurrying to carry her to safety. Once in the kitchen behind the shop, he set her gently down. 'Oh Rita. I came as soon as I could. I got leave after all, the plans were changed at the last minute so I couldn't send word. Then as I was coming along the dock road I saw Ruby, and she's told me the strangest things have been going on. But never mind that now. Let's take a look to see how badly you're hurt and worry about everything else later.'

Rita felt the tears begin to fall, of pain, of relief, but also of sheer happiness at being in his arms again. She felt as if she would never let him go. 'Jack, you're back,' she sighed against the warmth of his shoulder. 'I needed help and you were there. My rescuer. Oh Jack, I can't begin to tell you how glad I am you're here.'

'You don't have to,' he said, his breath warm and soothing against her ear. 'I'm as glad to be here and to see you. I've dreamed and dreamed of seeing you again, and holding you close, showing how much I love you.' He broke off, releasing her from his strong arms, leant back and smiled at her. 'All right, I didn't dream you'd be in such a state. But I don't care – I'm back, and with you, which is where I belong, and now I'm going to fix you up.' He glanced up as Ruby slowly made her way into the kitchen. 'Here, Ruby, you sit with Rita for a minute. You'll be right as rain, Rita, just you see.' He kept his voice light and encouraging, not commenting on the weal on her face. From what Ruby had told him, he could well imagine what had gone on. But there would be time enough for explanations later. For now he had to make sure the woman he loved above all others was safe and protected.

'Oh Jack, thank God you're back,' sighed Rita.

CHAPTER THIRTY-THREE

Kitty bowed her head as the organ finished the final bars of the closing hymn. She was grateful for the support of Laura and Marjorie, who stood one either side of her, all three of them in their Wren uniforms. Now, if she could just keep control of her emotions as they formed up to leave the church and went into the graveyard, she would have managed to get through the public part of the day.

She wasn't sure exactly what had changed her mind about going to Elliott's funeral, but now she was glad she had done so. Thinking it over, as she had done incessantly for the past few days, she'd decided it was important to be there not only because of her relationship with him, but to represent how Elliott's life had been in the period immediately before his death. All around were those who'd known him as a boy or a medical student, but there were few who'd known what he was like as a doctor in Liverpool – the kind, knowledgeable professional, widely respected and admired, who had loved her. Nobody could be spared from the hospital on Linacre Lane; they were under too much pressure now one of their key members of staff had been taken from them. So Kitty, Laura and Marjorie were there to remember him as he had been in his last months of life.

Mrs Fitzgerald, Elliott's mother, had been keen for all three of them to come back to her house afterwards along with other family and friends, but Kitty had not felt able to accept. She kept remembering how she was to have gone to that very house for a celebratory lunch, and the contrast with reality was a step too far. So she had politely declined, saying that they were needed back on shift, and if Mrs Fitzgerald had detected the lie, she had been too discreet to comment on it. Kitty thought the woman was exactly how she'd imagined Elliott's mother would be: elegant, courteous, dignified even in her grief.

Elliott's father was a more remote figure who had retreated into silence as a way of coping with bereavement. Kitty had exchanged a handful of words with him, the briefest of condolences, but neither of them wanted to prolong the conversation. Kitty knew there was little point. They were unlikely to meet again. She registered the physical likeness between the man and his son, from the thickness and wave of the hair to the set of the eyes, but that was no surprise. Mrs Fitzgerald had assured her she must keep in touch and Kitty had smiled and thanked her but really did not want to. If Elliott had not been killed, she had no doubt that she would have got on well with his parents, but there was no reason to continue to see them now he was dead. The only thing they had in common was the wish that he hadn't died, and it was too painful a bond.

Numbly she joined the others as they processed out of the church, following the crowd as they made their way to the grave site. It was almost over. She had dreaded this day, but now she was glad she had come because, just as people said would happen, it made her feel as if that chapter of her life had finished. Her grief was no less real, but she trusted that slowly it would fade – not vanish, but not invade every waking moment. Slowly her sense of self was returning. She was still Kitty Callaghan, still a Wren, still sister to Jack, Danny and Tommy. Even if she was no longer the girlfriend of Dr Elliott Fitzgerald, she would go on with her training; she had to throw herself into every opportunity that life offered, as a way of paying tribute to his loving trust and support.

'Go on, it's your turn.' Laura touched her arm and Kitty realised she was expected to throw a little earth on to the coffin. If someone had told her even a day or two ago that she would be able to manage to do this without breaking down, while everyone looked at her – including Elliott's former professor, father of his late fiancée – she wouldn't have believed them. Yet she came forward and performed the necessary ritual without faltering and then returned to Laura and Marjorie's protection. Sombrely she said a mental goodbye to Elliott, and she clutched her new handkerchief in her pocket. But she did not cry. She had finished crying. Now she would set her sights on the future

– not the one she thought she would have, but a different one. She recognised that this year of knowing Elliott had changed her, and for the better. Now it was up to her to live the life he had helped to give her. Men and women like Elliott were making the ultimate sacrifice, both at home and many, many more on the front. Kitty knew it was up to her and thousands of people like her to make sure that it was a price worth paying – they'd show Hitler what they were really made of.

'Oh Jack, I can't thank you enough.' Rita gazed at him with gratitude added to her deep love for this wonderful man. He'd done his best to dress the wound on her leg, but had realised it was too serious for him to manage alone. So he'd borrowed Pop's horse and cart and taken her to hospital that way. She'd protested that he could just have left her at the VAD nursing station where Sarah could have looked at it, under Rita's own instructions, but Jack would have none of it. He wanted a fully qualified, experienced doctor to see to it, and she was ultimately glad he had insisted, as the main cut was very deep and the others also continued to bleed. She'd had three separate sets of stitches in the end, and had been given the strictest instructions to rest the leg for several days to prevent any of the injuries opening up again. They'd also done what they could for the angry red mark on her face where Charlie had slapped her so hard, although she knew it would turn into a bruise that would last for ages. She'd had enough of them before from him – just not as obvious and prominent.

Now she was propped up on one of the comfier chairs in what Winnie used to call the breakfast room, a stool next to it with her leg resting on an old cushion and a towel under it for extra padding. It didn't feel too bad. She thought she had come off lightly, compared to what might have happened if the military police hadn't arrived, when they did. At least the ride to and from the hospital had given her a chance to explain to Jack what had gone on, and he had filled in some of the details he'd heard from Ruby.

Ruby was now over at Dolly and Pop's, something she would never have dared to do only a few weeks ago, but the events of the day had given her courage. Besides, Violet was there, and she trusted her, along with little Georgie, who was a constant source of delight to her. Dolly had wisely surmised that Rita needed some time alone with Jack, and had asked Ruby to stay on for a few hours, 'to help look after Georgie', but really to make sure Rita had her privacy. Dolly wasn't daft; despite Rita's efforts to play down her feelings for the young man, Dolly could tell something was up. It was the way her eldest daughter's face lit up at the very mention of him. Dolly had very strict views on the sanctity of marriage and knew her daughter was deeply moral – but if anyone deserved some time alone with the man she so clearly adored and who adored her right back, it was Rita.

'You don't have to thank me,' said Jack seriously. He sat in the chair next to hers and took her hand. 'Just being with you is thanks enough. Knowing what danger you were in has made me realise just how easily I could have lost you, and I can't even begin to think about what would have happened then. You're the most important person in my world, Rita. I'd do anything for you, taking you on a short ride to the hospital and back is nothing. I'd walk across burning coals.'

'Please don't do that.' Rita's eyes were bright with love. 'You're the most important person to me too – well, along with Michael and Megan of course.' She stopped, reminded of how Charlie was going to kill her son. But now he could do no more harm. 'I don't know what I'd do without you. When your leave got cancelled it felt like the end of the world. I'd been looking forward to seeing you so much. It hurt more than my leg did this morning. It was all I'd been thinking about. It's like a miracle, you turning up when you did.'

'Just as well I did,' he said seriously, squeezing her hand.

'But imagine Ruby doing what she did. She's scared stiff of the police or anyone in authority, but she somehow got herself out of the house on those crutches without me knowing anything about it, and then convinced the ARP warden that something bad was about to take place. I've completely underestimated her.'

'So you didn't think she knew what she was talking about?'

Rita shook her head. 'It wasn't so much I didn't believe her, it was more that I thought it couldn't be anything terrible. So a bit of stock was going missing. I was angry about it, but after everything that's happened recently, the air raid, Elliott dying, it was more of an annoying puzzle. I sup-

370

pose I imagined it was just Winnie dabbling in the black market again. It was different for Ruby, she didn't usually leave the house, so she must have overheard more than she'd let on. I knew she'd worked out the stock would probably be taken today – but not that Winnie had been giving food to Charlie, or that he was so desperate. It means Ruby was braver than ever as she was terrified of him. I don't know what he did to her before we brought her back from Southport, but she used to go white if anyone said his name. So to think she ran the risk of bumping into him – that took a lot of courage.'

'It did.' Jack stroked her hand gently. 'So did trying to help Winnie and Charlie when the building collapsed. I don't think I'd have been so selfless, Rita. I'd have left them to it, if they'd done to me what they did to you. But you're so kind, you put yourself at risk to help your enemies.'

Rita looked gravely at him. 'No you wouldn't. You'd have tried to help, the same as I did – that's the sort of person you are. Besides, I didn't really think I'd be at risk. I was just doing what any nurse would have done. It wasn't courage or kindness, it was what we are trained to do – our duty. And it turned out I couldn't help anyway.' She gave a deep sigh, recalling the scene: Winnie's lifeless arm hanging down, covered in dust. The stupid horror of it. The terrible waste of lives needlessly lost.

'Don't think about it.' Jack could tell what was going through her mind, he knew her so well. 'Rita, we should think about something else instead. Heaven knows I wouldn't wish anyone dead, but you know what this all means, don't you?'

For a moment Rita's mind was blank. 'What, Jack?'

'Rita, you're free,' Jack said, holding her hand more tightly. 'You don't have to go against your beliefs and get divorced – you're legally a widow. You can do what you want. You're not tied to a husband who was never there, you're out of limbo.'

'I'm free.' The enormity of it began to dawn on her. She hadn't been free since she was a teenager – pregnant with Michael, with Jack abroad and not there to help her, and forced to marry Charlie in a hurry. How she had paid for that decision – although she could never have stood the shame of bearing a child out of wedlock. She stared at him in dawning astonishment. 'It's true, Jack. I really am free.' Then she sighed, her eyes downcast. 'But I'm not sure I feel that yet. Whatever I felt about Charlie, he was still my husband for all that time, and he was Megan's father. Without him, she wouldn't be alive.'

Slowly, deliberately, Jack rose from his chair and got down before her on one knee. 'Rita, this isn't how I imagined it happening and I'm not exactly prepared, but it's a day I sometimes thought would never come. Now it has. I don't want to rush you into anything, and you know I'll respect your wishes above all, but I'm only on a short shore leave. So I'm going to ask you now: will you be my wife? I love you more than words can say. I would be proud to have the most beautiful woman in Liverpool as my wife. Say you will. Say you'll marry me.'

Rita felt the tears well up, and for once they were of pure, undiluted happiness. She had lain awake many nights wondering if she'd done the right thing by refusing to seek a divorce, knowing how much Jack wanted her, and how much she wanted him right back, but also knowing that she would have felt it was fundamentally wrong. Was she being selfish in denying this to Jack, when he was out there every day putting his life on the line to defend his country? Or would she live to regret it if she went against her most profoundly held principles? The dilemma had eaten away at her. Now it was resolved. She didn't have to choose between her beliefs and the man she loved. The dreadful events of the morning had brought about this wonderful truth.

'Of course,' she said simply. 'I'd love that more than anything else in the world.' She stared at him, this handsome, brave man who cared for her so tenderly and made her feel safe. He rose again and kissed her, gently but intensely, avoiding brushing against her so as not to move her leg.

'Jack, I don't think we should rush off for a special licence before you return to your ship. I want us to wait a little,' she said, turning to him and then wincing as pain shot through her wound once more. 'As long as I know we're going to be married at last, after all these years, let's wait just a bit longer.' Her face grew solemn. 'Charlie might have done some truly awful things, but I owe him some respect, for the children's sake – we need a bit of time to let all the wounds heal a little. It's the proper thing to do, and when they're older I want the children to know that we both did right by him.'

'You're too kind to Charlie, even in death. But it's why I love you so much.' Jack encircled her as best he could with his arm. 'I tell you what. I will be due a couple of days' leave around Christmas or just before. Will that be long enough? Will you marry me then?'

'Yes,' she said immediately, not even having to think it over. 'We won't need a big do. It will be the best Christmas present ever.'

'Do you mind if it isn't in church?' he asked. He knew how important her beliefs were, even if she didn't attend very regularly.

'No, I don't mind if you don't. It'll be easier to plan if we don't have a church wedding,' she said decisively. 'Father Harding will understand. It's more important that we're married than where the ceremony takes place. Oh Jack, it's going to be wonderful.' She leant into him as best she could. 'You and me together at last. I can't quite believe it. I'm so sorry Charlie died the way he did, but now we can start planning our future. Oh Jack, sometimes I thought it would never happen. That we'd be apart for ever. Now it's a dream come true.'

He shook his head and gave a little laugh. 'I always knew,' he said. 'I had faith we'd manage it somehow, some day. Rita, you've made me the happiest man alive. I'm going to treat you as you deserve for the rest of your life. And I can't wait to show you just how much I love you.'

CHAPTER THIRTY-FOUR

Laura made her way down the spotlessly clean hospital corridor as she had done many times before. It had been a few days since she had visited; she'd used up some of her free time to go to Elliott's funeral and of course she didn't begrudge that, but it had meant she hadn't been able to visit the captain. Even though she knew he had been progressing well, she was never quite sure what she'd find when she went through the door to his room. Although reason told her she would have been told if he'd taken a turn for the worse, she couldn't be certain how he would be and she bit her lip in anxiety. She hesitated as she reached the door and then told herself not to be so silly. There was nothing to worry about. She knocked softly and heard his voice call her to come in.

'Oh!' She stopped abruptly. 'You're up and about! Nobody said!'

He was standing by the window, in his uniform trousers and pressed shirt. She registered how well he looked – his thick hair shining, his broad shoulders back, as if he'd never had a serious chest injury. He'd drawn himself up to his impressive full height, which she'd almost forgotten for all the time he was bedridden.

'I told them not to tell you,' he said with a wide smile. 'It would have been too dreadful if you'd got your hopes up and then I had a relapse. But

I've been able to stand and get around for a couple of days now.'

'That's wonderful.' Then her eyes clouded. 'But you mustn't overdo it. Shouldn't you sit down again now that you've proved your point? I don't want to be the one to cause you to relapse – your uncle would never forgive me for a start.' She came across to him and stood beside the window, through which they could see the last of the autumn leaves falling and being blown in haphazard patterns around the hospital grounds.

'Oh, I think my uncle would forgive you quite a lot, as it happens,' he said lightly, making no move away. 'Seriously, Fawcett, you mustn't fret. I'm quite capable of knowing if I need to sit down or not. That's what happens when you're promoted to captain. They acknowledge you have full control of your bodily functions.'

'Well, yes, of course, sir.' Laura didn't know where to look. She knew he was teasing, but he was so close to her and somehow it was different to when she'd sat close to him when he'd been ill. She could feel the heat from his body.

'Fawcett,' he said, looking down at her, 'I realise this is very informal but I have a distinct memory of you calling me Peter. We even talked about my name, if I recall rightly.'

'We did, sir.' She couldn't tell which way this conversation was heading.

'I also realise that when we are in public I am of superior rank to you and it is fitting that you call me "sir" or "captain". However, when we are alone, I do think you should drop the formality and call me Peter. Would you do that?'

She gazed up at him, conscious that she was only up to his shoulder. 'As a way of aiding your recovery, you mean?'

'Most definitely.' He seemed to step even closer to her. 'And maybe I should address you by your first name. Seems as though I'm always giving you orders if I call you Fawcett all the time.'

'It's Laura, sir. I mean Peter.' She could feel her legs trembling now; she couldn't help it.

'Well, yes, I knew that, Fawcett. Laura.' He gazed at her and suddenly that sense of close connection that had blazed between them at the police station after the fire was back, and she tipped her head back as he bent his mouth to hers and kissed her – not gently, not carefully like an invalid might, but a full-blooded kiss of barely restrained passion, such as she had never received in her life, and she found herself responding fully, brazenly, despite the nearness of the window. For a few moments she could think of nothing else. Then slowly she pulled away, catching her breath, unsure of what to say.

'Laura,' he breathed against the top of her hair, his breath hot and catching a little. 'I've wanted to do that for a very, very long time. Almost since I saw you, in fact. Definitely since the first time you answered me back when I asked you to reverse into a tight spot.'

'I never did!' she objected. 'I was always a paragon of propriety and obedience.' Her eyes danced as she gazed up at his.

'Maybe. But I had to have you with me whenever possible,' he confessed. 'Surely you guessed why? That I'd asked for you to be transferred from driving lorries to permanent chauffeur duties? Surely you saw I couldn't bear to be without the sight of you for a day?'

'No, I thought you hated me. You were always so silent or else so rude,' she told him honestly. 'You used to stare at the back of my head, I could see you in the rear-view mirror.'

He laughed at being caught out. 'I did. Not out of hatred though. Out of ... admiration.'

She shook her head, unable to believe how wrongly she'd read him. 'I complained about you all the time. All those evenings when you stopped me going to the cinema with my friends.'

'I bet you did. I was impossible, I admit.' He gazed softly at her. 'I wasn't sure if you had a chap or not, to be honest. You've never said. Or if you'd lost somebody, like your friend did.'

With a sinking feeling Laura turned away. She didn't want to break the magic of the moment, but his words had brought back to her the ache she always carried.

'I'm sorry,' he said at once. 'Did I say the wrong thing? Is there someone? Laura, you have to tell me. I'm showing you my heart here. There's nobody in my life, I've never met anyone like you. But if you have someone else, then tell me now. Don't let me believe you feel the same and then break my heart.'

She gasped at the meaning of his words – that he was declaring himself in the most open way and laying himself open to hurt. How brave he was to make himself vulnerable like this. That took courage, a different sort of courage to the one needed to race into a burning building to save a child.

'Sort of,' she said, looking away. 'No, not like that, but ... you know when we found the baby and it was safe, and its blanket was alight? We wrapped it in my scarf.'

'I remember.' His voice was full of uncertainty, not knowing what was coming next.

'My brother gave it to me. I don't have much else of his. He's missing, presumed dead,' she said quietly. 'We were very close. So, while I don't have a chap, I have lost someone, or I probably have. The not-knowing is the worst.'

'Oh, my darling girl.' His arms were around her in an instant, stroking her back, his beautiful shirt absorbing her tears. 'I'm sorry. It's rough, isn't it? My best friend is missing, has been for months, and it's torture. I do understand.'

'Yes.' She lifted her head once more. 'There, now you know. I don't tell everyone, only Kitty and Marjorie realise, but there we are, it's part of everyday life now. Too, too grim. Maybe one day we'll know for sure and then at least we can grieve properly.'

He reached into his pocket, drew out a pristine linen handkerchief and wiped her eyes. 'Yes, that would help.' He kissed her softly on the forehead. 'Don't cry, my beautiful Laura. Not when we've just found each other.'

She sighed. 'I can't believe it. All those weeks, months, I thought you were setting out to make my life hell.'

'No, Laura.' His voice was deadly serious now. 'It was selfish of me to commandeer your presence so often, but I never wanted to make your life hell. The very reverse. We'll have to work out something once I'm out of here, but once I'm fully better, I want to make your life as wonderful as you deserve it to be. What do you say?'

Laura felt her sorrow fade away and a bubble of happiness rise within her. 'Yes, Peter,' she said. 'Yes, with all my heart.'

Then, in case there could be any doubts left, he kissed her again, as strongly as he dared, and she responded with all the passion that had built up inside her since realising on that fateful night of the fire that here was the man she would love for the rest of her life.

Epilogue

CHAPTER THIRTY-FIVE

December 1941

Kitty Callaghan got to her feet in the swaying train carriage and reached up for her case. She swung it down and took it through to the corridor, which was packed with passengers who'd had to stand all the way from London. Now they were almost into Lime Street Station. The journey had taken twice as long as it used to do before the war, but nobody was complaining. There had been many longer than this and Kitty reflected she was home earlier than she'd expected to be.

The train pulled up at the platform and she

scrambled down, bowled along by the crowds disembarking. She had told nobody she was coming, deciding that she would surprise them, and after all there was always the chance that her leave would be cancelled at the last minute or the trains wouldn't be running. She couldn't bear the thought of disappointing them, not after she'd been away for the best part of the year.

Gazing around the familiar station, she could see men and women in uniform hugging wives, girlfriends, children, husbands, boyfriends. Until recently that might have been her. But the person she would have wanted to welcome her back wasn't here – would never be here again.

She straightened her shoulders in resolution. Even if this wasn't how she had imagined her homecoming, she was still glad to be back, despite it being for such a short while. She hadn't admitted to herself how much she'd missed everyone. She'd worried about Tommy, of course, wondering if he was behaving himself, worried he'd be ill again. Although Danny was old enough to look after himself, she'd worried about him too, as he'd been far from recovered when she'd last seen him. His letters assured her he was getting better by the day and that his new job suited him, so she'd tried to put his underlying heart condition out of her mind, as there was nothing she could do about it. All the same, she was keen to see him, to check for herself how he really was.

As for Jack – she had gasped with delight when she'd got the letter telling her he was getting married to Rita at last. It had almost distracted her from her own sorrow to hear such wonderful news. She'd been too young to understand what had gone on when the couple had first got together in their teens; she only knew she had missed her big brother when he'd moved away, and then Rita had married Charlie. Later on, when the age gap between herself and Rita didn't matter any more, she realised how unhappy her friend was in her marriage and that she still carried a candle for Jack, even if she did her very best to hide it. She'd willingly helped her by passing on his letters – never judging them, as some self-righteous people might well have done. Now finally they were getting married. God knew they deserved their happiness after what they had both suffered, Rita in particular. Kitty hadn't shed any tears over the deaths of Winnie and Charlie. She knew without any shadow of a doubt that Jack would make her friend happier than her first husband ever had.

Stepping out of the station entrance she gasped again, this time in shock. She had heard about the destruction visited on the city centre by the Luftwaffe's raids, but nothing could have prepared her for the actual sight of it. It was like another world. She'd seen bomb damage in London, of course, but the harm done to Liverpool was like a dagger in her heart. A wave of deep sadness washed over her, that her beloved city should have endured all this. How would it ever be put back together? For a moment she shut her eyes, not wanting to believe that the familiar streets of her childhood were so drastically changed.

Then she strode forward, swinging her case, determined not to give in to the overwhelming emotion. She'd done enough crying over the past few weeks. All about her people were milling around, some in uniform, others in clothes that had last been fashionable in 1939, but none looked demoralised. These were the people of Merseyside, and while their city might have been flattened, they were not defeated. They were fighting back and refusing to be cowed by a powerful enemy. She was part of that fight, and she had her part to play now too: sister of the groom, close friend of the bride, celebrating their wedding with all the goodwill she possessed. Squaring her shoulders once more, she set off to find what public transport had survived the destruction so she could make her way back to Bootle.

'Pass me that plate of sandwiches, pet.' Dolly was in her element, organising the preparations for the wedding feast. Everyone had contributed their ration coupons to make sure there would be a proper celebration for Jack and Rita. She was determined that they should have a party every bit as good as the ones before the war. It would just take more ingenuity.

Luckily Tommy, Michael and Megan had arrived from the farm laden with parcels of food from Joan and Seth. As there had been no more raids over Bootle since October, Rita had decided they could risk coming home for a short visit, as long as they brought their gas masks. She dearly wanted her children with her when she said her vows to Jack. Tommy had threatened to run away and come along anyway if they'd not been allowed back. He was beside himself with happiness now that he'd be as good as properly related to Michael and Megan. While he'd taken full advantage of being the youngest by far of the Callaghan siblings, he'd grown into the role of big brother to the Kennedy children. Rita thought it was good for him – he was more responsible when he was looking after them or showing them what was what, and heaven knew he had been in need of calming down. No adult had ever managed to do it, but this new position of big brother was bringing out a whole new side of him.

Now she was being urged to sit down by Dolly. 'You don't have to make your own party food,' she said. 'You take the weight off your feet and stay out of the way. Save your energy for this afternoon. We've got it all under control, haven't we?' She turned to Violet and Ruby, who nodded without stopping what they were doing. Violet was cutting slices of bread and then buttering them with real butter, while Ruby was opening tins. After the dreadful events of Charlie's return and the building collapsing, Rita had had to face going through Winnie's things. To her surprise, there were boxes and boxes under the old woman's bed, filled to the brim with luxury foodstuffs. It seemed she had never lost the habit of squirrelling tins away, and now they would all reap the benefit. Winnie would be turning in her grave to think her precious salmon was to be used for Rita's second wedding, but Rita thought it was only justice. There would also be a generous amount of sherry for anyone who wanted it – Winnie had hidden the bottles behind her wardrobe. No wonder she'd been able to drink from first thing in the morning.

'When are you going to start getting ready?' Violet wanted to know. 'You aren't getting married in your old cardigan with patches on the elbow, are you?'

Rita shook her head. 'No, although Jack said he'd marry me whatever I wore, he wouldn't care.' She knew he'd meant it as well. She was lucky beyond her wildest dreams to have such a man. 'Nancy took me shopping – she knows all the best places in the city centre now. She found me a lovely frock and it wasn't even too expensive. I'm going to borrow her green coat so I'll look smarter than I have done for years. She's coming over in a moment to paint my nails, she's got a bottle of polish put away that goes really well with the pattern of the frock.'

'I'm amazed she has the time,' said Dolly. 'She's been busier than ever with the WVS now that the Americans are in the war good and proper.' Just a couple of weeks ago the Japanese had bombed Pearl Harbor, taking everyone by surprise, and this had prompted the United States to declare war on Japan and throw its weight behind the Allied cause. Nobody was in any doubt that this would mean many more American servicemen and -women arriving in Britain, and that many of them would pass through Liverpool. Nancy would be right in the midst of it.

'She couldn't *not* come to the wedding, and she's the best person to help me look glamorous.' Rita stood and posed like a model. 'I want to look right in all the photos, don't I? And to do Jack proud, of course.'

'I do hope Sarah will be back in time,' Dolly said, wiping her hands on a tea towel. 'She promised she would be here by midday. You know what she's like, she always stays on if they're short-staffed.'

'She'll be here,' Rita said confidently. She wondered why she wasn't more anxious, as there was still so much to do and the wedding was booked for three o'clock. Yet she felt completely calm. It was the exact opposite of when she'd married Charlie in such haste. Now she had no doubts at all. She adored Jack and couldn't wait to be his wife, and she knew he loved her more than anything. Her children loved him too, and they would finally have the most wonderful man as their father. After everything that had happened, she didn't mind if her sisters arrived late, or wearing the wrong thing. Such small details would not mar her joy on her wedding day. Nothing would.

As if on cue, the back door opened and Sarah came into the kitchen, her cheeks flushed by the cold outside. 'Sorry I'm a bit late,' she gasped. 'Some silly accident down on the dock road. They asked me to help this afternoon but I said no.'

'Well then, I am honoured,' grinned Rita. 'You never say no. Bet they were shocked.'

'Just a bit.' Sarah came across and hugged her sister. 'How's the blushing bride? Do you need any help getting ready?'

Rita shook her head. 'No, as soon as Nancy gets here we're going over to my place and she'll doll me up. You just make sure you're as gorgeous as possible.'

'And you could fold some napkins if you've a

386

moment,' Dolly told her youngest. 'We don't want anyone saying we don't do things properly round here.'

'Where are the children?' Sarah asked.

'I wanted them out of the way,' said Dolly honestly. 'It's lovely to have them back but they aren't much use at a time like this. So Danny's taken all three of them down to the victory garden. Not that there will be much to bring back at this time of year, but you never know.'

'That's good of him,' said Sarah, knowing how hard Danny had been working recently. But he'd be pleased to see his little brother and spend some time with him. She just hoped they didn't get too filthy down there. 'Right, I'll go and get changed out of my uniform, put on my glad rags and then grab an apron and help out.'

There was another sound at the door and she turned to open it.

'That'll be Nancy now,' Dolly predicted, glancing at the clock. 'She's cutting it fine.'

But it wasn't Nancy who stepped into the kitchen. For a moment nobody spoke and then they all exclaimed at once – except Ruby, who was confused.

'Kitty!' Rita ran across the room to hug her friend, who was still in her Wren's uniform. 'I didn't think you'd be able to come! You should have said, we'd have sent someone to meet you.'

Kitty's face glowed with happiness. How wonderful it was to be back, and it was all the sweeter for having been away for so long. Now it hit her just how much she had missed everyone, and this place in particular. She'd always loved Dolly's kitchen, which had been like a home from home since she was a little girl. Dolly had promised to look after her when her own mother had died so tragically young, and had always welcomed her with open arms. 'That's why I didn't tell you,' she replied now, taking in Rita's changed appearance – her loss of weight, but the deep contentment that radiated from her in a way she'd never seen before. 'I wasn't sure if I'd make it in time. It's no trouble. I just dropped my case at home and thought I'd come across to see if I could make myself useful. But I can see you've got it all under control.' She gazed at the spread on the kitchen table and every available surface: sandwiches of every sort, meat pies, vol-au-vents, and the luxury of tinned fruit in Dolly's best cut-glass dishes.

'Well...' Dolly glanced at the clock once more. 'Thanks to Joan and Seth, we've got eggs and butter, and everyone's donated sugar, so ... there might just be time. Kitty, would you make us a cake?'

'Oh!' Rita couldn't help herself. The memory of Kitty's famous cakes made her mouth water. Surely her friend would be too tired – if she'd just got off the train she must have been up at an unearthly hour.

But Kitty was taking off her jacket and rolling up her sleeves. While it could never be anything like the three-tiered iced confection she'd produced for Nancy's wedding to Sid, back when the country had still been at peace, she was sure she could come up with something. 'For Rita's wedding? I'd love to.'

The parlour rang with laughter and the sounds of everyone eating, drinking and having a good time. Gloria's parents had donated bottles of beer and the menfolk were cheerfully opening them. Someone had got hold of some whisky as well. Kitty's cake stood in pride of place at the centre of the table. By a miracle it had been ready to come out of the oven just as they couldn't wait to set off any longer, and she'd been relieved to find it hadn't sunk in the middle when they'd returned from the civil ceremony. She'd surreptitiously lifted off the dome of netting and dusted it with a precious teaspoon of icing sugar, and tied a beautiful satin ribbon around it, which Dolly had procured from somewhere. Now it was ready for Rita and Jack to cut, once they'd finished receiving everyone's congratulations. That might take a while, Kitty thought. She had never seen so many people crammed into the house. Some were in the parlour, some in the kitchen or narrow back kitchen, and some were even in the back yard, even though it was a cold day. Everybody, it seemed, wanted to wish the young couple well; Rita was well liked locally and the story of how she had tried to rescue Winnie and Charlie, despite him being a deserter and everything the pair had done, had gone around like wildfire. Of course Jack was known as a serving airman and people admired him for his daily dicing with death.

'You've done them proud with that cake,' Violet said in admiration, coming to Kitty's side. 'Rita's made up about it.'

'Well, you've made all those sandwiches,' Kitty responded, 'so you must take the credit for feeding all these guests.'

Violet smiled at the appreciation of all the work she'd put in; she knew that the fruit they'd grown in the victory garden had been turned into jams and chutneys which were being served alongside the rest of the food. She had good reason to feel satisfied. If only Eddy were here to share this moment with her. She would not cry or even give a little sigh – she couldn't show her sadness in front of this, her new family, who had welcomed her so warmly and made her feel part of them. But how she missed Eddy, his quiet humour, his acceptance of her for who she was and not who she'd tried to make herself out to be. Gazing at Rita, who had one arm around Michael and the other around Megan, both of whom were dressed up in their very best, Violet wondered for the thousandth time if she would ever have a family of her own, the children that she longed for so keenly. Eddy would be such a good father, anyone could see that. He'd be patient and loving, firm when he needed to be, and fiercely protective, just as he was of her. There was no sense in dwelling on it though; she'd just have to look forward to his next leave, whenever that might be. He'd tried to come home for the wedding but had been turned down, much to his disappointment. They'd just have to wait to be together again, like so many couples all across the country.

Sarah came carefully through the crowd, carrying a tray laden with a collection of mismatched glasses full of sherry. She offered one to her sister-in-law but Violet declined, pulling a face.

'Kitty, how about you?' Sarah cautiously turned

round. 'Some of Winnie's ill-gotten sherry? We might as well make the most of it.'

Kitty shook her head. 'I know what you mean, but even the thought of Winnie cursing us from wherever she is now can't persuade me to like the stuff.' She gave a mock shudder as Danny came up behind them.

'Here, Sar, I'll take that. You don't want "Winnie's ruin" down your best frock,' he grinned.

Pop, passing by, made a tutting noise. 'Now let's not speak ill of the dead.' But he smiled to take the sting out of his remark, before moving off to open more beer.

Sarah turned gratefully to Danny. 'Thanks. They're heavier than they look and you're right, I don't want to spoil this on its first outing.' She was wearing a beautifully soft wool dress in a yellow so pale it was almost cream, with delicate crocheted collar and cuffs in white. It suited her slender figure and set off her colouring, but it would no doubt show every mark. Kitty smiled at her brother's chivalry. His manners had improved since she'd left home. Not for the first time she noticed how close he seemed to Sarah, but more likely than not there was nothing in it – Sarah was still very young, and from what everyone said was following in her big sister's footsteps and devoting herself to nursing.

'Frank should be here at any minute,' he went on. 'He couldn't get the afternoon off, they were expecting something through that only he could deal with.' He stopped, knowing that he shouldn't have said even that much – but Sarah had a pretty good idea of what he and Frank did, and Kitty would be utterly trustworthy. As a Wren she must have to deal with complex levels of security all the time.

'Is he bringing Sylvia?' Sarah asked.

'Don't think so, she's on late shifts this week,' Danny said, failing to notice the expression on his sister's face.

Immediately Kitty forced her smile to remain in place, so that her flicker of emotion would remain unseen. So Frank had a girlfriend – that should come as no surprise. He was handsome and clever, and had always been popular with the opposite sex; of course he would have someone by now. He'd been back on Merseyside for as long as she'd been away. The only surprise was that she hadn't heard about it before. Of course there had been a time when such news would have caused her distress, but she reminded herself that she was a different person now, after everything Elliott had taught her, and also after the experience of living and training away from home. She wasn't a silly kid longing for the gorgeous boy-next-door to notice her. So when, a moment later, she caught sight of Frank's head of molasses-coloured wavy hair above the crowd, she simply told herself it was the excitement of the day that made her heart beat a little faster, and that standing near the fire had caused her face to flush. She looked calmly at him as he made his way steadily over to them and wondered if anyone had tipped him off that she was here.

'Kitty. You made it, then,' he said, and she still wasn't sure if he'd been caught off-guard or not, but he appeared pleased to see her. The atmosphere seemed to change imperceptibly around them, but she told herself she was imagining it. She reminded herself that she was done with all of that, and that there was no room to think of any future attachments; she needed to be free to go wherever she was posted. But, much as she tried, Kitty couldn't stop the tremble that had crept into her legs, or fail to be conscious of Frank's larger-than-life presence as they stood so near to each other. Frank was so close she could touch him if she wanted to...

Frank schooled himself not to react to Kitty's unexpected presence. Of course he knew she'd been asked to come, but when nobody had heard from her he, like everyone else, assumed she would be unable to make it. Now here she was, as beautiful as ever, but with something else behind those lustrous eyes: a sorrow and maturity that was new. The loss of her doctor boyfriend must have hit her hard. It had only been a couple of months ago, so she must be deep in grief still. His heart went out to her and for a moment he almost said something that would give away how he felt – but then he reminded himself that she would be unlikely to welcome it when she was so recently bereaved. Besides which, he was now seeing Sylvia as often as they could manage, and if he wasn't quite head over heels in love, he was most definitely 'in like'. All their lives had changed and he had to accept that.

'Wouldn't have missed this for anything,' she said lightly, and her voice was still as musical as ever, although maybe her accent wasn't quite as strong. He realised he was staring and snapped out of his reverie.

'Of course not. It's good to see you,' he replied, cursing himself for being so dull, but unable to come out with anything better. Just being next to her made him as tongue-tied as a schoolboy.

'You too.' She was just being polite, nothing else. He mustn't monopolise her. So now he smiled again in acknowledgement of her presence, resisting the sensation that she was still so magnetic to him, and moved across to congratulate his sister and old friend, now his brother-in-law. Kitty, for all her beauty, could form no part of his future. He had to steel himself to accept it – although every cell in his body screamed against the idea.

Jack had chosen to get married in his Fleet Air Arm uniform, and had never looked more handsome as he stood with one arm around Rita, now that the children had run off to find more treats. Rita looked simply radiant. Utilising all her finest skills from when she had worked in George Henry Lee, Nancy had ensured that her big sister was as beautiful a bride as had been seen, war or no war. She'd found the dress in Lewis's warehouse, a silk bias-cut with softly puffed sleeves, in a subtle but elegant pattern of corals, creams and greens, which suited Rita's Titian-red hair and blue-green eyes to perfection. Everyone had pooled their coupons for it. She'd matched the coral shade exactly for Rita's nail polish. Rita herself had one good pair of black shoes with heels that she rarely wore, as for nursing and working in the shop she needed flat, comfortable ones – and she had rarely done anything other than nursing or working in the shop for years. Nancy had given Rita a precious pair of nylons which one of the US engineers had given her, and Rita had wisely asked no questions about what exactly Nancy had done to receive such a valuable gift. There would be time enough after the wedding to quiz her wayward sister about her behaviour. Rita had taken off the fine new coat that Nancy had lent her, joking that with that, the dress and nylons, along with the shoes, she'd got the 'something old', 'something new', and 'something borrowed' – at which point Kitty had stepped forward and pressed a gold chain into her friend's hand. Attached to it was a tiny locket with a blue stone.

'There you are. Something blue. Wear it and you'll have all the luck in the world.'

'Really, Kitty? This is gorgeous. It's so delicate.' Rita held it up to the light to admire it.

'It will suit you much better than me, I never have anywhere to wear it,' Kitty assured her, bending the truth a little, as Elliott had given it to her, saying the stone echoed Kitty's own dark-blue eyes. Part of her wanted to keep it as a memento of him, but in her heart she knew he had given her gifts far more precious than jewels: confidence, self-belief, a doorway to another world. It was utterly right that Rita should have the locket.

So now Rita wore it at her throat and it gleamed in the light from the parlour gas lamps. Frank noticed it as he made his way to the happy couple, and automatically registered its fine quality, but thought no more of it. He reached to shake Jack's hand.

'You're a lucky man, Jack,' he grinned, then his

face grew more solemn. 'Make her happy, won't you—'

Rita interrupted before Jack could reply. 'He's going to, I'll see to that. How could he do anything else?' She gazed up at the man she loved more than any other, now her husband, and the proud expression on his face almost took her breath away.

Frank tore his thoughts away from Kitty and smiled at his sister, delighted and hugely relieved to see her so happy at last. He'd been worried for her, as had everyone in the family, and felt guilty that he couldn't do more to help her, especially when Charlie upped and disappeared. Now things had finally come right for her. Impulsively he leant in and gave her a swift kiss on the cheek. 'Congratulations, Rita.' He could tell he was surplus to requirements and, having said what he'd wanted to say, he backed away again to talk to Danny.

Jack looked down at his bride, her face slightly flushed with the heat of the room and also with the excitement of the day. 'Fancy stepping out for some fresh air?' he asked quietly.

'Good idea.' Rita smiled apologetically as they edged their way through the scrum. She picked up Nancy's lovely coat from the hook beside the front door and they slipped outside into the street, now nearly dark with the shortest day being so close. Seeking shelter from the biting westerly wind, they tucked themselves into the entrance to the alley that separated the Feeny household from the corner shop. Jack drew her to him and breathed in the scent of her beautiful hair, which shone in the remains of the twilight.

They could hear the sounds of the party from the house and voices rising from the Feeny back yard.

'So, Mrs Callaghan.' Jack smiled as he said the name. 'How did you like your wedding day?'

'Oh, Jack.' Rita hugged him close, almost unable to believe that it was true. 'It was better than I'd ever hoped for. Standing there before the registrar, all our family and friends looking on, made me the proudest woman in the world. I have to keep pinching myself that it really happened. It was the best day of my life – well, that and when the children were born.'

'I've never been so happy, Reet. I've wanted this for us since we were sixteen.' He sighed in satisfaction. 'I always knew we'd be together somehow, but I never guessed what you'd have to go through first.' His voice changed, becoming charged with fierce emotion. 'You'll never suffer like that again, my darling. I'm going to make sure you're safe and protect you for the rest of your life.'

Rita didn't reply, just gazed up at him hungrily, and he brought his head down to hers and kissed her slowly and then with more passion, until they were leaning against the wall of the alley like the couple of teenagers they had been the first time they'd realised how they felt about one another. 'Oh, I could...' Rita shuddered in anticipation. What with her injuries when he'd last been home and him getting leave from only the day before the wedding, they had not had the chance to make love all the time they'd been engaged, with her a free woman desperate to make up for all those years they'd been apart. 'I want you so badly, Jack

Callaghan, and I'm not ashamed to say so.'

'I should hope so too, now you're my wife.' He kissed her again, more gently this time. 'But we've got all the time in the world now. We'll wait a few more hours and then I can show you how much I love you in style.'

'In style? What, have we got the room above the Sailor's Rest?' she asked. 'No, it'll be Bent-nose Jake's, won't it? Somewhere really classy.' She laughed, sure that they'd be spending their first night together in Jack's old room on Empire Street.

'Even better.' He couldn't keep the delight from his voice. 'Nothing but the best for you, Mrs Callaghan. We're going to the Adelphi.'

'What? Really? Jack, do you mean it?' Rita almost let go of him in surprise. She'd never been into the hotel in all of her life. She'd heard all about it from Nancy and wondered at who would actually go to stay there in such opulence. She couldn't believe it might be her.

'Of course.' He held her tightly again. 'I love my old house, but I didn't want us to spend our first proper night together with Tommy and Danny on the other side of the wall, or at yours with Ruby and the kids able to listen to everything. Why not treat ourselves? You're the most beautiful woman in the world – why wouldn't you want to spend the first night of our marriage in Liverpool's finest? The perfect place for you, I'd say.'

'Oh, Jack.' She was speechless with love for this man. He would do anything for her, she'd known that for a very long time, but for him to have taken the trouble of such an extravagant gesture, such a luxurious treat – words could not describe her wonder at all she had to learn from him. 'Jack,' she said very quietly, 'just stay alive, won't you? I never, ever want to lose you.' Suddenly she wanted to cry at the enormity of what losing him would be like.

'You don't get rid of me that easily,' he said, holding her so passionately that they could barely breathe. 'Now that I've got you, I'm never letting you go. The thought of you will always keep me safe and bring me home.' He rubbed his face against her hair and then smoothed it back. 'Come on, let's get back to the party. We're so lucky, you and I. There's all those people come to wish us well and make sure we're happy.'

Rita let him take her hand and lead her back to the front door. 'We are lucky, Jack. We're lucky because we found each other and we don't have to hide it any more. Jack Callaghan, I love you to the ends of the earth and I'm the luckiest, luckiest woman alive.'

This Large Print Book for the partially sighted, who cannot read normal print, is published under the auspices of

THE ULVERSCROFT FOUNDATION